"There's a really good reason why I don't know anything about this house or the life we shared together other than the fact that I know it was brief."

"Well, then, you need to clue me in because I have no idea how you could forget the fact that you never lived in this house. You looked at Laurel like you've never seen her before and yet the two of you used to work side by side and talk for hours."

"I'm sorry. I'm seeing how difficult all of this is for you—"

"You can spare me your sympathy, Autumn. Just tell me the truth."

"Well, then, let's start right there. My name is not Autumn." She held up the necklace and took a step toward him, noticing how the grooves in his forehead deepened. "My name is Summer."

"You lied to me?" He gripped the edge of the counter like he needed to ground himself.

"No, I didn't. I've never met you before in my life. You were married to my identical twin sister."

LONE STAR THREAT

USA TODAY Bestselling Author

BARB HAN

Previously published as *Texas Target* and *Texas Law*

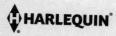 HARLEQUIN®

ISBN-13: 978-1-335-42726-7

Lone Star Threat

Copyright © 2022 by Harlequin Enterprises ULC

Recycling programs for this product may not exist in your area.

Texas Target
First published in 2020. This edition published in 2022.
Copyright © 2020 by Barb Han

Texas Law
First published in 2020. This edition published in 2022.
Copyright © 2020 by Barb Han

For questions and comments about the quality of this book, please contact us at CustomerService@Harlequin.com.

Harlequin Enterprises ULC
22 Adelaide St. West, 41st Floor
Toronto, Ontario M5H 4E3, Canada
www.Harlequin.com

Printed in U.S.A.

CONTENTS

TEXAS TARGET   7

TEXAS LAW   235

USA TODAY bestselling author **Barb Han** lives in north Texas with her very own hero-worthy husband, three beautiful children, a spunky golden retriever/ standard poodle mix and too many books in her to-read pile. In her downtime, she plays video games and spends much of her time on or around a basketball court. She loves interacting with readers and is grateful for their support. You can reach her at barbhan.com.

Books by Barb Han

Harlequin Intrigue

An O'Connor Family Mystery

Texas Kidnapping
Texas Target
Texas Law
Texas Baby Conspiracy
Texas Stalker
Texas Abduction

Rushing Creek Crime Spree

Cornered at Christmas
Ransom at Christmas
Ambushed at Christmas
What She Did
What She Knew
What She Saw

Visit the Author Profile page at Harlequin.com for more titles.

TEXAS TARGET

All my love to Brandon, Jacob and Tori
the three great loves of my life.

To Babe, my hero, for being my greatest love
and my place to call home.

To my mom, you're almost there and you got this!

I love you all.

Chapter One

The sun blasted on what had turned into a pavement melting summer day in Austin. Texas was legendary for its August heat. This day was going to be one for the books. Despite the triple-digit temperatures, navigating Congress Avenue still felt like running through a horde. Summer Grayson didn't have time to care about the sweat literally pouring down the sides of her face and dripping onto her shirt. She didn't have time to register how dry her mouth already was or how great a drink of water would feel right then. All she could care about was breaking free from the men who were right behind her, gaining ground with every step as she darted through throngs of people.

There were two men behind her. Their eyes trained on her. *She* was their target. No matter how much she desperately wanted to escape, to live, those men had other plans. Were these the same men who'd made her sister disappear?

Summer should never have pretended to be her identical twin, Autumn. Rolling the dice and claiming to be Autumn was backfiring big-time. On a base level, she'd needed to know if there was any possibility her sister was still alive even though she knew in her heart it wasn't likely. Criminal investigations took months, sometimes years. In too many cases, the criminal was never found. After two months of her own investigation, she'd been no closer to finding answers than when she'd first started.

So, yeah, she'd decided to cut corners and step into her sister's shoes. Getting desperate for answers had caused Summer to make mistakes that put these jerks on her tail. Risking a glance behind her added another miscalculation to the growing list. It slowed her down enough for one of the men to gain more ground.

The closest guy was the shorter of the two. He had light blond hair, a tan and a swimmer's build. His long torso and shorter legs were clad head to toe in black. He was also the faster runner of the pair. He was quick and lean, his face set in a permanent scowl. Everything about him said he was scrappy. The other jerk was at least six inches taller and thick. Thick neck. Thick arms. Thick hands.

Summer picked up the pace and risked another glance behind her, tamping down the panic that had adrenaline bursts fueling her legs. Scrappy was gaining on her and his friend, Thick Guy, wasn't far behind. No matter how hard she pushed her legs she wouldn't be fast enough to get away from Scrappy. Repeating a protection prayer that she'd learned as a young child, she pushed harder against burning thighs. It would take a miracle to get away.

No such marvel came. He caught hold of her. His grasp nearly crushed her bones. Icy fingers gripped her spine at the thought she would never know what had happened to her sister. As his nails dug into her skin, fear slapped her into realizing she might just end up in the same position. Gone.

A little voice in the back of her head picked that time to remind her how strong she really was. Despite being born prematurely and a minute later than her stronger, more athletic sister, Summer had enough fight in her to keep going despite the odds. Determination reminded her she'd survived then and would now, dammit.

Pushing harder, her thighs burned and her lungs clawed for air. She kept her pace, doing her level best to jerk her arm free. Giving in to pain could land her in a grave beside her twin sister, and she was certain that Autumn was dead. That was the only explanation for her sister's sudden disappearance. Granted, her sister had distanced herself from everything and everyone in the small town where they'd grown up years ago. She'd moved away from the Austin suburb and never looked back. Until recently.

Shutting out the past had been Autumn's way of surviving it—a past she'd refused to talk about even with her twin. Summer understood her sister's need for silence on a basic level, except for the part about closing off their relationship. The bond between twins was supposed to be ironclad. But Autumn was a grown woman capable of making her own decisions and Summer had no choice but to respect them.

Even so, no matter how rough it got for Autumn or how much time had passed in between communication, she'd always returned a 9-1-1 text from Summer.

"How are you still alive?" Scrappy's voice came out in a growl as he tightened the vise around her upper arm.

Those words nearly gutted Summer. Her sister had

been secretive for the past couple years and had only touched base a few precious times. There wasn't a scenario where Autumn was alive that included her going dark. Summer's gut instincts said her sister was gone but if there was a shred of hope that Autumn was out there, alive, there was no end to the lengths that Summer would go to find her. Hell would have to freeze over before she stopped looking.

And if her sister was dead, the same went for finding justice.

This jerk wasn't going to stop her from finding the truth no matter how tight his grip became. More of that Grayson resolve that had kept Summer alive through more situations than she could count kicked into high gear.

"Last time I checked hell hadn't frozen over." Summer jerked her arm as Scrappy caught her by the other elbow. She had about two seconds to react before he dug his bony fingers into her arms. All that came to mind was what she'd learned in second grade and it basically only applied to a fire, but it was all she had. Stop. Drop. And roll.

So that's exactly what she did. On her way down, it dawned on her that smacking the concrete at a dead run was going to hurt. There was no choice but to push through the pain. Give up now and thick hands would close around her this time. She'd be hauled backward, landing hard on her backside and at the mercy of these two jerks.

This way, she could trip them and create a scene.

Stabs of pain shot through her calves as she tripped over her own feet and prepared to hit concrete. At least this way she could control the fall. That was the little white lie she told herself. She'd gotten good at letting herself believe the little lies that her sister had told her. Ones like, *I'm fine.* And, *All I need is a little more time to clear up some bad karma in Austin.*

Summer should have forced her sister to talk. She should have cornered Autumn and not let her walk away until she came clean about everything that was and had been going on in her life. When her sister had emailed to say that she'd found a wonderful man and that they'd gotten married, Summer shouldn't have left it at that. She shouldn't have taken Autumn at her word that all of life was suddenly smooth. *Smooth* and *Autumn* didn't belong in the same sentence. Eventually her past would catch up with her.

Her sister had gushed about her new husband, saying how strong he was and how protected she felt. Looking back, Summer should've asked the question, *Protected from what?*

She could blame the fact that she'd been working two jobs to make ends meet. She could blame the fact that she was tired and not doing a heck of a great job managing her own life. She could blame her boss for keeping her late most nights. But the truth was that Autumn had always been a handful.

Until a year and a half ago when she'd announced the fact that she'd met *the one.* Learning that her sister had gotten married on a whim hadn't been the shock it should've been. Finding out she'd married into one of, if not *the* wealthiest cattle ranching families, had. Then again, Autumn had always managed to land on her feet.

Suspicion was second nature to Summer, who'd grown up watching over her shoulder for danger. And yet, her sister had sounded genuinely happy in her emails. That was something rare for a Grayson. And Summer had selfishly wanted a break from looking out for her sister. Autumn had a knack for placing herself straight-up in the middle of trouble. And trouble had a way of finding her. Like the time in high school when she'd made a pact with a star athlete on the soccer team to cheat off each other on a test. Adam Winston got caught and decided not to go down alone. He showed the principal his text exchange with Autumn. The funny thing was that Autumn had studied and could pass the test on her own merit. She'd played dumb because she thought he'd be more attracted to her.

As her shoulder hit the pavement, Summer unleashed a scream. She made the loudest noise that could come out of her mouth. The daytime crowd shuffled to get out of her way, like a sea parting. Summer realized the fall was going to be more than she expected, measured by the sheer number of gasps around her.

She did, however, elicit enough attention to make Scrappy think twice. In fact, his gnarly grip on her elbow released and he disappeared into the gathering crowd.

Summer's head smacked the ground harder than she'd anticipated. For a split second, she heard ringing in her ears. She could hop back up, but then what? The men would chase her again. This time, she might not be so lucky.

An authoritative female voice parted the crowd and a woman in uniform came into Summer's blurry vision.

"Ma'am, are you okay?" a female officer asked as she kneeled down.

"My name is Autumn Grayson and I need to confess to a crime."

The officer blinked shocked eyes at Summer. Those words seemed to grab her by the throat. "What was the offense, ma'am?"

The only thing that came to mind was the fire that had devastated a popular camping ground on the outskirts of Austin. It had been all over the news.

"Arson," she said.

"You're not going to believe who just confessed to arson." Dawson O'Connor's brother, Sheriff Colton O'Connor, had been one hundred percent correct. Dawson couldn't believe that Autumn Grayson would confess to a crime there was no way she could've committed. Because he couldn't believe that his ex-wife could be capable of breaking the law. Not to mention the fact that she was scared to death of fire and would go nowhere near a campsite.

She'd been a city girl through and through. But then, he was still trying to believe that she'd served him divorce papers out of what felt like nowhere last year.

As far as he'd known, their marriage could have been saved. He wasn't the giving-up-when-times-got-tough kind. So, he'd been all kinds of surprised when he found out she hadn't taken their vows as seriously as he had. The note she'd left said she'd made a mistake, not to look for her, and he should forget he'd ever met her.

How was he supposed to do that? He'd been fool enough to spend time with her, marry her. And then he was supposed to…what? Forget any of that had ever happened? Far be it from him to dwell on unhappiness. Heaven knew he'd seen the effects of not being able to let go of a painful past firsthand in his own family. He had a wonderful mother who'd never really recovered from the night her firstborn child had been kidnapped in her own crib decades ago.

Dawson had had a sideline view to real tragedy. His mother had picked herself up and moved on best she could, always reminding her six O'Connor sons about the sister they never had the privilege to know.

Granted, getting a divorce was nowhere near the tragedy of losing a child and, worse yet, never knowing what had truly happened or if the child was alive. He chided himself for still hanging on to the pain of mistakenly falling for the wrong person. That was more a bad decision than a tragedy.

What was worse? He couldn't believe that he was sitting in the parking lot of the Travis County Jail with a handful of jewelry pieces in a box that his wife—correction *ex*-wife—had told him were family heirlooms. He'd had the sense from her that she hadn't grown up with much when it came to money or family. But then the subject of family had been off-limits. It should've been his first sign something was wrong.

He also shouldn't care about returning the pieces to her.

As a matter of principle, he didn't feel right holding on to them. Since she'd cut off all contact last year, he hadn't had an opportunity to hand them over. Call it cowboy code but he didn't like the thought of keeping someone else's belongings.

Engine idling. Hand on the gearshift. Foot on the brake. Time to make a decision. Drive away or go inside?

Dawson muttered a curse under his breath and shut off the engine. He made the trek into the jail and walked directly toward the officer at the counter.

"I'm here to see my wi—" He stopped himself right there. "Someone in your holding cell. Her name is Autumn Grayson." Since inmates in a holding tank weren't allowed visitors, Dawson pulled out his badge. Professional courtesy might get him through the steel doors. "My name is Marshal Dawson O'Connor."

The jailor perked up, his eyes widening for a split second. He extended his hand. "Nice to meet you, sir."

"The pleasure is all mine." He gave a small smile. "Is there any chance I can have a short visit with Ms. Grayson."

"Yes, sir." The cop examined the US Marshals badge on the counter in front of him as Dawson pulled a coin from his pocket. It was a custom that started long ago to give out a department-stamped coin when visiting a cooperating agency.

"Are you picking her up? The crime she confessed to committing has already been solved."

"We'll see." He doubted she'd go with him voluntarily.

The jailor introduced himself and took the offering with a broad smile. The tall, thin man who wore a white Stetson nodded his approval. "I appreciate this." He tossed the coin in the air, caught it and then said, "You want to follow me?"

It was more statement than question and didn't require an answer. Dawson followed. He was led into a small room with a table, two chairs opposite each other and a pair of doors. There was one behind him and one in front of him.

"If you'll take a seat, sir, I'll bring Ms. Grayson." With a nod, the officer left the room.

Sitting in the interview room, it dawned on Dawson

just how much trouble Autumn might be in. She had, after all, confessed to arson. The who, how and why remained to be seen. He would ask routine questions and try to determine why she would volunteer to be charged for a crime she didn't commit.

There had to be more to the story, and he intended to get to the bottom of it. His mind snapped to self-defense. She was a beautiful woman who might've gotten involved in a bad situation. It happened.

Nothing could prepare him for the shot he took to the heart at seeing her again. She had changed a lot in the past year. Her shiny wheat-colored hair fell well past her shoulders in waves. Even with her eyes cast down to the white tiled flooring, he could almost see their violet hue. Her lips seemed fuller, pinker. Maybe it was the fact she had on no makeup and her hair looked natural, but this didn't seem like Autumn at all.

Maybe too much time had passed, and he wasn't remembering her very well. They'd had a whirlwind courtship before an even faster wedding.

She'd gained a few curves that made her even sexier. Hell, he didn't need to be thinking about those right now. He took in other differences, too. She no longer had bangs or wore designer clothing from head to toe.

Of course, those were cosmetic changes. He knew firsthand how a few little changes could make a person look completely different. He'd hidden enough witnesses in his day to know the value of a hat, scarf and pair of sunglasses.

Still, it struck him as odd that she wouldn't want to make eye contact with him. She had to know who was waiting in the room to talk to her. She would've been given the name of her visitor and even if she hadn't, that would give her even more reason to want to find out who would be sitting in the chair across the table from her.

Keeping her eyes cast down made her look guilty of something.

He cleared his throat and when she finally did glance up, the fear in her eyes was a second punch. What was she so afraid of? Him? Of his reaction to her walking out with no real explanation? He'd nursed a bruised ego longer than he cared to admit.

Dawson waited until the jailor instructed her to sit and then moved to the corner. Arms folded across his chest and feet apart in an athletic stance, he waited.

Autumn didn't sit. She stared at Dawson for a long moment and didn't speak, like they were playing a game and the person who spoke first lost. Her cheeks flushed, a telltale sign her body still reacted to him whether she wanted to admit it or not. Physical attraction had never been their problem. There was something different about the way she stood that he couldn't quite pinpoint. The oddities were racking up.

Even so, seeing her was a lightning strike in the center of the chest.

"Go away. You shouldn't be here." Hearing her voice again shouldn't send a shot of warmth through his heart.

"Really? Because I was about to say the same thing about you." He clasped his hands together on top of the table and leaned forward. "What's going on, Autumn?"

That question could go way back to their past but that wasn't what he was referring to right now.

"I don't know what you mean, and my life is none of your business." Her shoulders tensed and the lines on her forehead appeared like they did when she was concentrating. Her defensive posture spoke volumes about how she felt at seeing him again. He shouldn't have expected anything less. She'd been clear about her intentions when she'd walked out and then had divorce papers served.

Those violet eyes threw darts at him. "Why are you here?"

"I came to return a few things you left at the ranch and to see if I can help you get yourself out of this…" he glanced around "…mess."

"You don't care about me."

"That's where you're wrong, Autumn. I do care." He wanted to add that he wished like hell that he didn't. He'd known seeing her again was going to be hard on him. He just didn't know how bad it was going to get.

Chapter Two

"I'll sign whatever you need to let her go," Dawson said to the jailor who was standing quietly in the corner.

"You can't do that." Summer pushed off the desk and started pacing. Nothing prepared her for being in the same room with Dawson O'Connor. She'd recognized her sister's husband from the pictures Autumn had sent of their wedding day. There'd been two. One of the couple standing next to each other. Dawson's arm had been around the waist of his bride, who'd been dressed in all white. For some reason that one burned into Summer's memory. Could it have been the only time her sister had seemed remotely happy? And then there'd been one of Dawson that had been taken on the same day. His face was turned toward a wooded area. He didn't seem to care that a camera phone was aimed at him. He was strong, like the muscles-for-days type of body. But, it was his smile that struck her the most.

In the pictures, he'd been seriously good-looking. Tie loosened, top couple buttons on his shirt undone, he'd been leaning against a fence post looking all relaxed. Happy. Seeing him in person, she realized the snaps hadn't done him justice. There was a magnetism about him that drew her gaze and made it stick. His looks came through loud and clear on the digital files, but he was sinning-on-Sundays gorgeous in person.

"Like hell I can't. Just because we're divorced doesn't mean I can't help you."

Summer didn't bother to hide her shock. "Hold on. What did you just say?"

"I said I wanted to help—"

She waved her arms in the air, stopping him mid-sentence. "Not that part. We're divorced?"

A dark brow went up and she realized her mistake. Her sister never mentioned anything about a divorce.

Dawson O'Connor had that whole tall, dark and handsome bit nailed down. It was easy to see why Autumn would be attracted to a man like him. His rough, masculine voice traveled over Summer like warmth and sex appeal and temptation.

Summer folded her arms tightly across her chest. She turned toward the door. "I want to go back to my cell *now*."

"Go ahead and do that." There was something foreboding in Dawson's tone that stopped her in her tracks. "Call the cop over and have me kicked out of here. Then what? What's your next play?"

She didn't immediately answer, and he must've taken that as a sign she was hearing what he was saying and willing to keep listening.

He continued, "I sure hope you have a next move in mind because this one seems like an act of desperation."

She couldn't argue. She didn't have it in her to put up a fight. Plus, he was speaking the truth. In fact, no truer words had ever been spoken. She'd been desperate. Desperation caused her to pose as her sister. Desperation caused her to confess to a crime she didn't commit. The only reason she'd confessed was to escape the bad guys on her trail. And it was desperation that had her needing Dawson O'Connor to be as far away from her as possible.

And, no, she hadn't figured out her next move. Plus, she was starving. Her stomach growled, picking that time to remind her that she hadn't even figured out her next meal.

His tone softened when he said, "Allow me to get you out of here. We both know you didn't commit the crime you're confessing to and so do they. I don't know what you're up to and I don't know why this seemed like a good option." He waved his arms in the area. "Let's go somewhere we can talk and see if I can help you get back on your feet."

His unexpected kindness tapped into a long-forgotten place buried deep inside. A place that had no business seeing the light of day.

"I appreciate your willingness to help me after what I put you through." Summer had no personal knowledge of exactly what that meant but knowing her sister it was a lot. Based on the look in his eyes, it was far more than this man deserved. "I can't accept your help. We're divorced. What happens to me doesn't concern you anymore."

"Is that what you think? I'm the kind of person who could walk away from someone I cared about once? Because if that's true you clearly did us both a favor by walking out last year." He threw a hand up before she could answer. "Never mind. The past is the past. We both moved on. And now you find yourself here. You don't want my help. There's not a whole lot I can do about that. But let me ask you this. How long do you really think it's going to take for whomever you're running from to find you here?"

Those words were the equivalent of a bucket of ice water being dumped over her head. He was right. Hearing him say those words as plainly as he had brought home the fact that she wasn't safe anywhere anymore. The cops were onto her about the lie and she figured they'd boot her out soon anyway.

Autumn had gushed about life on the ranch. A remote location far away from Austin sounded pretty good right about now.

Summer took in a deep breath meant to fortify her nerves and prepared to shock him. "Fine. I'll let you pay my bail, but you have to take me home with you."

SUMMER WAS STILL surprised Dawson had agreed to her terms as she walked into his home on an expansive ranch property. Mental images of him sharing this place with her sister slammed into her—images she didn't like for reasons she didn't want to explore. An attraction was so out of the question.

She glanced around the room and was initially shocked to realize there were no photographs of the two of them. Then, it dawned on her that her sister had filed for divorce last year. Of course, any pictures that had been hanging on the walls would've been taken down.

The place was decorated in a surprisingly masculine style. Or, maybe it shouldn't be such a surprise. Again, he might've redecorated. Thinking her sister had walked in this very room not that long ago struck an emotional chord.

Summer tucked her chin to her chest and blinked her

eyes, trying to clear away the tears threatening. For the sake of Autumn's memory, Summer needed to hold it together. For the sake of the investigation, she needed to continue the lie even though after meeting Dawson it was increasingly difficult to hold the line. For the sake of her own sanity, she needed to keep her distance from him on both an emotional and physical level.

Getting too close to her sister's ex would only add to both of their heartbreak. Despite the tough exterior, one look in his eyes told her that his feelings had run deep for Autumn.

A sound in the next room caused her to jump over the back of the couch and drop to her knees. It took a second to register the fact that Dawson's eyes were on her, studying her. Analyzing her.

Of course, she should've realized her extreme reaction would draw his attention. She also shouldn't let it warm her heart that Dawson still cared enough about her sister to drive all the way to Austin to bail her out of jail.

"It's just Laurel. She's probably finishing up cleaning for the day." He didn't so much as blink.

"You have a housekeeper?" The raised eyebrow he gave her in response to her question told her she'd just made another mistake. She needed to keep the questions to a minimum. Lay low for a few hours until she could figure out her next move, grab a meal and definitely not talk to him more than she had to.

There was no way she would stick around and put Dawson or his family in danger. Was that the reason her sister had divorced him? Had she known trouble was coming and wanted to protect him? Cut all ties to save him from her fate? Had she married a US marshal thinking he could keep her safe?

"You know we did. I still do. Even though I've told Laurel a hundred times I don't need the help. She's stubborn that way. You remember that about her." From everything she could tell about the man so far, her sister was right. He was good-looking beyond a casual description. Carved-from-granite jawline. Check. Thick, dark hair—the kind that her fingers itched to get lost in. Check. Serious brown eyes with a hint of sadness. Check. He was kind. It was the only explanation for him going out of his way to help her after being served papers. He didn't seem like the kind of person who took divorce lightly. In fact, he seemed like the type who put family above all else.

A middle-aged woman padded into the room. She had a kind face and a stout build. In one hand, she white-knuckled the handle of a pail. In the other, she gripped a white cleaning rag.

Summer scrambled to her feet. The woman—Laurel—gasped. Her chin practically dropped to her chest. Mouth agape, she released her grip on the bucket. It tumbled onto the tile, crashing against the flooring.

"I'm sorry." Summer glanced around, desperate to find something to help contain the spill. She ran toward the open-concept kitchen and made it to the counter with the paper towel roll at the same time as Dawson.

He gave her a small look of approval, like she remembered something because she was home. That look nearly cracked her heart into two pieces. Getting out of there and out of Katy Gulch just jumped up her priority scale. She hadn't found paper towels because this was her home. Their location had been intuitive.

They'd been placed next to the kitchen sink—an obvious place. All she'd done was follow a line across the counter until she saw the paper towels.

It dawned on her that Dawson must've loved her sister and the divorce had to have been hard on him. Autumn had ended their marriage without explanation or ceremony.

This close, she could easily see the dark circles cradling his honey-brown eyes. She could almost feel the toll that caring for Autumn had taken on him, because the feeling was so familiar to her it was palpable. Caring for Autumn was hard. Draining at times. Still the question burned. What had Autumn gotten herself into?

Happiness had always been fleeting for a Grayson. It was beyond Summer's comprehension how her sister could've found it with this man and then walked away. She grabbed the paper towels off the counter and turned toward the mess. In all the commotion, Summer didn't notice the small black-and-white dog that had run behind Dawson.

She dropped to the floor and used half the roll of paper towels, trying to mop up the spill.

Laurel smiled nervously at her. She had kind eyes and what Summer was certain would be an equally kind heart.

Dawson joined them, the little dog by his side, which she could now see was a puppy. Since the dog was probably a safe topic, Summer decided to start there.

"Who is this little guy?"

"My shadow," Dawson said. "Hence, his name is Shadow."

"You should've seen this little guy when Dawson

first found him." Laurel made a tsk-tsk noise. "It's impossible to imagine what kind of person could just dump a little guy like this all alone in the country, leaving him unable to fend for himself."

"What happened?"

"Nothing," Dawson said, looking embarrassed by the attention. "He got into a tangle with something—"

"Dawson's being modest. Shadow was attacked by a coyote. Dawson heard what was happening and hopped off Mabel—" she flashed eyes at Summer when no recognition dawned "—you remember his horse."

"Oh. Right. Mabel. Yes." Lying to this sweet woman made Summer feel awful. There was no way she could keep up the charade. Telling Laurel, exposing the truth, might just put the woman in danger. Summer couldn't do that, either. This woman was all s'mores and campfires and the kind of person who probably baked cookies on a chilly day.

"So, Dawson here literally forced open the jowls of the coyote and ripped this little guy from its teeth." Laurel was clearly proud of him, not that Summer could blame the woman. "Never mind that the coyote's mouth then closed on Dawson's elbow. Tore him up pretty good before he managed to get free."

Summer didn't notice his left elbow until then. A pretty gnarly scar ran a solid four inches across his skin.

"Wild things are dangerous. It was really brave of you to take on the coyote." She tried to stifle the admiration in her voice. It was difficult. She also realized the statement covered more than just his coyote encounter.

"Laurel is making too big of a deal out of what happened. All I know is that helping this little guy out of trouble gave me a shadow I can't shake around the house." He nodded toward the black-and-white pup that had yet to grow into his oversize paws. The hint of annoyance in his tone seemed clearly just for show. Dawson scratched the dog behind his ears.

If the little guy had been a cat, he would've purred. She could think of worse problems than to have the adoration of an adorable puppy. And Summer figured little doggies weren't the only things willing to follow Dawson O'Connor around, eyes filled with admiration. With sex appeal in buckets, she suspected half the women in town would do the same thing. The other half were either married or dead.

Summer also couldn't help but notice how Laurel kept a tentative eye on her. The kind housekeeper looked like she'd seen a ghost. Based on her expression and reactions, the woman Laurel assumed was Autumn was the last person she expected to see. More proof that Summer's sister had left a mess in her wake. Autumn could be like a volcano. Mesmerizing to see and experience until she erupted. Then, it was pure devastation for anyone who got too close or landed in her path.

"The mess is all cleaned up now. Can I drop Shadow off at the barn on my way to the main house?" Laurel asked.

"He'd like that. Wouldn't you, little guy?" Dawson picked up the pup in one sweeping motion and brought him nose to nose.

"Having another dog to play with might be good for him." Summer could've sworn the puppy smiled.

"He loves playing with Apollo and it's good for him since he lost Daisy. Apollo has been moping around for weeks. The only time I've seen him perk up in the slightest is when Shadow comes around." Laurel walked over to Dawson, who handed over the sweet pup.

"Be nice to Apollo. No biting his ears with those sharp puppy teeth." Despite the warning, his voice was low and warm as he scratched the pup behind the ears. "Will you let me know when I need to pick him up?"

"I sure will." Laurel excused herself before gathering her supplies and making a quick exit.

Lying to the woman with kind eyes about Summer's identity was the equivalent of a physical stab. Perfection had never been her goal and heaven knew she got into her fair share of troubles growing up. Being her own parent from an early age had a way of teaching with a baptism by fire. No one would ever accuse Summer of being perfect. But she was not a liar.

Honesty rated highly in her book. Autumn, on the other hand, had always claimed that bending the truth never hurt anyone. It wasn't true. Summer knew from personal experience how her sister's tiny white lies left marks on the inside—marks that weren't visible to the naked eye.

So, she seemed to find herself between a rock and a hard place as she pushed to standing. Being in close proximity to Dawson, close enough to smell his warm, masculine scent, wasn't helping with the guilt racking her.

"You've been really kind, and I appreciate it. Especially after the way you were treated." There was something very primal in her that could not take the blame for her sister's actions. Maybe it was because standing in the light of Dawson's honey-gold eyes made her want to be honest with him. An important part of that was being authentic.

But honesty at this point in the game would have a price. It was easy to see that a man like Dawson wouldn't walk away easily from someone who needed a hand up. He would see it as his duty to help just as he'd seen it as his responsibility to get her out of jail and talk sense into her.

"Do you mean after the way *you* treated me?" He seemed to regret those words the minute they came out of his mouth. "Don't answer that. Whatever happened between us is water under the bridge. The reason I came to see you today wasn't as altruistic as you might think." He walked over to the counter where he'd placed his keys and picked up a small box. She'd noticed it in his hands earlier but with everything going on didn't think to ask about it.

She walked over to the kitchen counter and placed her hands on it to steady herself.

"These belong to you. You said they were important." He set the box on the counter next to her and walked away. "I'm about to make coffee. Do you want a cup?"

"No coffee for me. But, thanks." She had no plans to stick around long enough to finish a cup.

Summer stared at the box like it was a bomb about to detonate. Did she even want to know what was inside? Sadness was a physical ache. Summer of all people knew that even though her sister could be selfish and focused on all the wrong things sometimes, Autumn had also been her best friend and partner in crime growing up. Autumn's faults could so easily have been Summer's considering the childhood they'd shared.

Life had hardened them both at too young of an age. Broken them? There'd been times when Summer wondered if her sister had been capable of caring for anyone but herself. She'd asked the question countless times, wondering if she was wasting her time and energy on someone who would always be a taker.

"Your stomach growled earlier. You're here. You may as well eat and have some coffee before you take off again." She didn't want to hear the twinge of hurt in Dawson's voice. Especially since he did a fine job of covering it with a cough.

Trying to find out what had happened to her sister was becoming an exercise in stupidity. So far, all she'd done was attract the attention of very bad people. People who wanted her dead. Maybe it was time to move on. It would be easy enough to change her appearance and disappear off the grid for a little while. Could she, though? Could she walk away without knowing what had happened to Autumn?

Summer tapped her finger on the lid of the small box. She wrapped her fingers around it, still unsure if she wanted to see what was inside.

Her fist tightened around the top of the box as she opened it, memories assaulting her. These few pieces of jewelry were her sister's most prized possessions? It was all junk, worth nothing when it came to money. Memories were a different story.

Her fingers closed around a tarnished chain. The necklace that spelled out one word brought back a treasure trove of memories from the county fair.

This was considered one of her sister's most prized possessions? Because the name on the necklace read *Summer*.

Chapter Three

Dawson watched as his ex-wife stood in his kitchen, tracing the letters on the necklace using her index finger. Autumn had changed. A thought struck that maybe she'd been in an accident and suffered some type of head trauma. She pretended to know the house even though she never lived in it. In fact, he'd moved in three months ago after some tweaks to the original plan—a plan she'd helped him design.

The two of them had made big plans to move into the home that she was going to decorate. He'd even started contemplating the next logical step, a family. But those plans had never gotten off the ground.

After working with the contractor to make enough changes for the house to feel like *his* and not *theirs*, he'd moved in. It only took a few phone calls and clicks to cancel all the furniture and decorations she'd ordered. The custom pieces had been finished and donated to the House of Hope for abused women and their children.

With the addition of oversize leather couches and a large metal star hanging over the fireplace, the place had become home for the bachelor.

The twist of fate that brought Autumn into the space

he never thought she'd see had him off-balance. He needed to stay focused. He poured a cup of coffee and took a couple of sips. It was time for answers.

"Why did you say you did it?" He started right in with one of the biggest.

She ducked her head, chin to chest. Her mannerisms were different from a year and a half ago. It was an odd sensation to be staring at a woman he'd known intimately and yet feel like he was staring at a total stranger now. Could the fact he was looking at his ex through a new lens be the impact of divorce?

"I was desperate." Well, now he felt like he was starting to get somewhere. He'd been beginning to think this wasn't Autumn at all, which was crazy because she looked exactly like her.

"Why?"

"Believe me when I say you really don't want to know." There was no conviction in those words. There was sadness in spades and a lost quality that caused a knot to form in his gut.

"Why not let me be the judge of that? I think I have a pretty good handle on what I do and do not want to know." That came out a little harsher than he'd intended. He tried to soften his tone when he said, "Believe it or not, I'd like to help."

"You can't. This is something I have to deal with on my own." Now her intention came out loud and clear. Hurt and stubbornness laced her tone.

"Will you at least tell me why you have to deal with this by yourself?"

She shook her head and didn't make eye contact.

"Does this have anything to do with why you walked

out on our relationship?" His bruised ego needed to know because that darn thing still licked his wounds.

"I didn't give you a reason?" This time, she made eye contact. Eyes wide with a look of disbelief caused more questions to form in his thoughts.

"No. But it's not too late. Tell me why. Your note didn't explain what went wrong. I thought we had a good thing going. Granted, looking back, it wasn't perfect, but we had a base to build on."

"I'm sorry. I can't do this with you right now." The hint of fear in her voice didn't get past him.

"Do what? Finally answer a question? Give me the real reason why you left our marriage after exchanging vows? In case you didn't notice, I took those seriously." He pushed even though he knew better. As a seasoned law enforcement officer, he had developed and honed instincts that told him he was doing nothing but backing her into a corner. Just like the coyote, she'd bite.

"I didn't deserve you." She broke eye contact and guilt stabbed at him. But guilt for what? Why was he suddenly feeling like a jerk for making her feel bad? She'd walked away from their marriage not the other way around. Losing the pregnancy had been even harder on her than it had on him, but he hadn't seen a need for a divorce despite that being the reason for the marriage in the first place.

Her admission struck a nerve. It was impossible, though, not to feel like he was forcing his help on her right now. She was in a desperate situation and he'd been pushing her to take his aid.

"It's not fair of me to put you in the position of explaining yourself. You didn't ask for me to show up today—"

"Which doesn't mean I'm not grateful you did." She had the necklace draped over her opened hand. Giving her back something that she so obviously cared about made him feel like maybe this day hadn't been a total mistake.

"It seems like you've gotten yourself into a situation that maybe you're having a hard time figuring out how to get out of. We've all been there—"

She clucked her tongue. "Somehow I doubt that. I can't imagine a man like you would know anything about regret."

Dawson stood there for a long moment, taking in her body language. Shoulders tensed, her feet aimed toward the back door, everything about her said she was in for a quick exit. It was his fool pride wanting answers from someone who so clearly didn't care about the marriage as much as he did. *Hadn't cared.* Past tense.

"Okay, let me try this another way." He motioned toward the sets of keys. They hung on a key rack nailed to the side cabinet near the hallway that led to the garage. "There are several vehicles in the garage. I'm sure it won't be too hard to figure out which key belongs to what vehicle. Take whatever you want. No questions asked. You don't have to worry about returning anything. I'm not bringing in the law."

"You are the law. And didn't you just post bail for me? Won't you get into trouble if I disappear?"

"My lawyer can tie up the courts for years until they forget all about my connection to you and technically all I did was sign paperwork to get you released. We both know you're innocent, Autumn." A strange look passed behind her eyes when he said her name.

He didn't go into the fact that he'd put his reputation on the line to help her. "Tell me an amount and I can pretty much have as much money as you need at your disposal." He checked the clock hanging over the cabinets in the kitchen. "Bank is about to close." Of course, he could call up his banker at any moment and have the bank reopened for him. A selfish part of him wanted to stall for time, maybe wanted a little bit more time with Autumn before she disappeared again.

She just stood there, a blank look on her face. "You would do all that for me?"

He waved her comment off like it was nothing.

"Seriously?" She started pacing. "That's pretty much the nicest thing anyone's ever volunteered to do for me." She glanced up at him nervously. "I mean, there are so many nice things you did when we were married but I walked out on you."

His ex didn't seem to remember much about their past. Had something happened? Trauma? Working the angle that she'd somehow lost her memory, he asked, "Really? You remember nice things I did for you? Name one."

"I-UH—" SUMMER DREW a blank. And then an obvious answer smacked her between the eyes. "You asked me to marry you."

His eyebrow shot up.

"And there were so many other things that it's hard to remember them all right now." She gripped her forehead, trying to stave off the massive headache forming in the backs of her eyes. Headaches were like that. They had a way of taking seed and then sprouting tentacles that seemed to wrap around her brain and squeeze.

"Did something happen to you, Autumn? Were you in some kind of accident?"

His questions registered. He thought she was suffering from some kind of brain trauma, which basically meant Autumn never told Dawson about her. It would be so easy to go along with that line, a quick escape out of an almost unbearable situation. But she couldn't go there. "No. I wasn't, Dawson."

"You've changed a lot in the past year and a half. More than I expected. I mean, you look like my ex-wife. There's no debating that. But it feels like I'm talking to a complete stranger. On the outside, it's you but you don't act like her. Her mannerisms are totally different. And I just thought there had to be an easy explanation."

She wanted to give him one. She wanted to help him make sense of a marriage that had been cut short. She wanted to give him answers he seemed to crave in order to go on with his life. He seemed like the kind of person who deserved that and so much more. But how without adding fuel to an already blazing fire?

If she came clean with him right then and there, it would only lead to more questions. Worse yet, he might want to get involved and end up hurt or dead. That would be on her conscience for the rest of her life.

"Money would be a huge help, but only as a loan. You have to promise to let me pay it back." She could use a cash infusion to keep her off the grid. The investigation had to be put on the back burner until the situation cooled off. She'd riled someone up. Maybe she could rent a cabin in the woods until life chilled out again.

"Done. How much do you need?"

"A couple thousand dollars if you can spare it." She almost winced saying the number out loud.

"I can do a whole lot better than that. Twenty-five thousand—"

"I'd never be able to pay that much back." She blinked at him, a little bit dumbfounded. Her sister had said the man she'd married came from a wealthy family. Summer couldn't even fathom someone who could conjure up that kind of cash on a moment's notice.

"You don't have to. It's yours already. Remember? I put it in your account when we got married and you never used it."

"Now I know you're lying." Or testing her. The latter made more sense.

"The money is sitting in your account. What you do with it is your own business." There was a sadness to his tone she didn't want to pick up on. She couldn't afford to care about his feelings right now, not when there was so much at stake. The fact she was aware that he tried to cover with a sharp edge to his tone made everything so much worse.

"You said I could borrow a vehicle…"

"Take whatever you need. There are several in the garage to choose from. You didn't take your own when you left—"

She was already shaking her head before he finished his sentence. "I'd like to borrow one of yours. Preferably something I've never driven before."

He'd mentioned that the bank was almost closed. They needed to hurry if she was going to get out of there. "Is there any chance we can make it into town tonight?"

"It's too late to go through normal procedures." He glanced away from her when he spoke. What was he hiding?

Summer ran through possibilities in her mind. She could take twenty-five thousand dollars in cash and disappear for a while. Then what?

Keep on running the rest of her life? She'd been living a lie recently and it was coming back to bite her. Would she turn out exactly like her sister? Lying and then covering up the lies. Could she convince herself it was all for the best? That the only reason she lied was to help other people? Could she walk away from investigating her sister's disappearance? Because if she did that, she wouldn't recognize herself anymore.

Staring at a pair of honest honey-brown eyes standing a few feet in front of her, she realized that she could never be the kind of person who could look into them and lie. That even little white lies meant to protect others ended up hurting them more than anything else.

Telling Dawson the truth was risky. It could put him in danger. Not telling him seemed like it could also put him in harm's way. Especially if he started digging around to figure out what was really going on.

Ignorance wasn't always bliss. Sometimes, it could kill.

She decided to clear up this whole mess by coming clean with him. He worked in law enforcement and he seemed to care about her sister. He would know how to protect himself if he was aware of a threat. When she really thought about it, he was a US marshal. Weren't they involved in witness protection? She personally had no idea.

"Dawson, I'm going to tell you something that you

might not be ready to hear. You deserve to know the truth." Just saying those words caused her heart to hammer her rib cage.

He set his coffee cup down on the granite countertop and crossed his arms over his chest like he was bracing himself for the worst.

"I don't know much about your marriage except that I know you got married on the last day of January." She held her hand up to stop him from speaking before he could respond because she could already see the questions forming in his eyes. "I was honest before. I haven't been in an accident or had any kind of head trauma."

"Then, what?"

Speaking the words out loud was proving to be so much harder than saying them in her head. She was trying to think of a way to ease him into the news rather than blurt it out and completely shock him. "There's a really good reason why I don't know anything about this house or the life we shared together other than the fact that I know it was brief."

"Well then, you need to clue me in because I have no idea how you could forget the fact that you never lived in this house. You looked at Laurel like you've never seen her before and yet the two of you used to work side by side and talk for hours."

"I'm sorry. I'm seeing how difficult all of this is for you—"

"You can spare me your sympathy, Autumn. Just tell me the truth."

"Well then, let's start right there. My name is not Autumn." She held up the necklace and took a step toward him, noticing how the grooves in his forehead deepened. "My name is Summer."

"You lied to me?" He gripped the edge of the counter like he needed to ground himself.

"No, I didn't. I've never met you before in my life. You were married to my identical twin sister."

Chapter Four

Dawson studied the woman in front of him, trying to give his brain a minute to process what he'd just heard. He must've looked her up and down like she was crazy, because she put her hands up in the surrender position.

"I know how that must sound but it's true. I should probably be surprised that you don't know about me. In a normal family, we would. My sister kept secrets. We're identical twins and I absolutely know something happened to my sister. I tracked her to Austin where a pair of men found me. They said I wouldn't die and that they intended to finish the job." Those honest violet eyes blinked up at him and his heart stuttered. "If my sister was alive, I would've heard from her by now."

There were so many questions mounting. This one popped first. "I need to rewind for just a second. Your name is Summer, and I was married to your identical twin sister. You're here to find out what happened to your sister, who you believe is gone?"

She nodded. "I'm sorry to say this to you, because I know you lov—"

"Thing of the past." He cut her off right there. There was no use going down that road again.

"She is gone." Her chin quivered and she ducked her head to one side.

Summer's answer caused his chest to squeeze. He didn't have to have the same feelings for Autumn as he once did.

"How do you know?" Disbelief washed over him as he studied her for any signs she was lying. His brain couldn't process the news. More questions flooded him as his past unraveled. He narrowed his gaze and studied the woman in his kitchen. He'd noticed something different the second he saw her at county lockup.

"Hear me out. I've been living in Washington State where I work as a waitress. My sister and I always stay in touch."

"And yet I had no idea you existed," he said low and under his breath. Had she planned to leave all along?

"I'm sorry about that. I'm puzzled about that part as well because she told me about you. Granted, it was after you were married. We may go a while in between connecting but we always circle back. She'd been leaving cryptic messages lately about her past."

"A past you knew very little details about if I had to guess." A picture was emerging. Autumn would classify herself as a free spirit, forgetting all about the hurt and questions she left behind.

His comment seemed to offend Summer based on her deep frown lines. Hell, he hadn't meant to add to her hurt. It was obvious she cared about her sister or she wouldn't be here trying to find out the truth.

"My sister was far from perfect. No one knows that better than I do." She folded her arms across her chest and leaned back on her heels.

He was taking all this new information personally.

How could he not? He'd met someone, had been told he was going to be a parent long before he was ready and with someone who he'd only known a handful of months.

Autumn had been good, though. When he'd popped the question, she said she had to think about it. Over the days that followed, she'd seemed genuinely anguished about the decision to rush their relationship and that had only made him want to protect her more.

How stupid was he?

Normally, liars gave themselves up. There were signs. The direction of their gaze when they responded to a question would tell him how truthful they were being. Or how fast a verbal response came. A liar paused in the wrong places. They were also good at hiding their eyes or mouth during questioning. There were other telltale signs like coughing or clearing their throat before answering.

A practiced liar could get around most of the signs. A pathological liar—someone who believed the lies— was the most difficult to detect.

Summer was a valuable witness and now that Pandora's box had been opened to his past, he needed answers. She was the fastest route and they both had the same goal.

"It'll take me a minute to get my head around this… situation. I don't take vows lightly and I'm currently in a tailspin, which doesn't mean I don't want to help. Please, continue."

Summer eyed him warily and his heart squeezed. Her pain was obvious. He wasn't the only one Autumn had hurt.

She took in a breath before her next words. "The

last time I heard from her she said that she was going through something with an ex but not to worry. Everything was fine and she was happy with you."

He shot her a look but quickly apologized for it.

It was impossible to believe she ever cared about him, considering the fact she'd walked away without a backward glance. If she'd been in trouble, he couldn't think of a better person to help than a member of law enforcement. If she'd needed to hide, who better to ask than a US marshal? Relocating witnesses was one of his specialties.

"For what it's worth, I do think she loved you," Summer clarified.

Now he really shot her a look.

"What? You don't believe me?" she asked.

"No, I don't. How could anyone be happy who is living a lie? The woman I married told me she was an only child and that her parents were killed in a car crash on the interstate a few years after she went to college." He stopped right there because the woman's jaw looked like it was about to smack the floor. "Explain that."

"She doesn't like to talk about the past. It was hard for both of us. I think there was a year in California where we got passed around to four different foster homes and there was this point where I saw it break my sister. I think she shut down some critical emotions and never could get them back. She wasn't a bad person. She was just…" Her gaze shifted up and to the right like she was searching for the right word.

"Lost?" The way Summer, if he could believe that was her name, spoke about Autumn made him realize she *did* know her sister. As identical twins, it stood to reason the two would have known each other intimately. "Why would she suddenly move to Texas if she grew up in California?"

"You want my best guess?"

He nodded.

"We're originally from here. Our parents were together when we were really young, and we lived in Austin as a family. Our dad took off when we were still little. My mom had a cousin in California. She thought she could make a better life for us there. She was a very beautiful woman and she felt like maybe there was easy money out there in Los Angeles as a model."

"But there wasn't?"

"LA was harder than she expected, and she got depressed. Four of us lived in a one-bedroom apartment and her cousin wasn't happy Mom wasn't pulling her weight. There were some parties in our apartment complex, and I remember coming home from school to find her passed out on the couch. Her drinking got out of control and she couldn't keep it together."

Again, this was something Dawson came across in his line of work more than he cared to. Despite his frustration at the situation, he had sympathy for Summer and Autumn. No kid deserved a father who turned his back on the family or a mother who couldn't cope with the demands of bringing up children. There were resources out there for those who would use them but it was always the kids who suffered and they were the innocent ones in the equation.

"Someone called child protective services when my sister and I were locked out of our house. Our mom got in a really bad fight with her boyfriend, so he pushed us outside and locked the door while he broke her nose and her jaw. I think our neighbors were afraid of what might happen to us next, so they called the authorities."

His heart broke for their lost childhood. It was obvious that Summer was Autumn's identical sister. Put the two of them facing each other and it would be like one of them looking into a mirror. But they seemed like exact opposites in terms of personality despite growing up under the same conditions.

What he couldn't figure out was why his wife would lie to him. In fact, their entire life was built on lies. More of that anger and frustration built up inside of him.

"Autumn was in trouble based on the texts. What makes you think she's gone?" He couldn't imagine a scenario where this would be Autumn standing in front of him.

"She stopped all communication. She never would have done that." Summer seemed convinced on that point. Dawson couldn't say one way or the other. He should've known his wife better than that. Autumn had shown up in his life and tore through town, his heart, like a tornado.

"With all due respect, she married a man who never knew you existed," he countered.

"I see your point." She was rocking her head. "But I have known my sister for the past twenty-nine years. Even when she spirals, she answers my texts. And especially our emergency signal."

Well she obviously knew her sister a hell of a lot better than he'd known his wife. Had she been in real trouble? Was that the reason she'd taken off?

Dawson's mind was still spinning. He couldn't help but think he'd been taken for a fool. The unproductive thought wouldn't help matters.

He wasn't in love with her anymore. That ship had sailed. Lick his wounds? He'd done that. Being burned had a way of bruising the ego.

As weeks had turned into months with no word from Autumn after divorce papers had been signed, he realized his mistake had been marrying someone he barely knew.

There were other things that she told him and he now wondered if there was any truth to her words.

"Can I ask you a question?" Dawson wasn't exactly sure he wanted to know the answer.

She shrugged. "Why not?"

"Did she talk to you about me before the wedding?" He studied her, trying to decide if he could trust her.

"I didn't even know about you until after you were already married. She did send me a picture. Two actually."

"But did you communicate? Did you talk on the phone or whatever it is you guys did?" The question burning through him shouldn't matter. He wanted to know if she'd cared about him at all. Would he have been trying to build a life with someone who was callous? Or had there been something real between them? It might not have been that all-consuming something he thought he'd have with the woman he loved. He'd convinced himself that he could build a future with Autumn and their child.

"Nope, just the wedding pictures. I asked her if I could meet you and I never got a response. Whatever was going on with her back then was obviously big. It wasn't like her to go dark for too long. Although, to be perfectly honest, my sister could be unpredictable."

A shocked cough came out before he could stop it.

"Did she mention the baby?"

Now it was Summer's turn to be floored. Her violet eyes were huge and again her jaw seemed like it was about to hit the floor. "Are you saying what I think you are?"

"That your sister was pregnant? Yes. At least that's what she told me." Everything she'd told him was suspect now. Their entire relationship was tarnished with the latest information he was receiving.

"I'm so sorry." There was so much compassion in those eyes. "Did you ask for verification, like from a doctor?"

"She showed me a positive result on one of those stick tests. I didn't question much after that," he admitted.

"I'm sorry to tell you this." She glanced around like she was searching for the right words. The knot tightening in his gut that told him this was about to get a whole lot worse. "That would have been impossible. We were in a car crash with one of our fosters and my sister took an impact to her midsection. We were in the hospital for weeks. I got these scars." She rolled up her sleeve and showed him a four-inch scar running up her left arm. "My sister injured her abdomen. She had emergency surgery and the doctors had to remove most of her female parts including her fallopian tubes. There's no way my sister was pregnant."

The baby bombshell had been the reason Dawson had asked her to marry him. Looking back, he'd been a fool and he sure as hell felt like it right now. He'd been played in one of the worst possible ways. He muttered a few choice words under his breath, unable to suppress his frustration.

In his line of work, he spent the bulk of his time

locking up people who lied, cheated and manipulated. How could he not have realized he was living with one of them?

The answer came quick. She'd been the best. He hadn't seen her deceptions coming. Most criminals were locked up because they weren't smart enough to pull off their crimes. Autumn had been intelligent and, if he was being honest, wounded. She'd brought out all his protective instincts by making him feel like she was alone in the world. He'd let his primal instincts take over, pushing logic out of the way in the process.

When he really thought about it, he deserved everything he was getting.

But, damn, he had to be suspicious of everyone he came across in his line of work. One of his favorite things about living in Katy Gulch and still being connected to his family's ranch was that he could leave work behind him and live a normal life.

In Katy Gulch, he let his guard down. He *could* let his guard down. Almost everyone in town knew each other. There were a few outliers who lived outside town and were very private about their business. They'd learned recently that a woman thought to be a little old lady turned out to be connected to an illegal baby adoption ring. Mrs. Hubert's case had brought up all kinds of questions about his sister's kidnapping decades ago.

Now he felt like he'd been duped in the place where he felt the most relaxed and himself.

"How long did you know my sister before the two of you got married?"

"Clearly not long enough."

Chapter Five

"I'm so sorry," Summer started but was stopped with a warning look from Dawson.

"You already apologized," he pointed out.

"Yes, but I—"

"Feel responsible?" he asked.

She nodded.

"Why? Did you know your sister lied about a pregnancy to get me to marry her?" His question came out more like he'd issued a challenge.

"No." Summer's heart sank. She shouldn't feel responsible for her sister's actions. "It doesn't make me hurt any less for what she put you through."

It was hard to look into his eyes with the admission, but she did anyway. He needed to know how badly she felt.

"I hate to break this news to you, but your sister is a grown woman capable of manipulating grown men. I'm not trying to brag but I'm good at my job. The fact that I lived with a con artist shows how good she was." He didn't add the fact she'd lied to a member of law enforcement and gotten away with it. Or that he must feel so burned right now even though the fact was written all over his face. "If you didn't know or weren't involved, it's not your fault."

Summer issued a sharp sigh. "How could I have not known how much trouble my sister was in?"

"I lived with her and didn't know. If what you're saying is true, and I believe it is, then she disappeared—" He put his hand up to stop her protest. "She tricked me into believing we were going to have a baby *and* a real marriage. Although, I was fool enough to volunteer for that last part to the point she had me thinking getting married because of a child was my idea."

No matter how hard or frustrating this had to be for Dawson, to his credit, he didn't raise his voice. Summer still flinched if there was conflict and especially the sound of a man yelling. Chin out, she could handle whatever came her way but those were hard-won skills.

Whatever had happened to the marriage was one thing, at least he'd cared about her sister.

"I have a lifelong habit of feeling responsible for my sister's actions. I can promise to try to do better and that's as far as I can go right now."

"That's all anyone can ask." He stopped as her stomach reminded both of them she hadn't eaten in a while. His gaze dropped to her midsection. "How about we grab some food and start searching for answers?"

"You'd still help me?" She couldn't hide her shock.

"I have a few days owed to me at work and no big cases pending. It won't hurt to request time off. Besides, there's a private family matter that has been needing my attention. Maybe we can kill two birds with one stone." He seemed to regret his word choice when he shot a look of apology.

She shook her head. He didn't mean to dredge up

bad feelings and he didn't seem convinced that Autumn was gone anyway. With his help, she could get to the bottom of things quicker. If it was any other person besides Dawson O'Connor, she would have doubts about taking his help. The man was a US marshal. He knew how to protect himself. Heck, the ranch had its own security if it wasn't enough that he worked in law enforcement.

"I probably have some leftovers in the fridge if you're not opposed—"

"Anything sounds fine as long as it's not too spicy. I don't do hot." She looked at him and her face flushed.

A ghost of a smile crossed his lips. "How does meatloaf sound?"

"I haven't had meatloaf in… I can't remember how long." Getting help breaking down the details of her sister's case gave Summer the first burst of hope in weeks.

"Meatloaf it is." He pulled out a container and dished food onto two plates. After pushing a couple of buttons on the microwave, the smell filled the kitchen.

"Can I help with anything?" she asked, not used to letting someone else wait on her.

"I'm almost done." He moved to the cabinet and located two glasses. The cotton of his shirt stretched and released over a strong back. Summer diverted her eyes. She had no business ogling Dawson O'Connor's backside.

Looking down at her hand, she realized she was gripping the necklace so tightly there were deep indentations in her left palm. She loosened her grip on the necklace and placed it on top of the small box of her sister's possessions.

"Water okay?" he asked.

"Perfect."

"I figure we can have coffee after we eat while you tell me what you know up to this point and we move on from there."

More of that dangerous hope blossomed. Summer wasn't kidding herself that her sister was out there somewhere still alive despite the fact her heart wanted it to be true. Scrappy and Thick Guy had made it abundantly clear about that. They seemed to have first-hand knowledge that Autumn was gone. It had been a long couple of weeks and more than anything else, she needed answers. Justice had been too much to hope for. Now? There was hope.

Since she'd learned early in life just how slippery a slope hope could be, she wouldn't get too comfortable.

Dawson set a plate down in front of her along with silverware and a glass of water. It was foreign allowing someone to do something for her. Even something so simple as serving food had been off-limits with anyone else.

Summer tried to convince herself that she was too tired to protest. A tiny voice in the back of her mind called her out. There was something easygoing and honest about Dawson that made her relax a little bit around him.

The food was beyond amazing. Before she knew it, she'd cleared her plate. "Did you make this?"

That ghost of a smile returned to his lips—lips she had no business staring at. She refocused.

"Not me. I'm not the best in the kitchen. Laurel cooks up a few meals so it's easy for me to heat something up after work. Other times, I eat at the main house with whoever shows," he said.

Summer wanted to know more about Dawson. She tried to convince herself it had to do with understanding the man who'd made her sister happy, even if it had been for the briefest amount of time.

Again, that voice called her out. She was curious about him for selfish reasons. Reasons she couldn't allow herself to go into now or ever.

"Does your family own this whole ranch?" she asked.

"We're fourth generation cattle ranchers," he said with a nod. She could've sworn his chest expanded with what looked a lot like pride. He finished the last bite of food and took a drink of water. He'd said those words like they were common knowledge. Maybe growing up here in Katy Gulch, it was. She was an outsider despite Dawson making her feel right at home.

It was easy to see why Autumn had fallen for him.

"A dynasty?" The question was meant to be a joke. One look at him stopped her from laughing.

"Something like that." He was serious.

"Okay, what does that even mean?"

"That we're comfortable." So basically, rich.

"Can I ask a question?" Trying to word this without being offensive proved tricky.

"Yeah." It didn't help matters that even when he spoke one word his masculine voice traveled all over her.

"If you own all this land and your family has all this money…why become a US marshal?" Her question caused a low rumble of laughter to escape his serious mouth.

"You said it."

She cocked her head to the side and her eyebrows pinched together.

"My family is wealthy. That gives me a roof over my head that I don't have to pay for and privileges that make life a whole lot easier, like Laurel. But it stops there. I may inherit money, but I have my own life. I live off my own paycheck and invest the money I would've spent on a mortgage. I know how fortunate I am, and I don't take it for granted. If my parents never left me a dime, I'd do just fine on my own. Better than fine."

"Your attitude is impressive. Most people would just ride their legacy out." Summer had even more respect for Dawson now. Even though she'd barely met him didn't mean she didn't know him. He was one of the most down-to-earth people she'd ever met, despite growing up with all this and standing to inherit what must be one of the biggest fortunes in Texas.

He had honor beyond any man she'd ever known. The fact that he would bother to drive to Austin to bail out a woman who'd coldly left him, and to return a box of her prized possessions, struck her heart. He was showing incredible kindness to Summer, despite everything he'd been through. He was concerned about her having a decent meal when he could just try to pin her for answers—answers he deserved.

"Yeah? Seems like a waste of a life to me," he said, like his outlook toward life was no big deal.

"How many siblings do you have?" Getting to know him wasn't helping with her attraction.

"There are seven of us in total but my only sister was kidnapped when she was six months old. She was the firstborn and I doubt Mom would've survived the ordeal if she hadn't found out she was pregnant with my oldest brother a few weeks after."

Summer was stunned. "I can't even imagine what that would do to a mother, let alone being new parents." She studied him. He hadn't even been born at the time of the kidnapping and yet she picked up on something in his voice—a palpable sadness—when he mentioned his sister. "What happened? Did they find her?"

"The case was never solved." He shook his head before picking up the plates. "My father recently died."

"I'm so sorry." She stopped him with her hand on his arm. The sheer amount of electricity that pulsed through her fingertips startled her. She pulled her hand back and flexed her fingers.

She cleared her throat that had suddenly gone dry. "I can do those."

"Don't worry about it." His voice was trying to come off as casual but there was enough tension for her to realize he'd had the same reaction to physical contact.

"At least let me help."

He stopped for a second and the left corner of his mouth curled. She wondered if he even realized he'd done it. "How about this…you rinse these off and I'll make coffee?"

"Deal." It would give her something to do besides feel like she was betraying her sister with the strong attraction she felt toward Dawson.

Dishes done, fresh coffee in hand, Dawson motioned toward the sofa as she bit back a yawn. She caught him staring at her on the walk over, so he seemed to think it was a good idea to speak his mind when he asked, "When was the last time you slept?"

"It's been a couple of days." She suppressed another yawn. Now that she had a full belly, her body craved rest. Or, maybe it was being around Dawson that allowed her to let her guard down enough to think about dozing off. She'd been sleeping in thirty-minute intervals since arriving in Austin seven days ago.

Seven was the number of days it apparently took to show up in enough places to attract the interest of who she suspected were her sister's killers.

"Think you can sleep now?" He watched as she tried to bite back another yawn.

She took a sip of coffee. "This should help. I want to work on figuring out what happened to Autumn."

"First things first, I need to clear time off with my boss. I'll still have access to law enforcement resources and my guess is we'll need all the help we can get."

Summer didn't feel alone for the first time since this whole ordeal started. And maybe the first time in her whole life, but she didn't want to try to analyze that sentiment now. She sat up straighter and took another sip of coffee. The sofa was made to sink into. She blinked her eyes a couple of times. They'd gone dry on her.

"What do you need me to do?"

There was a laptop on the coffee table that he grabbed and then balanced on his thighs. "You believe your sister was murdered."

He was restating the obvious. "Yes."

"But you don't have proof?"

"No." Again, this was obvious. She wondered where he was going with all this.

"So, I'm looking for a Jane Doe in Austin."

Hearing those words were a hit to Summer's heart. It took a minute for her to be able to respond. "Yes."

A Jane Doe meant an unidentified body.

"She could be in a hospital somewhere." He seemed to be able to read her thoughts. Then again, he was a seasoned investigator. "She would be tagged as Jane Doe if she refused to give her name."

"Hospitals are a good place to start." Summer didn't have it inside her to hope after what the two men chasing her had said.

"And morgues." He was staring at the laptop screen when he seemed to realize how hearing that word might affect Summer. He glanced up and locked eyes. "I'm sorry. I've learned to distance myself from investigations. It's how we get through the rough ones. It doesn't mean that I don't care what happened to Autumn."

"That makes a lot of sense to me actually." Hadn't Summer been doing that on some level for most of her life? Tucking away her emotions. Forcing them somewhere down so deep she couldn't feel anymore. She and Dawson weren't so different.

"It can come off as uncaring but it's really all about focusing every ounce of energy and brain power on finding out the truth."

"And then what?"

"The really bad cases cause you to spend a lot of time at the gym trying to work off the frustration," he said honestly. It also explained why he was in amazing shape.

"Does your work cause you to have a lot of intense days?"

"Yeah," he said with another half smile. "It does. But there's a pretty big payoff when you take a criminal off the streets and give justice to a family that has been waiting. Everyone deserves that."

She thought about his sister and the fact that her case was never solved. It occurred to her that he brought justice to families when he'd never gotten it for himself or his family.

If she had to guess, he was in his early thirties, which meant the case was several decades old. That was a long time to go without knowing what had happened to a loved one. Her sister's lies to him about a pregnancy when he was the kind of person who wouldn't take that lightly made her angry.

"I'm sorry about your sister, Dawson."

"Thank you." He paused long enough to look at her, catching her gaze and holding on to it. "Now, let's find out what happened to yours."

Chapter Six

Dawson checked the last on his list of hospitals and came up empty. He and Summer had divided the names, working side by side and making call after call. In all, there'd been four Jane Does admitted in the last week to three major hospitals in Austin.

Patient privacy made it tricky to get information but Dawson had a few tricks up his sleeve. He was able to rule out all four Janes, which didn't mean Autumn wasn't in a bed somewhere under a false name.

So, that was a dead-end trail.

The morgue was easier to navigate. There'd been nine Jane Does this month, none of whom fit Autumn's description. If she was dead, her body hadn't shown up anywhere in Austin. There were plenty of places to dump a body in and around Austin. He gave his contact information to the coroner in the event a body showed up that might be a hit.

By eight o'clock, he'd filed a missing persons report and made sure she'd been entered into the database.

It was obvious to him that Summer was running on fumes, but she refused to go to bed. So, when he saw her slumped over on the couch with her eyes closed, he put a blanket over her and dimmed the lights.

Getting into the groove of treating this like any normal investigation helped. He had a rhythm that went along with ticking boxes off a checklist. Routine was good in times like these.

When he'd made every call on Autumn's behalf that he could, he decided to do a little digging into her personal life. For instance, their marriage.

They'd had a small ceremony. She'd insisted on getting married in Austin and he was beginning to see that the city held a special place in her heart. Especially if that's where she went after she left him. He probably could've traced her, considering they were still legally married for a time. He'd been too busy licking his wounds.

But, now that he thought about it, a few of her actions seemed suspect. Like how she'd insisted on being the one to arrange everything. She'd said that she wanted to be married before they told his family about the pregnancy, insisting that it would lead to less embarrassment in the long run.

He hadn't cared one way or the other. He'd been busy with work and the ranch. So, he'd let her take the lead. She'd also insisted the wedding be just the two of them and Laurel. Again, he'd thought it was a little odd at the time but the most important thing to him had been to become a family so they could get ready for their baby.

The loss Dawson felt when she'd told him she'd lost the baby not long after the wedding still felt real. It had hollowed him out in unexpected ways. For one, he'd known that he wasn't ready to become a father, or a husband for that matter. He was still far too married to his work and kept way too busy on the ranch.

So, the devastation he'd felt when he'd learned about the miscarriage had caught him off guard. Don't get him wrong, he'd been scared as hell after first learning Autumn was pregnant. But he figured no person was ever truly ready for such a life-changing event.

And from firsthand experience he could tell anyone who asked that no one was ever truly ready for the loss, either. Looking back, Autumn had sure played the part. She'd seemed so broken after the news that he felt the need to protect her even more.

The fact she'd played him both ways still stung.

Dawson pulled up the copy of the divorce papers figuring he needed to interview anyone and everyone connected to Autumn. It had been so early in the pregnancy he hadn't been to a doctor's appointment yet. She'd said she had someone she trusted in Austin and had taken several daylong trips to tie up loose ends.

Katy Gulch had an incredible doctor that Dawson's mother had recommended. Autumn had burst into tears at the suggestion of changing doctors. At the time, Dawson's mother reassured him that pregnant women had all kinds of hormones and told him not to take it too personally.

Now he wished he'd asked for the name of her doctor in Austin. Of course, the pregnancy was a sham so she most likely would've made something up. He couldn't exactly count on anything she'd told him.

Which also made him wonder about the friend of hers, supposedly a minister who she'd insisted marry them. Dawson had asked for the marriage certificate so he could add her to his work benefits and she'd stalled big-time.

Had she backed herself into a corner?

The obvious reason someone would want to pin him down for marriage was money. But she hadn't asked for or taken a dime. Looking back, it was also the reason he'd signed the divorce papers so easily. She'd wanted nothing but her freedom. He'd been too hurt and angry to fight back. His pride had been wounded. He'd scribbled his name on the dotted line after reviewing the document and then mailed it back after making a copy for his records.

He wouldn't make the mistake of not fact-checking another relationship.

There'd been no need to cancel her insurance at work because he'd never officially added her to anything. Considering he'd never been married before, he took her word for everything. Why wouldn't he? She was his wife. Adding her to his insurance was a simple thing to him. She'd said something about being covered under a different policy that didn't run out until the end of the year.

In his personal life, he'd never been betrayed. Had that made him naive?

Dawson pulled up his divorce file and searched for the name of her attorney. Matt Charley Shank. There was no address on the letterhead, which was odd. He found it in the body of the second page.

Dawson typed in the name to get a phone number. He shouldn't be surprised at the search results. There was no Matt Charley Shank listed as an attorney in Austin.

He flexed and released his fingers a couple of times to work out some of the tension. He needed to hit the gym for a good workout but there was no time. He could, however, fire off a few push-ups. He had a set of weights in the garage for those times when he needed a quick workout.

This seemed like one of those times. But first, he checked the internet for the name of Autumn's minister friend, Grover Hart, to see what church he belonged to. Not a huge surprise at this point when Dawson learned Grover Hart's services could be bought and paid for. His big claim to fame? Weddings, no licenses required.

If the attorney was a sham and the minister was a sham, the marriage had to be a sham.

SUMMER STOOD IN the opened doorway leading into the garage. A heavy metal band played low in the background. It was the middle of the night. A shirtless Dawson pumped weights. Her gaze lingered a little too long on his muscled chest, mesmerized by the tiny beads of sweat.

She forced her gaze away and cleared her dry throat.

"Sorry to interrupt, is it okay if I use the restroom to freshen up?" she asked.

He didn't seem surprised that she'd been standing there and that made her cheeks burn with embarrassment. Getting caught staring at him didn't top her list of things to do when she woke up. She was still trying to figure out how she'd fallen asleep in the first place.

She'd woken to a dimly lit room with a blanket placed over her.

"Make yourself at home." He sat up and grabbed a towel.

Summer forced herself to look away as he toweled off his face. He stood up. He still had on jeans that hung low on lean hips. He had the kind of body she'd expect to see on a billboard somewhere. His abs were cut. His arms strong. His waist lean. Don't even get her started on how gorgeous he was.

Dawson O'Connor was the total package. Intelligent. Decent. Smokin' hot. And fierce. He had a look in his eyes that said he wouldn't hesitate to go all in to protect someone he cared about. He also had the kind of confidence that said he could back it up, too.

An attraction to her sister's ex-husband couldn't happen. The electricity she felt radiating from him was most likely residual desire that he felt for Autumn, not Summer. He had, in fact, loved her sister enough to marry her. Granted, Autumn had played a dirty trick to get him to ask. But his feelings for her sister must run deep.

"I can show you where everything is." He tossed the towel onto the weight bench and headed in her direction. She immediately took a few steps back to allow him room to pass by. She needed to put as much distance between them as humanly possible.

Dawson paused long enough to make eye contact as he walked by. There was something in his eyes she couldn't quite put her finger on. Was looking at her in the home they were supposed to share like seeing a ghost?

"I'm sorry. I must remind you of her," she said softly.

"You'd think that would be the case but I couldn't help noticing how different you both are. Beautiful without a doubt, but now that I've had a chance to get to know you, I was just thinking how different you look to me. Strange how personality affects looks once the initial impression wears off. You know?"

"Yeah." She did know. She couldn't count the number of times she met an attractive man only to get to know him and never see him in the same light again. That wasn't the case with Dawson. His personality enhanced already drop-dead gorgeous looks. The saying that beauty was only skin deep came to mind. It was so true. There was so much more to a person and she'd been turned off countless times by outwardly attractive, inwardly awful people.

Summer followed Dawson to the opposite side of the main living area and down a hallway. There were several opened doors revealing an office, a bedroom and a bathroom.

"This is the guest suite. Make yourself comfortable."

She had little more than the clothes on her back and her handbag. He looked her over and moved to the closet.

"Laurel's niece is probably about your size. Rachel is a grad student in Houston and has stayed here a few times. She left behind a jogging suit if you want to borrow it."

"Thanks. I'll take you up on that offer," she said.

"I can throw your clothes in the wash while you shower if you want." The thought of Dawson handling her undergarments had her shaking her head. That was a hard no. She didn't want the image of him touching any of her personal belongings anywhere in her thoughts. Fighting the attraction when he stood this close was difficult enough. She didn't need to add mental images to the equation.

"I'll take care of it when I'm out of the shower if you point me in the direction," she quickly said. Too quickly.

He studied her for a long moment before he spoke again.

"I didn't find a Jane Doe in any of the hospitals I called or at the morgue."

"Any hits on the missing persons report or is it too early?" she asked.

"Never too early to hope but no."

"I can draw them out again if—"

"Hell, no. I won't risk your safety."

"It might be the fastest way to find out who we're dealing with," she countered.

"I won't argue your point and it's easy to see that you care about your sister. Let me do this the right way and investigate in a way that keeps you safe in the process. Okay with you?" Those intense penetrating eyes swayed her away from running off half-cocked. Doing that so far had almost gotten her killed. She reminded herself that she wasn't alone in this. Dawson had resources she didn't. Plus, she couldn't bring justice for her sister if Summer was dead.

She took in a deep breath. "Okay."

"I'll let you know if anything comes in while you grab a shower."

Thanking Dawson didn't seem nearly enough to cover her gratitude. It was a starting point.

He nodded before stepping into the hallway. With his hand on the door, he said, "You have this whole wing to yourself. Do you want the door open or closed?"

"I'll close it." She did before getting her bearings in the oversize guest room. One door led to a walk-in closet and another led to a large bathroom. There were fresh towels hanging and, she noticed, a white bathrobe on the back of the door.

There were shampoos on hand as well as fresh toothbrushes and toothpaste. The place was stocked and ready for company. Mostly likely Laurel's doing. Summer doubted someone who kept a full-time job as a marshal while still working the family ranch had time to think about stocking a guest bath.

She was grateful for Laurel. Now that she really thought about it, she'd like to circle back to the woman and have a conversation. If she and Autumn used to talk, maybe there was some hint there as to what Autumn's life had been like.

Again, guilt struck that Summer hadn't been more in tune with her sister. To be fair, Autumn was complicated. She marched to her own drum and had a tendency to go all-in before going all-out. She could be charming. And, although she and Summer shared the same genes, Autumn knew how to make the most of their looks.

To Summer's thinking, her sister had always been the prettier one of the two despite starting from the same blank canvas.

She showered in record time, thinking how great a cup of coffee would taste about now. She'd only managed a few sips of the other one before she'd conked out on the sofa. Like everything at Katy Bull Ranch, the coffee tasted better than anywhere else.

Autumn had found a sanctuary here. Why would she ever leave?

Had she gotten bored of the ranch? Best as she could remember about the timeline, Autumn and Dawson had only been together a few months before she'd played the pregnancy card. Summer was still mortified and embarrassed on her sister's behalf for that one.

And then what? How long had they been together before her sister had broken the news to him there was no baby? The web of lies was going to take some time and some untangling to find the truth. An honest man like Dawson would be frustrated by her sister's antics. Someone else might not handle the situation the same. Which begged the question, *was there someone else?*

Summer needed to sit down and develop a timeline. She always did her best thinking when she could see everything written on paper.

After meeting Dawson, even more questions simmered. One bubbled to the surface. Had Autumn come to Katy Gulch to hide and then found protection in Dawson O'Connor too good to pass up?

Chapter Seven

"Coffee smells amazing." Even the sound of Summer's voice was different from her sister's. He couldn't believe he'd ever thought she was his ex. And she looked even more beautiful after a few hours of sleep.

"I waited for you to get out of the bathroom to pour a cup." Dawson turned toward the voice and his chest tightened when he saw Summer standing at the kitchen doorway wearing the sweat suit on loan from Rachel. She had wadded up her clothes into a ball that she held.

There shouldn't be anything sexy about the clothes she had on. The material was standard cotton, and the top was tight at the waist. She had the zipper gripped so tight with her free hand there was no way the thing was moving.

He chalked up his reaction to her to simple biology. She was a beautiful woman, even more so as he got to know her. There was enough electricity pinging between them to light an entire house anytime the two stood close to each other.

Even at this distance, his body heated. And it was more than physical attraction. His heart fisted and he was in trouble. Then again, after the case was solved, she'd go back to living her life and he'd go back to his.

"Washer and dryer are down the other hallway." He was pretty damn certain there was no annual Christmas card obligation to his ex-wife's sister. He hadn't even known about her until she'd dropped the bomb on him that she was Autumn's sister. He'd shot off an email to one of his buddies to verify what he already knew in his heart, she was being honest about her identity.

His need to verify every new person in his life sat hard on his chest. He was used to being suspicious in his job but had always surrounded himself with good people. With Autumn, he'd had a lapse in judgment.

Something else had been gnawing at the back of his mind. A pathological liar believed their own lies. It was what made them so good at delivering them. The fact that she was a pathological liar made him think twice about what he'd discovered from the internet last night as he poured a cup of coffee for Summer and tried to shake the fresh-from-the-shower image out of his thoughts.

Work started on a ranch at 4 a.m. sharp so waking up at this time wasn't uncommon. To a normal person, this was the middle of the night and Grover Hart would fall under the category of "normal" person when it came to sleep patterns. That was as much leeway as Dawson would give the man.

Again, Dawson was kicking himself for letting his guard down with the wrong person. Those mistakes felt the worst. Trusting someone when he should've known better made him kick himself twice as hard.

By the time Summer returned, he'd gotten hold of his frustration enough to hand over the mug he'd filled.

Fresh-faced, her skin practically glowed. Thick, black lashes hooded violet eyes he could stare into for days.

She took a sip and he cleared his dry throat.

"Can you eat something?" he asked, trying to deflect much of his out-of-control reaction to her. Long, silky hair was still damp from the shower—a shower he didn't want to think much more about for obvious reasons.

"I couldn't eat another bite after filling up on that meatloaf a few hours ago. I'm still full." Her voice was a little too husky, a little too sexy. "It was heaven. Laurel must be a great cook."

Dawson had to fight every instinct he had not to lean in and kiss her. He imagined the horror on her face if he followed through with the impulse and that was a reality slap. Good. He needed to keep a clear mind.

"Did your sister ever mention any names to you in the past year or two?" he asked.

"Besides you? No. And she only gave me your first name in the beginning. I finally matched your picture to a news article." She took a sip of coffee and leaned her hip against the counter.

"How about Matt, Charley or Shank? Do any of those names sound familiar?" Following along the lines of Autumn being a pathological liar, she would use names that she wouldn't mix up easily. It was part of believing the lies.

Summer closed her eyes like she was reaching back as far as she could into her memory bank. "Seems like there was a Charley at some point."

Dawson retrieved a notepad and pen from the small built-in desk in the kitchen. He set them on top of the granite island and scribbled the names in those variations.

"You like to write stuff down?" she asked.

"Seems like everyone uses computers now. Call me old-fashioned but I like pen and paper," he admitted with a small smile.

"Same here. It's just easier for me to look at something when it's on paper for some crazy reason." She shook her head. "Go figure."

He didn't want to notice the similarities between him and Summer. He didn't want to notice how naturally beautiful she was or how a small line creased her forehead when she really concentrated. Or how sexy it was when it happened. He didn't want to notice how full her pink lips were or how sweet they would probably taste.

Dawson refocused on the piece of paper.

"What is it? Is there something on my face?" she asked.

"Nope. Your face is perfect." He caught his slip a few words too late. They were out there and he couldn't reel them back in now.

"Oh." The one word was all she said. He wished she'd said it with a little more shock or maybe even disgust. Instead, it was surprise and something that sounded a lot like hope.

Dawson's cell buzzed, a welcome break into the moment happening between them. He walked over to the sofa where he'd left it and then checked the screen.

"Hey, what did you find out?" he asked his buddy from work, Anderson Willis. Law enforcement worked round the clock and Anderson was one of the few people Dawson could call at this hour.

"I'm sorry to break the news to you, Dawson," came the familiar voice. "There's no record of you ever being married."

It was a double-edged sword. He shook off the shock and said, "I owe you one for tracking this answer down for me."

"You know I have your back."

"I appreciate it." Dawson ended the call and then looked to Summer. "Turns out, the wedding was a fake. I was never married to your sister."

"Why would she go through all that?" she asked.

"It explains a lot actually. She only wanted the two of us there for the ceremony with Laurel as a witness. Autumn insisted on handling all the details herself. I learned a few hours ago that the man who 'married' us was a for-hire and not a longtime family friend."

"But why trap you into marriage with a fake pregnancy story only to find out there'd never been a wedding in the first place?"

If he knew the answer to that question, he'd be so far ahead of the game. Investigations were like puzzles. Evidence often came one or a few pieces at a time. Sometimes the motive didn't make sense until all the pieces were in place.

This would most likely be one of those complicated cases.

"We'll start with the name Charley. It isn't much to go on but we'll know to pay special attention if his name comes up."

She moved over to the notepad, picked up the pen, wrote down the name.

"There was a coffee shop on Capital Avenue where my sister used to go. One of the workers did a double take when I showed up and it made me think he knew her. It could just be that she got coffee there when she was in town but the way he looked at me with…*surprise*… I guess is the right word…made me think there was something more to it."

"Capital Coffee?"

She nodded.

"I know that place," he said, trying to think of any politicians he knew with the first name of Charley. A political tie could explain her murder if she'd rubbed a politician the wrong way or if this was someone from her past. Austin was the capital. If she hung out at a coffee shop that was a known hangout for politicians, it could give them a direction.

"We need to look up any politician with the name Charley." That wouldn't be too difficult. Their names were public record.

"Or a political aid." She was right. And it made the list a whole lot longer and harder to track down.

"The only other people who frequent that coffee shop are UT professors. I doubt she'd have a run-in with one of those." Ideas started churning and they were making progress. Inching along at this point but he'd take what he could get. "How'd you find out about the coffee shop?"

"She sent me a picture from there a couple of times."

"It's a starting point. I don't like the idea of taking you back to Austin, though. Not while this situation is hot." He didn't doubt his skills in protecting a witness. One of the most important rules of the program was that the witness not return to the town from which they were relocated.

Technically, she wasn't the one being tracked. The

men chasing her didn't seem to know that. If Autumn had hid her twin sister from her so-called husband, she probably didn't talk about her family member with any of the men she'd dated.

That might mean no one would ever go looking for Summer. She could be safe if she went back to her life in Washington. Even though he highly doubted she'd go for what he was about to pitch, he had to do it anyway.

"What do you think of letting me take over the investigation from here?" He'd barely finished his sentence before she started shaking her head.

"No way." The finality in those words told him not to argue.

"Would you at least think about stepping back?"

The look she shot him made words unnecessary.

"The only reason I bring it up is because I can protect you better if you go back to your normal life and let me lead the investigation into your sister's case." He had a moral obligation to make her aware of her options.

She didn't immediately respond. Her lips were set in a thin line. She'd made up her mind. Instead of overreacting, she seemed to take a minute to pick apart his reasoning. The small crease appeared on her forehead. "I think I understand what you really mean. I understand the risks I'm taking. Believe me. I barely got away and I know that was sheer dumb luck. I got even luckier that, despite what my sister did to you, you are a decent enough human being to actually want to help. So, I'm not taking it for granted."

He was impressed with how well she'd thought out her response.

"You have a big family, right?"

"Yes," he confirmed.

"You guys are all close based on what you've told me so far." Her argument was already being laid out for her the minute she brought his family into it.

"That's right."

"My sister is all I have in the world. She might not be perfect. Believe me when I say that I can count the ways in which she isn't. But we made a pact to have each other's backs. I told her that I'd always be there for her. I've let her down in the worst possible way. There's so much that I'd do differently now. I can't go back. I can't change what has happened. I can't bring her back. All I can do is nail the bastards who hurt her."

There were only two words appropriate as a response. "Fair enough."

THE WASHING MACHINE BUZZED. Summer forced her shoulders to relax. "I know where to go."

The washing machine was down the same hallway as the garage. The hallway was longer and there was a window at the end. She moved her clothes through to the dryer, pushing the sexy sweaty images of Dawson out of her thoughts. It was probably good that she would only know Dawson for a few more days before heading back to Washington and to her life there.

Not that she had much of one. She'd been saving tips to take a few computer classes so she could get a nine-to-five job. She wasn't particular about where she worked as long as it didn't involve hustling drinks or food. She'd done both. Often at the same time to make rent.

Summer and her sister had had a crazy dream when they were little of owning their own shop. When they were super little, the dream had been to open a toy store and then they'd wanted a small bookstore. At least, Summer had. Autumn had said she didn't care as long as there was a coffee shop attached for her to manage.

Then, her sister started drifting around and moved farther and farther away, not just physical distance. The calls had stopped coming. Autumn was later and later returning Summer's calls.

The reason Summer had been working in restaurants and bars was to save up enough to start their business. She'd been working every job from waitress to assistant manager trying to learn everything she could about running a business.

Everything came to an abrupt stop after Autumn sent news she got married. Her life was going to be with her husband and she said that Summer shouldn't worry about finances because Autumn had married well.

At first, Summer questioned whether or not her sister had married for a bank account. The look on her face in the wedding picture had given Summer hope that wasn't the case. Finding out her sister had forced Dawson's hand still didn't sit well. Now there was the fact she'd actually never truly been married in the first place.

But she'd wanted Summer to believe she was married, and still was married. She turned on the dryer and headed back to the kitchen. She walked over to the pen and wrote down the word *married*.

"My sister didn't tell me about the divorce." She flashed eyes at him. "Even though it was all fairy tale or smoke and mirrors, however you look at it."

"It wasn't real," he seemed quick to confirm.

"But she wanted me to believe it. I'm wondering if she wanted someone else to believe it, too."

"Possibly someone named Charley?" he asked.

"It's all I can think of," she said. "It worked with me. I really thought she was happy and I stopped worrying about her." The fact she'd rarely returned messages in the past year had barely registered with Summer. "I was busy coming up with a Plan B for my life after hers seemed settled."

"So, her wanting you to believe she was married was important," he agreed.

"It's also strange that she left this box here." She motioned toward the wooden box with what was supposed to be her sister's most prized possessions. "She knew she was leaving. Right?"

"I believe so."

"Then, why take off without something so personal? I'm guessing the way she left things with you that she never intended to come back," she said.

He rocked his head. "That's been my assumption this whole time. The main reason someone leaves something of value behind is the person is in such a rush they forget it."

"I'm probably just wanting to see the best in my sister but I wonder if she left my necklace because she wanted to protect my identity." She picked up the pendant and let it rest on her flat palm.

"It's highly possible." He reached for the pen she'd set down and wrote "protect loved one."

"Have you considered that she might have been trying to protect you?" she asked him.

"It crossed my mind that she picked me for my ability to protect *her*." His response was honest, and she could give him that. There was far more hurt in his tone when he talked about Autumn now. He'd said before that he was in full-on investigator mode.

"That might be true. She seemed like she was hiding and making rash decisions. Some of it feels illogical."

"We have a lot of puzzle pieces missing," he agreed before glancing at the wall clock. "In a couple of hours, we leave for Austin."

His cell buzzed and this time it was still sitting on the granite island. He walked over to it. The look on his face when he checked the screen nearly stopped her heart.

Chapter Eight

"Thank you for letting me know."

Those six words were going to change Summer's life forever. She just knew it. Her legs gave and she smacked her hand on the island to stop herself from going down. All along, she'd known it. And yet confirmation of her sister's death nearly pulled her under.

Dawson was by her side in the next second, his strong hand steadying her, helping her stay upright.

"I'm sorry." Two words she hated more than anything in that moment.

He helped her to the couch and brought a fresh cup of coffee. For a long time, she couldn't speak as tears streamed. Dawson gave her space. He set his laptop up at the granite countertop and took a stool. He'd moved it to the side presumably so he could keep an eye on her.

Summer didn't want to know the details of what had happened just yet. She just sat there, suspended in time, unable to think or speak. Her brain refused to process. A fog descended, cloaking her with a heaviness that pressed so hard on her chest she could barely breathe.

Sipping coffee to try to jar herself out of the haze of grief, she hugged a pillow to her chest.

The dryer went off at some point. She didn't care. She heard Dawson move around without really registering what he was doing. The coffee in her cup had long since gone cold. She rolled the mug around in her palms.

Tears dried up at some point. She couldn't be certain when and didn't care. The sun came up and she cursed the fact. How could life go on when her heart had just been ripped out of her chest?

Come on, she finally tried to rally. She'd known this news was coming. She'd had time to deal with it. There was something extra devastating about that final blow, something extra cruel and final. She curled up on her side and pulled the blanket from last night over herself, suddenly feeling very cold.

The details could wait. In a few hours, she'd learn the condition of what would now be referred to as *the body*. She hoped like hell there was some evidence, a fingerprint or piece of DNA that could bring closure to the case and justice for her sister.

A small part of her didn't want this investigation to end. She didn't want to go back to the nonlife she'd had in Washington. The one where she had no real purpose anymore.

But then if wishes were being granted, she wanted her sister back. No matter how irresponsible Autumn had been or how lost, there had been something very good inside her that had been worth fighting for. At least Summer thought so.

Summer leaned forward and set the mug on the coffee table. A few seconds later, Dawson brought over a plate of food. She glanced at it, figuring there was no way that a breakfast sandwich was going down. It could go down but she highly doubted it would stay there for long.

The glass of water, on the other hand, she decided to try.

"Okay if I sit with you?" Dawson asked.

"I'd like that a lot." She meant it, too. The only light in this dark situation was the fact she hadn't been alone when she'd heard the news. Having been on her own for most of her life caused her to learn to depend on herself early. Being completely alone for the rest of her life was one of her worst fears. She'd been so afraid that if she lost her sister she would fade away, too.

She scooted over enough for him to sit next to her. It was unexpected for him to be her comfort. But she didn't hesitate for a second when he tugged her toward him.

Burying her face in his chest, she released the pent-up frustration that had been simmering for years.

DAWSON KNEW BETTER than to be Summer's comfort for too long. It was dangerous territory for him because it would be all too easy to get lost in her violet eyes. He couldn't argue how right she felt in his arms. Instead of giving in to what he wanted, he put up a wall.

His mind was still spinning from everything he'd learned in the past twenty-four hours. Autumn's lies stacked up from the fake pregnancy to the fact she never went to college or had a living relative. There was a lot to unpack and try to digest. Even though a year had passed, learning he'd been lied to and tricked caused all his old walls to shoot up. The thought of letting anyone else in seemed about as appealing as drinking motor oil.

Except, when it came to Summer, he found that he wanted to trust. There was a quiet strength and vulnerability in her that touched him in a deep place. Losing Autumn had hurt his pride. Losing Summer would break his heart.

Dawson's cell buzzed where he'd left it on the granite island. Summer tensed and then pulled back as though she realized the worst blow had already been delivered. It had. He couldn't imagine losing one of his brothers out of the blue like that.

He pushed up to standing and got to his phone in time to answer after a glance at the screen. "Hey, Colton."

His older brother was sheriff but there was no need for formalities.

"I wish I had better news." The fact that Colton was getting right to the point sent an icy chill racing down Dawson's spine.

"What is it?" Dawson asked.

"It's Dad. A private investigator came forward and said he gave Dad information about possible known associations of Mrs. Hubert a few weeks before Dad's death. Someone might've come onto the property to stop him. And there's more."

"What else?" The question had to be asked.

"Someone used his credit card two days ago, so we're diving in to figure out who and how the person got it." Colton said.

"If Dad was following up on a lead and that's what got him killed, would the killer be crazy enough to use the credit card?" Dawson asked.

"It's a reasonable assumption. The fact that his credit card was used a few days ago could mean a lot of things. He might've dropped his wallet and someone found it before he was murdered."

"True." There was no need for them to go over all the possibilities since both worked in law enforcement and both had seen plenty in their time on the job.

"Where was his credit card used?" Dawson asked.

"Convenience store in Beckridge."

"That's not far. There'd be camera footage. Right?"

"The Mart doesn't keep the recordings. They wipe them out every day. It would be impossible to know who used the credit card based on any footage," Colton explained.

"We could determine if the person was male or female, though. And the clerk might have a description. Let's see, the highway runs straight through there." Dawson was grasping at straws, hoping for a witness.

"The clerk couldn't remember who used the card. And, I talked to mother and she wanted to increase the size of the reward for information about Dad's murder. What do you think about that?" Colton asked.

"Ten thousand dollars is already a lot of money for someone to do the right thing."

"You won't get any arguments out of me there." At least he and his brother were on the same page.

"Did you tell her that might invite gold diggers into the party? The amount of false leads would go through the roof if we increased it five or ten thousand dollars?" Dawson asked.

"I sure did."

Dawson was preaching to the choir. His brother was a top-notch sheriff and would have already thought of all those things.

"For the record, I'm against the idea. I think it'll

bring too many quacks out of the woodwork. You probably have your hands full as it is with a ten-thousand-dollar reward," Dawson said.

"All of us are in unison on that," Colton confirmed. He, no doubt, would have contacted their other siblings.

"Changing subjects. Are you doing okay with *everything*?" Colton asked. The emphasis he'd placed on the last word gave a strong hint that he was talking about Summer.

Dawson wasn't ready to discuss anything about the sisters with his brother just yet. Especially not where he was on a personal level with Summer and he knew that was the real question Colton was asking. Dawson paused for a minute and the pieces started clicking together. Given how many of his brothers worked in law enforcement, the news about Autumn's death would've traveled through the family by now. He'd intended to call his brothers once he got his mind around the news. For now, Summer had been and still was his priority.

"We have a lot going on over here. I'm planning a road trip to Austin in a couple of hours. There are a few people I want to interview over there," he said. "And if we can keep the news about Autumn as quiet as possible, I'd appreciate it. And that goes for everyone who knows, not just the family."

The news about Autumn had been hard but not because of any residual emotions. He'd turned those off a while ago and was down to a bruised ego. Any anger he had toward her dissipated the minute he heard she was in trouble. It explained a lot about the way she'd acted. He was down to being genuinely sorry for her and her family on a human level rather than as an ex-husband. Hell, their marriage had been too brief for him to put down roots in the relationship. She'd swept in and out of his life like a spring thunderstorm.

"It's true. What you heard about Autumn," he said to his brother.

"I saw Laurel yesterday. I was in the barn when she brought Shadow over."

"Then you've probably pieced together the fact that Autumn has an identical twin sister. She's here and I'm going to help her see this through." Dawson braced himself for the argument that was sure to come from his brother—a brother who would have Dawson's best interest at heart without a doubt.

"You know each and every one of us is here if you need *anything.*" The way he emphasized that last word suggested the offer covered more than their brotherly bond. There was a hint of confusion in Colton's tone, which was understandable under the circumstances.

Dawson had no way to discuss something he didn't understand for himself. That "something" was his need to make this right for Summer.

"You say you're heading to Austin in a little while?" Colton brought the subject back to the investigation.

"That's right."

"You want any of us to tag along?" Colton asked.

"I got this. I appreciate the offer, though." Dawson figured he had enough contacts in Austin to get backup if anything went down. For now, he wanted to visit a coffee shop and a so-called minister. An internet search of Texas lawmakers didn't reveal anyone with the first name of Charles or Charley.

"You know I'm just a phone call and a couple of hours away if you need anything. I'm also pretty decent with the database, so if you need any help with research, I'm here for that, too," Colton offered.

"I appreciate you more than you know."

"It's what we do for each other. Right?" Colton said. It was true. Any one of them would drop what they were doing on a moment's notice for the other one.

Dawson thanked his brother before ending the call. He moved to the sink and filled a glass with water, and then polished it off. He'd pace if it would do any good. Frustration built when he thought about someone using his father's credit card like it was nothing, like they knew they wouldn't get caught. Finn O'Connor was strong and tough for any age. Under most conditions, he would have been able to hold his own. *Most* being the operative word.

Anyone could be taken down under the right conditions no matter how strong or well prepared. He needed to make a pit stop at the convenience store on the way to Austin. Shadow would be okay hanging out in the barn for a couple of days. He'd have to let the ranch foreman know, but that was easy enough. Shadow loved being at the barn so no reason to feel bad there. Apollo could certainly use the company.

From behind him, he heard the sound of Summer's bare feet on the wood floor. He could sense she was moving toward him. Her clean, fresh-flower smell filled his senses when he took in a breath meant to calm himself.

"Was that news about your father?" Summer's voice traveled over him, detonating in his heart.

"Yes. His credit card is in play a couple of towns over." He heard the hurt in his own voice when he spoke about his father—hurt he was usually so good at masking.

He set the glass down on the counter and released his hold on it for fear he might break it. He gripped the bullnose edge of the granite countertop instead.

There were a whole lot of *should not*s rolling around in Dawson's thoughts. He should not turn around. He should not take a step toward Summer. He sure as hell should not kiss her. But that's exactly what he did.

Dawson dipped his head down and captured those sweet, full, pink lips. He exhaled against her mouth as her tongue darted out.

Now it was Summer's turn to take in a breath as he pressed his lips against hers harder and the two melded together. She pushed up on her tiptoes and brought her hands up, tunneling her fingers in his hair as she took the lead, deepening the kiss.

Electricity pulsed through his body, bringing him back to life. He looped his hands around her waist as she pressed her body flush with his. Through the cotton material of the robe, he could feel her full breasts against his stomach. She was perfection and fit him perfectly.

She parted her lips, which gave him better access, and he drove his tongue inside her mouth. She tasted like dark roast coffee and a little bit of peppermint from brushing her teeth earlier. Dark roast coffee mixed with peppermint was his new favorite flavor.

Dawson's pulse skyrocketed and his heart jackhammered his ribs. Summer molded against him. When she opened her eyes and pulled back just enough for him to see those incredible violet eyes of hers, his heart detonated.

She seemed to search his gaze and he knew what was coming next.

"Is this a good idea, Dawson?" she asked.

Looking into those eyes, he couldn't imagine doing anything with her would be a bad idea. Bad timing? Now that was a thing.

If he'd met her two years ago or a year and a half ago, it would be so much easier to get lost in her. Now timing was a problem. He couldn't go back and undo the past. Normally, he understood the value of life lessons and hard situations. He could appreciate how deep he had to reach and how much he had to grow when times were tough.

Selfishly, he wanted Summer. He wanted those bright violet eyes and sweet lips. He wanted to get lost and forget how complicated all of this was.

Dawson muttered a curse under his breath. Because timing.

"Probably not." It was difficult to say that, considering their kiss brought him to life in places that had been dead too long. No one had caused that kind of reaction from him with something so simple before Summer. Timing.

"Then, we should probably put a stop to this." The uncertainty in her voice made him want to convince her otherwise. It didn't seem like it would take a whole lot and it definitely wouldn't on his part.

Her body pressing against his wasn't making it any easier to think straight. She had the kind of curves that made her feel like a real woman. Long legs, soft round bottom, she was perfect, sexy…

Dawson stopped himself right there. His arms still looped around her waist, he dipped his head down and feathered a kiss on her bottom lip. "I want to do this. I sure as hell don't want to stop. But, the last thing I want to do is confuse the situation any more than we already have."

Those words were a bad idea. He heard how they sounded coming out of his mouth and the hurt in her eyes compounded it. The thing was, he could see himself going *there* with her. He could easily see himself doing the get-to-know-her-better thing. He wanted to know all those little details about her that made up a relationship. Could he?

Could she? Could she stick around long enough to see if there was anything deeper than spark between them? Could she stay in one place long enough to figure out if this could ignite into a flame? See if there was any substance to turn initial attraction into something so much more?

There was nothing inside Dawson that wanted to jump into another serious relationship. He would doubt his own judgment every step of the way because of Autumn. She'd burned him enough to back away from the stove the second time.

An annoying voice in the back of his head told him he was making up excuses. Was he?

Hell, maybe he was the one who needed some distance. Nothing in his body or mind or heart wanted to take a step back from Summer. And that was dangerous under the circumstances.

He could make all the arguments he wanted to. The truth was that while he was standing toe to toe with Summer, he couldn't force himself to be the one to step back. She would have to do it. And she did.

Which also told him she could.

If he was going to guard his heart, he was going to have to do a better job than that.

Turned out Summer Grayson was his weak spot. Dawson needed to get more control over his emotions. The phrase "get a grip" came to mind.

What he needed was to get a handle before this became a runaway train.

The first time he'd seen Summer opened up a sore wound. Although, to be honest, she had seemed different from Autumn from the moment he laid eyes on her. He'd noticed all those quirks that were uniquely hers. Her personality could not be more opposite her sister despite a likeness. And he stopped there at a resemblance.

Dawson couldn't think of Autumn and Summer as identical because they were so different. Summer had that fresh-from-the-shower face. She looked like she ran a brush through her hair and let it flow.

Autumn, on the other hand, spent quite a bit of time in the bathroom tinkering around with her looks. Being around her triggered his protective instincts, but that wasn't the same as love. She'd been helpless and he'd stepped in. To be fair, he'd always seen himself with an independent, spirited wife for the long haul. Someone who could challenge his thinking and yet be silly enough to laugh at herself because life was guaranteed to deliver some hard knocks.

Summer, on the other hand, was strong. Yes, vulnerable, too. There was a certain undeniable vulnerability about her, which wasn't the same as helplessness. Summer was the roll-up-her-sleeves type. If something needed doing, she was going to do it. She was far from a helpless victim.

Her personality couldn't have been more opposite from her sister's. Summer was quick-witted and resourceful. She was beyond intelligent. And, man, did she possess a strength about her, a dignity that he'd rarely ever witnessed.

He had to fight every instinct that had him wanting, no needing, to be as close to her as he physically could. Summer just had that way about her. She was like the sun. He wanted to tilt his face toward it and take in its warmth.

Dawson reminded himself once again that Summer lived in Washington and he lived in Texas. Those were a lot of miles to cover. And that was the easiest part about a relationship between the two of them.

"Where to first?" Again, her voice traveled over him, bringing to life those places that had been dormant far too long.

"I'd like to interview Grover Hart first. See if he knew your sister beyond her locating him on the internet. Maybe he can give us some insight into where she hung out and what she did while she was in Austin."

"It sounds like a good place to start." She paused for a few seconds and he could almost see the wheels spinning in her brain. "Is there some way we could change the way I look? Is there something here like a scarf or maybe a ball cap that I can wear?"

"I'm already a few steps ahead of you on that one. I do have to get witnesses to safety from time to time so I keep a duffel bag full of supplies in the closet. We'll be traveling during the day and it's sunny, so I have a variety of sunglasses for you to choose from. I definitely have scarves and a few other things I think you might find helpful," he said.

Dawson turned toward the front door and motioned to the closet. He also had to force his gaze away from her backside when she headed over to the closet.

Watching her walk away wasn't going to do good things to Dawson. He was still kicking himself for not having a better answer when the two of them had been close. And he probably would be for a very long time if he let her get away.

Chapter Nine

Summer didn't realize she was tapping her finger against the window on the passenger side of Dawson's truck until he glanced over at her. His look was one of concern, not annoyance. She realized her nervous tick was in full swing.

She'd like to say her thoughts were consumed with what they were about to face in interviewing Grover Hart, the internet minister, but that wouldn't exactly be true. Her thoughts kept winding back to the kiss she'd shared with Dawson in the kitchen and the way it held the kind of passion that had been missing in every kiss for her entire life.

Since that was about as productive as squeezing a turnip and expecting blood, she did her best to shove those thoughts aside.

Grover Hart lived far north of Austin in a small town called Bluff. His house sat on what looked like at least an acre of land, and mostly resembled a junk-yard. There were tractor parts and what she assumed were truck parts littering the lawn. There was a couch that looked like an '80s relic sitting next to the front porch steps of the small bungalow.

Dawson parked and kept the engine idling. He

glanced over at Summer one more time, his gaze lingering a little bit longer this time.

"This should be interesting," he said.

"I couldn't agree more."

On the east side of the house was a small white gazebo. There were fake flowers wound through the slats. She imagined this was a place Grover performed quick ceremonies. Her sister and Dawson had married on his family's ranch. She shuddered, thinking about the kind of person who would be on the outskirts of town needing a quickie wedding in basically a junkyard. She also wondered how legal the nuptials would be. That was a whole different issue altogether.

"Guess we better do this." Dawson shut off the engine and exited the driver's seat. By the time he got around to the passenger side, she'd let herself out. There was a small look of disappointment in his eyes. Opening a door was still considered chivalrous in Texas.

They hadn't made it more than a few steps when the front door to the small green-siding bungalow popped open. A man who looked to be in his late forties or early fifties bounded out the door. He had on a variety of brightly colored prints and a matching cloth headband tied around his head. His hand was extended in front of him. He had a tanned, weathered face and a gap-toothed smile.

Grover had the whole Keep Austin Weird vibe down pat. He also looked like a bona fide hippie and she half expected him to offer them something besides the usual water or alcohol fare.

"How can I help you?" He looked at Dawson and then her. There was no hint of recognition.

Summer realized she had on a scarf, a ball cap and

sunglasses. Her hair was tucked inside the hat as best she could. She removed a few articles and studied the man for any hint of recognition.

"Beautiful day," Dawson said, shaking Grover's hand. Dawson was stalling for time, waiting to see if Grover recognized her or him.

He looked from Summer to Dawson and back again before throwing his hands out to the side. "Would you like a tour of the wedding gazebo?"

The man looked confused when neither one of them answered.

"You married us a while back," Dawson began, and Grover really did seem caught off guard with the statement.

"Oh." He seemed to be searching his memory, trying to find a match to the couple standing in front of him. "I'm real sorry. I hope everything is okay with the—"

"It's all fine," Dawson reassured. "I was just hoping you could remember talking to my wife when you set up the arrangements."

Grover Hart seemed genuine enough, looking like he'd rather shoot the peace sign than anything else. He had flower child written all over him and she figured he was probably too high to remember much of anything most of the time.

"I could check my records if you'd like." He shrugged. His bushy eyebrows knitted together. "Was there something specific you were hoping I'd remember about the day?"

"No, I just thought you might recognize me. That's all," Summer said, figuring this was a dead end.

Dawson seemed to reach the same conclusion when

he stuck out his hand and plastered on a smile. "Nothing to worry about here. We were driving by and thought we'd stop in and check with you. She lost her favorite earring on the day of the wedding and hoped you might remember seeing it. Since you don't, we'll be on our way."

Grover let out his breath like Dawson had just twisted a relief valve. She didn't think Grover was up to anything, but he did seem genuinely disappointed that he couldn't be of help.

"Thanks for trying," Summer said as she turned and headed toward the truck. Once inside, she said, "It's safe to say he didn't know my sister from Adam."

"I got the same impression." Dawson drove down the gravel lane, to the farm road leading to the highway. "Maybe we'll have better luck at the coffee shop."

She hoped.

The rest of the drive was quiet, save for the horns honking and general congestion of Austin where the term *rush hour* implied traffic actually let up at some point.

Using the map feature on her phone, it was easy to find Capital Coffee and not so easy to navigate downtown traffic, especially in a vehicle that took up much of the road.

By some miracle, Dawson found parking. The coffee shop was half a block away. It was midafternoon on a sunny day. Temperatures hovered around the mid-seventies.

He reached for her hand and laced their fingers together. His touch reassured her as she walked the downtown street with her glasses, hat and scarf. It was crazy to think Autumn had walked this same path countless times on her way to her favorite coffee shop.

It was reaching for another miracle that any of the employees would remember Autumn. Turnover in a coffee shop in a town with mostly college students had to be off the charts. Then again, maybe a good job with decent tips was hard to find.

For whatever reason, Autumn had come back to Austin after leaving Dawson. Summer could only think of one reason why her sister would do that...a man. Charley? Autumn was never the type to be alone and the divorce papers had Austin as the address of the 'lawyer.' She hated it and moved from relationship to relationship. Summer had hoped the marriage would stick, but now that she knew the details, she realized how naive she'd been to think her sister would've settled down.

Again, Summer was struck by how crazy her sister's actions had become over the past few years. She'd been straight-up crazy to leave Dawson. He was literally the perfect man.

Had she gotten herself into some kind of trouble? Autumn might have been lost and unpredictable but she'd never been one to break the law. Evidence would say otherwise, but Summer still knew her sister deep down. Autumn wasn't capable of doing much more than her little white lies.

A thought struck. How well could she say that she knew her sister? She was still scratching her head over Autumn leaving Dawson. Granted, her sister had built a mountain of lies—a mountain that she had to know would come tumbling down eventually.

She tugged at Dawson's hand for him to stop walking as she surveyed the street. "My sister had to know her lies would eventually catch up to her."

"It's possible they already were," he said, and she was already nodding. She'd been thinking the exact same thing.

Again, she couldn't for the life of her figure out what her sister had to lie about. "I've been thinking about what happens when people get married."

"Aside from the obvious part where they spend the rest of their lives together?" he asked.

"I'm thinking on a more practical level. The first thing people have to decide is whether or not to change their last names."

"Autumn was insistent on taking my name—"

He stopped cold.

"But she really wasn't. She only wanted people to *think* she was Autumn O'Connor."

Dawson was already nodding his head. "She wouldn't have to tell people her real last name if I believed we were really married."

"And we already know that the ranch is a safe haven. There's more security there than at the average bank." She didn't say Fort Knox even though she thought it.

"She never wanted to leave the property. A lot more makes sense about how squirrely she got when I tried to get her more involved in the plans to build. She kept saying that was my part. She only cared about the decorating."

"She might have been avoiding it because she had no plans to move into the house, after all."

"My thought exactly." There was no hint of regret in Dawson's voice. He spoke matter-of-factly about his past relationship with Autumn.

The realization gave her the sensation of a dozen butterflies releasing in her stomach.

"THIS EXPLAINS A LOT about her behavior." Dawson remembered how reluctant Autumn had been to commit to anything that had to do with the house or their future. At the time, he'd assumed her sadness about losing the baby was the cause. Now he realized she had been wriggling out of making those commitments possibly because she didn't want to stick him with her choices and her taste.

The strangest thing about the whole situation was that he would've done anything in his power to help her if she'd just asked. She didn't have to go through a fake pregnancy and a fake wedding to get him on her side. That was just how Dawson was made.

But it did make him think that she must not have felt like she had another choice. Her lies stacked on top of lies. He was one hundred percent certain that he wasn't the only person she'd been lying to. Or rather, in the other case, lying to get away from.

Signs pointed to her doing something against the law or...

Dawson had come across plenty of types of liars in the course of his career. Most of the time, people lied to save their own behinds. Other times, they did so in order to save someone else's behind. He had to wonder which way it went with Autumn.

"Who am I looking for once we get inside the coffee shop?" Dawson motioned a few storefronts ahead where the sign read Capital Coffee.

"The guy at the coffee shop is tall and skinny. He has long, brown wavy hair that is usually pulled up in a man bun. He looks more like a local than a student to me. He seems to always have a red bandana tucked in the back pocket of his jeans that I don't think he ever uses." Summer's grip around Dawson's hand tightened as she gave the description.

Dawson hoped like hell this would be a lead. Otherwise, they'd driven a heck of a long way for nothing. He scanned the crowded sidewalk to see if anyone looked twice at Summer. They were at a distinct disadvantage considering this had been Autumn's stomping ground.

Summer might not realize who she was looking at and she could be staring into the eyes of her sister's killer. The worst part was that someone could mistake Summer for Autumn, just like what had happened the other day.

It had only been a few days, but they didn't seem any closer to figuring out who killed Autumn. He didn't have to remind his brother or anyone in law enforcement to keep the news of Autumn's death quiet, but he'd done it anyway.

Summer took the first step toward the coffee shop and Dawson kept hold of her hand. He also realized he'd know immediately if she recognized one of the men from yesterday based on involuntary muscle spasms. Her grip would tighten on his hand. He would have a couple extra seconds of warning with physical contact that he wouldn't have had otherwise.

He opened the door for her and followed her inside. The coffee shop was at the end of the street and had a fairly large outdoor space from what he could see. The temperature inside was no different than out.

Several hipster-looking waiters and waitresses moved through the crowded space. The inside of the coffee shop was relatively small. There was a long bar-height counter with a couple of people working the register and another pair manning the machines.

There were roughly a dozen tables. Several of them had two or three chairs nestled around them. There was a long green velvet sofa along one wall with several small laptop-friendly tables in a line. There were outlets galore.

Outside was impressive. There were more tables than he could count and lots of trees in planters. They hid people's faces. It was harder to stand at the front door and get a straight-shot look at everyone.

He took note of the other little nooks and corners. A couple of people in suits were hunkered over a table in one corner. There was pretty much every type of person in the coffee shop. The corporate types nestled around small tables and chatted. There had to be at least a couple of politicians, along with several political aids. At least one older gentleman had a hardback book the size of *War and Peace* in his hands as he sat with his legs stretched out and crossed at the ankles. His coffee mug sat on the table in front of him. He had that intellectual look with his sports coat and nylon slacks. He was most likely a professor at UT, which was a short walk from here.

Other than that, there were all manner of tattooed people milling about or at the chairs. Blue hair. Pink hair. Nose piercings. One lip piercing. Then, there was the usual crush of backpack-wearing students.

Dawson took it all in. He was used to sizing everyone up and evaluating all threat as a matter of habit. He knew where every exit door in the room was located.

Summer squeezed his hand. He glanced toward her

and she nodded at a guy behind the counter. Man Bun was so busy manning the machines and frothing milk that he didn't bother to look up. He had an AirPod in one ear and seemed to be jamming out in a zone as he made orders and checked what looked like order ticker tape.

Time to see if Man Bun recognized Summer.

Chapter Ten

Dawson wanted to see Man Bun's unfiltered reaction to seeing Summer. He would be able to tell a lot about Man Bun's involvement or lack thereof in Autumn's death based on his initial reaction.

"I'm not sure how much I look like her like this. She never stepped out of the house without being all done up with full hair and makeup." Summer removed the glasses and ball cap. She fluffed her hair.

"In my opinion, the two of you don't look much alike. But there's enough of a resemblance to trick an acquaintance." He meant every one of those words. Autumn and Summer couldn't be more different as people. Summer had a warmth about her despite being very reserved. Autumn was more of an in-the-moment type. She had a bigger personality. The thought she'd been abused in her young life and that had caused her to become a bigger-than-life person on the outside with that same trapped little girl on the inside nearly gutted him.

Her defense mechanisms were well honed, and she'd had a lifetime to polish them. Knowing this helped ease the frustration he felt from being burned by her lies. Trauma could do that to a person. He'd seen it too often in his line of work where someone detached from society to protect themselves.

Those tendencies usually caused folks to fall into the trap of abusing drugs or alcohol, sometimes both. Based on what Summer had said so far, he believed Autumn had developed an alternate persona instead.

It was a shame she'd had to do that in order to survive their upbringing. He had even more respect for Summer as he got to know her. She embodied strength and probably a little bit of stubbornness, too.

Any survivor had to have a stubborn streak. Used the right way, it could be very helpful because they didn't give up once they set their mind to a goal. Sometimes, that goal was simply not to let the past break them.

It was a rare quality to have that kind of determination when it seemed the world was against a person. *She* was rare.

There was no arguing Summer Grayson was special.

She squeezed his hand before letting go, took in a breath and then closed the distance to the counter. Standing right in front of Man Bun, she cleared her throat.

Dawson stood back and to the side, pretending to study something on the screen of his cell phone.

"Can I help y—"

Man Bun looked up. A hint of recognition passed behind his eyes before he plastered on a smile. Fake? Or was it the kind that people gave when they couldn't remember someone who obviously knew them?

"Hi. Remember me?" Summer plowed ahead through the awkward gaze. He had to give it to her. The stubborn streak made her strong when she probably wanted to bolt. The streak in her also meant justice was coming for her sister because Summer had the kind of tenacity normally seen in a starving pit bull going after a slab of meat.

Man Bun cocked his head to the side and squinted at her. This looked like he was trying to figure out if they'd dated or not. He gave the impression that she looked familiar but he couldn't place her.

"Autumn Grayson," she persisted.

Dawson scanned the room for anyone within earshot who took notice of the name. Nothing there. He sure as hell hoped this trip would be more productive in the investigation than it was turning out to be. He was about to take Summer to identify her sister's body. He couldn't think of a more awful thing for someone to have to do.

The only bright spot about this trip was supposed to be coming home with a lead to bring them one step closer to justice.

Man Bun threw his head back and smiled, genuine this time.

Dawson took a step closer to the counter so he could more clearly hear what Man Bun had to say.

"You remember me?" Summer did her best to sound perky. *Perky* wasn't a word he'd use to describe her personality. She was playing the part well, offering a bright smile as she put her hands up on the counter.

Dawson had no idea if she realized what that meant with her body language. But it was a show of trust, instinct at its finest, showing the person she was connecting with that she wasn't carrying any weapons.

"I do now." Man Bun stepped to the side where the counter was lower and nodded for Summer to follow.

She did. He leaned across the smaller table like he was about to tell her a secret.

Dawson leaned a little closer and for reasons he didn't want to examine, the green-eyed monster reared its ugly head. He didn't like Summer getting anywhere close to Man Bun. The guy would be considered attractive by most. He looked like one of those celebrity soccer players from Latin America who made millions for his ability on the playing field.

"Where have you been?" Man Bun seemed to recognize Summer now.

"Around. You know how it is." Summer shrugged her shoulder, playing nonchalant.

"I almost didn't recognize you. Did you get a haircut?"

"How long has it been since the last time I was in here?" She paused, playing the ditz. She reached up and twirled a long strand of her wheat-colored hair. "I know it hasn't been so long that you would actually forget me."

Dawson stepped forward interrupting their conversation. He reached into his pocket and pulled out his wallet, flipping it open so that Man Bun would get a glimpse of his badge.

"How well do you know this person?" He nodded toward Summer.

Man Bun's eyes darted over toward someone on the line who was wearing a slightly nicer shirt and Dawson assumed was in management.

"Is that your boss?" Dawson followed the man's gaze.

Man Bun nodded. "One more strike and I'm out of a job."

"I can speak to him. This is official business."

"Nah, man. I don't want to make him suspicious. Just ask me what you want so I can get back on the line."

"How do you know Ms. Grayson?" Dawson asked.

"She's a regular. Comes in here all the time. Vanilla latte with whipped. It took me a second to recognize her because she looks different today."

"You talk to her a lot when she comes in?" Dawson asked.

"Sure." He shrugged his shoulder casually. "You know, when it's not busy. She's a good tipper and we like to treat our customers more like family."

Man Bun's eyes kept darting back toward his boss. Obviously, the guy was on his last strike and Dawson didn't want to be the reason he ended up without a job. The guy's answers were genuine and as much as Dawson wanted this to go somewhere, it wasn't going to.

"One last question. Did you ever see her come in here with anyone?" Dawson asked.

Man Bun looked at Summer as though she'd lost her mind. It was pretty obvious she was standing right there and his question was written all over his face, *Why not ask her?*

"She never really came in with anyone. Every once in a while, she would go outside, and I would lose track of her. People come in here all the time." He glanced around as though the crowded room was his proof. "As you can see, we're pretty busy."

He nervously glanced over at his boss and then the ticker tape machine that was kicking out orders. "If that's all, man, can I get back to work? My orders are stacking up."

"That's all I need for now. We'll be back in touch if we have more questions." Dawson produced a business card from his wallet. "If you think of anything else, I'd appreciate a call."

"Yes, sir." Man Bun's gaze bounced from Dawson to Summer and back. "Can I go now?"

Dawson nodded before reclaiming Summer's hand. He linked their fingers and turned to walk out the door.

Man Bun did an about-face. "Hey, now that I think about it there were a couple of dudes in here the other day asking around if anyone had seen her. I was thrown off a minute ago and forgot all about it."

"Can you describe what they looked like?" Dawson asked.

The descriptions fit the men Summer had encountered to a T.

"Have you ever seen them around before?" Dawson continued.

Man Bun shook his head.

"Thanks for the information."

Summer's hand tightened around Dawson's. She had a death grip on his fingers. The men who'd tried to attack her and who'd planned to kill her had come looking for Autumn in the coffee shop. The killer must not know Autumn was dead.

She didn't speak until they got outside, walked half a block and made sure no one was around to overhear their conversation. She'd already replaced the ball cap and sunglasses, and he could almost feel her heart racing through her fingertips.

"He was being honest, wasn't he?" she asked.

"I believe so. I didn't detect any deception in his behavior."

The disappointment on her face was a gut punch. He squeezed her hand for reassurance and his heart took another hit when she looked up at him with those big violet eyes.

"Then, we'll keep going until someone has information about her."

DEAD ENDS WERE EVERYWHERE.

Summer took in a deep breath as she and Dawson made their way back onto the highway and toward Katy Gulch. The body suspected to have belonged to Autumn Grayson had, in fact, belonged to her sister. Decisions had been made about her sister's arrangements, despite the thick fog that had settled over Summer. Dawson had been a rock and she couldn't imagine doing any of this without him. The fact that he knew her sister at least on some level provided comfort. He seemed to genuinely care about what had happened to Autumn, despite her lies. That was the thing, underneath all those lies was a terrified person. The lies were like a wall that Autumn had used to keep everyone at a distance.

All Summer felt since was a deep dread and a sense of being completely numb. At some point, her brain might get to the point it could process what it had seen. Not without justice. Not without making those bastards pay.

Summer realized she'd been gripping the seat belt strap across her chest. At least she wasn't tapping the window. As far as nervous ticks went, hers were on full tilt.

About halfway home, Dawson's cell phone rang. He

fished it out of his pocket and handed it over to her. "Do you mind checking to see who that is?"

She checked the screen. "It's your brother Colton."

"Would you mind answering and putting it on speaker?" Dawson's grip on the steering wheel was as tight as hers had been on her seat belt moments ago.

Obviously, seeing Autumn at the coroner's office was affecting him. He'd cared about her sister once. He was a decent human being. And he was being incredibly understanding about Autumn's personality layers.

She pushed the button to put the call on the truck's speaker.

"Hey, Colton. You're on speaker and I'm in my truck with Summer Grayson."

"I look forward to meeting you at some point, Summer." There was not a hint of judgment in Colton's voice.

"Likewise," Summer said. She'd like to have the chance to meet all of Dawson's siblings. If they were half as decent and kind as Dawson, she couldn't think of a better caliber of men to be acquainted with. It was a foreign feeling to have one person who had Summer's back for a change. She couldn't even fathom having an entire support system in the form of a big family.

She'd never given much thought to having kids of her own. She always figured she'd get to a point financially where she could take care of herself and her sister. Open that small business they'd dreamed about. Then, she could think about a husband and possibly children down the road.

"What's going on?" Dawson asked his brother.

"Are you heading home?" Colton asked.

"On our way now," Dawson confirmed.

"You might want to make a U-turn."

Dawson navigated into the right lane and took the next exit. "What did you find out?"

"Gert has been doing some digging. You know Gert. Once she's on a scent, there's no stopping her."

Dawson glanced toward Summer. "Gert is his secretary."

Gert sounded like Summer's kind of person.

"I'm guessing she found something." Dawson said to his brother. His grip on the steering wheel tightened.

"It might be nothing, but it's worth checking into and I know you'll want to follow up on this yourself." Colton paused. "I apologize in advance for being frank with—"

"Please, don't worry about me. All I care about is justice for my sister," Summer said.

"Okay. Here's what Gert found. There was another strangulation victim in the Austin area. The tool used was a violin string. There was no DNA evidence in the case. The victim was twenty-eight years old and she had violet eyes."

"Same MO," Dawson muttered under his breath as he flipped on his turn signal and then banked a U-turn under the bridge.

Chapter Eleven

"I'll send you the file so you can take a look at witness statements." Summer wiped a stray tear as Colton continued, "It's a cold case."

She turned her face toward the passenger window like she was listening intently. In truth, she was trying to hold it together.

"How old is the case?" Dawson tapped his flat palm against the wheel.

"The murder happened two and a half years ago." The timeline could mean this guy moved on to Autumn. She might've gotten away and relocated to Katy Gulch to hide out where she met the one man who she believed could protect her. That would explain her wanting to stay on a secluded ranch and all the lies.

"What was her name?" Summer asked. She couldn't help herself. People in law enforcement would refer to her sister now as *the victim*. Summer wanted to know the young woman's name.

"Cheryl Tanning," Colton supplied.

Cheryl Tanning. She didn't deserve what happened to her, either.

"There were several suspects."

"Which one do you like?" Dawson asked.

"She used to frequent a coffee shop called Capital Coffee. Didn't you say you were visiting a place downtown that Autumn used to go to?" Colton asked.

Summer put her hand over her mouth to cover her gasp.

"We were just there," Dawson admitted.

In Summer's mind, the coffee shop would be a great place to scout a target for someone with an agenda. It was busy. All types of people came in and out. So much so, that people hardly noticed each other.

"So, it's the same place," Colton confirmed. "Okay."

"Is there mention of any other spots Cheryl used to hang out?" Dawson asked.

"That was the main place. There was a guy in her life, but her friends said she was very protective of him. No one knew who he was. A few names came up in the investigation. You'll see those in the file notes."

"I'll grab a place to stay. We might want to settle in for the night," Dawson said on a sigh. "I appreciate the information and tell Gert she did good work."

"She'll be tickled," Colton said before saying goodbye and ending the call.

The signs for Round Rock, a large suburb north of Austin, showed they were close to Austin again.

"Thought we might grab a place here for the night. We can take a look at the files and then follow up on any discoveries. There's every kind of food imaginable, which I can pick up. I'd rather you be seen as little as possible while we investigate." There was so much warmth and compassion in his voice. "And now it looks like we need to circle back and visit the coffee shop again."

She couldn't agree more with what he said. There

was no reason for her to be exposed more than necessary.

His cell phone buzzed and she assumed that meant the file was coming through.

"I have a laptop and an overnight bag in the backseat."

She quirked a brow.

"Don't always get a ton of notice when I have to head out. I keep most everything in the trunk of my sedan. The bag here is just for backup," he explained.

Her mind was still churning over what they'd just learned but she nodded. She was interested in hearing the details of his job. Staying focused when her mind was reeling proved harder than expected.

A serial killer? That couldn't be. How would she explain the two men chasing her yesterday if Autumn was killed by a serial killer? Hit men weren't serial killers and they usually didn't have henchmen.

Oh, Autumn. More of those fresh tears sprang to her eyes. She blinked them back. At least she felt something besides numb. Had her sister been in a relationship with a murderer and not realized it until it was too late? What kind of person seduced his intended victims?

Dawson pulled off the highway and into a big chain hotel. She straightened her baseball cap.

"I'll check us in and be right back." Dawson left the truck idling and headed inside the lobby. He was back a few minutes later, card keys in hand. He slipped into the driver's seat and then pulled ahead to a parking spot.

Summer kept her chin to her chest as she exited the truck and waited for Dawson. He quickly grabbed his emergency bag from the backseat before locking up the truck and joining her.

He put his arm around her, shielding her from other eyes. To onlookers, the move might seem intimate. A husband and wife stopping off at a roadside hotel on their way somewhere else.

She knew he was covering as much of her as was humanly possible. She was able to hide more of her body and face.

Their room was on the fifth floor, number 510. Dawson opened the door to the small suite. There was a microwave and a mini fridge in the entryway along with a coffee maker and an assortment of coffees and teas. The bathroom was larger than the one in her Washington apartment. The shower was travertine tile and the vanity area was large enough for half a cosmetic store.

The main room had a work desk, a small table with four chairs and a seating area. A flat screen TV took up half the wall in the living room. There was a comfortable if slightly worn sofa and two armchairs along with a marble coffee table.

This place was larger than her apartment back home. *Home.* Where was that anymore? Home was a foreign word to her now. Thinking about a future without Autumn was like walking forever in the dark, knowing light was out there in the distance but too far for her to see it.

Until she looked at Dawson and saw a glimmer of hope. Hope that she might somehow find her way through this darkness and toward the sun again. Hope that she might not want to spend the rest of her life alone. Hope she could have things she'd long ago dreamed about but never believed would be.

Anger seeded because she didn't want to think about a future that didn't involve her sister. Where did she even start?

"There's only one bed in the suite. It's yours. I can make myself comfortable here on the couch," Dawson said by way of explanation.

"That won't be a problem. I trust you. You can sleep in the same bed. I don't want to put you out." She was rewarded with a smile.

"It's no trouble." Dawson set his bag down, unzipped it and pulled out his laptop. He positioned it on the marble coffee table.

Summer moved next to him on the sofa and curled her left leg underneath her bottom.

"I want you to be prepared for the fact there are going to be graphic pictures. There's nothing wrong with skipping that part if you—"

She was already shaking her head. "I need to look at them. There might be something about her that reminds me of my sister. Something you wouldn't catch that I would."

Nothing in Summer wanted the images of a murdered Cheryl Tanning imprinted in her mind. But this was important. She would do whatever it took to find justice for her sister. This was the best way to see if there were any similarities.

He looked into her eyes like he was searching for confirmation it was okay to move forward. She gave him a slight nod before he fixed his gaze on the screen and opened a protected link.

There were two files in the one marked, Tanning Murder. The picture file contained two folders: evidence and victim. He clicked on the one marked Victim, and the screen was filled with thumbnails. He pulled up the first.

Cheryl Tanning's lifeless violet eyes fixed on a point above her. Her eyes were striking. Summer was always told that she and her sister had very rare-colored eyes. There was something haunting about the pair she was looking at.

Other than that, Cheryl Tanning was a beautiful young woman. She had pale skin and ruby-red lips. She had slightly darker hair than Summer and Autumn, and blunt-cut bangs. She was stunning. There was no question about that.

Dawson clicked on another photo and it was a full-body shot at the crime scene. Based on the photo, she looked to be about the same size as Autumn. Similar figures.

"This bastard likes a certain type." Dawson muttered a few more choice words under his breath.

She'd picked up on the similarities, too.

Her heart battered her rib cage as a weight dropped down around her arms. There was what looked like a wire wrapped around Cheryl's neck. They now knew it was a string from a violin.

What were the odds that Autumn would be killed by a similar method, two and a half years later? They had to be slim.

An icy chill gripped Summer's spine as she looked through the crime scene photos one by one. Dawson opened the case file next. A short description of the murder outlined that Cheryl Tanning had been found in an old dried up well on the back of someone's land. A group of teens who routinely rode dirt bikes on the property had stopped because of what they described as a smell that made them physically sick.

When they investigated, expecting to find an animal carcass, they received the shock of a lifetime when they found a body instead. All of the teens had been traumatized by the finding and during the course of the investigation had been cleared of any involvement.

There'd been a mystery man, who Cheryl's friends confirmed she'd been very secretive about.

"Do you think he was married?" Summer asked as she pointed to the screen.

"It's possible. A married man could have a lot to lose if word got out that he was having an affair." Dawson confirmed.

"It's Austin, so my mind snaps to a married politician," she admitted.

"Can't be ruled out. But those aren't the only powerful men in the capital or men with something to lose if word of an affair got out. There are three things we look for in a murder investigation: means, motive and opportunity," he stated.

"Opportunity wouldn't be difficult in a secret affair. The person would be used to meeting one-on-one in possibly secluded locations," she reasoned.

"True. Affairs are sticky. She was hiding his identity and was protective of him, which gives me the impression he was the power broker in the relationship."

"Someone older than her? Someone smarter or more cunning? Someone used to getting exactly what he wants from people?" she asked.

"That's along the lines of what I'm thinking," he confirmed. "I'd add to that someone who stands to lose a lot, be it money, prestige or social standing if an affair is uncovered."

"A murder conviction would rock his world." She caught herself tapping her finger on the marble coffee table as her brain started working overtime.

"Attorneys, bankers, anyone with a professional license would be in jeopardy."

"Look here." Summer pointed to the screen. "It says at least one of her friends thought she was getting depressed. He blames the affair."

"The jerk could've been manipulating her, asking her to do things she didn't want to. She might've complied for fear of losing him."

Autumn could be a manipulator. But the shoe could easily have been on the other foot. She wasn't strong mentally, and when it came down to it, a person could exercise power over her.

CHERYL TANNING HAD no visible signs of molestation. There was no DNA left on her body or found on the scene. Nothing under her fingernails. No sign that she'd fought back.

She'd been secretly dating someone. There was nothing in her cell phone record that would indicate she'd been seeing someone. Her credit cards showed no unusual activity. At least one of her friends regretted teasing her about being a call girl, saying she started having a lot more cash than usual. The response had been that Cheryl stopped returning calls and texts for a while.

The strangulation came from behind. The method of killing was personal. The killer would have to have been literally standing right behind Cheryl. She didn't fight back, so maybe she thought her lover was playing a joke or trying to arouse her.

There were several bruises on Cheryl's body in varying stages of healing. She worked as a waitress and took night school classes. A waitressing job could explain the bruises on her thighs and arms. But so could sexual exploration.

A defense attorney might argue Cheryl Tanning liked it rough in the bedroom. Or, at the very least, participated. Even if her lover had been identified, he wasn't necessarily guilty. Although, this kind of killing was personal. Staring at the evidence and the summary, Dawson was convinced the murderer was someone inside her circle despite the way the body had been dumped down the well.

The killer might have panicked. The police officer's report stated there'd been leaves tossed into the well after her body. Covering her up? Or covering her? As strange as it sounded, the sicko might have been covering her so she wouldn't get cold.

Dawson had seen enough deranged and sadistic people to last a lifetime. So, the leaves could actually be a sign of caring in a twisted way. Or a type of burial depending on religious affiliation. Even some cold-blooded killers believed they were spiritual. Hell, some killed out of ritual.

In this case, though, this bastard seemed well on his way to becoming a serial killer. The rule of thumb was three murders spread out over time.

If this killer believed that Autumn had lived, he would stop at nothing to silence her. There were all kinds of questions racing around in Dawson's mind.

"She didn't have a family, either," Summer noted.

"But Autumn did have a family. She had you."

"He didn't know that. Think about it, she hid me from you, too. I barely knew about you and the two of you were married." She made a good point. "Except that you weren't really."

"True." He rocked his head. "Then, that's part of his MO."

"Maybe he thinks no one will notice that they've gone missing and it'll give him more time to cover his tracks."

"I was thinking the same thing." Dawson pulled out the notepad and pen that he'd tucked into his emergency bag. He jotted down the fact the perp isolated his victims.

"Why did he decide to kill her, though?" she asked. "Like when did he know? The minute he started the affair?"

"It's possible. If Cheryl is his first victim, and so far Gert hasn't found any other that match this MO, he might have started the affair not knowing how it would end. At some point, he knew he was going to kill her."

"When he was done with her?"

"It's likely." He feared those words were like a physical blow. Of course, Summer would take them personally considering her sister was involved.

"My sister must've been scared of him. She might have felt backed into a corner with no way out," she continued.

It explained a lot about how she'd acted when he'd first met her and her actions after the fact. More of those puzzle pieces were clicking together.

"Do you think she figured out what happened to his former girlfriend?" she asked.

"It's highly possible."

"I just don't understand why she didn't go to law enforcement and explain her situation or tell me."

"Abusive men are master manipulators. He could've made her feel like he'd find her no matter where she went—"

"She could've come to me. I would've helped her find a way out of this."

"And she might think she would be bringing him right to your doorstep," he countered.

"The necklace. My name. You said it was one of her most prized possessions." Puzzle pieces were clicking together in her mind, too.

She tapped on the words they'd written on the notepad earlier. *Protect loved one.*

Chapter Twelve

A picture was emerging. Autumn had gotten into an unhealthy relationship that possibly even turned abusive. She didn't want Summer to know and so a couple of years ago, she withdrew.

The relationship became more than Autumn could handle. Luckily, she must not have told the guy about Summer. She'd kept her sister's identity safe and the necklace bearing her name locked in a box that she'd most likely kept hidden.

One day, Autumn decided enough was enough, or maybe things got heated between them and she began to fear for her life. Rather than go to Summer, and bring that blaze along with her, Autumn found a small town to hide in. Maybe she wanted to lay low.

Then, she met Dawson. He was honest and kind. It probably didn't hurt matters that he was smokin' hot. Maybe she even fell for him, fast and hard. He was everything she didn't have with the other guy.

There were perks to living with Dawson. He lived on a remote property and worked in law enforcement. As did several of his brothers. Autumn couldn't have asked for more or better protection. Her conscience got the best of her and she couldn't commit Dawson to an actual marriage, so she made up a pregnancy story, insisted on a low-key affair and then hired an internet guy who didn't care if proper papers were filed or not. It was a lot but sounded just like her sister to do something like this.

Summer relayed her theory to Dawson. It was met with nods of approval and that meant she was on the right path.

"The divorce makes no sense to me, though," she confessed.

"It was possible that he'd found her, or that she thought he would. She wasn't acting right in those last few weeks we were together. At the time, I chalked it up to her losing the baby. I tried to give her time and space to heal. I figured she would talk when she was ready but she just closed up. She stopped leaving the property and slept a lot of the time."

"Your logic sounds reasonable. Except that we both know there was no baby. So, he must've gotten to her somehow." How? was the question of the day. There was another bigger question...who?

"There were three suspects at the top of a short list in Cheryl's murder," Dawson said, pointing to the screen. "Sean Menendez, a creepy janitor, Jasper Holden, coffee shop worker and Drake Yarnell, ex-boyfriend."

"Okay. Where do we even start?" Something had been gnawing at the back of Summer's mind. She stared at the notebook page rather than the screen. Why was the name Charley bugging Summer?

"Is this exactly how my sister spelled the name, Charley? Just like it's written?" she asked Dawson.

"Yes. Why?"

She picked up the pen and wrote Cheryl next to Charley. "Does anything about this strike you as odd?"

"If I rearrange the letters and add an *a* the names are alike?" He rocked his head. "Look at that."

"She knew about Cheryl." That was the reason her sister was afraid. She knew about the murder.

"It's possible. She might have stumbled on a name and went to investigate. I can't imagine why she'd go back to Austin under the circumstances." Dawson tapped his finger on the screen. "We can start by interviewing Menendez, Holden and Yarnell."

More of those puzzle pieces Dawson had talked about before were being discovered. Finding where they fit and how they fit together was another story. Summer would take the progress. "I'm wondering why my sister went to the same coffee shop as Cheryl. Autumn didn't seem afraid to make her face known."

"It's possible she found evidence linking the murderer to the crime. If the perp found her in Katy Gulch, she had to know he would find her anywhere."

"Maybe he didn't know she'd found him out," Summer reasoned. "He could've convinced her to come back to Austin. Possibly even set her up in an apartment. Wine and dine her. She technically got away once. If this guy is a master manipulator, he might have convinced my sister that he loved her. He might have brought her back under his control."

Dawson nodded some more.

"He wasn't able to finish the job before. He wouldn't be able to let it go if he intended to kill her all along."

"What a sick bastard," Summer said.

"Agreed." The muscle in Dawson's jaw clenched.

"Then we're thinking that he lured her back in

town." Summer hated the thought her sister could be manipulated. If the jerk said the right things, though, she could see her sister going back to him unless she knew he'd killed his other lover.

Autumn had had a knack for picking up guys who obsessed over her. At least until she'd met Dawson. He was the most levelheaded and down-to-earth person she'd ever met.

Summer hated all the secrets her sister held inside and all the lies. She hated that her sister couldn't just live a normal life and follow through on the dream of opening their own business. And she hated that she hadn't been able to protect her sister.

There was no use looking back now. A tidal wave of emotion was building inside Summer behind the wall that had kept her safe. There were cracks—cracks that threatened to pull her under and toss her around until she didn't know up from down anymore.

"You know, she wasn't always like this," she said on a sharp sigh.

"Tell me about it." Dawson clasped his hands together and rested his elbows on his thighs.

"The two of us were inseparable growing up. Our parents used to fight. I don't remember the details because we were so young when my father left. But I do recall feeling a sense of relief once he was gone."

"Kids pick up on so much. I've noticed it with my niece and nephew and they're only a year old. It's like a Record button has been hit in the back of their minds and someday, when they're much older, an invisible finger will hit Play. They won't even know why they're acting a certain way—it's just programming," he said.

"That's a really good point actually." Autumn had

definitely recorded a lot of sadness. She seemed to take it more personally. "I can't say my sister even had good taste in the opposite sex." She flashed eyes at him, realizing how that would sound to him.

He feigned heartbreak before chuckling. "You really know how to hurt a guy's pride."

"Except for you," she quickly added.

"Right. Of course." Now he really laughed.

"No, seriously, I mean it. Don't take this the wrong way but I'm surprised you two were ever in a relationship. And what I mean by that is you're not normally her type. She always seemed to date guys who were edgy, you know, a little rough around the edges. Looking back, she always dated complicated people—a musician down on his luck or a guy in between jobs who needed her help. I used to always worry about her taste in men and told her she deserved better. Maybe that was part of the reason she came and found you. To protect her and show me that she was capable of finding someone who was amazing." She made the mistake of looking into his eyes as she said the last word.

DAWSON'S CHEST FISTED at the compliment. He couldn't afford to keep looking into those violet eyes without falling deeper into the well.

So, he coughed to clear his throat and asked, "What made you decide to work as a waitress?"

"I wanted to get experience in food service. I guess I saw it as my duty to take care of my sister and so we... *I*...dreamed of opening a small coffee shop together. Looking back, I did all the planning and talking about the coffee shop. She went along with it." There was a wistful quality to her eyes now. "She might not have wanted to hurt my feelings by saying she didn't want to open a business together."

"It sounds like you were trying to give her something to look forward to."

"True. I was. Now I'm wondering if I ran her off because I steamrolled over her."

"Don't do that to yourself. None of this is your fault."

"Oh, I doubt that. I should've done some—"

"I'm going to stop you right there. You didn't ask for this. You didn't contribute to this. As much as you might have felt responsible for your sister, you didn't do anything wrong. She had the will and the right to do whatever she wanted, and the person I knew did exactly that."

Summer paused and he hoped like hell she was letting his words sink in. This wasn't the first time she'd blamed herself for her sister's actions and if he could do anything else, he wanted to leave the impression with her that she didn't have to feel responsible. Adults were capable of making their own choices and did. Not all of those choices were good, and Autumn certainly made bad ones, but down deep, he didn't believe she was a bad person. Mixed up? Hell, yes. Confused? Absolutely. Bad? Not in his opinion.

"I hear what you're saying, and I know that in my mind. My heart is another story." She ducked her chin to her chest and turned her face away, a move he'd noticed she did to hide when she was getting emotional.

"It's okay to be upset. It's easy to see how much you love your sister. That's not going away and nothing will change that." He offered more words of comfort and when she turned to look at him, his heart took a dive.

She sat there, gazing at him, exposing her vulnerability to him. All he could offer by way of reassurance was a few words and his arms. He looped his arms around her, and she buried her face in his chest.

They stayed in that position for a long time. When she was ready to pull back, he feathered a kiss on her forehead. Being together with Summer like that, vulnerabilities exposed, was the most intimate moment in Dawson's life.

"Thank you." Her voice was shaky despite her chin jutting out.

"I'm here anytime. I mean that, Summer." He did. He meant long after this case was behind them and the grief settled in. Long after they were gone from this hotel room, from Austin and back into their normal everyday lives. He wanted to be there for her.

Summer and her sister didn't seem to have had a whole lot of breaks in life. He regretted that he'd missed so many signs with Autumn, but he would be there for Summer anytime she needed a friend.

"You can't know how much I appreciate it, Dawson." He could tell by the way she said those words she had no plans to take him up on his offer.

Why did that sting so much?

"So, Charley could possibly mean Cheryl." Summer brought the conversation back on track. "Which meant my sister either knew about Cheryl or heard the name."

Dawson nodded. "We're missing the connection, if there is one. Since you don't know much about your sister's daily habits, it's difficult to figure out where her and Cheryl's lives might have overlapped."

"That's true. It's interesting to note that Cheryl doesn't have any relatives who she was close to." Summer frowned and he immediately realized why. "So, they have that similarity. And we know that they both visited the same coffee shop. Maybe they lived near each other. Maybe that's another link. So, the perp lives or works in the area of the coffee shop."

Dawson wrote the question down on the pad of paper: "Did they live near each other or possibly know each other?"

"We know they looked alike and spent time in the same area of town. They might have had a few other touch points."

"Your sister left the money I gave her in the bank. She never touched it. I still can't figure out why. She must've needed it," he said.

"Unless she went somewhere she didn't, which would mean she left you to go back to the perp."

"Why?"

Good question. One he intended to find an answer to.

Dawson didn't realize how late it was getting and neither one of them had really slept last night. He'd be fine running on a few minutes of sleep here and there but Summer looked absolutely wrung out. She needed food and rest.

"What do you think about taking a break and grabbing some dinner?" he asked.

"I seriously doubt I could eat anything," she countered.

"Would you be willing to try?" It was important and she might surprise herself like she had with the meatloaf.

"I probably should but I don't want to be alone right now." Her violet eyes pleaded.

Taking her with him carried risks. One could argue leaving her alone in a hotel room also left her vulnerable. The mental debate going on in his head was a force to be reckoned with and yet he knew in his heart he couldn't leave her there alone.

He thought about ordering food and staying in. That could draw unwanted attention and expose them should someone be watching the room. It was dark so the sunglasses wouldn't work. That, too, would draw attention. Granted, Autumn had always been done-up with full makeup and her hair done to the nines, and Summer went with an all-natural look. It was possible the perp could recognize her.

"You could wrap the scarf around your hair," he said.

She was on her feet faster than he could say, "Boo."

Her violet eyes were red rimmed. He wanted her to know how brave she was. Most would buckle under the circumstances and yet she kept pushing forward, searching for answers for her sister.

When she was finished covering her hair, he linked their fingers and walked with her outside. Glancing around, the hair on the back of his neck stood on end. Not exactly a warm and fuzzy feeling, but he was on high alert.

The feeling persisted during the entire walk to the truck. Again, he put his arm around her to shield her as much as possible from view. Being this close to Summer, breathing in her clean and flowery scent, filled his thoughts with the kisses they'd shared.

Under different circumstances, she was exactly the kind of person he'd want to spend time getting to know better. Now?

It was complicated. His feelings were complicated. And despite their off-the-charts attraction, acting on it any further would make things between them even more complicated.

And the crazy thing was that a very huge part of him didn't want to care about the consequences.

Chapter Thirteen

The restaurant was one of those taco chain spots found in every major Texas city. Loud music was playing when they entered and, unlike everyone else, she didn't love tacos. They were okay. Edible.

Summer pointed toward the booth in the corner where she and Dawson could continue talking about the case. The images of Cheryl Tanning would haunt Summer for a very long time. Erasing those wouldn't be easy.

And her mind drew the parallels to her own sister's case. Obviously, the bastard had killed Autumn in a similar way. It was impossible not to imagine Autumn's face instead of Cheryl's.

She'd tucked the notebook and pen under her arm before leaving the hotel room, just in case they wanted to jot down more notes. She placed the items on the table and scooted them toward the wall in case a server brought their order.

One word jumped out at her. *Suspects*. Below the word, there were three names. Dawson had explained that law enforcement officers had interviewed everyone they could find. Cheryl Tanning might not have had a family to stand up for her but she'd had a voice in the detective who had taken the case.

"Drake Yarnell, what do you think of him?" she quietly asked Dawson.

"He was an ex-boyfriend who was in a biker club. He had a jealous streak and I didn't like that at first. But the timeline of their relationship ending? They'd broken up almost a year prior. I doubt he still had the kind of feelings or possessiveness required to circle back and murder his ex-girlfriend."

"Even though their neighbors overheard him threaten to kill her if she walked out the door when they lived together?" she asked.

"He was a hothead. I can't see him waiting almost a year to act on his threat. It was idle, said in the heat of the moment. I still want to talk to him but he isn't sending up any red flags to me so far."

"Okay. How about Sean Menendez?"

"He was the creepy maintenance worker in her apartment complex." Dawson tilted his head toward her and then looked down at the pad of paper.

"Right."

"It's possible he had a thing for her and even more possible he was stalking her. Going down that path, she rebuffed him and that's the reason the detective thought he was a good suspect." Dawson made a face.

"You don't think so."

"Not really. Why would anyone cover the body with the leaves? And what's the connection to the violin strings?" he asked.

"This detective believed he might've found the strings in one of the trash bins," she stated.

"Which makes sense and would be possible. But

then, what about your sister? How is she connected to the apartments and this guy? Did she live there? He's a creep, don't get me wrong. If I was a beat cop, I'd be keeping an eye on him. But, I can't connect him to Autumn and we're banking everything on these two cases being connected." His lips formed a thin line.

The waiter brought their taco baskets, so they tabled the discussion for the moment. The minute he left, they started up again.

"So, Jasper Holden? What are your thoughts about him?" she asked.

"He was a server at the coffee shop and that meant he would know both of the victims. He might not *know* them but he was acquainted with them both. Or at least, we think he was. He would've seen both of them coming and going, except that they might not have been there at the same time," he said. "He was a biochemistry major, which meant he was smart."

"Did he graduate by now?" she asked. It might be harder to track him down if he'd moved on. People came from all over Texas and beyond to attend UT in Austin. It wasn't an easy school to get into and a major like biochemistry would be even harder. Jasper would've had to have been pretty brilliant to pull that off. She wondered if he'd played in his high school band.

"I can't remember off the top of my head if he was a junior or senior at the time of Cheryl's murder. Could rule him out if he'd graduated and moved away at the time of Autumn's murder."

"There's another thing that's been bothering me about my sister. How did she have money for things like coffee? As far as we know she didn't have a job.

And she didn't touch the money you put in the account for her." The fact he'd done that despite how her sister had treated him was above and beyond honorable.

"It's possible she had a job. The coroner's office had very few of her personal belongings. No purse, no wallet and no cell phone. It's a big part of the reason he was having trouble identifying her."

"And also unheard of not to carry those items around everywhere. I can't live without my cell." She nodded toward her purse.

"We could talk to the detective in the Tanning case. She might be able to give us insight into Jasper's current whereabouts."

"That seems like a good idea," she agreed.

"She also seemed especially thorough in Cheryl's investigation. It signals to me that she didn't want to give up on the case."

"What do you think happened?" Summer must've been hungrier than she realized because she finished off the beans and rice that came on her plate alongside her pair of tacos.

"Austin's a fairly large city with higher crime rates than what we see in smaller towns. These things generally come down to available resources. Detective Libby was most likely pulled from the case when she stopped making progress. She might've worked it on her lunch breaks or after hours but eventually leads dry up."

Summer shivered. An icy chill ran down her spine. The thought that Cheryl Tanning had died alone nearly broke Summer's heart. Their lives were not so different now. It wasn't like there was anyone at home waiting for Summer. No life that extended much beyond a small group of coworkers at the diner who she spent hours on end with but barely knew on a personal level.

Actually, that wasn't entirely true. She knew about Marta's boyfriend who revved his motorcycle engine out front to signal he was ready to pick her up after her shift was over. She knew that Dane, one of the cooks, had tattoos running up both arms. He used to joke that he'd gotten them so no one would try to chat him up in line to get his morning coffee. He was the biggest teddy bear once she got to know him.

Summer, on the other hand, shared very little about her private life with her coworkers. She'd always seen the diner as a temporary stop, a place she shouldn't get too comfortable. She'd always played her cards close to her chest, sitting quietly in the breakroom while the others talked about weekend plans or bills due.

She'd gotten so good at keeping everyone at a distance, not unlike Cheryl or Autumn. Cheryl probably had goals. She was probably working toward something when her life had been cut short. Everyone had a dream. Didn't they? Everyone deserved to live out their potential.

Seeing two lives cut so drastically short sent a hot, angry fireball through her veins. Her eyes were too dried up to cry. She let those tears flow earlier in sweet release.

The anger motivated her to find answers. If Sean Menendez wasn't the killer, or Jasper Holden, or Drake Yarnell, Summer wouldn't stop until she figured out who was. The small amount of money she'd socked away for the business would be enough to get by. She'd been afraid to turn up at the bank after the jerks had chased her.

An idea struck.

"I could draw him out, Dawson."

"We talked about this before. This bastard isn't getting within five feet of you."

"Think about it. I could hang out at the coffee shop. My sister used to go there and so did Cheryl. That means this jerk might go there, too," she countered.

"Yeah? What if that's true. Do you really want to walk right into his hands?"

"I could dress up like my sister—"

"I think the words you're looking for are *a sting operation* and it would be way too risky. No responsible law enforcement officer would use you as bait to bring out a deranged killer and I might not be able to cover you from every angle. He knows what you look like, which puts us at a huge disadvantage."

"You're right." She needed to do something. Sitting here, doing nothing, would drive her insane.

"We have to be patient."

IMPATIENCE ROLLED OFF Summer in waves. Dawson understood. They were still studying the facts of the case and it wouldn't feel like they were making any progress to her. The way she was twisting her fingers together, picking up her food just to put it down before eventually taking a bite told him that her nerves were on edge.

It was easy to feel like they were spinning their wheels at this stage of the investigation. They were making progress, though. Slow, steady progress. Inch by inch but he'd take it. They had a similar and linked case to work with. It was a lot more to work with than what they'd had twelve hours ago.

Getting a strong lead with no real break was frustrating. Dawson had been involved in enough investigations over the years to know not every case was solved. As sad and frustrating as it was, there were times when the trail went so cold there was nothing left to follow.

And yet, he couldn't let himself think they wouldn't find the truth. Besides, they had a secret weapon. They had Colton and Gert back in Katy Gulch. Once Gert latched on to a case, her nickname quickly became Pit Bull.

The name responsible for Cheryl's and Autumn's murders were not in that file. Dawson was almost one hundred percent positive, which didn't mean he wouldn't retrace Detective Libby's tracks. He had every intention of interviewing Jasper Holden, Drake Yarnelle and Sean Menendez. Dawson never knew when a seemingly insignificant piece of evidence or interview might blow the case wide-open.

When he glanced over at Summer and realized she'd cleaned her plate and was studying the paper that contained their notes like it was the night before a final exam, he knew it was time to go. Her finger tapped double time on the wood table, a sign her stress levels were hitting the roof again.

The waiter stopped by the table and asked if they needed anything else.

"Just the bill," Dawson said, noticing how much the good-looking waiter kept staring at Summer.

She was beautiful, and he'd noticed most men checked her out when she walked into a room. Not exactly easy to keep her on the down low. Dawson tried to convince himself that was the reason their stares burned him up and not because a piece of him—a growing piece at that—wanted them to stake a claim on each other.

The waiter disappeared, returning a minute later with the bill. Dawson always carried cash. He never knew when he would need it on the road or in a small town, so he'd learned to keep a small stash with him at all times. This was one of the times he was grateful for the habit because he was ready to get her back to the hotel and out of plain view.

He wrapped his arm around her as they headed out the door, again noticing how right she felt in his arms. Again, ignoring the part of him that wanted this to be permanent.

It was dark outside and would be easier to move around at night without risking her. Most of the time, his witnesses were moved under the cover of night. Of course, it all depended on where he was going. Night in a big city still bustled with activity and no one really paid much attention to each other after a quick, primal is-this-person-a-threat-to-my-safety check.

Clean-cut couples barely hit the radar. That was always a good thing in Dawson's line of work and generally the goal. Colton had been in touch with Detective Liddy to let her know about the connection to Autumn and what they were now investigating. Dawson had to follow the right channels.

"I want to make a pit stop before heading back to the hotel." He'd scratched down Drake Yarnell's address on the notepad.

"Oh, yeah?" Summer's face lit up and he wondered if she realized how much danger she was in, *still* in, despite being with a US marshal.

"Yarnell lives in downtown, on the southwest side of Austin. I'd like to swing by his last known address. Detective Libby wrote down that he'd taken over the family home once his mother passed away five years ago. I'm thinking it's a safe bet he still lives there if the house is paid for. Holden and Menendez could be more mobile, especially Holden." They already knew one was a college student and the other worked at the apartment complex where Cheryl lived. A few years after the fact, he might've moved on. It was a safe bet he would stay in the same line of work but that didn't mean he would be at the same place of employment.

She nodded quietly and he wondered what was going through her mind. It took him a second to register that she would be wondering if she was about to come face-to-face with her sister's killer.

He walked her to the passenger side of the truck, and opened the door. Not because he didn't think she was capable of doing it for herself, but it was part of that cowboy code that required putting others first. It was a tradition well rooted in a Texan and one he hoped would never die.

Aside from being ingrained in him, it was protection for Summer. The less she was visible, the better.

He ignored the fact that he liked being in constant physical contact with her.

Chapter Fourteen

The southeast area of Austin's downtown was a row of bungalow-style houses in various states of disrepair. Rentals to university students—the kind who used lawn furniture inside the house and might have a keg on tap at all times but no food in the fridge—ensured the area was prone to crime.

As always, there were a few residents who'd decided to stick it out and whose social security checks or pensions weren't enough to cover new sod when needed or paint.

It was an interesting mix on Fourth. There was a steady wail of sirens in the background and, despite being what most might consider a rough area, an almost constant stream of foot traffic regardless of the late hour.

He pulled the truck up to the house across the street from Yarnell's place and pointed. "His is that one."

The porch light wasn't much more than a bulb hanging from a wire, and it kept blinking. Not exactly a good sign for stable electricity. He reminded himself to ask Yarnell to step outside. Getting fried by electrical current wasn't high on his list of favorite things.

Lights were on inside the house. Didn't necessarily

mean Yarnell himself was home but someone had to be. One of the lights in the front window turned off. Proof someone was moving around.

The front door opened, and a big burly guy stepped out.

"Wait here," Dawson requested as he hopped out of the driver's seat. The person's back was to him. The guy wore a black leather jacket with a massive orange logo covering the entire back. It explained the motorcycle parked in the front yard and they already knew Yarnell was a biker from Cheryl's case file.

Dawson crossed the street and made it to the metal fencing with overgrown scrub brush winding through the slats.

"Excuse me," he said.

Motorcycle Guy turned his head to one side but didn't look at Dawson. "Can I help you?"

"I hope so. I'm looking for Drake Yarnell." This guy fit the physical description of five feet eleven with a stocky build. His arms were covered by the jacket so Dawson couldn't tell if there were tattoos. But then, tattoos in Austin were commonplace so they didn't exactly stand out necessarily as an identifier. According to the files, Yarnell had a snake winding up his left arm, the tail of which stopped at the middle finger on his left hand. Now that was distinctive.

Dawson's question got the guy's attention. He slowly turned, looking ready for a fight. Dawson noticed his right hand fisted around his key. There was no reason to poke the bear.

"You found him."

Yarnell had grown a beard and mustache since the photos of him were taken two years ago. He looked like he'd aged more than two years but hard living could do that and, based on the condition of his home, it looked like he was doing just that. There were empty beer cans littering the yard. Dawson wasn't sure he wanted to know what else was.

"I'm a friend of Detective Libby's. My name is US Marshal Dawson O'Connor." He pulled out his wallet and produced his badge.

Yarnell's dull blue eyes widened. His skin was sunworn, his hair a little too long, and it looked like he'd just gotten off tour with a heavy metal band with a red bandana keeping his hair out of his eyes.

"I told the detective I wasn't involved then and nothing's changed, man." Yarnell put his hands in the air, palms out, in the universal sign of surrender. "But I hate that Cheryl's gone and hate the bastard that killed her."

"Good. Because I'm here in the hopes you can help us find him and lock him away forever."

"I'd like to help out but I'm late for work. You know how it is." If Yarnell was waiting for Dawson to ask him to schedule an appointment and give another statement he had another think coming.

"All I need is a couple minutes of your time," Dawson said.

Yarnell glanced at his watch before glaring at Dawson. "I'll do it for Cheryl. But, damn, I thought this whole thing would go away by now."

There was a weariness in Yarnell's voice that said he'd been put through the ringer. He'd been the prime suspect for a while according to the file. His shoulders deflated and it looked like the wind was knocked out of him.

"Not until her killer is behind bars," Dawson said, matching Yarnell's intensity.

"Fair enough." Yarnell relaxed his hand by his side. "What do you want to ask me that can't be found in my statement or in the files?"

"There's been another murder." Dawson figured coming out with the truth was the best way to gain Yarnell's cooperation.

"Who?" Yarnell asked.

"Autumn Grayson. Do you know her?"

Yarnell shook his head. His response was instant, which made Dawson believe the man was telling the truth.

"Do you think I did it?"

"No. But, to be honest, I would've interviewed you, too. Possibly more than once. Because Cheryl deserves justice and in talking to you, I might have found a clue." Using her first name would bring this conversation onto a personal level. It was personal, too. Any time a life was taken, it was personal for Dawson.

Yarnell's gaze traveled over Dawson like he was sizing him up for a fight.

"Good," he finally said. "Because she didn't deserve what happened to her."

"How did you first hear about the murder?" Dawson asked.

"When four cops showed up at my house with a battering ram," he stated matter-of-factly. "No one seemed to care that we'd been broken up for a while. I'd thought she was cheating on me and I said some things I shouldn't have. An older couple used to live next door and they were always calling the law on me. I guess my shouting at her gave them ammunition."

Dawson already knew Yarnell didn't retaliate against the neighbors. No additional reports had been filed against him despite the fact he'd been watched like a hawk.

"I'm a day late and a dollar short but I care about your history with Cheryl. When the two of you broke up, did you have any proof she was seeing someone else?"

"Nah, just a suspicion. She started acting weird. Secretive. She would disappear for a morning and get offended if I asked where she'd gone." He tucked his hands in his pockets. "Hell, I was just curious at first but after a while I started to think something was up. She would tell me she had to work an extra shift at the hospital where she checked patients in and then I'd show up to surprise her with dinner but her coworkers said she wasn't on the schedule. She got real upset about me going to her job."

"Did you stop?"

"Yeah." He shrugged. "I'm not going to lie. I waited out in the parking lot for her a few times with my lights off. I got caught by the night guard once and he threatened to turn me in if I did it again."

"Was that the end of it?"

Yarnell shrugged. "I'm not proud of the fact now but I used to drink and I waited for her more than once across the street from the hospital. She always parked in the south lot. I'd cruise through with a friend to see if her car was there."

"Was it?"

"Sometimes. Others not so much. She would make up some lame excuse about having to leave early. I guess she got tired of all the questions and moved out."

"She lived with you here?"

"For a few months. She didn't have enough saved up for her own place. She needed first and last month's rent, which was pretty steep. So, she stayed here and cooked instead of pitching in for rent. My roommates weren't crazy about it at first but they got over it. It's my house."

Dawson nodded. The report never said she'd lived with Yarnell. The detective must not have thought the fact was important. He couldn't say he would agree with the assessment and it also indicated a sloppier investigation than he would've liked to see.

"Over the course of your relationship, were you ever physically violent with Cheryl? While you were drinking?" He added that last part after catching the look of disappointment in Yarnell's eyes. He seemed like the kind of guy who'd partied a little too hard and became something he wasn't proud of. The report said he couldn't hold down a job and Dawson wondered if the drinking was a big part of that.

"I left marks on her arms a couple of times from grabbing her too hard. If you're asking if I roughed her up, the answer is no. She did come home with bruises sometimes. It got worse after she moved out. Suddenly, she had enough money to pay the deposit on her apartment. I stayed over once or twice and there was cash in her nightstand—"

Again, Yarnell put his hands in the surrender position.

"Hey, I was just looking for a condom. I wasn't rooting through her stuff like some crazed stalker."

"When was the last time you saw Cheryl?"

"Alive or dead?" He was goading now, understandably angry at having to dredge up what must've been a painful past.

Dawson didn't respond. There were times when it was a good idea to shut someone down and remind them to be respectful and there were times when the law had chewed someone up and spit them out on the other side. Yarnell would pull it together if given a minute to regain his composure. His stress level was through the roof and he looked like he was about to blow. He needed a release valve. In this case, a few minutes to blow out a sharp breath and reset was all it took.

He covered his mouth with his hand, a move someone did right before they were about to lie. In this case, though, he seemed like he didn't want to say the words he had to say next.

"I saw dead pictures of her. The detective, the blonde...what was her name again?"

"Libby."

"Right." He blew out another breath and looked up to the stars. "The Big Dipper."

"Excuse me? I'm not following."

"It was Cheryl's favorite. She pointed it out every time we went outside at night. She would stop in the middle of the street and search for it." He hung his head. "I can't count the number of times I had to pull her out of the road before she got hit by a car."

Dawson had seen this before in investigations. The person interviewed needed to remember something good about the deceased. The memories just bubbled up and it was like they had to come out. Remembering was a good thing. It connected Yarnell to Cheryl's memory. It would rekindle his anger that her life had been cut short.

"I can't say that I remember anymore. Whatever I said in the report is right. It had been months since I'd seen or heard from Cheryl, but I lost track of how many." He glanced down at an empty beer can with a deep longing. Like he needed one of those but couldn't because of work.

"The report says she called you a week before her murder. The call lasted forty seconds," Dawson pointed out.

"My girl answered when she saw my ex's name. She said a few choice words and Cheryl never tried to call back. Detective Libby brought that up a lot before. She swore I was lying but it's the truth. I never spoke to Cheryl before..." His voice broke on that last word and he turned his face away before clearing his throat and regaining his stiff composure. "I never got a chance to say goodbye."

Drake Yarnell's suffering could be seen in his weary eyes. "What if she was calling for help or to get back together. If she'd come back to me, I could've taken care of her."

It was easy to see Yarnell cared for Cheryl and that he'd been racked with guilt ever since her death.

Dawson brought his hand up to Yarnell's shoulder in a show of comfort. "You didn't know what was about to happen. There's no way to go back and undo the past. Try to make peace with it if you can."

"I appreciate that, bro." Yarnell seemed genuine and his honesty touched Dawson. One of the bright spots in his job was being the one to help someone see a tragedy wasn't their fault or helping a family find answers or justice.

He was frustrated that he hadn't been able to do that for Summer, or for Autumn for that matter.

"If you ever need to talk." Dawson pulled a business card out of his wallet. "I'm around."

Yarnell looked Dawson in the eye like he couldn't believe his ears.

"That's cool, bro. Uh, thanks."

What was the point of his job if he couldn't help people? He was usually picking up some lowlife with a felony warrant who'd evaded law enforcement and was considered dangerous. Yarnell had made mistakes in his past and Dawson would never condone being physical with the opposite sex.

He did, however, believe in second chances if any person was serious about cleaning up his or her act.

"I'm serious. Use it."

"I will." Yarnell took the offering. Those dull blue eyes held a momentary spark of hope—hope that he might get some relief from the hell he'd been living in since the dark day Cheryl was murdered.

This was the hell of investigations. A suspect who was innocent. The toll it took on a person's life.

"I'll let you get to work on time."

Yarnell nodded and tucked the business card in the inside pocket of his leather jacket. As Dawson left the yard, he accidentally stepped on a beer can, crushing it with his boot. He kicked the can aside before making his way back to Summer.

"He's innocent. There's nothing more to get out of him," Dawson said as he reclaimed his seat. He'd left the keys in the ignition in case Summer had needed to make a quick getaway.

"I'm wondering if the coffee shop is still open. Maybe we could stop by there and ask around for Holden."

He glanced at the clock as he navigated down the small residential street. There was barely enough room to get through with cars parked on the street and being in his truck wasn't helping. This part of Austin had the most narrow streets. He was used to it, having been here countless times to apprehend a criminal. But it was making Summer nervous based on her expression as he squeezed through.

As he turned on his blinker and pulled up to the light of a busy intersection, Summer gasped.

She pointed her finger at a guy who was walking behind a young woman. She seemed to be alone. Earbuds in, she didn't seem to be paying attention to her surroundings.

"That's him. That's one of the guys who was chasing me the other day," Summer said.

Chapter Fifteen

Summer's pulse raced as adrenaline pumped through her veins. She flexed her fingers a few times, trying to release some of the pent-up nerves as she sat ramrod straight in her seat. The guy who'd almost grabbed her stared at the back of the head of the woman walking ahead of him.

Thick Guy's arms extended, his focus laser-like, about to grab the unaware young woman. An icy chill raced through Summer and an involuntary reflex caused her to shout. No one would hear her inside the truck with the windows rolled up.

Dawson cut over to the other side of the street, and then pulled alongside the curb. He was out of the truck before Summer had a chance to take her seat belt off. The burst of adrenaline that put her body on high alert also caused her hands to shake.

She fumbled with the clasp but finally got the thing off. It pulled back with a snap against the door, but she was already shoving her shoulder into the door to open it.

Summer was out of the vehicle and gunning toward the young woman in seconds. She stumbled over the curb and nearly face planted. Taking a few steps to right herself, she glanced up in time to see a sneer on Thick Guy's face. Another chill raced down her back.

Thick Guy's gaze bounced to Dawson. A look of shock and then anger crossed his features before he turned and bolted in the opposite direction. For a sturdy guy, he had a superfast gait. Dawson turned up the gas and was right behind the perp.

The young woman glanced around and seemed to realize what had been about to go down. Her mouth fell open, her eyes widened and her skin paled. She tapped the white bud in her ear and started crying.

"You're okay," Summer soothed as she wrapped the young woman in an embrace. "Nothing happened. You're fine."

The young woman bawled in her arms. Summer was keenly aware that Thick Guy had had an accomplice last time. She scanned the area, searching for Scrappy. She also keenly realized she and the young woman were alone. Dawson had disappeared down the dark street.

"What's your name?" Summer asked, trying to get the young woman to focus on something besides what had almost just happened.

"Harper."

"Here's what we're going to do, Harper. We're going to go into my friend's truck and wait for him. Don't be scared. He works in law enforcement," she said as calmly and evenly as she could.

"Okay," came out through sobs.

Harper looked to be no older than nineteen. Summer walked the young woman over to the truck and locked them both inside.

"Do you live around here, Harper?" Summer asked.

"No." Harper shook her head. "I was walking to the UT shuttle after a study group meeting a few blocks away from here."

There were bus stops all over the city for UT students.

Right about then, Summer caught sight of Thick Guy walking toward them. Head down, hands behind his back, he looked to be in handcuffs. He heaved for air.

Dawson shoved him across the hood of the truck and wiped blood from his busted lip. Panic washed over Summer at the thought anything could happen to him. She reminded herself that he was standing right there, on his phone, most likely calling in what he'd seen so Thick Guy would be taken in.

Face down, Summer couldn't see Thick Guy's face. But she knew it was him. He had the same height and build. The same black hair. He turned his head to the side and tried to look through the windshield. She caught a glimpse of those same dark eyes.

"Is that him?" Harper asked even though the answer was obvious. She was practically hyperventilating.

"Yes. He's handcuffed and going to jail." If not for what he was about to do to Harper, then what he'd almost done to Summer.

Was hers a random attack? There was no way. She distinctly remembered him and his friend talking about Autumn. What had they said? *She just won't die.*

Summer couldn't imagine her sister getting involved with Thick Guy or Scrappy. Were they for hire? Had Thick Guy seen a pretty young coed walking down the street and decided to take one for himself?

She shivered and her skin crawled at what could have just happened to Harper.

"I need to call my roommate and let her know that I'm going to be late." Harper's voice sounded small and scared.

"Okay. Where's your phone?" Summer asked when Harper didn't immediately make a move.

"My backpack." Harper shrugged the floral-patterned quilt-like material backpack off her shoulder. She unzipped it as tears streamed down her face.

"Hey, he didn't get to you. You're going to be all right. You're safe." Summer looked into Harper's eyes, willing her to be strong. She looked even younger with red, puffy eyes.

"Thank you for stopping. I didn't even hear him over my music, and he must have been right behind me."

"He's done this before. He didn't want to be heard," Summer said.

"I don't know what I would've done if you hadn't shown up when you did."

Summer didn't want to think about it. Thick Guy seemed strong. Harper probably didn't weigh more than a hundred pounds wet. She was five feet two inches in heels.

"Call your roommate so she doesn't worry. We'll give you a ride home," Summer said. She doubted Dawson would mind that she'd made the offer.

Harper made the call and got through it with a few more sobs. Her roommate promised to be home and to wait up for her. Summer was relieved the young woman wouldn't be alone. She would be experiencing the effects of that trauma for a long time to come if Summer had to guess.

"Is it okay if I call my mom?" Harper asked.

"Of course, it is. Where are you from?" Summer

wanted to calm Harper down before she worried her parents.

"San Antonio," Harper said, gripping her phone like it was a grenade.

"Is this your freshman year?"

Harper nodded. Her eyes were still saucers and she was probably still in a little bit of shock.

Lights with sirens filled the air. A patrol car pulled up alongside the curb. An officer got out and within a few minutes, Thick Guy was seated in the back of a squad car. The officer took statements, and then thanked them.

Dawson introduced himself to Harper once the dust had settled.

"I said we'd take her home," Summer said.

There was no hesitation in Dawson's voice as he agreed. Within twenty minutes, he reached the address on campus and deposited Harper at her dorm. He returned to the truck and asked, "How are you doing with all this?"

"Fine. It's crazy to run into him."

"I'm sure as hell glad we did. He invoked his right to remain silent," Dawson said as he navigated them back onto the freeway that, even at this time of night, was stacked with vehicles.

"He's obviously been in this situation before."

"Wouldn't surprise me if he had a rap sheet longer than my arm," Dawson admitted.

"The officer said he'd see us at the station. Does that mean we're headed there now?" she asked.

"No. He won't talk and there's nothing we can do about it. You already gave your statement. We'll swing by tomorrow morning when the detective who worked

Cheryl's case is in. I have a few questions I'd like to ask her."

"You don't like how she handled the investigation, do you?" It wasn't really a question.

"Not really. I think she tried to pin the whole thing on Yarnell. He was a little too easy to try to nail. But the guy didn't do it. An experienced detective would've seen it right away. I'd like to know what I'm dealing with when it comes to Detective Libby and that's best done in a face-to-face meeting."

Despite cars as far as she could see on either side of her, in front of her and behind her, they were still moving. The progress was slow but she'd take it.

Forty minutes later in a drive that should've taken fifteen, Dawson pulled in front of the hotel and then around to the side of the building to park.

"I hope Harper called her mom." It was a strange thought to have now. Summer wondered what is was like to have that. She'd known that her mother had loved her children in her own way. She'd just been so broken that she kept herself too medicated to show it.

If Summer ever became a mother, she'd be the kind a child wanted to call in an emergency. Someone a child could lean on during tough times. She'd want to be part of her child's life like she imagined Dawson would be. His entire family was a support system for each other. What was that even like?

If she had a child, and she'd never really given it much thought, she'd want to have one with a man like Dawson. He'd be an amazing father.

Summer gave herself a mental slap to root herself back in reality.

Where did all that come from? She'd never once

thought about what it would be like to have children. Now she couldn't help but wonder if it was because she'd never been around a man she trusted enough to try.

DAWSON WALKED SIDE by side with Summer through the hotel lobby. At this hour, there were very few folks downstairs. The only group he saw was a family of four with their luggage being wheeled to the check-in desk.

He and Summer made it to the room without anyone giving them a second look.

"Do you think it's an odd coincidence that the guy who was after me was in Drake Yarnell's neighborhood?" she asked.

"His name is Jesse Lynch." Dawson couldn't say he was surprised. "It's one of the worst neighborhoods in Austin. We got lucky running into Lynch when we did but I can't say I'm surprised we saw him in that general area."

"Do you think he was behind the murders?" she asked.

"Not Lynch. I do believe he's for hire and someone used him to get to your sister and possibly Cheryl. A violin string might be his MO."

"Autumn and Cheryl didn't know each other as far as we can tell." Summer kicked off her shoes and reclaimed her seat on the sofa.

Dawson joined her, opening the laptop and entering the password to bring the screen to life.

"They were connected by the killer," she continued. "That's obvious. But it was someone they'd both dated."

"There's the coffee shop," he added.

"I can't help but think we need to park it there tomorrow and watch everyone who comes through those doors." The lines in Summer's forehead deepened as she concentrated. Her lips pursed and her unfocused gaze stared at the screen even though she wasn't really looking at it. "If he walks in, he's bound to have some kind of reaction to seeing me alive."

"It will also alert him to the fact you exist. Your sister seemed to go to great lengths to keep you hidden and I'm certain it was for good reason."

"What about the necklace, though?" she asked. "She had to know you'd go through her stuff eventually even if it was just to toss it in the trash."

"It's possible she wanted me to figure out the connection with you." It was all speculation but that was all they had at the moment.

"What about Sean Menendez?" she asked.

"We can stop by the apartment complex on our way in town," he said. He also made a mental note to check with Detective Libby about the name Matt Shank, the fake lawyer name that Autumn had put on the divorce papers.

Summer glanced at the clock on the wall and bit back a yawn. "What time do you want to head downtown tomorrow?"

"We could get a jump on traffic. Say, six o'clock in the morning. If the apartment complex doesn't net any leads we could stop for breakfast before heading to the station." He wanted to stay up and peruse the files to get a better handle on all the statements and evidence.

Summer excused herself to the bathroom, returning twenty minutes later wearing a hotel bathrobe. She had the waist cinched up tightly. She stopped at the doorway to the bedroom. She bit her bottom lip and shifted her weight from side to side. Was she nervous?

"Will you lie down with me until I fall asleep?" she asked. "Every time I close my eyes, I see those pictures in my head." She motioned toward the laptop and he immediately knew she was talking about Cheryl.

"Yeah, sure." He said the words casually like lying down next to Summer in bed would be no big deal. His pulse kicked up thinking about being in such close proximity to her. Since he no longer ran on hormones and caffeine like in his younger days, he told himself he could handle it. And he could. There was no way he'd cross a boundary with Summer that she didn't want.

The problem was that when he stood up, he saw desire in her eyes. Desire for comfort. Desire to get lost in someone. Desire to shut out the world for just a few hours.

Dawson took her by the hand and linked their fingers, ignoring all the electrical impulses firing through him as best he could. It wasn't easy. Being this close to Summer wasn't easy. But the easy road was underrated.

He lifted the covers for her, and she climbed into bed. He knew better than to follow, so he toed off his boots and propped up a couple of pillows. He sat on top of the comforter and even then his heart detonated when she curled her body around his.

Dawson watched as she fell into a deep sleep beside him. He closed his eyes, telling himself a catnap would do him some good.

The next sound he heard was the snick of a lock.

Chapter Sixteen

"Housekeeping." The small voice along with a knock on the door caused Dawson to shoot straight up to standing.

The sun was already up and he realized he'd fallen asleep. He couldn't remember the last time that had happened when he'd intended to stay awake. He missed the feel of Summer's warm body the minute he stood up.

A cursory look said he hadn't peeled his shirt off in the middle of the night and his jeans were still snapped. He was decent enough to face the person coming into their room. He cursed himself for not putting the Do Not Disturb sign on the door handle.

He moved to the doorway, trying not to wake Summer as he glanced at the clock. Seven a.m.

"Sorry," he said to the short, middle-aged woman standing at the door. She couldn't be much taller than five feet. "My wife is still asleep. Do you mind coming back in about an hour?"

"No problem, sir." The round woman with the graying hair and kind eyes waved as she took a backward step in the opened door. "I'll come back."

"Thank you." Dawson followed her to the door and

put the sign out. When he returned, Summer was sitting up and rubbing her eyes. Seeing that honey-wheat hair spill down the pillow he'd been sleeping on moments ago didn't do good things to his heart this early. He made a beeline for the coffee machine and raked his hand through his hair.

As the coffee brewed in his cup, he made a quick pit stop to the bathroom to wash his face and brush his teeth. Splashing cold water on his face helped shake him out of the fog that had him going down a path of real feelings for Summer.

She was in trouble and he was helping her out. That was all. She needed answers to what happened to her sister. That was all. He was going to nail the bastard who killed Autumn and then walk away from the Grayson family. That was all.

Too bad his mantra wasn't working. There were so many cracks in the casing around his heart there was no threat he'd use it instead of his Kevlar vest for protection.

As he exited the bathroom, Summer stood on the other side of the door. She squeezed past him as soon as he opened it.

"Coffee?" he asked.

"Yes, please." The door closed and he heard the water running as he moved into the next room. He didn't need to stick around the door and think about the fact she was naked underneath that robe any more than he needed the image of her waking up next to him etched in his brain.

Because it felt more right than anything had in longer than he cared to remember.

A couple of sips of fresh brew should shake his

brain out of the fog and keep it on track. He brought both cups over to the coffee table and retrieved his cell phone. He called the station and identified himself. He was immediately transferred to a supervisor, which he'd expected.

"This is Sergeant Wexler. How may I be of assistance?" Wexler had one of those voices that made him sound like he'd been on the job longer than he cared to and had seen just about everything. He was the two *C*s: curt and courteous.

"My name is Marshal O'Connor and I'm calling to check on a suspect by the name of Jesse Lynch."

"Right." There was an ominous quality to Wexler's tone. "I'm sorry to be the one to tell you but Lynch hung himself last night."

This news was the first indication this case was bigger than Dawson realized. He'd been thinking the perp was someone small-time who'd dated Cheryl and then Autumn. He got a taste of what it was like to kill with Cheryl. It had possibly even been an accident or an argument that had gone too far. By the time he got to Autumn, he'd developed a taste for it. The guy was someone who had access to a violin string, an unlikely murder weapon. A musician or music teacher? It also made a statement because strangulation was a very personal method for murder.

"I'm sorry to hear the news." Dawson had no doubt in his mind that Jesse Lynch was not the type to hang himself in his cell, especially considering they'd caught him before he'd done anything to the young coed. The case against him wouldn't stick if he had a decent lawyer.

Summer was a different story altogether. But then

all he'd done was chase her. He hadn't actually caught her. All the evidence against him was hearsay.

"It's a shame," Wexler said in a tsk-tsk tone. "Young people today have a lot of emotional problems. A university kid was sitting on the side of the road the other day with a flat tire. He was bawling and pacing. I calmed him down and told him I'd help him. I was tired. On my way home from a long day but if it was my kid, I'd want someone to stop. So, I'm working on the tire and he stops crying but instead of jumping in to help, do you know what he does?"

Wexler paused.

"Can't say that I do," Dawson supplied.

"He gets on his cell and starts snap-ticking a friend…or whatever that social media site is. The one where the kids send messages to their friends instead of calling."

Dawson wished Wexler would get to the point.

"I had to tell him, no-no. Get the hell off that thing and get over here. You're going to learn how to change a tire." He finished his sentence in ta-da fashion.

"Next time he'll know how to do it himself." Dawson had no idea how to respond or how this story was linked to Jesse Lynch's hanging.

"Yeah, that's what I was thinking. I can do it for him and he'll never learn or I can tell him to put the damn phone away and pay attention. These kids are lazy and the minute anything goes wrong, they fall apart." Wexler might believe that about Jesse Lynch but Dawson didn't.

Based on what he knew so far, Lynch was street-smart. He got by working the streets and taking what he wanted. He was from the wrong side of the tracks though. Not a kid who got busted for a dime bag of weed and thought his parents would never speak to him again.

This kid knew how to survive.

"Was he alone in his cell all night?" Dawson asked.

"According to the night watch, he was."

Dawson didn't like the sound of that. It could mean the killer was someone on the inside or had connections. The violin string bothered him, though.

"Thank you for letting me know about Lynch. That's unfortunate," Dawson said.

"Such a waste," Wexler said.

"Can you do me a favor?" Dawson asked.

"Sure, anything."

"Transfer me to Detective Libby." The quiet on the line sent another warning flare.

"She isn't around."

Dawson wasn't so sure what that meant but it sounded like a sore subject.

"When will she be back?" he asked.

"She's not with the department anymore," Wexler supplied.

"What happened?" Dawson asked.

"She left the department about two years ago."

"Do you have a forwarding address?"

"I can transfer you to personnel," Wexler offered.

Now Dawson needed to decide if the sergeant was involved or just complacent. His instincts said the latter was true.

"I'll call back another time." Dawson wanted to give the impression he didn't care all that much, so he added, "It's not that important."

Wexler seemed satisfied with that answer. "You take care."

"Will do." He ended the call. When he glanced up, he saw Summer studying him.

"What happened to Jesse Lynch?" Her forehead was creased with concern that their first lead had just dried up.

"He was murdered in his cell last night, but the department is calling it a suicide."

Stunned, Summer took a couple of steps backward until she sat in a chair at the small table. She seemed to pick up on the implication.

"I checked all the names of the politicians in Austin and didn't find a single Charles, Charlie, Charley or Matthew and no relation to the last name of Shank." Dawson reviewed his findings or lack thereof with her.

"So, Lynch is gone." She paused like she needed a minute for the news to sink in. Like saying it out loud made it that much more real and scary. "What about the detective on the case?"

"She quit the department six months after Cheryl's murder." The timing of her resignation was suspect as hell. The whole situation reeked of foul play.

"And this is the same department that is going to investigate my sister's murder?" Summer brought her hand up to her face.

"They gave Cheryl's case to a young detective. I'm guessing they didn't expect her to do a very good job being so green," he stated.

"Except that she stayed with it. We thought she was pulled off the case and it was marked cold, when it turns out she left the department. What would make her do that?"

"I'll ask Colton to look into it and see if he can dig up some information. He has a trusted contact at Austin PD and that might be our best route. I can call human resources but they won't be able to give out personal information about the detective." Her exit must have been the reason the investigation stalled.

"What would make her up and leave like that?"

"Bribery. Threats. Your guess is as good as mine. If we can figure out where she landed after leaving and how she's living now, we'll have a better idea of the reason."

And just who the department was trying to protect.

THIS NEWS WAS BIG. It screamed cover-up. And if the same person killed Autumn, there'd be no justice for her. If the person was so big or connected that he could make a detective leave her job and a witness be killed in jail and marked as a suicide, how could they bring him down? Who would listen?

"I got away," she said under her breath. "He must've had eyes on the jail in case one of his minions got picked up."

"Or Lynch used his one phone call to the wrong person."

"Why not just kill him before?" she asked.

"He wasn't done with the job, for one. Plus, the body count was racking up."

"There were two guys chasing me." She wondered what had happened to the second one.

"It's possible he's still out there. Once word gets out in their circles that Lynch is dead, the others will likely go underground for a few months. Maybe even hop over the border." He referred to Mexico. "There are plenty of little towns to get lost in."

She'd read about Americans living in both countries. It was easy to move back and forth with US citizenship. She'd also read about young people going over to party and never coming back. Many border towns were dangerous. But then, Scrappy wasn't exactly a college coed and he wasn't exactly innocent.

"I doubt Sean Menendez has the kind of connections necessary to pull off a jail murder." Dawson was right about that.

"Agreed." She didn't care how creepy the maintenance man was, he'd be hard-pressed to find the resources it took to kill someone while in a jail cell. "Do you think we can stop by and talk to him or the property manager anyway? Maybe I can get some information about my sister from the staff."

"It doesn't hurt to stop by for an interview. I also need to let my brother know what's going on." Dawson paused and stared at his phone. "No one at Austin P.D. knew your sister had been murdered."

"The coroner must be honest," she observed.

"I've known him a long time. He's always been one of the good guys."

"If you ever needed proof the coroner reported the death but it was covered up by Austin P.D, I think you just got it." She picked up her coffee cup and took a sip. The burn felt good on her throat. "You said Yarnell has been living in hell ever since Cheryl's murder. I can't imagine what he must've gone through with a department bent on hanging a crime on him."

"The guy was in pain learning about his ex. She'd tried to call him and his new girlfriend picked up. She said a few choice words to Cheryl and that was it. She never tried to contact him again and then she shows up dead." Dawson studied his cell phone screen. It started going off in his hand like crazy.

He immediately stood up and started pacing. A feeling deep in the pit of her stomach caused her to be nauseous because the look on his face said it was bad news—news about his beloved family.

"Sorry, I need to—"

"Don't apologize, Dawson. Your family is just as important as mine."

He stopped and looked at her, a bit shell-shocked. And then he nodded, smiled and made a call.

Summer was confused by his look of surprise. His family was important to him, and to her. He was becoming important to her. There was something about living in fear of her life for the past few weeks that made the grand scheme of things crystal clear. Family came first.

And maybe clarity had to do with the fact that she'd lost hers. Summer had always believed in family. She'd just never really had more than her sister.

She couldn't help but overhear Dawson's conversation despite the fact he'd gone into the bedroom for privacy. There was news about his father's case. An address came up for a possible suspect.

Dawson ended the call before walking into the room, a look of despair darkened his eyes.

"I overheard bits and pieces of your conversation. I'm sorry—"

He shook his head before raking a finger through his thick curls. A couple laps around the room later, and he seemed to calm down enough to tell her what was going on.

"Do you need to go investigate?" She didn't expect Dawson to stay with her under the circumstances.

"One extra person would just be in the way. My brothers are all over it and I'm needed here." The look on his face said he wanted to be with his siblings.

"You don't have to do this, Dawson. Your family needs you and I wouldn't want you to have any regrets about—"

He wheeled around on her so fast, she stopped midsentence.

"Last time I checked, you were family, too." His voice was sharp, and his eyes shot daggers. "But if you don't want me here then say the word."

Her entire body stiffened as she geared up for a fight. Before she could open her mouth to argue Dawson shot her a look of apology. He put a hand up and took another couple of laps.

Summer drew in a few breaths meant to calm her but all she ended up doing was breathing in more of his spicy and clean scent. She tried to form words but none came.

All she wanted was to stand up and put her hand on his chest to stop him and get him to breathe. So, that's exactly what she did. Summer stood up and then stepped in front of him, forcing him to stop. Hand to his chest, she locked gazes with him.

He started to speak and clamped down, compressing his lips instead.

She could feel the moment the air changed from anger and frustration to awareness. Awareness of their hearts pounding against their rib cages. Awareness of the chemistry that had been sizzling between them since the moment they'd met. Awareness of their raspy breathing.

Call her wrong, but one look in his eyes made her think he wanted to reach out to her as much as she needed to feel him. She ran her fingers along the muscled ridges of his chest. There was only a thin layer of cotton preventing her from skin-to-skin contact.

Dawson brought his hands up to cup her face. He looked at her with a longing so deep it robbed her breath.

The need to feel his lips move against hers was a physical ache. She tilted her face toward his and he brought his lips down on hers.

Summer brought her hands up to his shoulders to brace herself, digging her nails in when he deepened the kiss. His hands dropped and his arms looped around her waist, bringing her body flush with his. She could kiss this man all day. She *wanted* to kiss this man all day.

She couldn't.

Reality lurked and they'd come to their senses in a minute. But for right then, Summer didn't care about his past or hers. Nothing mattered except this moment happening between them, a moment they both wanted so badly they could hardly breathe.

She felt that kiss from her crown to her toes and when his tongue dipped inside her mouth, heat spread through her. She ignored the fact he was the best kisser in her life and the other obvious fact that he'd be mind-numbingly amazing in bed.

The other facts, she couldn't ignore so easily.

They didn't have a lot of time to waste. Kissing him

had been a luxury. And she needed to pull back while she still could.

Easier said than done.

With a deep breath, she managed to break away from those full lips of his—lips too soft for a face of such hard angles.

One look in his eyes said they were playing with fire.

Chapter Seventeen

Dawson pressed his forehead to Summer's while he took a minute to catch his breath. Being with her was doing things to his heart that he never knew possible. Rather than get inside his head about what that meant, how that changed things for him, he refocused on just breathing with her.

He knew one thing was certain. He'd had great sex in his life before and none of it would compare to what he would have with Summer. He meant that on every level. She had that rare kind of beauty that started on the inside.

Her smile, rare as it might be, was so genuine she radiated. She smiled from her soul, if that made any sense. Hell, he'd never been the poetic type, but she made him want to put his attraction to her into words. He just needed to find the right ones first.

There hadn't been much to laugh about lately but when she did he could swear it was the most beautiful sound. There wasn't a musical instrument in existence that compared to her, and hearing it did things to his heart that he'd tried to shut down long ago. It made him think of foreign things like forever—something he'd thought would never be possible after the way his marriage ended.

He'd cared about Autumn and had been determined to make things work because of the child he thought she was carrying. There was no forcing his feelings when it came to Summer.

Her face was blue skies and sunshine after a storm. Her mind kept him on his toes. And the fire burning inside her made him think life with her would never be dull.

But that wasn't on the table. He wasn't sure he could go down that road again with anyone. If he did…he'd want it to be with Summer.

After feathering a kiss to her lips, he cleared his throat and took a step back, hoping for a little clarity. Looking into her eyes only muddied the waters for him even more.

Damn.

He needed more coffee to wake him up because he wasn't thinking clearly. He'd promised himself that he wouldn't let things get out of hand with Summer and he had every intention of keeping that commitment to himself.

Besides, with his personal life in upheaval, this was the worst possible time to add more confusion into the mix. Summer didn't deserve that, either. She needed a strong shoulder to lean on while she got her bearings. The woman was fully capable of handling herself and yet he wanted to be her comfort in a storm.

Best not to confuse the sentiment with emotions. He'd keep himself in check better than he had been. For Summer's sake.

THE APARTMENT COMPLEX downtown wasn't exactly the kind Summer could see her sister living in. It was most likely what she could afford, and that broke Summer's heart even more. Why hadn't Autumn reached out for help? Why did she live like this? Was this place better than being with Summer?

She reached inside her purse where she kept the "Summer" necklace and rolled it around in her fingers. In a strange way, touching this piece of junk jewelry made her feel more connected to a sister who she admittedly didn't know very well.

This was the last place she would've looked for Autumn. Maybe that was part of the reason her sister rented an apartment here.

Dawson parked the truck and they both got out. The office was a small brick building with double glass doors. The sign said it was open. She took a deep breath and started toward the entrance.

For the life of her she couldn't figure out why her sister would've left twenty-five thousand dollars sitting in a bank account in her name without touching it. The money had been a gift from Dawson. It was free and clear with no expectation of payback.

Had Autumn regretted getting him involved in her life? Had she walked away and tried to minimize the damage?

If she didn't take anything from him, did she think she could convince herself the lies she'd told him were for his protection? It was possible she convinced herself that her disappearing act was harmless.

Did she leave Dawson to go back to the secret boyfriend she'd been involved with in the past? All signs pointed to just that. She remembered what Dawson said about women in abusive relationships. She just wished she'd known what her sister was going through. She could've been there for Autumn. Her sister wasn't alone.

A rogue tear escaped thinking about Autumn.

Summer wiped it away and stepped inside the glass doors. A little bell rang when Dawson opened the one on the right. Inside there was a tiled foyer. Beyond that was a great room overlooking a small pool. There was a kitchenette and two offices.

An overeager youngish woman dressed in a pantsuit bounded into the room. She had Shirley Temple curls and wore too much makeup to pull off the innocent look.

"Hello, I'm Marcy." She stuck out her hand toward Dawson.

Her gaze lingered a little too long on his face and Summer wanted to snap her fingers at the woman to get her attention.

"Dawson, and this is my wife—"

"Sandy." She nodded like she'd just answered the last question correctly on a game show. "I know."

Summer reined in her confused look because she realized this person might know her sister.

"I just didn't realize you were married." Marcy had one of those voices that grated. Fingernails on a chalkboard sounded like a relief after hearing her speak.

"Oh, right. I forgot to mention it because we've been separated. You know, trying to figure things out."

Marcy looked from Dawson to Summer and laughed. "You've been busy."

She flexed and released her fingers as she felt Dawson's hand clasp hers. He gave a little squeeze and it grounded her. They had a purpose and the ever-annoying Marcy didn't get to detract from that. Besides, she didn't seem very bright, which was a potential gold mine of information for them if they played it right.

"Your things have been boxed up. Headquarters makes us hold on to them for ninety days after eviction." Marcy shrugged.

"Oh. Right. I guess I forgot to keep my rent payments up once I got back together with my husband," Summer said by way of explanation, ignoring the fact that calling Dawson her husband had just rolled right off her tongue like it was truth. Not being honest hit her at her core but couldn't be helped if she wanted access to Autumn's things.

"I almost didn't recognize you at first. You look so…different." Marcy made a show of looking Summer up and down.

"Well, it's me." She had to tamp down the urge to come back with a snarky remark. This wasn't the right time for pride. "Is it possible to see my belongings?"

Marcy blew out a sharp breath and gave Summer a death stare.

"It's against policy when there's an overdue rent situation," she huffed, making her disgust with anyone who was late on rent clear as if the glaring eyes hadn't done it already.

"Do you take a credit card?" Dawson stepped up immediately. "I didn't bring a check with me today."

The annoying woman perked up at the sound of payment.

"We add 3 percent to the outstanding balance," she warned like that might be a tipping point that caused them to turn around and walk out the door.

Summer almost laughed out loud. Dawson O'Connor could cover 3 percent and so much more. He could keep the twenty-five thousand dollars in Autumn's bank account, and Summer would figure out a payment plan to cover her sister's expenses.

"Just give me a total." Dawson smiled and Marcy practically beamed back at him. It was enough to make Summer hold his hand a little tighter. And, yes, she was being territorial.

Dawson's smile was meant to disarm Marcy. Summer figured that part out on her own and yet a streak of jealousy still crept in. Keeping a safe distance from her emotions had always been a matter of survival for Summer.

Despite the magnetic pull toward Dawson and the absolute fire in every kiss that promised so much more than great sex, breaking down her walls would take time and patience. She didn't even know if it was possible anymore. In every past relationship she'd been afraid of heights and there'd been a cliff in the distance.

Before Dawson, she wouldn't consider getting anywhere near the edge. Now? She was starting to think that maybe it could happen. The problem wasn't the relationship. She knew being with a person as intelligent, kind and respectful as Dawson would set the bar for every future date. When the shine wore off and it ended, she would be shattered.

Because she wouldn't be able to keep Dawson at a distance. He was the sun, drawing everything that got near into his orbit, spinning faster and making her forget that if she stepped out, she'd spiral out of control.

"Let me check with my property manager," Marcy

chirped. Suddenly, fingernails on a chalkboard didn't seem so bad to Summer.

Dawson thanked her before tugging Summer a little bit closer and dipping his head to press a kiss on her lips.

Marcy exited quickly and it made Summer smirk. The move from Dawson was most likely meant to sell the marriage story but damned if it didn't feel like the most natural thing for him to kiss her. Summer was in his orbit all right. Pulling away from him when this came to a close might be more difficult than she'd anticipated.

Still, walking away would be the right thing to do, she reasoned. There was no other choice when she really thought about it. This case would end. She needed to get used to a new normal and a life without Autumn. Her sister had been preparing Summer for this in many ways over the past few years.

Autumn had been difficult to get ahold of and she'd disappeared for long periods. She'd been putting more and more emotional distance between them. The notion of looking through her sister's last possessions hit her so hard it nearly knocked her breath away. So many thoughts raced through Summer's mind about what her sister had held on to. How had her sister lived in those final months? What had been important to her?

Irritating chirp lady walked back into the lobby.

"You owe three months' rent at one thousand five hundred and fifty dollars a month. Plus, four hundred and fifty dollars in late fees and a thousand dollars for us to release your belongings. The total comes to six thousand, one hundred dollars." She produced an invoice.

Dawson pulled his wallet out of his back pocket. "Do you have a preference when it comes to plastic?"

"We'll take whatever you have available as long as the charge is approved." Marcy beamed at Dawson but when her gaze shifted to Summer, her forehead creased with disapproval.

He didn't hesitate to hand over his card.

"I'll be right back as soon as I run this," Marcy said before bebopping out of the room.

"I'd like to pay you back," Summer said in a whisper.

"You don't have to worry about that. It's the least I can do," he said and there was regret in his voice.

"What do you mean?" she asked.

"I let your sister down. She came to me for sanctuary and I couldn't protect her." His serious tone said he meant every word. Here, Summer had been so focused on the fact she'd let her sister down she hadn't once stopped to think Dawson might be in the same boat.

"You didn't know her. She walked out. You believed her. You did nothing but trust her and she betrayed that. Don't get me wrong, I love Autumn with all my heart. That doesn't mean I'm naive to the fact she made a lot of bad decisions in her life. But believe me when I say that you're the last person on earth who should feel responsible for her."

"Your card is good," Marcy interrupted the conversation.

Logic said Summer should be able to forgive herself for not being there when Autumn needed her. The advice she'd given to Dawson seconds ago was true for him and somewhere down deep she could acknowledge it was true for her, too.

Dawson took the card Marcy held between them. He tucked it back inside his wallet at the same time Marcy seemed to catch sight of the badge. She looked up at Dawson and studied his face.

Summer couldn't tell what the woman was thinking but the badge seemed to make her stand up a little straighter.

"Where do you keep eviction belongings?" Dawson asked. It was the question on Summer's mind.

"You'll have to wait thirty days and then you can buy them back from us." Marcy sounded a little less certain of herself and a lot less bubbly than she had a few minutes ago.

"We paid up my rent with late fees plus the thousand dollars to release those belongings. There's no reason to keep my stuff." Summer tensed up, ready for a fight.

Dawson squeezed her hand.

"How much to buy all of her belongings?" he asked.

Marcy glanced around. "I'm not really supposed to—"

"I don't trust that you've taken care of my stuff. I'd like to check on it to make sure everything's there." Summer was grasping at straws here but there might be something in her sister's personal items that could give a hint of who she'd been seeing. Leaving empty-handed wasn't an option.

"We have the right to dispose of your items. We sent out a notice of our intentions—"

"Which technically I never received."

"Your..." Marcy's gaze bounced from Summer to Dawson and back "...*boyfriend* stopped by a couple of months ago and emptied out your storage. There isn't much left but some makeup and toiletries. There

are a few towels and some clothing. I don't think my
boss would be too mad if I showed you what was left."

The wheels were already turning in Summer's mind
as to how to tactfully ask what her "boyfriend" looked
like.

"That would be great if it's not too much trouble."
Summer softened her tone, reminding herself she'd get
more out of Marcy with honey than vinegar.

"Stay right here and I'll get my keys." Marcy disappeared long enough for Summer to make eyes at
Dawson.

He seemed to read her apprehension even though
he didn't speak. How had he become so important in
such a short time? She'd tell herself the desperate life-
and-death situation she'd been in would cause her emotions to be all over the place. But that wouldn't be fair
to her feelings for Dawson.

Marcy returned and motioned for them to follow
her. She led them to a golf cart parked out front. Summer climbed inside and looked around. The person
who'd killed her sister had walked around on these
same paths. Cheryl's killer had been here.

No way to bring up Summer's "boyfriend" came
to her tactfully. So, Summer took the front seat and
leaned over when Marcy claimed the driver's side and
popped the key in the ignition.

"I don't want my husband to hear this but can you
tell me which one of my boyfriends stopped by. I dated
around a lot after my husband and I separated. We got
married straight out of high school and needed to find
ourselves as people." She was overexplaining, adding
details to convince Marcy of the untruth.

Marcy mouthed an *Oh*.

The woman winked and smiled, looking a little too happy that "Sandy" seemed to be a little loose.

Chapter Eighteen

"He introduced himself as Matt…um, hmm. That's weird. I'm not sure he ever told me his last name. If he did, I sure don't remember it. He was gorgeous, though." She glanced back at Dawson, who was making a show of checking his cell phone.

Luckily, the backseat faced the opposite direction so they couldn't see his face. It gave the illusion he couldn't hear.

Marcy backed out of the parking spot. The beep, beep, beep of the golf cart masked their conversation.

"If you ask me, this one's the best. Hands down." Marcy blushed as she nodded back toward Dawson. "But then I've always been partial to tall, muscled men. Matt looked like he stepped out of one of those Abercrombie and Fitch ads if there was one for middle-aged men. You know?"

"Yeah." Summer didn't have a clue. She'd gotten a first name, though. Matt. The name of the so-called attorney who'd handled the fake divorce had been Matt Charley Shank. The first two names were clues. What did Shank mean?

For some reason, Summer doubted it was his actual last name. In fact, she was certain that Dawson would have checked every Matt or Matthew Shank in Texas. She tabled that thought, figuring Marcy was feeling chatty.

"I never liked his hair, though," Summer said.

"Too curly?"

"Exactly. And the color—"

"Black never bothered me. It was a little long for a guy who wore a suit, though," Marcy stated.

Summer committed the details to memory. Matt, last name unknown, who looked like he'd walked off an Abercrombie and Fitch ad for middle-aged men, had curly black hair.

"His eyes were nice, though," Marcy continued in a hushed tone as she whipped around a corner and toward the back side of the complex. They passed a row of mailboxes before Marcy made another turn. "I don't normally like blue eyes on a man but his were so light. They looked good on him. And he had just enough gray at the temples to be sexy."

She added the extra details, repeating his description to seal it into her brain. Matt, last name unknown, who looked like he'd walked off an Abercrombie and Fitch ad for middle-aged men, had curly black hair. He also had light blue eyes and wore a suit. And he had just enough gray at the temples to be sexy.

A picture was emerging.

"He turned out to be a creep." Summer fished for any signs there'd been fighting between her sister and Matt. Marcy seemed like the nosy type who would know if a couple had problems.

"Really?" Marcy seemed shocked. She took a minute to think about it and then said, "You know, that explains all the flowers."

"His way of apologizing," Summer continued.

"My mom always said never trust a man when he sends flowers out of the blue. It means he's doing something wrong." Marcy looked at Summer in a show of solidarity.

Summer noticed there was no ring on Marcy's left hand.

"Dating is hard," Summer continued.

"It's the worst." Marcy smacked her palm on the steering wheel. "Right?"

"There are so many jerks out there," Summer agreed.

"And they take all shapes and forms." Marcy was really into the conversation now. Good, Summer had gotten good information out of the woman so far. And Summer was getting used to her nasal tone of voice. Fingernails on a chalkboard still had a better sound but Marcy was growing on her.

Summer repeated her new mantra. Matt, last name unknown, who looked like he'd walked off an Abercrombie and Fitch ad for middle-aged men, had curly black hair that was a little too long. He also had light blue eyes and wore a suit. And he had just enough gray at the temples to be sexy.

"You think you can trust a guy in a suit and then he turns out to be more of a jerk than you could ever have imagined." Summer kept pouring it on. She was always so careful when she met a new person and was always guarded if someone tried to interact with her for the first time online. She'd been too busy working extra shifts and socking away money to have much free time. When she did have a day off, she usually spent it at the library researching how to start her own business or under the covers trying to catch up on her sleep.

Marcy rocked her head as she pulled into a parking spot. Dawson, who'd been quiet up until now, was off the cart first. He clasped hands with Summer the second she exited.

"Right this way." Marcy took them to a storage building with five large doors. Keys clanked as she searched for the right one. "Hold on just a minute. Where'd you go?" She was talking to herself as she checked keys, one by one, and occasionally glanced over at Summer with an awkward smile.

At least Marcy was focusing on Summer now instead of Dawson. He moved behind Summer and looped his arms around her. The feel of his masculine chest against her back sent sensual shivers racing through her.

In the move, he also slipped his cell phone into her hands and swiped so that the screen came to life.

"Are you from Texas, Marcy?"

Summer could feel his chest vibrate when he spoke. More of those inappropriate shivers raced down her back.

"San Angelo originally." She beamed at him before refocusing on the keys. She slid one in and said, "Finally."

When her back was turned, Summer glanced at the screen of Dawson's phone. He'd written down the description of Matt, which was basically the same as the mantra she'd repeated a couple of times since getting off the cart.

He ran his thumb inside the palm of her hand, and it sent a trail of warmth.

"And, we're in," Marcy said after wrestling with the door. "Be careful. We don't usually let people back here, so it's a mess. Maintenance is supposed to clean up but Jared has been calling in sick lately and it's all we can do to keep residents happy."

"What happened to Sean?" Summer took the opportunity to ask another question that had been on both her and Dawson's minds.

"We had to let him go," Marcy said with a frown. "He made a few of our female residents uncomfortable, so he wasn't working out." She paused. "I didn't realize you liked him all that much."

"Can't say that I knew him very well." She shrugged. "Now that you mention it, he was a little creepy."

"That's the same word a few other residents used to describe interactions with him," she admitted. Those few minutes in the golf cart had won over Marcy's trust.

Steeling her nerves, Summer followed Marcy into the space. She flipped on a light, which was one of those basic builder installs hanging from the ceiling. The walls inside weren't finished. There were only boards and posts.

The storage shed was large and there was enough dust on the flooring to cover half the state. People's belongings were stacked in piles, some were wrapped in what looked like oversize pieces of Saran wrap.

Marcy navigated around a few of the piles until she located Autumn's belongings.

"Here's your stuff," she said to Summer.

The stack consisted of a pile of clothing on top of shoes. There was makeup, like Marcy had mentioned before. There wasn't a whole lot else. A couple of purses, some blankets and toiletries.

"I'll go get the truck," Dawson said as an icy chill

raced down Summer's spine. All of her sister's belongings could easily fit in the back.

Summer didn't have much, but she'd worked for her small apartment and filled it with things she loved. Her neighbor was looking after Summer's plants. She had a wall of bookshelves with her favorite paperbacks. There were a few shells from the beach along with art she'd bought on the street. She'd made a few pieces herself, nothing fancy, just pottery she'd painted and fired. She had the most comfortable bed and her blanket was the softest thing she'd ever felt.

Again, nothing extravagant but everything in her home meant something to her. She still had a white starfish blown from glass that she'd picked up in Seattle at the Pike Place Market. Clothes weren't her big thing and neither were purses and shoes. She carried a handbag, of course, but back home she usually just stuck her wallet inside her backpack and moved on. It was easier to carry and keep track of that way.

Nothing really stood out in her sister's personal effects but she wanted to take them home with her anyway. This was all she had left of Autumn.

She glanced up in time to see Marcy studying her.

"If you don't mind my saying so, I like the natural look on you much better than what you did before."

"I'll take all the compliments I can get." Summer realized if there was anything important, Matt would have picked it up when he came and got Autumn's stuff. He must've been worried something might link her back to him.

"Don't take it the wrong way. You were always beautiful, but you never really talked much."

"I was going through a lot while deciding if we were

going to give our marriage another shot." Summer felt defensive of her sister, which was silly. Marcy didn't mean anything by it and she didn't come across as the most sensitive person.

"There are earrings in the makeup holder that I had my eye on to buy," she admitted and then seemed to catch herself. "Before I realized you were coming back for your stuff, of course. Most people never do. Once they skip out on rent, we don't see them again. Their stuff ends up in here and we eventually sell it. My boss takes forever to get rid of this stuff."

All Summer could figure was that was Marcy's way of offering an apology.

"Which earrings did you like?" Summer knelt down beside the makeup container and then opened it, kicking up a small storm of dust.

Summer coughed.

"Sorry about the dust. No one has run a broom through here in forever." Marcy waved her hand in front of her wrinkled nose.

The makeup container had pockets like a tackle box. Summer unfolded it and in the bottom were several pairs of earrings.

"Those are beautiful." Marcy pointed to an art deco throwback. The pair she was talking about were like chandeliers. They had more sparkle than a craft store's glitter aisle.

Summer picked them up, figuring she could buy a little more good will. "They're yours if you want them."

"Are you serious right now?" Marcy was ecstatic. If a pair of cheap free earrings could do that for her, so be it.

"Definitely." Summer picked them up and held them out.

"I'm not sure I should. I mean, I want to…but… I don't know what the company policy is."

"How about this? They belong to me. I don't want them anymore since I wore them on a date with my ex-boyfriend. I don't think my husband would appreciate me bringing them into our home and I don't want the reminder of a horrible relationship. So, you'd be doing me a favor if you took them off my hands." Summer could tell she was winning Marcy over with her logic.

"Well, if I was doing you a favor…"

"You would be." Summer meant it, too. They were not her style one bit and she'd rather they bring someone else joy than end up at a garage sale. She wouldn't even begin to know what to charge for them.

Marcy took the offering and splayed them out on her flat palm. "They're so gorgeous."

"They'll look better on you than they would on me." Summer caught her slipup, but Marcy was too busy admiring her new earrings to notice.

The door opened and Summer's heart dropped. She stood up a little too fast and scared Marcy.

"Is that you, Dawson?" she asked as she heard boots shuffling across the dusty floor.

"It's me. Pickup is outside. We can gather up your things and head home." He must've noticed the panic in her voice because he was a study in calm when he got to them.

She flashed her eyes at him and he walked straight over to her and kissed her. It was another couple move and probably for show but being with him and especially when he made contact in any way made her feel like she'd found home.

"Truck is backed up as close as I could get it." Dawson realized his mistake in leaving Summer alone the minute he looked into her eyes. He wouldn't do that to her again. He'd jogged back to the front parking lot and gotten back as fast as he could.

A bad feeling caused the hair on the back of his neck to prick. He'd scoped the area without seeing any cause for alarm and yet that uneasy feeling wouldn't let up.

He was keenly aware that he had Summer at a known hangout of her sister's. The killer was powerful and had connections. He might have eyes everywhere and especially his old haunts.

Dawson was ready to get Summer out of there.

With three of them, loading the truck only took three trips. Marcy had warmed up to Summer, who she believed was Autumn. He noticed Marcy had a pair of earrings tucked into her shirt pocket. They seemed like prize possessions considering she patted her pocket after every load to make sure they didn't fall out somewhere along the way.

When they'd tucked in the last load, he thanked her for her help.

"No problem." She patted her pocket again and looked straight at Summer. "Thank you for these."

Summer smiled one of those genuine, ice-melting smiles that was unique to her at the exact time the crack of a bullet split the air.

Chapter Nineteen

Before Summer had a chance to process what she'd heard, Dawson's arm wrapped around her and he was taking her and Marcy down. He covered them with his heft and the next thing she knew she was on all fours being ushered around the side of the truck.

The sight of blood normally made her sick to her stomach. This time, it sent panic rocketing through her. In the crush of the three of them, she couldn't tell which one of them was bleeding.

Everything started happening fast after that.

"Stay down." Dawson had drawn his weapon and was on his feet in a heartbeat. He made eye contact with Summer. "You got this."

And then he seemed to see the blood, too. He clenched his back teeth and took in a sharp breath.

A bullet whizzed by over his head. In another second, he'd held up his index finger to indicate he'd be right back and then moved toward the driver's side of the truck.

Head low, weapon leading the way, he glanced over the hood of the truck, fixated on someone and then fired.

Despite originally being from Texas, Summer didn't

know much about guns. She couldn't tell what kind Dawson had except that it fired real bullets, one at a time. She scanned her own body looking for signs of a bullet wound but when she looked at Marcy, her stomach sank.

Marcy had that shocked expression that Summer had only seen in movies—a look that said she realized she'd been shot but the news hadn't quite been absorbed yet. Eyes wide, mouth open, she grabbed at her side.

There was a lot of blood. Too much.

Summer jumped into action, sitting on her back haunches and lifting Marcy's blouse on her left hip to assess the damage. The minute she saw the wound area, she knew she needed to stem the bleeding.

She dropped her shoulder, letting her purse fall onto the pavement.

"I need you to do something for me, Marcy," Summer whispered. When that didn't work, she brought her hand up to Marcy's chin and forced her gaze to meet her own. "Find my phone in my purse. I have to put pressure on your wound to stem the bleeding."

Dammit. She wasn't getting through to Marcy.

Oh, well, she didn't have time to waste. She glanced around looking for something she could use. The answer came to her. The scarf. She quickly untied it and then wadded it up into a ball.

"This might hurt but I need you to stay with me, Marcy." Summer had no idea if the woman understood a word, but she had to try to explain. This must be what shock looked like.

The minute Summer put pressure on the wound, Marcy let out a scream and tried to slap away her hand.

"I'm so sorry." Summer had to fight to keep the

scarf in place. She took a hard slap to the face. Ringing noises sounded in her ears, but she spun around to her side instead of giving up. She realized Marcy wasn't rational.

With one hand keeping pressure on the wound and the other trying to keep Marcy from digging her fingernails into Summer's shoulder, it was all she could do to contain the situation. And then, out of nowhere, Marcy seemed to snap.

"It's okay," she said.

"Yes. You're going to be okay," Summer confirmed firmly. Marcy needed to hear that Summer believed those words one hundred percent. No question about it. No hesitation.

"Sorry," Marcy said.

There was no time to worry about being polite. Summer didn't fault Marcy one bit for her panic.

"Can you grab my phone out of my purse and call 9-1-1?" Someone in the apartment complex might have already done it by now but Summer had no plans to chance it. She needed to get back up on the way for Dawson.

"Yes. Where?" Marcy glanced around and her eyes landed on the purse. "Oh. Here."

"Just reach in and feel around for it," Summer instructed.

"Got it." Marcy came up with the phone. Her skin was pale but her eyes were bright. She held out the phone. Summer put her thumb on the pad to get through the security feature because it was easier than explaining the step wasn't necessary for emergency calls. The screen came to life and Marcy called for help.

With Marcy's cooperation, Summer could risk a

glance toward Dawson. Most of his head and body would be covered by the truck and yet she still panicked that exposed sliver of him could be hit. Realistically, the shooter would have to be an excellent marksman.

He'd missed his mark, Summer. Despite the fact he'd shot Marcy, he clearly wasn't accurate. Summer would have been his target.

Dawson identified himself as a law enforcement officer as Marcy relayed what was happing to the dispatcher on the call.

"Tell them you need an ambulance," Summer urged.

Marcy complied. Now that she'd snapped out of the temporary shock, she seemed to be rational again. Good. They would need all the help they could get.

"She wants to know how bad it is," Marcy said to Summer, glancing down at her wound.

"You're going to be okay. I've stopped the bleeding for now but we're in a situation that could blow up any second. Tell them we don't have any more time."

She did.

"Do they have an ETA?" Summer asked.

Marcy nodded. "An officer is en route. He's five minutes out."

"And the ambulance?" she asked.

"Oh, right." Marcy asked the dispatcher. "Right behind him. They might get here first."

"Okay. We need to get you to a safer spot." Summer glanced around. The storage shed?

No. That wouldn't work. They could be shot while on the move. There was enough furniture inside to hide, though, and it would provide much-needed mass between them and bullets.

Whatever gun this shooter was using seemed to fire

one at a time. That was a saving grace that could turn at any second if he had accomplices on the way.

And the storage shed could also trap her and Marcy. What about inside the truck?

It seemed dangerous but offered a getaway.

"Put your hands where I can see them," Dawson commanded.

The response came in the form of a shot being fired.

And then she heard the glorious sound of sirens wailing in the distance. Backup would be there in a matter of minutes.

The sounds of tires squealing from across the parking lot sent an icy chill racing down her spine. The shooter was going to get away.

Dawson hopped into action. He was by her side in a second and pressing a small handgun into the flat of her palm.

"This is the safety and how you take it off. Use the gun if you have to. Go inside the storage shed and find a hiding spot until help arrives." His voice was a study in calm, but his words sent another chill down her back.

Dawson was going after the shooter.

He pressed a kiss to her lips and then he was gone. He climbed into the driver's seat as she helped Marcy to standing.

Summer glanced around as the truck pulled away. Relief washed over her when no one was standing on the opposite side of the parking lot like she'd half feared. The respite was a temporary feeling at best. And it was shattered when she heard another shot ring out.

Marcy flinched.

"We need to tell dispatch where we're going," she

said to Marcy, who had a death grip on the cell phone. Within a few seconds, Marcy and Summer were back inside the shed. Marcy mumbled into the phone and, best as Summer could tell, she provided a good update.

At least Marcy knew her way around the storage. Summer flipped off the light and they felt their way around, kicking up enough dust for both of them to cough.

Summer's nose and throat burned but she figured they had more pressing problems at the moment.

DAWSON GUNNED THE ENGINE. He had dispatch on the line. He'd given them a quick rundown of the situation. A uniformed officer was being sent to Summer and Marcy's location along with an ambulance.

He was currently giving chase to a late model SUV, all black with blacked-out windows. The SUV was heading toward the highway where it could get lost in all the traffic. There were temporary plates on the vehicle that, up close, looked like homemade jobs.

The SUV was already onto a road that led to the highway. Dawson cursed under his breath because it had sped up and navigated through enough traffic that he was having difficulty keeping pace. The engine must have been modified.

"I'm losing him," he said to dispatch. And then he saw something he didn't expect. The SUV made a U-turn over the median despite traffic and honking horns. Most people had the sense to get out of the way, but the vehicle was heading right toward him. "Scratch that. He did an about-face."

Dawson ducked low as the driver fired at him. The

bullet pinged the top of his truck missing the windshield but nailing the metal roof.

"Are those shots fired?" dispatch asked.

"Yes, they are." He filled her in on the SUV's new direction. "Heading southbound."

"Copy that."

The sound of a chopper roaring toward them clued Dawson in on the change in direction. The SUV weaved in and out of traffic before popping a curb and nearly wiping out a sidewalk full of people.

Folks scattered as the SUV came to an abrupt stop. From this angle, Dawson had to make a U-turn to see the driver's side but he'd bet money on the fact the guy just took off.

"I'm going on foot." He glanced up and then provided the street name before parking. He jumped out of his vehicle, caught sight of a guy full-on running, and gave chase.

Runner was fast. The man was in good shape. He also had a weapon and wasn't afraid to turn and shoot, which he did.

The bullet took a small chunk of brick out of one of the buildings they were cutting in between. It was a wild shot, far off the mark.

Weapon drawn, Dawson wouldn't risk injuring an innocent person. But he sure as hell wasn't letting Runner get away when he was this close.

This was the first mistake and real break in the case.

Staying back far enough for Runner not to be able to get off a good shot was key. Dawson could keep running for a long time without a break. He hoped Runner's stamina was weak.

Runner spun around and fired. Dawson flattened

his back against the wall. He'd gotten a little too close for comfort that time, the bullet pinging a couple feet away. He muttered a curse and froze when he realized Runner had stopped.

This time, the man slowed down enough to take aim when he fired. Except nothing happened. Nothing but a click noise came out of the gun.

Dawson made his move. He charged toward Runner and dove at him, tackling him at the knees as he tried to turn and run. Pavement bit hard. Pain shot up Dawson's elbow where he took the brunt of the fall. That was going to leave a mark, he thought wryly.

The weapon in Runner's hand went flying. It was no good to him anyway unless he wanted to use the butt of it as a hammer against Dawson's skull. The thought probably occurred to Runner as his gaze seemed to search for something to use.

And because everything that could go wrong usually did, Dawson's weapon flew out of his hand, too.

His target spun like an alligator with prey in his mouth. Runner might be middle-aged, but he was in great shape. Dawson could almost hear the crack as his head slammed into the concrete alley. A raging headache would spoil the rest of his day. He tried to shake off the ringing noise in his ears as Runner's hands wrapped around Dawson's neck.

Oh. Hell. No.

Curling up in a ball, despite Runner's best efforts to stop him, Dawson launched the heel of his boot at Runner's chest like it was on a spring. Impact knocked Runner back.

Hard contact loosened the man's grip on Dawson's throat. He sucked in a burst of air just in time to stave off the dizziness threatening. He coughed the minute air hit his lungs. His throat burned. But he couldn't focus on that right now. Runner was scrambling to his feet and reaching for Dawson's Glock.

Chapter Twenty

Summer kept pressure on the wound as she and Marcy crouched down behind a dresser. Marcy had led them to the middle of the room and to a spot where there was heavy furniture.

The door opened when they'd barely had time to squat down. Since she didn't hear sirens right outside, she feared someone had been left behind to deal with her and Marcy.

Fear tried to clasp its icy talons around her chest and squeeze her lungs. She forced herself to breathe and prayed Marcy would stay quiet.

Whoever was in the shed was stealth. There was no sound and Summer couldn't tell if the person had just opened the door to see if anyone was inside.

The light flipped on and Marcy gasped. Their location had been compromised. Summer scrambled to move them to a new location. She needed to get them out of there. Being locked in the small space with a killer wasn't going to end well.

Marcy's wound started bleeding again and Summer was certain they were going to leave a trail of blood. Could she secure Marcy somewhere, maybe in an empty cabinet? Summer could draw attention to herself and then run out the door.

It was risky. There wasn't enough time to go through all the reasons this was a very bad idea. Or, map out all the ways in which this plan could backfire.

All she knew for certain was that if they stayed together, they would most likely die. Trying to move the both of them as a unit might be certain death. Marcy was getting weaker, slower. Her panic was setting in.

Then again, emergency workers would be there in a matter of minutes. A thought struck. Had the driver left the scene to throw law enforcement off the track?

Summer was grateful for Dawson as she helped Marcy move toward the far right corner of the building. He wouldn't be easily tricked and yet he had no idea what was going down.

Inside the small space that seemed to shrink by the minute, she'd never felt more trapped. She scanned the area, looking for any kind of hiding space for Marcy. She could give her the small handgun Dawson had left with Summer.

Summer's hands were shaky as it was. Marcy might be the steadier shooter.

Another wave of panic engulfed Summer when the light flipped off. Whoever was inside the shed seemed to have gotten his bearings and decided moving in pitch-black was his best option.

More of those icy chills raced down Summer's back at the implication. It would also make identifying him that much more difficult should Summer and Marcy survive.

Another thought struck and it lit a fire deep in her

belly. This could be the bastard who'd murdered her sister. At the very least, he was involved.

More of that white-hot anger licked through her as she placed the gun in Marcy's shaking hand in case things didn't go the way Summer planned. She felt around for a cubby space that she could tuck Marcy inside.

Waiting it out for emergency personnel who might show too late was not an option. Not when this guy was inside the building. Besides, EMTs could be shot on arrival.

Summer had no idea how it all worked or who would show up. She wasn't willing to risk her or Marcy's life to find out. With a deep breath, she helped Marcy into a small space before crawling away. She made sure to swipe her hands on the floor to mess up the dirt trail just in case this guy decided to use a light. Every cell phone had a flashlight app.

This guy might find them, and he might kill them, but she didn't have to serve both of them up on a silver platter.

Winding through the tall stacks of furniture, she ran her hand along the plastic wrapping. Moving from bundle to bundle, she tried to get her bearings. It didn't take long to realize she was completely turned around. She stopped and listened for signs of him breathing.

She couldn't see her own hand if she held it out in front of her face. Hope that she could find the exit fizzled.

And then Marcy screamed and fired a shot.

Summer's bearings came real quick after that. She oriented herself and immediately beat feet, backtracking to Marcy. She could only hope Marcy's aim was on point.

Then again, she might have panicked and gotten off a wild shot.

"Sandy!" Marcy screamed.

Adrenaline spiked. It wasn't good that Marcy just let the creep know there was another person in the room. Now he would expect her to show.

It didn't matter, because she heard the sounds of a struggle and more screaming came from Marcy. Summer had no choice but to get back to the corner as fast as she could.

Glorious sirens sounded right outside the shed, close enough to know that help was so near she could almost reach out and touch it. Marcy might not have any more time. Summer might be too late. But she had to try.

So, she kept moving toward the scuffle.

The door opened. Light peeked in and she saw Scrappy three feet in front of her. He'd pinned Marcy to the ground and was running his hand along the floor, no doubt trying to find the gun.

Summer launched herself on top of him, screamed at the top of her lungs for help, and dug her fingernails into his eyes.

The light flipped on as Summer continued to scream for help.

"Everyone step outside, hands up." An authoritative female voice made the demand.

"There's a gun. He's...he killed my sister..."

This wasn't the movies. No cop would risk their own life by running in blind.

Time was the enemy.

Scrappy refocused all his attention on Summer. He

twisted around, his height and weight giving him an advantage. After a grunt, he knocked her flat on her back, but Summer kept digging her fingernails in his face anyway. She clawed at his cheeks when her hands slipped from his eyes.

Even if he killed her and got away, she'd have enough DNA underneath her fingernails for police to nail him. Justice would be served.

He drew back his fist and before he could get off a jab, she bucked and rolled. He regrouped a little too quickly as Marcy started kicking.

It gave Summer the advantage she needed to knock him off balance and roll away from him. Something hard dug into her left arm. She moved away enough to check. It was the gun. Her hands were no longer shaky when she thought about her sister's senseless murder.

Scrappy's hand gripped her shoulder and when he spun her around this time, he met the barrel of a gun. Using her thumb, she clicked off the safety.

"You better back up right now or they'll be scraping your brains off the ceiling," Summer said through clenched teeth.

His gray eyes widened in shock but he listened.

"Put your hands in the air," she demanded. That part of all cop shows rang true.

Scrappy's eyes darted from left to right, no doubt looking for an escape route.

"Don't even think about it. I'll shoot."

He seemed to debate that for a split second.

"Give me a reason," she said, not backing down an inch.

A female officer poked her head around one of the heavy chests.

"Drop your weapon," she demanded.

Summer had no plans to argue. She moved slowly so the officer would be clear on her intent, lowering the gun to the floor. "Can I move it away from him?"

"Slide it toward me," the officer said, her weapon trained on Scrappy.

Summer complied. "My friend was shot. She's bleeding pretty badly. Is there an ambulance? She needs medical attention right now."

Another officer rounded the other side of the stack of furniture. He didn't speak but his weapon was trained on Scrappy.

The door opened.

"My friend took off. He's a US marshal. Is he okay?" Summer was desperate for information about Dawson.

The first cop shook her head.

"Lace your fingers on top of your head," she said to Scrappy. He placed his hands up and shot a go-to-hell look at Summer.

Officer number two moved in and took Scrappy down. In a half second, he was face down chugging dust through his nose and out his mouth.

"I'm certain this guy was involved in my sister's murder." Summer realized that her nose was bleeding. "And he hurt my friend."

Marcy was sitting up, hands in the air.

"She needs medical attention," Summer repeated just as EMTs arrived on the scene.

The female officer patted down Summer and then Marcy. She signaled for waiting emergency workers to go ahead and treat the patient.

Within minutes, Marcy's bleeding had stemmed and

she was being carried out of the building. Summer followed outside to the waiting ambulance.

"I'll come to the hospital as soon as I can," Summer said, praying she wouldn't be visiting two people in there.

Marcy grabbed hold of Summer's hand.

"You've got this. You're going to be okay. This is just a speed bump," Summer reassured.

Marcy squeezed Summer's hand and smiled through the oxygen mask.

"Sorry, ma'am. We've gotta roll," one of the EMTs said.

"I'll see you soon," she said to Marcy, who nodded.

Summer took a step back and watched as Marcy was loaded into the ambulance, the doors closed and one of the men in uniform bolted around to the driver's side. Lights on, the ambulance took off.

She reminded herself that Marcy was in good hands then turned to the female officer to give her statement.

"Is there a way you can check on my friend the marshal?" she pleaded with the officer, who was beginning to realize Summer wasn't a threat.

The officer nodded and spoke low into her radio, and then she listened. "Ten-four. Thank you."

"What is it?" Whatever was going on didn't sound good.

"Marshal O'Connor was involved in a vehicle chase. The suspect abandoned his vehicle and Marshal O'Connor pursued him on foot. Witnesses near the scene reported shots being fired. The whereabouts of the suspect and Marshal O'Connor are unknown at this time."

Summer's legs turned to rubber and she had to take

a step back until she found the golf cart to keep herself upright. She leaned against the solid vehicle with the feeling that it was the only thing connecting her to Dawson.

"I'm sorry, ma'am." The officer was short, five feet three inches if Summer had to guess. Her long black hair was in a braid that ran halfway down her back.

Although she might be tiny, Summer had no doubt the woman could take care of herself.

"I'll need to take your statement if you want to help the marshal." The officer was sympathetic. "I'm Officer Williams."

She stuck out her hand.

"Summer Grayson." She took the offering.

Officer Williams looked Summer up and down, focusing on the bloodstain on her pale blue shirt. "Do you need medical care?"

"It's Marcy's blood, not mine. Other than a bloody nose, I'm not hurt." Summer scanned her body just to be sure. There were going to be a few bruises but nothing that a warm bath and some antibiotic ointment couldn't handle.

"Okay. Start from the beginning and tell me everything that happened." Officer Williams pulled a notepad out of her pocket along with a small pen.

Summer relayed everything that had happened since they showed up at the apartment complex. "Dawson." She flashed eyes at the officer. "Marshal O'Connor wrote down the description Marcy provided. Matt visited my sister's things and most likely took evidence if my sister had any against him."

Officer Williams nodded as she jotted down key words along with the description.

Minutes ticked by with no word on Dawson or the guy he'd abandoned his truck to chase. Summer could barely breathe.

DAWSON TIGHTENED HIMSELF into a ball and rolled back onto his shoulders. Lifting his lower back off the ground, he sprang to his feet in a martial arts kip-up maneuver. He didn't have time to thank his training when he landed on his feet and in ready position. Runner's hand was within inches of the Glock.

He plowed into Runner, closed his arms around the guy's midsection like a vise, and rolled forward, bringing Runner with him. Dawson dug his fingers into the man's ribs before tucking and rolling.

Runner practically howled in pain.

Unwilling to let up or give the man an inch, Dawson rolled them both onto their sides and wrapped powerful legs around his target in a scissor leg lock. Runner squirmed and tried to break free from Dawson's grip.

Not this time.

Runner twisted and turned, and Dawson squeezed harder, waiting him out. The saying, patience won wars, was as true in hand-to-hand combat as it was in any battle.

Adrenaline would fade and, at this pace, Runner would deplete his energy. Both were already heaving for air. Dawson made a point to slow his breathing so he could control his racing pulse.

The struggle started to ease, and Dawson tightened his grip even more. This was where his endurance training would kick in and he damn sure needed it.

Dawson managed to wrangle one arm around Runner's elbow, locking it into place. The man was lying on his other arm, rendering it useless. There was still a loaded gun in the vicinity and Dawson couldn't risk Runner getting to it first.

Reaching back, Dawson felt around for his Glock. He knew it was close behind him. He just didn't know how close.

Arching his back, he reached a little farther. Unfortunately, the move gave Runner enough room to break his elbow free. He jabbed it into Dawson's chest, knocking the air from his lungs.

Well, that just angered him even more.

Dawson bucked as his hand landed on the butt of his weapon. The cold metal felt good in his right hand. He spun around onto his back, bringing Runner with him. The move freed his right hand to bring the Glock up to Runner's temple.

"Go ahead. Make another move. Flinch the wrong way and this is all over. I'll put a bullet through your skull." The last thing Dawson wanted was to give this guy the easy way out with death.

"Don't do that." Runner grunted, his muscles stiffening. "I can explain this whole mix-up."

Mix-up? Dawson grunted.

Runner, whoever the hell he was, needed to serve his time and spend the rest of his freakin' life locked behind bars. It was the only way to bring justice to Cheryl, Autumn and their families.

Despite what Summer had said, Autumn had family. She'd had her sister and no O'Connor would've turned their back on her. She'd become part of the family, a rare club that took care of its own. Her legacy was complicated, but that didn't mean she didn't have family.

Tying this bastard to the crimes was another story

altogether. A slick guy like this would lawyer up. Running away from a crime scene wasn't exactly the same as murder.

"Roll over onto your stomach and keep your hands where I can see them at all times," Dawson instructed.

Runner did.

"Hands behind your back." Gun trained to Runner's temple, Dawson rolled onto his side and then he sat up on his knees.

He was winded, but that didn't stop him from pulling zip cuffs from his back pocket and tying up Runner's hands. He patted the man down next and felt in his pocket for a wallet or some form of ID. There were no other weapons. All Runner had on him was a money clip with close to a thousand dollars in mostly hundred-dollar bills.

It figured there'd be no ID. If Dawson had to guess there wouldn't be anything tying the SUV back to this guy, either. He was smooth. This had been well thought out. And it might've worked against a civilian.

"What's your name, sir?" Dawson knew to dot every i and cross every t when it came to this guy. There was no way he was making a mistake that could cost the case.

When Runner didn't answer, Dawson identified himself one more time as law enforcement before Mirandizing him.

Chapter Twenty-One

Backup arrived.

Dawson had never been so happy to see fellow law enforcement officers. And they came running. A pair who looked opposite in every way possible came bolting toward him and Runner.

"Marshal O'Connor, sir, I'd be honored to help you with this suspect," the first one said. He was on the short side. Dawson would guess him to be in his early twenties. What he lacked in height he made up for in brawn. He had the body of a world-class gymnast. His nameplate read Smith.

"Be my guest." Dawson moved back enough to lean the back of his head on the nearest building to try to catch his breath. Every place he'd been kicked, punched or jabbed was waking up, making its presence known, bringing all kinds of pain to the forefront. He couldn't focus on any of that right now. "I had to leave behind my…" Words failed him on exactly how to describe his relationship to Summer. He decided on, "Girlfriend and an office worker at an apartment complex. One of them was shot and I don't know how bad the injury is. Do you—"

The second officer, Jenkins, was tall with dark skin

and a mustache. He was nodding his head. "We've been following along on the radio. One of the victims was taken to the hospital by ambulance, the GSW. The other is giving her statement to a colleague, Officer Williams."

"Is there a way I can talk to her?" Dawson needed to hear Summer's voice. For reasons he couldn't explain, he needed to know she was all right. *Hells bells, O'Connor.* The reason was obvious. He loved her. He wanted to know she was all right because the thought of losing her knocked him in the chest so hard he couldn't breathe.

"I can call Officer Williams," Jenkins offered.

Dawson nodded.

"What's your name, sir?" Officer Smith asked Runner.

Apparently, the guy was invoking his right to remain silent.

"He didn't talk for me, either," Dawson said as he watched Jenkins make the call.

When the officer turned the phone over, Dawson immediately listened for Summer's voice.

"Dawson, are you there?" Her voice was like velvet.

"I'm here." He took a second to breathe as relief flooded him. Hearing her voice set things right inside him that he didn't realize had been broken. "I heard Marcy's on her way to the hospital."

"She looked pretty bad, Dawson. There was so much blood and then the skinny guy from—"

"Hold on a second. What skinny guy?" All his internal alarm bells sounded. The thought he'd left them alone and vulnerable tightened the knot in his gut. And then it dawned on him who she was talking about. The two guys who'd chased her were nicknamed Scrappy and Thick Guy. "The one from a few days ago?"

"Yes—"

"Are you hurt?" Fire raged through him at the thought.

"No. I'm okay. A couple of bumps and bruises, a bloody nose… I'm just worried about Marcy. She lost a lot of blood."

"I'll pick you up as soon as I'm cleared here. Did they say which hospital she was going to?" he asked.

"No. I forgot to ask. The EMTs got going with her really fast. She was so pale," she said, and he heard the worry in her voice.

"I can find out. I'm on my way to my vehicle right now." He pushed up to standing. "I'll see if an officer can stay with you until I get there."

"Okay." There was hesitation in her voice. This wasn't the right time to tell her how he felt about her. Not while Marcy was in a hospital fighting for her life. "Dawson…"

"Yeah?"

"I—uh…never mind. I guess I'll see you in a few minutes," she said. He needed to ask what that was all about but everything could wait until they got a status update on Marcy.

Plus, he needed to get to her. He needed to hold her in his arms. He needed to be her comfort.

And he hoped like hell she needed the same from him.

"I'll be there as fast as I can." Dawson had caught his breath and his truck was in good shape. He could jog back to his ride and get to her inside of fifteen to twenty minutes if the roads were clear.

"I'll see you soon." Summer ended the call.

Dawson turned to Officers Jenkins and Smith. "Can you guys handle this from here? I need to pick up my… *someone* and get her to the hospital to check on our friend. I'll be there for a little while if you want to swing by for my statement. Or, I can come down to the station."

Jenkins was already shaking his head.

"No, sir. You go take care of your *friend*. We got this suspect from here."

"Thank you." He'd never meant those pair of words more. He took off back toward his truck and started feeling the effects of the fight with Runner.

This guy refused to identify himself. He carried no ID. One look at him said he had plenty of money to smooth over any bumps in the road.

The fact the evidence against him was all circumstantial burned Dawson's gut. A sympathetic jury pool would acquit in a heartbeat. If the runner was powerful enough to have a detective leave her job and someone killed in county lockup, he could find a way out of this.

Dawson made it to his vehicle, thankfully right where he left it. He fished keys out of his pocket and slid into the driver's seat. He navigated back onto the road and backtracked using his GPS.

His pulse galloped the entire ride back to the apartment complex. He pulled up to the scene where a female officer stood outside her squad car, arms folded as she talked to Summer.

The second Summer locked gazes with him, she started toward him. He didn't bother parking, he just stopped in the middle of the lot. He wasn't concerned about turning off his truck, either.

All he wanted was to feel Summer in his arms where she belonged. Dawson had never felt home in another person before Summer.

And the world righted itself for just a moment when she buried her face in his chest. He looped his arms around her and she pressed her body flush with his.

This was what love was supposed to be. Not obligation. It was supposed to feel like this, like he didn't want to spend another day without her in his arms.

Even though she'd ran straight to him and held on to him like there would be no tomorrow, he had no idea if she needed a friend or if she needed him. Big difference.

Dawson would take whatever she was willing to give. But first, they had to get to the hospital and check on Marcy.

Officer Williams walked over and introduced herself. Dawson thanked her for staying with Summer.

"You're welcome, sir. It's a pleasure to meet you." Officer Williams had stars in her eyes when she looked at him. Other departments gave him a healthy amount of respect and he appreciated them for it. His division prided themselves on cooperating with other agencies and it had bought them a helluva lot of good will over the years.

"Take care," he said as he walked with Summer to the truck. She climbed in on the driver's side and scooted to the middle of the bench seat. She seemed to need physical contact as much as he did. He hoped that was a good sign.

He also had bad news to deliver but that could wait until they checked on Marcy.

THE HOSPITAL WAS a ten-minute drive that took twenty in traffic. Summer sat scooted up against Dawson, thigh to thigh. Her heart had fisted when she'd seen his face and then relief flooded her that they were both alive.

"I just realized something. We don't even know Marcy's last name," she said to Dawson.

He gripped the steering wheel as he navigated through the heavy traffic. "I can get us past the lobby with my badge. I'm guessing there aren't a whole lot of GSWs in the middle of the day at the hospital."

"GSW?" She had no clue what that meant.

"Gunshot wound." His reply was low and reverent.

"Oh." Those weren't exactly her favorite words to hear right now. Seeing the scared look on Marcy's face would haunt Summer long after this ordeal was over. She leaned into Dawson, drawing as much strength from him as she could. Her body started shaking and she imagined it was because her adrenaline finally wore off.

Exhaustion hit like a motorcycle going a hundred miles an hour and then slamming into a wall.

Dawson pulled into the ER bay and parked. He threw his shoulder into the door to open it and grunted. She realized he must've taken a few blows. His face was perfect unlike hers. Officer Williams had given Summer a few wipes while they waited for Dawson.

Summer was able to wipe off the blood, but her busted lip couldn't be cleaned so easily. That was sticking around.

He opened the door before helping her step out of the truck. As soon as her shoes hit concrete, he blew out a breath and then kissed her. His lips were gentle on hers but that didn't mean there wasn't a sizzle below the surface.

He locked gazes, holding for just a few seconds before linking their fingers together and heading inside the ER.

With his free hand, he pulled out his wallet and flashed his badge. "You had a GSW come in during the last hour via ambulance."

The nurse at the intake station was already nodding her head. "There's a waiting room through those doors, all the way down the hall and to the left. I'll update the file to let the doctor know you're waiting."

"Thank you," was all Dawson said before heading down the hall.

The waiting room was small. There were only about a dozen chairs. Everything was blue. The chairs, the carpet, the curtains. The wallpaper had hints of blue. None of which mattered because all she cared about was Marcy being well cared for.

There was coffee. She and Dawson seemed to notice it at the same time because they both made a move in that direction.

He poured two cups and handed one over. She took a few sips, welcoming the burn on her throat.

"Do you want to sit or stand?" he asked.

"I'm not sure my legs can hold me up much longer." She wasn't kidding. The past few days had caught up to her and she could barely stand. She also glanced down at her shirt and realized she must be a sight.

A nurse stepped inside the room and identified herself as Ramona. She was late thirties, with kind eyes and a round face.

"I brought you something to change into if you'd

like," she said to Summer, holding out a shirt that looked like scrubs.

"Thank you." Summer took the offering and hit the bathroom. She washed off more of the blood and splashed cold water on her face.

"She's in surgery but the outlook is good," Dawson said as soon as Summer returned. Ramona had already left.

"That's great news." Summer reclaimed her seat and took another sip of coffee, anything to wake her up.

He nodded. Then said, "There's not so good news about the case."

Dawson's serious expression sent a wave of panic rippling through her.

"What is it?" Bad news only got worse with age.

He explained the situation with the guy he called Runner, and her heart literally sank.

"Marcy can ID him. He came to the apartment complex to go through my sister's personal belongings," she said.

"Won't make a difference. It's all circumstantial evidence. We don't have anything directly linking this guy to the murders. Our Runner did try to kill a US marshal and that should be enough to jail him for a long time. And Scrappy tried to kill Marcy and Summer. The police officers in the shed are witnesses, as well." There was so much frustration in his voice. "With a good lawyer, he could get out of jail in a few hours."

"Even though he shot at a US marshal?"

"Trust me, an expensive lawyer could create doubt." Dawson issued a sharp sigh. "That's how the legal system works."

"Well, that's messed up."

"At times, it is. Most of the time, though, it works. That's why I still do this job," he explained.

"We need proof that he's tied to my sister or Cheryl." She sat up straighter and took another sip of coffee. It was strong and black.

"I'd hoped we would find something in your sister's personal effects."

"But he got there first." Of course, he had. The bastard.

Chapter Twenty-Two

Summer felt around in her handbag, needing to feel the necklace in her fingers and some connection to Autumn. A thought came to her. "My sister would've known him well enough to realize he'd go through her stuff at the apartment complex."

She pulled out the necklace and stared at it for a long moment.

Dawson's cell buzzed. He fished it out of his pocket and stood up. "This is Dawson O'Connor."

He paused for a long moment before saying a few uh-huhs into the phone. He thanked the caller and then ended the call. "The runner's name is Mateus Hank."

"Sounds a lot like Matt Shank." The wheels started spinning in Summer's head. "She left clues, Dawson. She wanted us to figure this out."

The cold metal warmed in her hand and she traced the letters with her index finger. Holding the necklace in her hand gave her an idea.

"What if she wasn't protecting me? What if my sister tucked this inside the box as a clue?" There was no need for coffee now with the way her mind clicked through theories.

"It's possible." He nodded. "But where does the clue lead?"

"I don't know yet. My first thought is the place where we bought these. The fairgrounds." She flattened out her palm and looked at the dull piece of metal. "I can't let that bastard walk away scot-free."

"Agreed."

The door to the waiting room opened and a man in scrubs walked inside. He was average height with a runner's build and a full head of gray hair. "Good afternoon, my name is Dr. Warner."

Dawson stood and Summer followed suit. Each shook the doctor's hand.

"Your witness is doing well. She's out of surgery now and did great." He went through the procedure using medical jargon that Summer couldn't understand if she'd tried. But she got the gist of what he was saying.

"We gave her a transfusion because she lost a lot of blood. All in all, we're expecting a full recovery. She'll be resting for a little while. We're keeping a close eye on her. No visitors for the next few hours until she gets out of ICU." He put a hand up to reassure them. "Out of an abundance of caution."

Dawson thanked the doctor. He reassured them, once again, that Marcy was expected to make a full recovery.

"I wish she had family here waiting for her," Summer said after he left.

"Her parents are being notified. I'm sure they'll be here soon." He walked over to where they'd been seated and drained his coffee cup. "We have a couple of hours. Are you ready to hit the fairgrounds?"

"I'm ready to find evidence that will nail that bastard to the wall."

"That's my girl." Dawson seemed to catch himself on those last words. Her heart performed a little flip at the term of endearment.

She walked over to him and pressed up on her tiptoes. He met her halfway and their lips touched so gently it robbed her breath.

This time, she linked their fingers.

WALKING ONTO THE empty fairgrounds brought on a rush of memories. The smell of funnel cake. Livestock. The bright lights and all those carnival rides.

Autumn's favorite had been the Tilt-A-Whirl. Nothing said the fair like strapping themselves into a ride that spun so fast and hard they almost tossed up their candy apples.

Cotton candy. Autumn couldn't get enough of it. She was terrible at games but never passed one she didn't think she could win anyway. Her seven-year losing streak was always on the verge of being over, according to Autumn.

The fair was the one place they'd gone every year without fail. They laughed and played. They would feed llamas and pet baby pigs. For that one day, they weren't poor or hungry.

Tears welled at the memories.

Walking hand in hand, she led him to where she remembered the necklace booth to have been. There wasn't much there now but a patch of grass. She looked around for a hiding place.

There was a light pole with a metal plate screwed onto the base. "Maybe in there, Dawson."

He'd brought a pair of gloves and a paper bag that he'd explained was used for collecting evidence. He'd grabbed a few other items that he explained were useful. Things like tongs.

Dawson moved over to the light pole and took a knee. He examined the plate. "There's a screw missing."

Her heart leaped in her throat at the possibility of this hunch panning out.

"It's loose." He jiggled the plate.

Chill bumps ran the length of her arms. Experience had taught her not to get too excited before she had something concrete but this was promising.

Somewhere deep in her gut, she knew that if her twin hid something anywhere that it would be here. She prayed someone else hadn't gotten to the evidence first.

Dawson snapped a few pictures of the plate from different angles. He pulled a screwdriver from his pack and went to work loosening the screws. He set the plate down carefully and shone a light inside the six-by-four-inch opening.

A small smile crept across his lips. Summer knew. There was something inside.

Using the tongs, he pulled out a freezer bag through the opening. He set it down and then checked for more. A second freezer bag came and then a third.

One of the bags contained what looked like a journal. It was labeled My Story.

The second bag was labeled Cheryl. It contained some type of bloody clothing along with pictures that had been taken of her after she'd been strangled.

In the final bag, there were pictures with labels on the backs.

Dawson flipped over the bag with the journal in it. There was a folded-up sheet of paper tucked in the back with Summer's name on it. He opened the bag carefully and, using the tongs, pulled out the note.

He set it down on the grass and smoothed it out for her to read.

Summer,
this is bad. I've gotten myself involved with a bad person and I don't know how to get out without him hurting the people I love. He's powerful and rich. And I just found evidence that he killed his last girlfriend, Cheryl. I put it in the bag with her name on it. I think he knows I've figured him out. He's been threatening to dig into my past and find all the dirt if the cops show. He's been to parties at the governor's house. He took me as his date. He can cover up anything he wants. His name is Mateus Hank and he's the CEO of some bank. Anyway, I think he has politicians in his pocket.

I can't risk him finding you. So, I have to figure something else out. I wish I could tell you about all this. But, knowing you, you'd just come here and get yourself in the same hot water I'm in.

I tried to get out with Dawson O'Connor. I thought he could keep me safe and I cared about him. No one can hide from Mateus for long. He knows too many people and I saw one of his friends at the O'Connor ranch. I knew then I had to get away from there or risk him getting hurt.

I have a lot of regrets, sis. I thought I could come back to Austin and handle Mateus. He says he loves me but it's not the good kind. Anyway, I have to go. Love you more than words.

Tears streamed down Summer's face as she read the note from her sister.

"Now we know. She said it herself. She collected evidence against him and probably threatened him. He knew she had something but he didn't know where," Summer surmised.

"He kills her and then you show up. He knows you are trouble for him so he hires thugs to take care of you," Dawson said. He glanced at the plastic bags. "These are proof. This is all we need to link him to the murders."

Summer took the necklace out of her purse and held on to it. Her sister had been protecting her all along.

AN HOUR HAD passed by the time the last officer had left the fairground. Summer looked up at Dawson as he walked over to her and pulled her into an embrace.

"Where do we go from here?" She realized this was the end of the road for them. There would be justice for Autumn and Cheryl. Her sister was gone. There was no reason to stick around Texas, except that she'd never felt more at home than since she'd been back.

"Look into corruption at Austin P.D. for one," he said. "Make sure the evidence is handled properly and justice is served."

"Agreed."

"I don't make rash decisions." Dawson looked into

her eyes and her heart fluttered like a dozen butterflies were trapped inside her chest.

"Good. Neither do I."

"So, I've given this a lot of thought. Over the past few days, we've had a crash course in getting to know each other. I feel like we skipped over all the formalities and dove straight in with both feet. I got to know the *real* you."

She nodded. About the only thing she was certain of was that she didn't want to walk away.

"I have to caution you right there, Dawson. This is my heart we're talking about and I don't normally *do* trust. But the thought of things ending right here—"

"Who said anything about ending what we have?"

"Weren't you about to?" Her heart really worked overtime now.

"No. I was about to ask you to stay. I haven't done a great job of expressing it but I'm in love with you, Summer Grayson. I've never been in love with anyone before you and I promise to love you for the rest of my life if you'll have me." He got down on one knee. "So, I'm asking you to stay. I'm asking you to consider making what we have permanent and official because I don't want to spend another day without you in my life."

Happy tears rolled down her cheeks now.

"I love you, Dawson O'Connor. You're my family and the only home I've ever known. Of course, I'll stay. And I'll spend every day of the rest of my life loving you."

Summer pressed a kiss to Dawson's lips, tender but with the promise of passion. He pulled back enough to smile at her and her heart took another hit. She could look into those eyes forever.

"My beautiful Summer," he said against her mouth. "Let's check on Marcy and then go home."

Summer couldn't think of a better plan. She'd found home. And she was ready to get started on forever.

* * * * *

TEXAS LAW

Chapter One

Sheriff Colton O'Connor took a sip of coffee and gripped the steering wheel of his SUV. Thunder boomed and rain came down in sheets. Seeing much past the front bumper was basically impossible. He'd had three stranded vehicle calls already—one of those cars had been actually submerged—and the worst of this spring thunderstorm hadn't happened yet. The storm wreaking havoc on the small town of Katy Gulch, Texas, was just getting started.

On top of everything, Colton's babysitter had quit last night. Miss Marla's niece had been in a car crash in Austin and needed her aunt to care for her during her recovery. The spry sixty-five-year-old was the only living relative of the girl, who was a student at the University of Texas at Austin.

Colton pinched the bridge of his nose to stem the thundering headache working up behind his eyelids. His mother was pinch-hitting with his twin boys, Silas and Sebastian, but she was still reeling from the loss of her husband, as was Colton and the rest of the family.

A recent kidnapping attempt had dredged up the unsolved, decades-old mystery of his sister's abduction, and his father was murdered after deciding to take it upon himself to take up the investigation on his own again. Colton was just getting started untangling his father's murder.

Considering all that was going on at the ranch, Colton didn't want to add to his mother's stress. As much as his one-year-olds were angels, taking care of little ones with more energy than brain development was a lot for anyone to handle. His mother had enough on her plate already, but she'd convinced him the distraction would be good for her.

And now a storm threatened to turn the town upside down with tornadoes and flash floods.

So, no, Colton didn't feel right about leaving his mother to care for his children, although Margaret O'Connor was strong, one of the toughest women he'd ever met.

He took another sip of coffee and nearly spit it out. It was cold. Bitter. The convenience-store kind that he was certain had been made hours ago and left to burn. That tacky, unpleasant taste stuck to the roof of his mouth.

This might be a good time to stop by the ranch to check on his mother and the twins. He could get a decent cup of coffee there and he wanted to check on his boys. His stomach growled. A reminder that he'd been working emergencies most of the night and had skipped dinner. He always brought food with him on nights like these, but he could save it for later. It was getting late.

Colton banked a U-turn at the corner of Misty Creek and Apple Blossom Drive, and then headed toward the ranch. He hadn't made it a block when he got the next call. The distinct voice belonging to his secretary, Gert Francis, came through the radio.

"What do you have for me?" He pulled his vehicle onto the side of the road. At least there were no cars on the streets. He hoped folks listened to the emergency alerts and stayed put.

"A call just came in from Mrs. Dillon. Flood waters are rising near the river. She's evacuating. Her concern is about a vagrant who has been sleeping in her old RV. She doesn't want the person to be caught unaware if the water keeps rising, and she's scared to disturb whoever it is on her own." Mrs. Dillon, widowed last year at the age of seventy-eight, had a son in Little Rock who'd been trying to convince her to move closer to him. She had refused. Katy Gulch was home.

Colton always made a point of stopping by her place on his way home to check on one of his favorite residents. It was the happiest part of his job, the fact that he kept all the residents in his town and county safe. He took great pride in his work and had a special place in his heart for the senior residents in his community.

He was a rancher by birth and a sheriff by choice. Both jobs had ingrained in him a commitment to help others, along with a healthy respect for Mother Nature.

Colton heaved a sigh. Thinking about ranching brought him back to his family's situation. With his father, the patriarch of Katy Bull Ranch, now gone, Colton and his brothers had some hard decisions to make about keeping their legacy running.

"Let Mrs. Dillon know I'm on my way." Actually, there was no reason he couldn't call her himself. "Never mind, Gert. I've got her number right here. I've been meaning to ask her how she's been getting around after foot surgery last week."

"Will do, Sheriff." There was so much pride in her

voice. She'd always been vocal about how much she appreciated the fact he looked after the town's residents. The last sheriff hadn't been so diligent. Gert had made her opinion known about him, as well.

"After I make this call, I need to check out for a little while to stop by the ranch and see about things there," he informed her.

"Sounds like a plan, sir." More of that admiration came through the line.

Colton hoped he could live up to it.

"Be safe out there," Gert warned.

"You know I will. I better ring her now." Colton ended the call. Using Bluetooth technology, he called Mrs. Dillon. She picked up on the first ring.

"I hear you have a new tenant in the RV. I'm on my way over." Colton didn't need to identify himself. He was pretty certain Mrs. Dillon had his cell number on speed dial. He didn't mind. If a quick call to him or Gert could give her peace of mind, inconvenience was a small price to pay.

"Thank you for checking it out for me. This one showed up three nights ago, I think." Concern came through in Mrs. Dillon's voice. "I know it's a woman because MaryBeth's dog kept barking and I heard her tell him to shush."

"Well, if she stays any longer you'll have to start charging rent," he teased, trying to lighten the mood.

The older woman's heart was as big as the great state they lived in.

"If I started doing that, I'd end up a rich lady. Then all the young bachelors would come to town to court me. We can't have that, can we?" Her smile came through in her voice.

"No, ma'am. We sure can't."

"I hope she's okay." She said on a sigh. "Not a peep from her. I wouldn't have heard her at all if it hadn't been for MaryBeth's dog." Mrs. Dillon clucked her tongue in disapproval. Normally, her neighbor's dog was a thorn in her side. This time, Cooper seemed to have served a purpose.

"Sounds like we have a quiet one on our hands. I'll perform a wellness check and make sure she gets out before the water rises."

"I always complained to my husband that he put the parking pad to the RV way too close to the water's edge. But do you think he listened?" Her tone was half-teasing, half-wistful. Mr. and Mrs. Dillon had been high school sweethearts and had, much like Colton's parents, beaten the odds of divorce and gone the distance. The Dillons had been schoolteachers who'd spent their summers touring the country in their RV. Anyone who knew them could see how much they loved each other. They were almost obnoxiously adorable, much like his own parents had been.

Losing Mr. Dillon had to have been the hardest thing she'd gone through. Colton's heart went out to her.

"I just didn't want her to be caught off guard. If this storm is as bad as they say it's going to be, the RV will be flooded again." She heaved a concerned-sounding sigh. "I probably should've gotten rid of that thing ten years ago after the first time it flooded. But Mr. Dillon loved his camping so he could throw out a line first thing with his morning coffee." Her voice was nothing but melancholy now at the memory.

"He was one of the best fishermen in the county." Colton swerved to miss a puddle on the road that was

forming a small lake. Flash flooding was a real problem in the spring. This storm was just beginning to
dish out its wrath. Mother Nature had a temper and it
was becoming apparent she was gearing to show
them just how angry she could become.

"That he was," she agreed.

"Who is driving you to Little Rock?" He changed
the subject, hoping to redirect her from a conversation
that would bring back the pain of losing her husband.
After seeing the look on his mother's face at hearing
the news her husband was dead, Colton didn't want to
cause that kind of hurt for anyone, certainly not for
someone as kind as Mrs. Dillon. His second grade
teacher deserved more brightness in her day, and especially after putting up with him and his brothers
when they were young. They'd been good kids by most
standards. And yet they'd also been a handful. After
having twins, Colton was more aware of the responsibility and sacrifice that came with the parenting job.

"Netty. You know her from my knitting club. She's
heading that way to stay with her daughter, so I'm
hitching a ride with her." He could almost see the twinkle in Mrs. Dillon's eye when she said the word *hitched*.

"Tell Netty to drive safe." He could barely see in
the driving rain and needed to close the call in order
to concentrate on the road ahead.

"I will do it, Sheriff. Thank you for checking on my
tenant." He could envision her making air quotes when
she said the last word.

"You're welcome. In fact, I'll head to your house
now." After exchanging goodbyes, he ended the call.

The rain was so thick he could barely see the end
of his vehicle now, let alone the road. The weather had

definitely turned in the last couple of minutes since he'd started the conversation.

It was a miracle he could see at all. His headlights were almost useless. If he didn't know the area so well, he'd pull over and wait it out. These kinds of storms usually came in waves. Radar didn't look promising on this one.

As he turned right onto Mrs. Dillon's street, a flash of lightning streaked across the sky, and a dark object cut in front of him so suddenly he couldn't stop himself from tapping it with his service vehicle.

A *thunk* sounded and then a squeal. The noise was quickly drowned out by the driving rain.

Colton cursed his luck, wondering if he'd been struck by debris. He hopped out of his vehicle to check. Rain pelted his face. He pulled up his collar and shivered against the cold front, praying whatever he'd hit wasn't an animal. Deer sometimes cut through town. At least he was on his way to the ranch. He could scoop it up, put it in the back and see what he could do about nursing it back to health.

Pulling his flashlight from his belt, he shined it around the area. It was next to impossible to see. Hell, he could barely see his hand in front of his face for the rain.

Squinting, he caught sight of something moving a few feet from his passenger-side bumper. Hell's bells. He hadn't nicked an animal at all…it was a person.

Colton dashed to the victim. He took a knee beside the woman, who was curled in a tight ball. Her dark clothing covered her from nearly head to toe. She was drenched and lying in a puddle.

"My name is Colton O'Connor. I'm the sheriff and

I'm here to help." He knew better than to touch her in case she was injured.

"I'm okay. You can go." He didn't recognize the voice, but then it was next to impossible to hear over the sounds of the rain. She kept her face turned in the opposite direction, away from him.

Considering she seemed anxious to not show her face to him, he wondered if she had something to hide.

"I'm not going anywhere until I know you're okay. And that means being able to stand up and walk away from here on your own," he said, figuring she might as well know where he stood.

"I already said that I'm okay. Go away," the woman shouted, and he heard her loud and clear this time. Her voice was somewhat familiar and yet he couldn't place it.

He dashed toward his vehicle and retrieved an umbrella. It wouldn't do much good against the torrent. Water was building up on the sidewalk and gushing over faster than the gutter could handle it. But it was something and might help with some of the onslaught.

And he believed that right up until he opened the umbrella and it nearly shot out of his hands. A gust of wind forced him to fight to hold on to it and keep it steady over the victim. Finally, it was doing a good job offering some shelter from the rain.

"Like I said, I need to see that you can walk away from here on your own and answer a few questions. I'm the one who hit you and there's no way I'm leaving. What's your name?" He bent down lower so she could hear without him shouting at her.

She didn't answer and that sent up more warning flares. Anyone could see she was injured. She'd taken a pretty hard hit. She might be in shock or maybe suffering head trauma. From his position, it was impossible to see if she was bleeding, and because of the way she'd fallen, he couldn't rule out a broken arm or leg.

Colton stood up and walked around to where she was facing. He dropped down on his knees to get a better look. Rain was everywhere—his eyes, his ears, his face. He shook his head, trying to shake off the flood.

"I'm calling an ambulance. I'm going to get some help." He strained to see her face, still unable to reach back to his memory and find a name that matched the voice. In a small town like Katy Gulch, Colton knew most everyone, which meant she was someone who'd passed through town.

She lifted her arm to wave him away.

"No can do. Sorry." He tilted his mouth toward the radio clipped to his shoulder. With his free hand, he pressed the talk button. "Gert, can you read me?"

There was a moment of crackling. He feared he might not be able to hear her response. And yet going to his SUV wasn't an option. He didn't want to leave the woman alone in the street in the soaking rain again. She looked like she needed a hand-up and he had no plans to leave her.

With the wind, his umbrella was doing very little, but it was something.

The woman, who had been curled up on her side, shielding her face, pushed up to sit. "See, I'm okay. I'm not hurt. I just need a minute to catch my breath and I'll be fine."

Colton wasn't convinced she was able to think clearly. Often after experiencing trauma, it took a while for the brain to catch up. That was how shock worked. She might not even realize it.

"What's your name?" he asked again, trying to assess her mental state.

She shook her head, which either meant she didn't want to disclose it or she couldn't remember. Neither was a good sign.

Since she hadn't answered his question, there was no choice but to have her cleared medically before he could let her go, even if she could walk away on her own, which he highly doubted at the moment.

"I'm just going to get somebody here to take a look at you, and if everything's okay, you'll be cleared in no time. In the meantime, you can wait inside my vehicle and get out of this weather." He'd noticed that she'd started shivering.

He slipped out of his rain jacket and placed it over her shoulders.

The woman looked up at him and their gazes locked. His heart stirred and his breath caught.

"Makena?"

WATER WAS EVERYWHERE, flooding Makena Eden's eyes and ears. Rain hit her face, stinging like fire-ant bites. She blinked up and stared into the eyes of the last man she'd expected to see again—Colton O'Connor.

Still reeling from taking a wrong turn into the road and being clipped by his sport utility, she felt around on her hip.

Ouch. That hurt. She could already feel her side bruising. Mentally, she tried to dust herself off and stand up. Her hip, however, had other plans, so she sat there, trying to ride out the pain.

"I just need a minute." There was no other option but to get up and fake being well. She had no job, no medical insurance and no money. And she couldn't afford to let her identity get out, especially not on a peace officer's radio. Then there was the other shock, the fact that Colton was kneeling down in front of her. How long had it been?

"Not so fast." Colton's eyebrow shot up and he seemed unconvinced. He was one of the most devastatingly handsome men she'd ever met, and her body picked that moment to react to him *and* remind her. This was turning out to be one red-letter day stacked on the back end of months of agony. One she'd survived by hiding and sliding under the radar.

"I don't want you to try to move. We need to get you checked out first." He snapped into action, tilting his chin toward his left shoulder to speak into his radio. She could hear him requesting an ambulance. For a split second, she wondered if she could run away and get far enough out of sight for him to forget this whole situation. *Wishful thinking.* It was so not good that he knew her personally. Granted, he knew her before she'd become Mrs. River Myers, but still...

Panic squeezed her lungs as she tried to breathe through the building anxiety. She couldn't let her name go down on record. She couldn't have anything that would identify her over the radio.

"I promise that I'm not broken. I'm shaken up." Before she could say anything else, he put a hand up to stop her.

Water was dripping everywhere, and yet looking into those cobalt blue eyes sent her flashing back to her sophomore year of college. The two of them had been randomly hooked up as partners in biology lab. Even at nineteen years old, it was easy to see Colton was going to be strong and muscled when he finally filled out.

Now, just seeing him released a dozen butterflies in her chest along with a free-falling sensation she hadn't felt since college. She could stare into his eyes for days. He had a face of hard angles and planes. Full lips covered perfectly straight, white teeth.

Looking at him was like staring at one of those billboard models. The man was tall. Six feet four inches of solid steel and ripped muscle. The only reason she noticed was the survival need at its most basic, she told herself. She was in trouble and had to assess whether or not Colton could defend her.

Icy fingers gripped her spine as she thought about the past, about *her* past. About *River*. Stand still long enough and it would catch up to her. He *would* find her.

Colton might look good. Better than good, but she wouldn't let her mind go there for long. There were two things that would keep her from the attraction she felt, other than the obvious fact they'd had one class and a flirtation that hadn't gone anywhere. A badge and a gun.

Chapter Two

Makena needed to convince Colton that she wasn't injured so she could get far away from him and Katy Gulch. Coming here had turned out to be a huge mistake—one that could get her killed.

How had she not remembered this was his hometown?

Being on the road for months on end had a way of mixing up weeks. Towns were starting to run together, too. They fell into one of two categories, big and small.

Dallas, Houston and Austin fit into the big-city category. They all had basically the same chain restaurants if a slightly differing view on life. Small towns, on the other hand, seemed to share a few characteristics. In those, she was beginning to realize, it was a little harder to go unnoticed.

Getting seen was bad for her longevity.

The other thing she'd noticed about small towns in her home state of Texas was the food. Some of the best cooking came from diners and mom-and-pop shops. Since she'd run out of money, she'd been forced to live on other people's generosity.

Makena hadn't eaten a real meal in the past three days. She'd sustained herself on scraps. The owner

of the RV where she'd been staying had been kind
enough to leave a few supplies and leftovers a couple
of days ago, and Makena had stretched them out to
make them last. Hunger had caught up to her, forcing
her to seek out food.

The fact that the owner knew Makena was staying
on her property *and* Makena had remained there anyway signaled just how much she'd been slipping lately.
Starvation had a way of breeding desperation. Not to
mention it had been so very long since she'd slept on a
real bed in a real room or in a real house that she could
scarcely remember how it felt. The RV was the closest
she'd come and she hadn't wanted to give it up.

Makena was drenched. She shivered despite having the sheriff's windbreaker wrapped around her. She
could sit there and be stubborn and cold. Or, she could
get Colton's help inside the SUV and wring herself out.
And at least maybe have him turn the heat on.

"If you help me up, I can make it to your vehicle,"
she said to him.

Colton's eyebrow shot up. "You sure it's a good idea
to move? I didn't realize how badly you were hurt when
I offered before."

"I'm so cold my teeth are chattering. You look pretty
miserable. There's no reason for me to sit here in a
puddle when I can be warm inside your vehicle." She
had to practically shout to be heard. She put her hands
up in the surrender position, palms up. "All I need is a
hand up and maybe a little help walking."

He opened his mouth to protest.

"Sitting out here, I may end up with the death of
cold." She realized she was going to have to give him
a little bit than that. "I'm pretty sure that I have

a nasty bruise working up on my left hip. It was stupid of me to run into the street. I didn't even see you."

"You must've darted out from in between the parked vehicles right when I turned." There was so much torment in his voice now.

"Sorry. I was just trying to stay out of the rain but I'm okay. Really." It wasn't a total lie. Mostly, a half-truth. Being dishonest pained Makena. She hated that she'd become the kind of person who had to cover her tracks like a criminal.

"What are you doing out on a night like this?" he asked.

"I-um…was trying to get back to my rental over by the river." The way she stammered was giving her away based on the look on his face.

He nodded as he studied her, but she could see that he wasn't convinced.

"My name is Makena. You already know that. It's Wednesday. At least, I think it is."

"Do you know where you are right now?" The worry lines on his forehead were easing up.

"Katy Gulch, Texas," she said. "And I've been out of work for a little while. That's the reason I've lost track of the days of the week."

It was her turn to look carefully at him.

"What do you think?" she asked. "Did I pass?"

Colton surveyed her for a long moment. Lightning raced sideways across the sky and thunder boomed.

"Lean on me and let me do the heavy lifting." He put his arm out.

"Deal." She grabbed hold of his arm, ignoring the electrical impulses vibrating up her arm from contact. This wasn't the time for an inappropriate attraction and especially not with a man who had a gun and a badge on his hip. She'd been there. Done that. And had the emotional scars to prove it.

Not taking Colton's help was out of the question. She had no car. No money. No choices.

Makena held onto his arm for dear life. As soon as she was pulled up to her feet, her left leg gave out under the pain from her hip.

"Whoa there." Colton's strong arms wrapped around her, and the next thing she knew he'd picked her up. He carried her over to his SUV and managed to open the passenger door and help her inside.

She eased onto the seat and immediately felt around for the adjuster lever. Her fingers landed on the control and she adjusted her seat back, easing some of the pressure from her sitting bones. Her hip rewarded her by lightening up on some of the pain.

Colton opened the back hatch, closed it and was in the driver's seat a few seconds later.

He then leaned over and tucked a warm blanket around her. "Is that better?"

"Much." She said the word on a sigh, releasing the breath she'd been holding.

"Be honest. How badly does it hurt?" he asked, looking at her with those cobalt blues.

"On a scale of one to ten? I'd say this has to be a solid sixteen."

The engine was still humming and at least she'd stopped shivering. She could also finally hear him over the roar of the weather, even though it seemed the rain was driving down even harder than a few minutes ago.

"I couldn't hear a word Gert said earlier." He flashed his eyes at her. "Gert is my secretary in case you hadn't sorted it out for yourself. And she's a lot more than that. She's more like my right arm. I'm the sheriff."

She glanced down at the word *SHERIFF* written in bold yellow letters running down her left sleeve. Even if he hadn't told her earlier, she would've figured it out. With a small smile, she said, "I put that together for myself."

"Is your car around here somewhere? I can call a tow."

"No." Talking about herself wasn't good. The less information she gave, the better. She hoped he would just drop the subject, let her warm up and then let her get back to her temporary shelter in the RV.

Her stomach growled, and surprisingly, it could be heard over the thunder boom outside.

"There's someone I need to check on. Are you hungry?" Colton asked.

"Yes. I didn't get a chance to eat dinner yet." She followed his gaze to the clock on the dashboard. It read 8:30 p.m.

With his left hand, he tucked his chin to his left shoulder and hit some type of button. "Gert, can you read me?"

Crackling noises came through the radio. And then a voice.

"Copy that, Sheriff. Loud and clear." The woman sounded older, mid-sixties if Makena had to guess.

"I need an ambulance on the corner of Misty Creek and Apple Blossom. Stat. A pedestrian was struck by my vehicle and needs immediate medical attention. She is alert and communicative, with a possible injury to her left hip. She's lucid, but a concussion can't be ruled out," he said.

"Roger that, Sheriff. You must not have heard me earlier. There's flooding on several roads. Both of my EMTs are on calls and even if they weren't, the streets aren't clear. No one can get to you for at least the next hour."

Relief washed over Makena. However, Colton didn't look thrilled.

"Roger that." He blew out a frustrated-sounding breath. "I'll drive the victim to the hospital myself."

"County road isn't clear. There's been a lot of flooding. I don't advise making that trip unless it's life-threatening," Gert said.

Flash floods in Texas were nothing to take lightly. They were the leading cause of weather-related deaths in the state.

"We probably need to close the road since the water's rising," she continued.

Colton smacked his flat palm against the steering wheel. "Roger that."

"As soon as I warm up, you can drop me off. I think my hip just needs a little chance to rest." Embarrassingly enough, her stomach picked that moment to gurgle and growl again.

Colton's gaze dropped to her stomach as he reached under the center console of his SUV and pulled something around. A lunchbox?

He unzipped the black box and produced what looked like a sandwich. He opened the Ziploc bag and held it out toward her. "I knew I'd be working late tonight with the storms. So I made extra. You're welcome to this one."

When she didn't immediately reach for the offering, he locked gazes with her. "Go ahead. Take it. I have more."

"I really can't take all your food." Her mouth was practically watering.

"It's no big deal. I can always swing by my house and get more. It's on the way to my office, not far from here."

"Are you sure about that, Colton?" The last thing she wanted to do was take his food and leave him with nothing. The sandwich looked good, though. And she was pretty certain she'd started drooling.

"It's fine," he reassured her with that silky masculine voice that trailed all over her, warming her better than any blanket could.

He urged her to take it, so she did.

"Thank you." She wasted no time demolishing the sandwich. Ham. Delicious.

He barely looked away from the screen on the laptop mounted inside his vehicle as he handed her an apple next.

This time, she didn't argue. Instead, she polished off the fruit in a matter of seconds while he studied the map on the screen. Just as she wrapped the remains of the apple in the paper towel he'd given her, he pulled out a thermos and handed her a spoon.

"Soup," was all he said.

Angel was all she thought.

COLTON ENTERED THE hospital's location into his computer. The screen showed red triangles with exclamation points in the center of them on more roads than not, indicating flooding or hazardous road conditions. Gert was a lifeline, going well above and beyond typical secretary duties. She'd become Colton's right arm and he had no idea what he'd do without her.

Makena needed medical attention. That part was obvious. The tricky part was going to be getting her looked at. He was still trying to wrap his mind around the fact Makena Eden was sitting in his SUV.

Talk about a blast from the past and a missed opportunity. But he couldn't think about that right now when she was injured. At least she was eating. That had to be a good sign.

When she'd tried to stand, she'd gone down pretty fast and hard. She'd winced in pain and he'd scooped her up and brought her to his vehicle. He knew better than to move an injured person. In this case, however, there was no choice.

The victim was alert and cognizant of what was going on. A quick visual scan of her body revealed nothing obviously broken. No bones were sticking out. She complained about her hip and he figured there could be something there. At the very least, she needed an X-ray.

Since getting to the county hospital looked impossible at least in the short run and his apartment was close by, he decided taking her there might be for the best until the roads cleared. He could get her out of his uncomfortable vehicle and onto a soft couch.

Normally, he wouldn't take a stranger to his home, but this was Makena. And even though he hadn't seen her in forever, she'd been special to him at one time.

He still needed to check on the RV for Mrs. Dillon... and then it dawned on him. Was Makena the 'tenant' the widow had been talking about earlier?

"Are you staying in town?" he asked, hoping to get

her to volunteer the information. It was possible that she'd fallen on hard times and needed a place to hang her head for a couple of nights.

"I've been staying in a friend's RV," she said. So, she was the 'tenant' Mrs. Dillon mentioned.

It was good seeing Makena again. At five feet five inches, she had a body made for sinning, underneath a thick head of black hair. He remembered how shiny and wavy her hair used to be. Even soaked with water, it didn't look much different now.

She had the most honest set of pale blue eyes—eyes the color of the sky on an early summer morning. She had the kind of eyes that he could stare into all day. It had been like that before, too.

But that was a long time ago. And despite the lightning bolt that had struck him square in the chest when she turned to face him, this relationship was purely professional.

Colton wasn't in the market to replace his wife, Rebecca, anytime soon. He was still reeling from the loss almost year later. He bit back a remark on the irony of running into someone he'd had a crush on in college but not enough confidence to ask out. He'd been with Makena for all of fifteen or twenty minutes now and the surge of attraction he'd felt before had returned with full force, much like the out-of-control thunderstorm bearing down on them.

He refocused. His medical experience amounted to knowing how to perform CPR and that was about it.

Even soaked to the bone, Makena was still stunning—just as stunning as he remembered from twelve years ago in biology lab.

However, it was troublesome just how quickly she'd

munched down on the sandwich and apple that he'd given her. She'd practically mewled with pleasure when she'd taken the first sip of soup, which she'd destroyed just as quickly.

Colton glanced at the third finger on her left hand. There was no ring and no tan line. For reasons he couldn't explain, given the fact he hadn't seen Makena in years, relief washed over him and more of that inconvenient attraction surged.

No ring, no husband.

It didn't exactly mean she was single. He told himself the reason he wanted to know was for the investigation. Here she'd shown up in town out of nowhere. She was staying in an RV and, based on the brightness in her eyes, he was certain she was sober. He hadn't expected her to be doing drugs or drinking. However, his job had trained him to look for those reasons first when dealing with uncharacteristic behavior.

Darting across the road without looking, in the middle of one of the worst thunderstorms so far this year, definitely qualified as uncharacteristic. Now that he'd determined she fell into that camp without a simple explanation, it was time to investigate what she was really doing in town and why.

Again, the questions he was about to ask were all for the sake of the investigation, he told himself, despite a little voice in the back of his head calling him out on the lie.

For now, he was able to quiet that annoyance.

Chapter Three

In the dome light, Colton could see that Makena's face was sheet-white and her lips were purple. Color was slowly beginning to return to her creamy cheeks. He took that as a good sign she was starting to warm up and was in overall good health.

"I thought you were in school to study business so you could come back and work on your family's ranch." She turned the tables.

"I realized midway through my degree that my heart was not in business. I switched to criminal justice and never looked back." Colton figured it couldn't hurt to give a little information about himself considering she looked frightened of him and everything else. As much as he didn't like the idea, she might be on the run to something or *from* something. Either way, he planned to get to the bottom of it and give her a hand up. "How about you? Did you stay an education major?"

"I stayed in my field," she said.

He would've thought that he'd just asked for her social security number and her bank passwords for the reaction he got. She crossed her ankles and then her arms. She hugged her elbows tightly against her chest.

To say she'd just closed up was a lot like saying dogs liked table scraps over dry food.

"Did I say something wrong?" Colton may as well put it out on the table. He didn't like the idea of stepping on a land mine, and the response he'd gotten from her was like a sucker punch that he didn't want to take twice.

"No. You d-didn't say anything wrong. You j-just caught me off guard." The way she stammered over every other word told him that she wasn't being completely honest. It also made him feel like she was afraid of him, which was strange. Innocent people might get nervous around law enforcement, but straight-up scared? He wasn't used to that with victims.

"Okay. We better get on the road and out of this weather. I promised one of our elderly residents that I would stop by and check on her property. The rain isn't letting up and we're not going too far from here. Her home is nearby. Mind if we—"

"It's okay. You can just let me out. I don't want to get in the way of you doing your job." Panic caused her voice to shake. Colton didn't want to read too much into her reaction.

"Makena, I hit you with my SUV and the fact is going to bother me to no end until I make absolute certain that you're okay. Check that. I want you to be better than okay. In fact, I'd like to help you out if I can, no matter what you need." He meant those words.

Makena blew out a slow breath. "I'm sorry. You've been nothing but kind. I wasn't trying to put you off. Honest. I'm just shaken up and a little thrown off balance." She turned to look at him, and those clear blue eyes pierced right through him. "Don't take any of this the wrong way. It's just been…" she seemed to be searching for the right words "…a really long time since I've had anyone help me."

Well, he sure as hell hoped she didn't plan on stopping there. If anything, he wanted to know more about her. He chalked it up to nostalgia and the feelings he'd experienced when he was nineteen, the minute he sat beside her in the bio lab, too chicken to pluck up the courage to ask her out.

He'd waited for weeks to see if she felt the same attraction. She was shy back then and he was even shyer. When he finally found his courage, a kid had beaten him to the punch. Dane Kilroy had moved in.

Colton couldn't say he'd ever had the best timing when it came to him and the opposite sex. Missed opportunity had him wanting to help her now. Or maybe it was that lost look in her eyes that appealed to a place deep inside him.

He knew what it was to be broken. His family had experienced a horrific tragedy before he was born. One that had left an echo so strong it could still be heard to this day.

A decades-old kidnapping had impacted the O'Connor family so deeply that they could never be the same again. The hole could never be filled after his six-month-old sister was abducted.

Colton figured the best place to start with Makena was the basics. "Is your last name still Eden?"

He opened up a file report on his laptop.

"What are you doing?" She seemed shocked.

"Filing a report." Colton forgot that she was a civilian. She would have no idea about the process of

filling out an incident report. "I need to file an accident report."

"No. That's really not necessary. I mean, I didn't get
a good look at your car but there didn't seem to be any
damage to your bumper. As far as me? I'll be okay in a
couple of days. There's really no need to file any type
of report. Won't that get you in trouble with your job?"

She was worried about him?

"My job isn't going to be on the line over a freak
accident. This is what I do. This is my job, my responsibility."

"What can I say to stop you from filing that report?"

Colton couldn't quite put his finger on what he heard
in her tone when she asked the question, but it was
enough to send a warning shot through his system.

"Are you in some type of trouble?" he asked.

Part of him wished he could reel those words back
in when he heard her gasp. Too late. They were already
out there. And consequences be damned, he wanted to
know the answer. Maybe he shouldn't have asked the
question so directly.

"Colton, this is a bad idea. My hip is hurting right
now, but it's going to be fine. There's really no reason
to make a huge ordeal out of this. Despite what you
said it can't be all that good for your career for you to
have a car crash on your record. I can't imagine someone who drives around as part of his job wouldn't be
hurt by a report being filed. I promise you, I would tell
you if this was a big deal. It's so not."

The old saying, "The lady doth protest too much,"
came to mind. Colton realized what he heard in her
voice. Fear.

And there was no way he was going to walk away

from that. "Makena, I can't help you if I don't know what's going on. Do you trust me?"

Colton put it out there. As it was, everything about her body language said she'd closed up. There was no way he was getting any information out of her while she sat like that, unwilling to open up. And since the person closest to a woman was the one most likely to hurt her, as angry as that made him, his first thought went to her hiding out from a relationship that had soured.

Domestic disturbances were also among the most dangerous calls for anyone working law enforcement.

"It's really nothing, Colton. We're making too big a deal out of this. I'm just passing through town." She heaved a sigh and pulled the blanket up to her neck. "You asked if I stayed with teaching as my degree and the answer is yes. I did. Until the music program was cut from the school where I worked, and I decided to see if I could make it as a musician on my own."

"Really?"

"I've been traveling across the state playing gigs as often as I can set them up. I don't have a manager and I've been living in an RV without the owner's permission, but I planned to leave a note and some money as soon as I'm able to." He noticed her fingers working the hem of the blanket. "I've fallen on hard times recently and jobs have been in short supply. Really, it's only a matter of time before I get back on my feet."

"Sounds like a hard life and one that's causing you to make tough choices. And the owner knows you've been staying there. She asked me to make sure you're okay." Colton nodded his head. Her explanation nearly covered all the ground of any question he could've thought of. She'd pretty much wrapped up her lifestyle in a bow and the reason she would be moving around the state. But was her story tied up a little too neatly?

He decided to play along for just a minute.

"I thought I remembered seeing you on campus a million years ago picking at a guitar." He tried not to be obvious about watching her response.

"You saw me?" The flush to her cheeks was sexy as hell. She was even more beautiful when she was embarrassed. But that physical beauty was only a small part of her draw. She was intelligent and funny and talented, from what he remembered years ago.

He wondered how much of that had changed...how much she'd changed.

Thunder rumbled and it felt like the sky literally opened up and dumped buckets of rain on them.

Tornado alarms blared. He owed his former father-in-law a call. It was impossible to know if there was an actual tornado or if this was another severe thunderstorm drill. Colton had warned Preston Ellison that overusing the alarm would lead people to disregard it, creating a dangerous situation for residents.

Had the mayor listened?

Clearly not. He hadn't listened to his daughter, Rebecca, either. The single father and mayor of Katy Gulch had overprotected his daughter to the point of smothering her. She'd rebelled. No shock there.

Down deep, Rebecca had always been a good person. She and Colton had been best friends since they were kids and married for less than a year when she'd died. Damned if he didn't miss her to the core some days.

But being with Makena again reminded him why he hadn't married Rebecca straight out of high school.

"ARE YOU COMFORTABLE?" Colton's question felt out of the blue to Makena, but she'd noticed that he'd lost himself in thought for a few minutes as he slogged through the flooded street. This must be his way of rejoining the conversation.

The windshield washers were working double time and had yet to be able to keep up with the onslaught.

"I'm better now that I'm inside your vehicle and we're moving toward safety. Why?" Luckily, the height of the SUV kept the undercarriage of the vehicle above water. The engine sat high enough on the chassis not to flood.

Makena strained to see past the hood. The sirens stopped wailing. The sound would've been earsplitting if it hadn't been for the driving rain drowning out nearly every other sound outside of the SUV.

"The storm's predicted to get worse." He wheeled right and water sloshed as his tires cut a path where he made the turn. The sidewalks of the downtown area and the cobblestoned streets had to be completely flooded now.

"Really?" Makena tried to shift position in her seat so that she could get a good look at the screen he motioned toward. Movement only hurt her hip even more. She winced and bit out a curse.

Colton's laptop was angled toward the driver's side and the only thing she could see was the reflection from the screen in his side window.

He seemed to catch on and said, "Sorry. I can't tilt it any closer to you."

"No need to apologize. Believe it or not, I'm not usually so clumsy, and I don't make a habit of running out in front of vehicles. Like I already said, give this hip a few days and she'll be good as new." Makena forced a smile.

"I hope you weren't planning on going anywhere tonight." There was an ominous quality to his voice, and he didn't pick up on her attempt to lighten the mood.

"Why is that?" Actually, she had hoped to figure out her next move and get back on the road. She'd ducked into the RV to ditch a few friends of her ex-husband, who was the real reason she'd been on the run. Her marriage to an abusive Dallas cop had ended badly. Hunger had caused her to leave the relative safety of the RV. She assumed it would be safer to travel in the rain and easier to cover herself up so she could travel incognito.

It was most likely paranoia, but she could've sworn she'd seen the pair of guys she'd caught in their garage late one night, huddled up and whispering with River. She'd surprised the trio and River had absolutely lost his cool. He'd demanded she go back inside the house and to bed, where he told her to wait for him.

River's decline had become even more apparent after that night. He was almost constantly angry with her over something. Yelling at her instead of talking. Not that he'd been great at it before. Gone was the charm of the early days in their relationship.

When River's attention was turned on, everyone noticed him in the room and he could make the most enigmatic person come to life. River's shadow was a different story altogether. It was a cold, dark cave. His temper had become more and more aggressive to the point she'd had to get out.

"According to radar, this storm's about to get a

whole helluva lot worse." Colton's voice cut through her heavy thoughts.

Leaving her husband, River, one year ago had been the best decision she'd ever made. Not a night went by that she didn't fear that he'd find her.

"How is that even possible?" she asked as a tree branch flew in front of the windshield.

"Apparently, Mother Nature isn't done with us yet. We're about to see just about how big this temper tantrum is going to get."

And just when she thought things couldn't get any worse than they already were this evening, the tornado alarms blared again. Rain pounded the front windshield, the roof. And in another moment of pure shock, she realized the winds had shifted. Gusts slammed into the vehicle, rocking it from side to side.

"Normally, I wouldn't leave the scene of an accident. However, if we want to live to see the light of day, we better get out of here." Colton placed the gearshift into Drive and turned his vehicle around. Water sloshed everywhere.

"Where to? You mentioned an elderly neighbor that you need to check on." Another gust of wind blasted the front windshield. Makena gasped.

"She asked me to check on her 'guest' who was staying in her RV. Since you're right here, a change of plans is in order. My place isn't far from here. The parking structure is sound and partially underground. We should be safe there."

Before she could respond, Colton had his secretary on the radio again, updating her on his new destination. Makena figured she could ride out the storm with Colton, giving away as little personal information as she could. Their shared history might work in her favor. Any other law enforcement officer in this situation would most certainly haul her in. Her name would get out.

Makena couldn't risk River figuring out where she was. With his jealous tendencies, it wouldn't be good for him to see her around Colton, either. The Dallas cop would pick up on her attraction faster than a bee could sting.

Colton stopped at the red light on an otherwise empty street. Everyone seemed to have enough sense to stay off the roads tonight. The only reason she'd left the RV at all was to find scraps of food while everyone hunkered down.

Makena had thrown away her phone months ago, so she'd had no idea a storm was on its way. The cloudy sky and humidity had been a dead giveaway but spring thunderstorms in Texas were notorious for popping up seemingly out of nowhere. In general, they retreated just as fast.

This one, however, was just getting started.

Chapter Four

"What do you think?" Colton asked a second time. He'd blame the rain for Makena not hearing him, but she'd been lost to him for a moment.

The prospect of her disappearing on him wasn't especially pleasing. After being in the vehicle with her for half an hour already, he barely knew any more about her or her situation than he had at the start of the conversation.

The fact that she deflected most of his questions and then overexplained told him the storm brewing outside wasn't the only one.

Since she seemed ready to jump if someone said boo, he figured some things were better left alone. Besides, they were trapped together in a storm that didn't seem to have any intention of letting up over the next twenty-four hours. That would give him enough time to dig around in her story.

Colton relaxed his shoulders. He needed to check in with his mother and see if she was okay with having the twins sleep over. Again, he really didn't like doing that to her under the circumstances no matter how many times she reassured him the twins were nothing but pure joy.

"About what?" Makena asked.

"Staying at my apartment at least until this storm blows over." Colton banked right to avoid a tree limb that was flying through the air.

"When exactly might that be?"

Colton shouldn't laugh but he did. "I'm going to try not to be offended at the fact that you seemed pretty upset about the prospect of spending a couple of hours alone with me. I promise that I'm a decent person."

"No. Don't get me wrong. You've been a godsend and I appreciate the food. I was a drowned rat out there." She blew out another breath. "I wasn't aware there was a big storm coming today. And especially not one of this magnitude. I got caught off guard without an umbrella."

He didn't feel the need to add, without a decent coat. The roads were making it increasingly unsafe to drive to Mrs. Dillon's place. It looked like there were more funnel systems on the way. A tornado watch had just been issued for this and four surrounding counties. He'd like to say the weather was a shock but it seemed folks were glued to the news more and more often every year and some supercell ended up on the radar.

"You didn't answer my question." The reminder came as she stared at the door handle.

Makena sat still, shifting her gaze to the windshield, where she stared for a long moment. She heaved another sigh and her shoulders seemed to deflate. "I appreciate your hospitality, Colton. I really do. And since it doesn't seem safe to travel in this weather, going to your place seems like the best option. I have one question, though."

"And that is?"

"It's really more of a request." She glanced at the half-full coffee sitting in the cupholder.

He knew exactly what she wanted. "I have plenty of coffee in my apartment. I basically live off the stuff."

"I haven't had a good cup of coffee in longer than I care to count."

His eyebrow must've shot up, because she seemed to feel the need to qualify her statement. "I mean like a really good cup of coffee. Not like that stuff." She motioned toward the cupholder and wrinkled her nose.

He laughed. At least some of the tension between them was breaking up. There was no relief on the chemistry pinging between them, though. But he'd take lighter tension because he was actually pretty worried about her. He couldn't imagine why she would be living even temporarily in an RV that didn't belong to her in a town she didn't know. She was from Dallas and they'd met in Austin. Again, his thoughts drifted toward her running away from something—he wasn't buying the broke musician excuse. And since he hadn't seen her in well over a decade, he couldn't be one hundred percent certain she hadn't done something wrong, no matter how much his heart protested.

Something about the fear in her eyes told him that she was on the run from someone. Who that would be was anyone's guess. She wasn't giving up any information. Keeping tight-lipped might have been the thing that kept her alive. Didn't she say that she'd been on the road for months with her music? There were more holes in that story than in a dozen doughnuts. The very obvious ones had to do with the fact that she had no instrument and no band. He figured it was probably customary to bring at least one of those things on tour.

"To my place then," he said.

The light changed to green. He proceeded through the intersection, doing his level best to keep the questions at bay.

His apartment would normally be a five-minute drive. Battling this weather system, he took a solid fifteen and that was without anyone else on the road. A call home was in order and he needed to prepare Makena for the fact he had children.

As he pulled into the garage and the rain stopped battering his windshield, he parked in his assigned parking spot, number 4, and shut off the engine.

"Before we go inside, I need to make you aware of something—"

Makena scooted up to sit straighter and winced. His gaze dropped to her hip and he figured he had no business letting it linger there.

"Now, there's no reason to panic." It was clear she'd already done just that.

"Was this a bad idea? Do you have a girlfriend or wife in there waiting? I know what you already said but—"

"Before you get too twisted up, hear me out. I have twin sons. They're with my mother because the woman who usually lives with me and takes care of them while I work got called away on a family emergency and had to quit. She hated doing it but was torn, and blood is thicker than water. Besides, I told her to go. She'd regret it if she wasn't there for her niece after the young woman was in a car crash."

"I'm sorry." Much to his surprise, Makena reached over and touched his hand. Electricity pinged. Turned out that the old crush was still alive and well.

"Don't be. It was the right thing for her to do." He debated these next words because he never spoke about his wife to anyone. "I was married. I didn't lie to you before about that. My wife died not long after the babies were born."

"Oh no. I really am sorry, Colton. I had no idea." She looked at him. The pain in her eyes and the compassion in her voice sent a ripple of warmth through him.

He had to look away or risk taking a hit to his heart.

"Why would you?" He'd gotten real good about stuffing his grief down in a place so deep that even he couldn't find it anymore.

When he glanced over at Makena, he saw a tear escape. She ducked her head, chin to chest, and turned her face away from him.

"I'm not trying to upset you..." This was harder than he wanted it to be. "I just didn't want you to walk into my place and be shocked. You've been through enough tonight—" longer if he was right about her situation "—and I didn't want to catch you off guard."

She sat perfectly still, perfectly quiet for a few more long moments. "You have twin boys?"

"Yes, I do. Silas and Sebastian. They are great boys."

When she seemed able to look at him without giving away her emotions, she turned to face him, wincing with movement and then covering. "I bet they're amazing kids, Colton."

It was his turn to smile. "They are."

"Are they at your house?"

"My mom is watching them for me at the family's ranch while I work. She'll be worried with all the weather. I need to check in with her and make sure the boys are asleep."

"How old did you say your boys were?" She seemed to be processing the fact that he was a father.

"One year old. They're great kids." He needed to contact his mother. But first, he needed to get Makena inside his apartment with the least amount of trauma to the hip she'd been favoring. "How about we head inside now?"

He half expected her to change her mind, especially with how squirrelly she'd been so far.

"It would be nice to dry off."

Colton shut off the vehicle's engine and came around to the passenger side. He opened the door. She had her seat belt off despite keeping the blanket around her. Color was returning to her creamy skin, which was an encouraging sign.

"It might be easier if I just carry you up."

"I think I got it. I definitely need some help walking but I want to try to put some weight on this hip."

Considering Makena knew her identity and didn't slur her speech—a couple of key signs she was lucid—his suspicion that she might have a concussion passed. Although, he'd keep an eye on her to be safe. He figured it wouldn't hurt to let her try to walk; he had to trust her judgment to be able to do that.

"Okay, I'm right here." He put his arm out and she grabbed onto it. More of that electricity, along with warmth, fired through him. Again, he chalked it up to nostalgia. The past. Simpler times.

Makena eased out of the passenger seat, leaning into him to walk. He positioned himself on her left side to make it easier for her. With some effort, she took the first couple of steps, stopping long enough for him to close the car door.

His parking spot was three spaces from the elevator bank, so at least she didn't have far to go.

"You're doing great," he encouraged. He couldn't ignore the awareness that this was the first time in a very long time that he'd felt this strong a draw toward someone. He hadn't been out on a date since losing Rebecca. He'd been too busy missing his wife and taking care of their boys. Twelve months since the kiddos had been born and soon after that, he'd lost his best friend and wife in one fell swoop. He never knew how much twelve months could change his life.

MAKENA LEANED HEAVILY on Colton. She couldn't help but wonder if he felt that same electrical impulse between them. If he did, he was a master at concealment.

Thankfully, the elevator bank was only a few more steps. Pain shot through her if she put any weight on her left leg. But she managed with Colton's help. Despite having told him repeatedly that she'd be fine, this was the first time she felt like it might be true.

The elevator did nothing to prepare her for the largeness of Colton's penthouse apartment. Stepping into the apartment, she realized it took up the entire top floor of the building, which was three stories on top of the parking level.

It felt like she'd been transported into a world of soft, contemporary luxury. "This place is beautiful, Colton."

She pictured him sharing the place with his wife and children. Losing the woman he loved must have been a crushing blow for a man like him. Colton was the kind of person who, once he loved you, would love you forever.

Why did that hurt so much to think about?

Was it because she'd never experienced that kind of unconditional love?

It was impossible not to compare Colton to River. She'd been so young when she and River had gotten together. Too naive to realize he was all charm and no substance. He'd swept her off her feet and asked her to marry him. She'd wanted to believe the fairy tale. She would never make that mistake again.

Colton's apartment comprised one great room and was built in the loft style, complete with a brick wall and lots of windows. The rain thrashed around outside, but the inside felt like a safe haven. In the space cordoned off as the living room, two massive brown leather sofas faced each other in front of a fireplace. In between the sofas was a very soft-looking ottoman in the place of a coffee table. It was tufted, cream-colored and stood on wooden pegs. She noticed all the furniture had soft edges. The light wood flooring was covered by cream rugs, as well.

There was a pair of toy walkers that were perfect for little kids to explore various spots in the room. A large kitchen, separated from the living room by a huge granite island, was to her right. Instead of a formal table, there were chairs tucked around the white granite island, along with a pair of highchairs.

Seeing the kid paraphernalia made it hit home that Colton was a dad. Wow. She took a moment to let that sink in. He gave new meaning to the words *hot dad bod*.

The worry creases in his forehead made more sense now that she knew that he'd lost his wife and was navigating single parenthood alone.

Makena had once believed that she would be a

mother by now. A pang of regret stabbed at the thought. She'd known better than to start a family with River once she saw the other side of him. She was by no means too old to start a family except that the pain was still too raw from dealing with a divorce. The dream she'd once had of a husband and kids was the furthest thing from her thoughts as she literally ran for her life. She still felt the bitter betrayal of discovering that the person she'd trusted had turned out to be a monster.

It had taken her years to extract herself from him. Now she'd be damned if she let that man break her. Her definition of happiness had changed sometime in the last few years. She couldn't pinpoint the exact moment her opinion had shifted. Rather than a husband and kids, all she now wanted was a small plot of land, a cozy home and maybe a couple of dogs.

"Are you okay?" His voice brought her back to the present.

"Yes. Your home is beautiful, Colton," she said again.

Now it was his turn to be embarrassed. His cheeks flamed and it was sexy on him.

"I can't take the credit for the decorating. That was my mother." Not his wife? Why did hearing those words send more of those butterflies flittering around in her chest again?

"She did an amazing job. The colors are incredible." There were large-scale art pieces hanging on the walls in the most beautiful teal colors, cream and beige. The woman had decorating skills. The best part was how the place matched Colton's personality to a T. Strong, solid and calm. He was the calm in the storm. It was just his nature.

She took a few more steps inside with his help.

"Can I ask a personal question?" she asked.

He nodded.

"Didn't your wife want to decorate?"

"She's never been here." She felt a wall go up when it came to that subject.

"How about we get you settled on the couch and I get working on that cup of coffee?" he asked, changing the subject. His tone said, case closed.

"Are you kidding me right now? That sounds like heaven." She gripped his arm a little tighter and felt nothing but solid muscle.

He helped her to the couch before moving over to the fireplace wall and flipping a switch that turned it on. There were blue crystals that the fire danced on top of. It was mesmerizing.

She tried to keep her jaw from dropping on the carpet at the sheer beauty of the place. It was selfish, but she liked the fact that he'd only lived here as a bachelor, which was weird because it wasn't like she and Colton had ever dated, despite the signals he'd sent back in the bio lab. She had probably even misread that situation, because he'd never asked her out. The semester had ended and that was that.

Makena again wanted to express to Colton how sorry she was for the loss of his wife. Considering he had one-year-old twins, his wife couldn't have died all that long ago. The emotional scars were probably still very raw.

"If you want to get out of those wet clothes, I can probably find something dry for you to wear for the time being." He seemed to realize how that might sound, because he put his hands up in the air. "I just mean that I have a spare bathrobe of mine you can wear while I throw your clothes through the wash."

She couldn't help herself. She smiled at him. And chuckled just a little bit. "I didn't take it the wrong way and that would be fantastic. Dry clothes and coffee? I'm pretty certain at this point you've reached angel status in my book."

He caught her stare for just a moment. "I can assure you I will never be accused of being an angel."

A thrill of awareness skittered across her skin. A nervous laugh escaped because she hoped that she wasn't giving away her body's reaction to him. "I wouldn't accuse you of that, but I do remember what a good person you are. I wouldn't be here alone with you right now otherwise."

She surprised herself with the comment as he fired off a wink. He motioned toward an adjacent room before disappearing there. He returned a few moments later with a big white plush bathrobe that had some fancy hotel's name embroidered on the left-hand side.

Colton held out the robe. When she took it, their fingers grazed. Big mistake. More of that inconvenient attraction surged. She felt her cheeks flush as warmth traveled through her.

He cleared his throat and said, "I'll go make that coffee now. You can change in here. I promise not to look."

Again, those words shouldn't cause her chest to deflate. She should be grateful, and she was, on some level, that she could trust him not to look when she changed. Was it wrong that she wanted him to at least consider it?

Now she really was being punchy.

Makena took in a deep breath and then slowly exhaled. Colton made a show of turning his back to her and walking toward the kitchen. Despite pain shooting through her with every movement, she slipped out of her clothes and into the bathrobe while seated on the couch. The wreck could've been a whole lot worse, she thought as she managed to slip out of her soaked clothing and then ball it all up along with her undergarments, careful to keep the last part tucked in the center of the wad of clothing.

"Do you still take your coffee with a little bit of sugar and cream?"

"Yes. How did you remember after all this time?"

He mumbled something about having a good memory. Was it wrong to hope that it was a bit more than that? That maybe she'd been somewhat special to Colton? Special enough for him to remember the little things about her, like the fact she took her coffee with cream and sugar?

Logic said yes, but her heart went the opposite route.

Chapter Five

"I'm surprised you don't live on the ranch." Makena watched as Colton crossed the room. He walked with athletic grace. If it was at all possible, he was even hotter than he'd been in college. He'd cornered the market on that whole granite jawline, strong nose and piercing cobalt blue eyes look. Based on the ripples on his chest and arms, he was no stranger to working hard or hitting the gym. His jeans fit snug on lean hips.

"I have a place there where I spend time with the boys on my days off." He handed over a fresh cup of warm coffee. She took it with both hands and immediately took a sip.

"Mmm. This is quite possibly the best cup of coffee I've ever had."

Colton laughed and took a seat on the opposite couch. He toed off his boots and shook his head, which sent water flying everywhere. He raked his free hand through his hair. He was good-looking in that casual, effortless way. "I got this apartment so I could be closer to my office, after..."

The way his voice trailed off made her think he was going to tell her more about his wife. He shook his head again and recovered with a smile that was a little too forced. He took a sip of coffee. "You don't want to hear my sad story."

Before she could respond, he checked his phone.

"I do, actually," she said softly, but he didn't seem to hear. Strangely, she wanted to hear all about what had happened to him since college. Even then, he'd been too serious for a nineteen-year-old. He'd seemed like he carried the weight of the world on his shoulders. His eyes had always been a little too intense, but when they'd been focused on her they'd caused her body to hum with need—a need she'd been too inexperienced to understand at the time.

He picked up the remote and clicked a button, causing one of the paintings to turn into a massive TV screen. Makena had known his family was successful, but she had no idea they had the kind of money that made TVs appear out of artworks on the wall.

Color her impressed.

It was a shock for many reasons, not the least of which was the fact that Colton was one of the most down-to-earth people she'd ever met. She was vaguely aware of the O'Connor name, having grown up in Texas herself. But being a big-city girl, she had never really been part of the ranching community and had no idea until she'd seen an article about his family years ago. That had been her first hint that they might be wealthier than she'd realized.

Makena had had the opposite kind of childhood. She'd been brought up by a single mother who'd made plenty of sacrifices so that Makena could go to college without having to go into massive debt. And then a couple of years into Makena's marriage with River, long after the shine had worn off and she realized there was no other choice but to get out, her beloved mother had become sick.

Leaving her husband was no longer the number one priority. Her mother had taken precedence over everything else, despite River's protests that helping her ill mother took up too much of her time. He'd had similar complaints about her work, but her job had kept her sanity in check while she watched the woman she loved, the woman whose sacrifices were great, dwindle into nothingness.

Makena reached up and ran her finger along the rose gold flower necklace she wore—a final gift from her mother.

Despite River's protests, Makena remained firm. But with a sick mother who needed almost round-the-clock care in her final months, Makena had been in no position to disappear. And she'd known that was exactly what she had to do, when she walked away from River after his threats.

When Makena looked up, she realized that Colton had been studying her.

"What's his name?" he asked. Those three words slammed into her. They were so on point it took her back for a second.

She opened her mouth to protest the question, but Colton waved her off before she could get a word out.

"Makena, you don't have to tell me his name. I'll leave that up to you. Just don't lie to me about him existing at all."

Well, now she really felt bad. She sat there for a long moment and contemplated her next move. Having lived alone for six months after losing her mother, barely say-

ing a word to anyone and focusing on the basest level
of survival, she now wanted to open up to someone.

She just wanted to be honest with someone and with
herself for a change.

"River."

She didn't look up at Colton right then. She wouldn't
be able to bear a look of pity. She didn't want him to
feel sorry for her. It was her mistake. She'd made it.
She'd owned it. She would've moved on a long time
ago if it hadn't been for her mother's illness.

"Was he abusive? Did he lay a hand on you?" The
seriousness and calmness in Colton's tone didn't convey pity at all. It sounded more like compassion and
understanding. Two words that were so foreign to her
when it came to her relationship with a man.

"No." She risked a glance at him. "He would've. We
started off with arguments that escalated. He always
took it too far. He'd say the most hurtful things meant
to cut me to the quick. I didn't grow up with a father
in the house. So I didn't know how abnormal that was
in a relationship."

"No one should have to." There was no judgment
in his voice but there was anger.

"Things escalated pretty badly, and one day when
we were arguing I stomped into the bedroom. He followed and when I wouldn't stop, he grabbed my wrist
like he was a vise on the tightest notch. He whirled
me around so hard that the back of my head smacked
against the wall. I was too prideful to let him know
how much it hurt. It wasn't intentional on his part.
Not that part. But he immediately balled his fist and
reared it back."

Makena had to breathe slowly in order to continue.

Her heart raced at hearing the words spoken aloud that she'd bottled up for so long. Panic tightened her chest.

"What did you do to stop him from hitting you?" Colton's jaw muscle clenched.

"I looked him dead in the eyes, refusing to buckle or let him know that I was afraid. And then I told him to go ahead and do it. Hit me. But I cautioned him with this. I told him that if he did throw that punch he'd better sleep with one eye open for the rest of his life because we had a fireplace with a fireplace poker and I told him that he would wake up one morning to find it buried right in between his eyes."

A small smile ghosted Colton's lips. "Good for you. I bet he thought twice about ever putting a hand on you again."

"Honestly, I don't think I could ever hurt another human being unless my life depended on it. But I needed him to believe every word of that. And he did. That was the first and last time he raised a fist to me. But his words were worse in some ways. They cut deep and he tried to keep a tight rein on who I saw and where I went."

"Can I ask you a question?"

"Go ahead." She'd shared a lot more about her situation than she'd ever thought she would with anyone. Part of her needed to talk about it with someone. She'd never told her mom because she didn't want her to worry.

"Why did you stay?"

"My mom. She was sick for a couple of years and then she passed away." Makena paused long enough to catch her breath. She tucked her chin to her chest so he wouldn't see the tears welling in her eyes. "That's when I left him. Before that, honestly, she needed me to be stable for her. She needed someone to take care of her and she needed to stay with the same doctors. I couldn't relocate her." Makena decided not to share the rest of that story. And especially not the part where River had threatened her life if she ever left him. He seemed to catch onto the fact that she'd at the very least been thinking about leaving.

But Makena didn't want to think about that anymore, and she sure as hell didn't want to talk about herself. She'd done enough of that for one night. She picked up her coffee and took a sip before turning the tables.

Catching Colton's gaze, she asked, "How about you? Tell me about your wife."

"There isn't much to tell. Rebecca and I were best friends. She lived across the street and we grew up together. Her father is the mayor. We dated in high school and broke up to go to different colleges. Her older sister had married her high school sweetheart and the relationship fell apart in college, so Rebecca was concerned the same thing would happen to us."

"And what did you think?"

"That I was ready for a break. I looked at our relationship a lot like most people look at religion. When someone grows up in a certain church, it's all they know. Part of growing up and becoming independent is testing different waters and making certain it's the right thing for you and not just what's ingrained. You know?"

"Makes a lot of sense to me." She nodded.

"Before I committed the rest of my life to someone, I wanted to make damn sure I was making the right call and not acting out of habit. That's what the break meant to me."

"Since the two of you married, I'm guessing you realized she was the one." Why did that make Makena's heart hurt?

"You could say that. I guess I figured there were worse things than marrying my best friend."

Makena picked up on the fact that he hadn't described Rebecca as the love of his life or the woman he wanted to spend the rest of his life with, or said the two of them had realized they were perfect for each other.

"We got married and the twins came soon after. And then almost immediately after, she was hit by a drunk driver on the highway coming home from visiting her sister in Austin. She died instantly. I'd kept the twins home with me that day to give her a break."

"I'm so sorry, Colton."

"I rented this apartment after not really wanting to live on the ranch in our home. The place just seemed so empty without her. I go there on my days off with the twins because we still have pictures of her hanging up there and I want the twins to have some memories of growing up in a house surrounded by their mother's things."

"Being a single dad must be hard. You seem like you're doing a really great job with your boys. I bet she'd be really proud of you."

"It really means a lot to hear you say that. I'd like to think she would be proud. I want to make her proud. She deserved that." A storm brewed behind his eyes when he spoke about his wife.

"How long were the two of you married?" Makena asked, wanting to know more about his life after college.

"We got married after she told me that she was pregnant."

Was that the reason he'd said he could've done worse than marrying his best friend? Had she gotten pregnant and they'd married? Asking him seemed too personal. If he wanted her to know, he probably would've told her by now. The questions seemed off-limits even though they'd both shared more than either of them had probably set out to at the beginning of this conversation.

Despite the boost of caffeine, Makena had never felt more tired. It was probably the rain, which had settled into a steady, driving rhythm, coupled with the fact that she hadn't really slept since almost running into the pair of men she'd seen with River, not to mention she'd been clipped by an SUV. She bit back another yawn and tried to rally.

"Losing her must've been hard for you, Colton. I couldn't be sorrier that happened. You deserve so much more. You deserved a life together."

COLTON HADN'T EXPECTED to talk so much about Rebecca. Words couldn't describe how much he missed his best friend. There was something about telling their story that eased some of the pain in his chest. He was coming up on a year without her in a few days. And even though theirs hadn't been an epic love that made his heart race every time she was near, it had been built on friendship. He could've done a lot worse.

Being with Makena had woken up his heart and stirred feelings in him that he'd thought were long since dead. In fact, he hadn't felt this way since meeting her sophomore year. He'd known something different was up the minute he'd seen Makena. Rebecca had texted him that day to see how he was doing and it was the first time he hadn't responded right away.

Rebecca had picked up on the reason. Hell, there were times when he could've sworn she knew him better than he knew himself.

Being here, with Makena, felt right on so many levels. It eased some of the ache of losing his best friend. Not that his feelings for Makena were anything like his marriage to Rebecca. He and Rebecca were about shared history, loyalty and a promise to have each other's back until the very end.

Colton felt a lot of pride in following through on his promise. He'd had Rebecca's back. He'd always have her back. And in bringing up the twins, he was given an opportunity to prove his loyalty to his best friend every day. Those boys looked like their mother and reminded him of her in so many ways. A piece of her, a very large piece, would always be with him.

He reminded himself of the fact every day.

Right now, his focus was on making certain the residents in his county were safe and that fearful look that showed up on Makena's face every once in a while for the briefest moment subsided. She'd opened up to him about living with a verbally abusive ex. Colton had a lot of experience with domestic situations. More than he cared to. He'd seen firsthand the collateral damage from relationships that became abusive and felt boiling hot anger run through his veins.

He flexed and released his fingers to try to ease out some of the tension building in him at the thought of Makena in a similar predicament. He'd also witnessed the hold an abusive spouse could have over the other person. Men tended to be the more physically aggressive, although there were times when he saw abuse the other way around. Women tended to use verbal assaults to break a partner down. He'd seen that, too. Except that the law didn't provide for abuse that couldn't be seen.

Texas law protected against bruises and bloody noses, ignoring the fact that verbal abuse could rank right up there in damage. The mental toll was enormous. Studying Makena now and knowing what she'd been like in the past, he couldn't imagine her living like that.

"How long were you married?" he asked.

"Nine years." The shock of that sat with him for a long minute as he took another sip of fresh brew.

"Was your mother the only reason you stayed?" he asked.

"Honestly?"

He nodded.

"Yes. She got sick and couldn't seem to shake it. I took her to a doctor and then a specialist, and then another specialist. By the time they figured out what was wrong with her, she had a stroke. It was too late to save her." She ran her finger along the rim of her coffee cup.

The look of loss on Makena's face when she spoke about her mother was a gut punch. She didn't have that same look when she talked about her ex. With him, there was sometimes a flash of fear and most definitely defiance. Her chin would jut out and resolve would darken her features.

"I miss her every day," she admitted.

Since the words *I'm sorry* seemed to fall short, he set his coffee down and pushed up to standing. He took the couple of steps to the other couch and sat beside her. Taking her hand in his, he hoped to convey his sympathy for the loss of her mother.

"She's the reason that I got to go to college. She, and a very determined college counselor. It was just me and my mom for so long. She sacrificed everything for me."

"Your mother sounds like an incredible person."

"She was." Makena ducked her head down, chin to chest, and he realized she was hiding the fact that a tear had rolled down her face.

"I can imagine how difficult it was for her to bring you up alone. There are days when I feel like my butt is being kicked bringing up my boys. Without my family by my side, I don't even see how it's possible to do it. I don't know what I'd do without my tribe and their help."

"Whoever said it takes a village to bring up a child was right. We just had two people in ours and it was always just kind of us against the world. It wasn't all bad. I mean, I didn't even realize how many sacrifices my mom made for me until I was grown and had my first real job out of college. Then I started realizing how expensive things were and how much she covered. I saw what it took to get by financially. She didn't have a college education and insisted that I get one. She worked long hours to make sure that it could happen without me going into a ridiculous amount of debt. I never told her when I had to take out student loans because I wanted her to feel like she was able to do it all."

"It sounds like you gave her a remarkable gift. Again, I can only compare it to my boys but I also know that I want to give them the world just like I'm sure your mom wanted to with you. The fact that she was able to do as much as she did with very little resources and no support is nothing short of a miracle. It blows me away."

He paused long enough for her to lift her gaze up to meet his, and when it did, that jolt of electricity coursed through him.

"It's easy to see where you get your strength from now." Colton was rewarded with a smile that sent warmth spiraling through him before zeroing in on his heart.

"Colton..." Whatever Makena was about to say seemed to die on her lips.

"For what it's worth, you deserve better, with what you got from your marriage and the loss of your mother so young," he said.

She squeezed his arm in a move that was probably meant to be reassuring but sent another charge jolting through him, lighting up his senses and making him even more aware of her. This close, he breathed in her unique scent, roses in spring. The mood changed from sadness and sharing to awareness—awareness of her pulse pounding at the base of her throat, awareness of the chemistry that was impossible to ignore.

He reached up and brushed the backs of his fingers against her cheek and then her jawline. She took hold of his forearm and then pulled him closer, their gazes locked the entire time.

When she tugged him so close, their lips were inches apart, and his tongue darted across his lips. He could only imagine how incredible she would taste. A moment of caution settled over him as his pulse skyrocketed. His caution had nothing to do with how badly he wanted to close the distance between them and everything to do with a stab of guilt. It was impossible not to feel like he was betraying Rebecca in some small measure, especially since his feelings for Makena were a runaway train.

He reminded himself that his wife was gone and had been for almost a year. It was a long time since he'd been with someone other than her, and that would mess with anyone's mind. Not to mention the fact he hadn't felt this strong an attraction to anyone. In fact, the last time he had was with the woman whose lips were inches from his.

Makena brought her hands up to touch his face, silently urging him to close that gap.

Colton closed his eyes and breathed in her flowery scent. He leaned forward and pressed his lips to hers. Hers were delicate and soft despite the fiery and confident woman behind them.

All logic and reason flew out the window the second their mouths fused. He drove the tip of his tongue inside her mouth. She tasted like sweet coffee. Normally, he took his black. Sweet was his new favorite flavor.

Makena moved toward him and broke into the moment with a wince. She pulled back. "Sorry."

"Don't be." He wanted to offer more reassurance than that but couldn't find the right words. Either way, this was just the shot of reality that he needed before he let things get out of hand. Doing any of this with her right now was the worst of bad ideas.

They were two broken souls connecting and that was it. So why did the sentiment feel hollow? Why did his mind try to argue the opposite? Why did it insist these feelings were very real? The attraction was different? And it was still very much alive between them?

"I'm sorry if I hurt you," he finally said.

"You couldn't have. It was my fault. I got a little carried away." Her breathing was raspy, much like his own.

He'd never experienced going from zero to one hundred miles an hour from what started as a slow burn. Don't get him wrong, he'd experienced great sex. This was somehow different. The draw toward Makena was sun to earth.

Colton was certain of one thing. Sex with Makena would be mind-blowing and a game changer. With her hip in the condition it was, there was no threat it was going to happen anytime soon. That shouldn't make his chest deflate like someone had just let the air out of a balloon. He chalked it up to the lack of sex in his life and, even more than that, the lack of companionship.

This was the first time he realized how much he missed having someone to talk to when he walked in the door at night. Having the twins was amazing but one-year-olds weren't exactly known for their conversation skills.

Colton took the interruption from the hip pain as a sign he was headed down the wrong path. Granted, it didn't feel misguided, and nothing inside him wanted to stop, but doing anything to cause her more pain was out of the question.

A voice in the back of his mind picked that time to remind him of the fact he'd struck her with his vehicle. He was the reason she was in pain in the first place.

The idea that she'd been adamant about not filing a report crept into his thoughts. As much as she'd insisted not doing so was for his benefit, he'd quickly ascertained that she didn't want her name attached to a report. Colton had already put two and two together and guessed she was hiding out from her ex. But living in a random trailer and hiding her name meant her situation was more complicated than he'd first realized. No matter what else, this was a good time to take a break and regroup.

"I'm sorry. That whole kissing thing was my fault. I don't know what came over me." Makena's cheeks flushed with embarrassment and that only poured gasoline onto the fire of attraction burning in him.

"Last I checked, I was a pretty willing participant." He winked and she smiled. He hadn't meant to make her feel bad by regrouping. In fact, the last thing he wanted to do was add to her stress. Based on what she'd shared so far, her marriage had done very little to lift her up and inspire confidence.

Was it wrong that he wanted to be the person who did that for her?

Chapter Six

Embarrassment didn't begin to cover the emotion Makena should be feeling after practically throwing herself at Colton. It was impossible to regret her actions, though. She hadn't been so thoroughly kissed by any man in her entire life. That was a sad statement considering she'd been married, but wow, Colton could kiss. He brought parts of her to life that had been dormant for so long she'd forgotten they existed.

She wanted to chalk up the thrill of the kiss to the fact that it had been more than a decade in the making, but that would sell it short. He'd barely dipped the tip of his tongue in her mouth and yet it was the most erotic kiss she'd ever experienced. She could only imagine what it would feel like to take the next step with him.

And since those thoughts were about as productive as spending all her paycheck on a pair of shoes, she shelved them. For now, at least.

Makena blew out an awkward breath. Yes, dwelling on their attraction was off the table, because not only was it futile, but there was no way she could compete with a ghost. Colton had said so himself. He'd married his best friend. His beloved wife had died shortly after giving birth to their twins and making a family.

Despite the fact that he hadn't described his relationship with his wife as anything other than a deep friendship, it would be impossible to stack up to that level of love.

Colton's gaze darted to his coffee cup. "Mine's empty. How are you on a refill?"

"I'm good. I think I've had enough." She bit back a yawn. "If it's okay, I'd like to just curl up here and rest my eyes for a few minutes."

"Make yourself at home." Colton stood. The couch felt immediately cold to her, after his warmth from a few moments ago. He scooped up his coffee mug and headed toward the kitchen. She could've sworn she heard him mumble phrases like "another time and place and things might be different," and "bad timing." She couldn't be certain. It might've just been wishful thinking on her part to believe there was something real going on between them.

An awkward laugh escaped. She'd never been the type to latch onto someone, but then this wasn't just anyone. Was she seriously that lonely?

This was Colton O'Connor and they shared history. And based on the enthusiasm in his kiss, an attraction that hadn't completely run its course.

Makena counted herself lucky that embarrassment couldn't kill a person. Actually, maybe it wasn't embarrassment she felt. Maybe it was that strong attraction that caused her cheeks to heat. When she really thought about it, she hadn't done anything to be embarrassed about.

The past six months, being alone, had done a number on her mindset. That was certain. But it hadn't knocked her out. And it wouldn't. She would get through this, rebound and pick her life up again. A life that seemed a little bit colder now that she'd been around warmth again.

Makena figured it was too much to hope that she'd find her feet rooted in the real world again. And real world started with a few basics. "Hey, Colton. Any chance you have a spare toothbrush and a washcloth I could use?"

Her clothes were in the dryer, so she might as well go all in wishing for a real shower rather than a bowl of warm soapy water by the river like she'd done the past few days at the RV.

"Like I said, make yourself at home." He tilted his head toward the hallway where he'd disappeared earlier to bring her the robe. "You'll find a full bathroom in there. Spare toothbrushes are still in the wrappers in the cabinet."

With some effort, Makena was able to stand. Colton turned around and a look of shock stamped his features.

"Hold on there. I can help you get to the bathroom."

"It still hurts, I'm not going to lie. But it's not as bad as it was an hour ago. I'd like to see if I can make it myself." She wasn't exactly fast and couldn't outrun an ant, but she was proud of the fact that she made it to the bathroom on her own. She closed the toilet seat, folded a towel and paused a moment to catch her breath. It was progress and she'd take it.

As she sat in the bathroom waiting for the pain in her hip to subside, she couldn't help but inhale a deep breath, filling her senses with Colton's scent. The bathrobe she wore smelled like him, all campfire and outdoors and spice. It was masculine and everything she'd remembered about sitting next to him in biology lab. His scent was all over the robe.

She needed to get her head on straight and refocus. Thinking much more about Colton and how amazing and masculine he smelled wasn't going to help her come up with a plan of what to do next.

It would probably be best for all concerned if she could put Colton out of her head altogether. She appreciated his help, though.

Taking another deep breath, Makena reached over and turned on the water. Using the one-step-at-a-time method, she peeled off the bathrobe and then took baby steps until she was standing in the massive shower. She had no idea what materials actually were used, but the entire shower enclosure looked like it was made of white marble. There were two showerheads. The place was obviously meant for a couple to be able to shower together. However, a half dozen people would fit inside there at the very least.

Now that really made Makena laugh. Images of single father and town sheriff Colton in a wild shower party with a half dozen people didn't really fit well together.

They tickled her anyway.

And maybe she was just that giddy. Exhaustion started wearing her thin, and her nerves, nerves that had been fried for a solid year and really longer than that if she thought back, eased with being around Colton.

The soap might smell clean and a little spicy, but it was the warm water that got her. Amazing didn't begin to cover it. She showered as quickly as possible, though, not wanting to keep too much pressure on that hip. Her left side bit back with pain any time she put pressure on it.

After toweling off and slipping back into the robe, she brushed her teeth. She had a toothbrush at the RV, in the small bag of shower supplies she kept with her at all times while on the move. But this was a luxury. It was crazy how the simple things felt so good after being deprived. Simple things like a real shower and a real bathroom.

Speaking of which, the cup of coffee that she'd had a little while ago had been in a league of its own.

Makena reminded herself not to get too comfortable here. It was dangerous to let her guard down or stick around longer than absolutely necessary. Being in one place for too long was a hazard, made more so by the fact her identity could be so easily revealed by Colton.

She tightened the tie on the bathrobe before exiting the bathroom and making her way back into the living room. She might move slow, but this was progress. If she could rest that hip for a couple of hours and let the worst of the storm pass, she could get back to the RV and then…go where?

Thinking about her next step was her new priority. She'd been so focused on surviving one hour at a time that she'd forgotten there was a big picture—an end game that had her collecting evidence against her ex. Time had run out for her in Katy Gulch.

Inside the living room, Colton was in mission control mode. He was so deep in thought with what was going on and talking into his radio that he didn't even seem to hear her when she walked into the room.

Rather than disturb him, she moved as stealthily as possible, reclaiming her spot opposite him on the couch. He glanced up and another shot of warmth rocketed through her body, settling low in her stomach. Colton's deep, masculine voice spoke in hushed tones as she curled up on her side on the sofa. He almost immediately shifted the laptop off his lap and grabbed the blanket draped on the back of the sofa.

He walked over and placed it over her before offering her an extra throw pillow. She took it, laid her head on it and closed her eyes.

With all the stress that had been building the six months and especially in the past couple of days since she thought she'd seen River's associates, there was no way she could sleep.

Resting her eyes felt good. That was the last thought she had before she must've passed out.

Makena woke with a start. She immediately pushed up to sit and glanced around, trying to get her bearings. Her left hip screamed at her with movement, so she eased pressure from it, shifting to the right side instead.

Daylight streamed through the large windows in the loft-style apartment. She rubbed blurry eyes and yawned.

Looking around, she searched for any signs of Colton as the memory of last night became more focused. She strained to listen for him and was pretty sure she heard the shower going in the other room. The image of a naked, muscled Colton standing in the same shower she'd showered in just a few hours ago probably wasn't the best start to her morning. Or it was. Depending on how she looked at it. Makena chuckled nervously.

The events from the past twelve hours or so came back to her, bringing down her mood. She opened up the robe to examine her hip on the left side. Sure enough, a bruise the size of a bowling ball stared back at her. Pain had reminded her it was there before she'd even looked.

Movement hurt. She sucked in a breath and pushed past the soreness and pain as she closed her robe and stood. Then she remembered that Colton had some of the best coffee she'd ever tasted. Since he'd instructed her to make herself at home, she figured he wouldn't mind if she made a cup.

Her stomach growled despite the sandwich, apple and soup he'd given her. She glanced at the clock. That had been a solid ten hours ago. How had she slept so long?

Makena hadn't had that much sleep at one time in the past year. Of that she was certain. She cautioned herself against getting too comfortable around Colton. She'd already let way too much slip about her personal life, not that it hadn't felt good to finally open up to someone she trusted and talk about her mother and other parts of her life. It had. But it was also dangerous.

A part of her wanted to resurface just to see if River had let his anger toward her go by now. If he'd let *her* go by now. Being on the run, hiding out, had always made her feel like she'd done something wrong, not the other way around.

Standing up to fight a Dallas police officer who ran in a circle just like him could wreak complete havoc on her life, so she had erred on the side of caution.

But should she start over now, after she'd found Colton again? There was something almost thrilling about seeing him, about finding a piece of herself that had been alive before she'd lost her mother...before River.

If Makena was being completely honest with herself, she could admit that part of her disappearing act had to do with wanting to shut out the world after losing her mother. She'd succumbed to grief and allowed fear to override rational thought.

But where to start over? Dallas was out. Houston was a couple hours' drive away. Maybe she could make a life there? Get back to teaching music. It was worth a shot.

Living like she had been over the past few months, although necessary, wasn't really being alive.

Makena saw a coffee machine sitting on a countertop. It was easy to spot in the neat kitchen. There were drawers next to it and so she went ahead and made the wild assumption that she'd find coffee in one of them.

She didn't. But she did find some in the cupboard above. It was the pod kind. She helped herself to one that said Regular Coffee and placed it in the fancy-looking steel machine. She glanced to the side and saw a plastic carafe already filled with water.

There was only one button, so that was easy. The round metal button made the machine come to life. It was then that she realized she hadn't put a coffee cup underneath the spout.

"Oh no. Where are you?" She opened a couple of cupboards until she found the one that housed the mugs. She grabbed one and placed it under the spout just in time for the first droplets of brown liquid to sputter out. "Good save." She mumbled the words out loud and, for the second time since opening her eyes, chuckled.

Her lighter mood had everything to do with being around Colton again. The kiss they'd shared had left the memory of his taste on her lips. And even though their relationship couldn't go anywhere, the attraction between them was a nice change of pace from what she usually felt around men. After being with River, she'd become uneasy interacting with the opposite sex.

Makena slowly made her way to the fridge. Quick movement hurt. Walking hurt. But she was doing it and was certain she could push through the pain.

In the fridge, she found cups of her favorite thing in the world, vanilla yogurt. She took one and managed to find a spoon. She polished it off before the coffee could stop dripping.

The carton of eggs was tempting, but she needed to take it easy on the hip. Standing in front of the stove was probably not the best idea. The yogurt would hold her over until she could rest enough to gather the energy to find something else to eat or cook.

Cup of coffee in hand, she slowly made her way to one of the chairs at the granite island. It would be too much to ask for sugar and cream at this hour, especially with the amount of pain she was in. She hadn't asked for ibuprofen last night, not wanting to mask her injury. Today, however, she realized the injury was superficial and she would ask for a couple of pain relievers once Colton returned from the shower.

Speaking of which, she was pretty certain the water spigot had been turned off for a while now.

Nothing could have quite prepared her for the sight of Colton O'Connor when he waltzed into the room wearing nothing but a towel. The white cloth was wrapped around lean hips and tucked into one side.

"Good morning." The low timbre of his voice traveled all over her body, bringing a ripple of awareness.

"Morning to you." She diverted her gaze from the tiny droplets of water rolling down his muscled chest.

"I see you managed to find a cup of coffee. It's good to see you up and around. How's that hip today?" His smile—a show of perfectly straight, white teeth—made him devastatingly hot.

"It's better. I managed the coffee minus the cream." She decided it was best to redirect the conversation away from her injury. "This coffee is amazing straight out of the pot. Or whatever that thing is." She motioned toward the stainless-steel appliance.

Colton's eyebrow shot up and a small smile crossed his lips—lips she had no business staring at, but they were a distraction all the same.

"You want cream and sugar?"

"It's really no big deal." She'd barely finished her protest when Colton moved over to the fridge and came back with cream that he set on the counter in front of her. He located sugar next and tossed a few packets in her direction.

She thanked him.

"You seemed pretty busy last night. Is everyone okay?" she asked.

"The storm was all bark and no bite thankfully. Roads were messy, but folks respected Mother Nature and she backed off without any casualties."

"That's lucky," she said.

"There were a few close calls with stranded vehicles. Nothing I could get to, but my deputies could."

"That's a relief." She took a sip of coffee and groaned. "This is so good."

He shot her a look before shaking his head. "That's a nice sound. But not one I need in my head all day and especially not after...never mind."

The words on the tip of his tongue had to be *that kiss*. She'd thought the same thing when she saw him half-naked in the kitchen.

"I can't remember the last time I slept as well as I did last night." She stretched her arms out.

"If you slept that well on the couch, imagine what it would be like in a real bed." He seemed to hear those words as they came out and shot her a look that said he wanted to reel them back in.

The image that had popped into her thoughts was one of her in bed with him. Considering he still stood there in a towel, she needed to wipe all those thoughts from her head.

Seeing him again was making a difference in her mood and her outlook. Somewhere in the past six months after losing her mother, she'd given up a little bit on life. Looking back, she could see that so clearly now.

This morning, she felt a new lease on life and was ready to start making plans for a future. She hadn't felt like she would have one, in so long.

She took another sip of coffee. "I know that I said last night was the best cup of coffee I'd had in a long time, but this beats it."

He practically beamed with pride. "Are you hungry?"

"I already helped myself to yogurt. I hope that's okay."

"Of course it is. I make a pretty mean spinach omelet if you're game."

The man was the definition of hotness. He cared

about others, hence his job as sheriff. And now he decided to tell her that he could cook?

"You're not playing fair," she teased. "I really don't want you to go to any trouble."

"If it makes you feel any better, I plan to make some for myself. No bacon, though. I'm out."

"Well, in that case, forget it. What kind of house runs out of bacon?" She laughed at her own joke and was relieved when he did, too. It was nice to be around someone who was so easy to be with. Conversation was light. This was exactly what she remembered about biology lab and why she'd been so attracted to him all those years ago. Sure, he was basically billboard material on the outside, with those features she could stare at all day. But how many people did she know who were good-looking on the outside and empty shells on the inside? A conversation with a ten on the outside and a three on substance made her want to fall asleep thinking about it.

Physical attraction was nice. It was one thing. It was important. But she'd learned a long time ago that someone's intelligence, sense of humor and wit could sway their looks one way or the other for her.

On a scale of one to ten, Colton was a thirty-five in every area.

Chapter Seven

Colton whipped up a pair of omelets and threw a couple slices of bread into the toaster while Makena finished up her cup of coffee at the granite island.

"Is there any chance I can have some pain reliever?" she asked.

"I have a bottle right here." He moved to the cabinet at the end of the counter. Medicine was kept on the top shelf even though his sons had only just taken their first steps recently. "Ibuprofen okay?"

"It's the only thing I take and that's rare."

"Same here." He grabbed a couple of tablets and then put a plate of food in front of her. "You probably want to eat that first. Ibuprofen on an empty stomach is not good."

She nodded and smiled at the plate. Tension still tightened the muscles of her face but sometime in the past twelve hours they'd been together, she'd relaxed just a bit. Given her history with men, it was wonderful that she could be this comfortable around him so quickly, and Colton let his chest fill with pride at that, although her ease was tentative, as he could tell from her eyes.

"Are you serious about these eggs?" She made a show of appreciating them after taking another bite.

Colton laughed. He realized it had been a really long time since he'd laughed this much. The roller coaster he'd been on since losing Rebecca and then his father had been awful to say the least.

To say that Colton hadn't had a whole lot to smile about recently was a lot like saying The New Texas Giant was just a roller coaster.

The exception was his twin boys. When he was with them, he did his level best to set everything else aside and just be with them. He might only have an hour or so to play with them before nighttime routine kicked in, but he treasured every moment of it. The last year had taught him that kids grew up way too fast.

"I'm glad you like the eggs."

"*Like* is too weak a word for how I feel about this omelet." Her words broke into more of that thick, heavy fog that had filled his chest for too long.

"The roads are clearing up. After you eat, I should make a few rounds."

"Can you give me a ride to the RV?" she asked.

"Happy to oblige," he teased. "I just need to get dressed."

Her cheeks flushed and he wondered if it had anything to do with the fact that he was still in a towel. A rumble of a laugh started inside his chest and rolled out. "I just realized that I'm walking about like I don't have company. Pardon me. I'll just go get dressed now."

"Well, it hasn't exactly been hard on the eyes." Now it was her turn to burst out laughing. "I can't believe I just said that out loud."

He excused himself and headed into his bedroom,

where he threw on a pair of boxers, jeans and a dark, collared button-down shirt. He pulled his belt from the safe and clipped it on. It held his badge and gun.

Colton located one of his navy windbreakers that had the word *SHERIFF* written in bright, bold letters down the left sleeve. He finger-combed his hair and was ready to go. Walking out into the living room and seeing Makena still sitting there in his robe was a punch to the chest.

"I'll go and grab your clothes from the dryer." His offer was met with a smile.

"I can go with you. Or you could just point me in a direction. I think I can find my way around," she said.

"Down the hall. Open the door in the bathroom. You probably thought it was a closet, but it's actually a laundry room."

"That's really convenient." She tightened her grip on her robe and disappeared down the hallway.

He was relieved to see that her hip seemed in better condition today. She was barely walking with a limp. Even so, he wondered if he could talk her into making a trip to the ER for an X-ray.

Ten minutes later, she emerged from the hallway. She'd brushed her hair and dressed in the jeans and blouse she'd had on yesterday. "Ready?"

"Are the pain pills kicking in yet?" he asked.

"It's actually much better. I mean, I have a pretty big bruise, but overall, I'm in good shape. The ibuprofen is already helping. I won't be riding any bucking broncos in the next few days, but it'll heal up fine."

"I like the fact that you're walking more easily, but I would feel a whole lot better if we stopped off at the county hospital to get it checked out. The roads are clear on that route." He hoped she'd listen to reason.

She opened her mouth to protest, but he put his hand up to stop her.

"Hear me out. You won't have to pay for the cost of the X-ray. It's the least I can do considering the fact that I hit you."

"Technically, I ran out in front of your car and you didn't have enough time to stop. You also couldn't see me because of the rain. So, technically, I hit you."

Well, Colton really did laugh out loud now. That was a new one and he thought he'd heard just about every line imaginable in his profession. He couldn't help himself, and chuckled again. It was a sign she was winning him over, and he didn't normally give away his tells.

"I'm glad you're laughing, because you could be writing me up right now or arresting me for striking an official vehicle. Does that count as striking an officer?" She seemed pretty pleased with that last comment.

"All right. You got me. I laughed. It was funny. But what wouldn't be funny is if there's something seriously wrong with your hip and it got worse because we didn't get it checked out." Was it him or had he just turned into his old man? He could've sworn he'd heard those same words coming out of Finn O'Connor's mouth for most of Colton's life. His dad was great at coaxing others to get checked out. He didn't seem to think he fell into the same category.

And it was only recently that Colton and his brothers had found out his father had been dealing with a health issue that he'd kept quiet about until his death.

"Don't you think we would know by now? Plus, what's the worst it could be? A hairline fracture? I had one of those in my wrist in eighth grade PE. It's an incident I don't talk about because it highlights my general inability to perform athletics of any kind. But there wasn't much they could do with it except wrap it and put it in a sling. It wasn't like I needed a cast. I'm sure my hip falls into the same category. I need to rest. I need to take it easy. Other than that, I think I'm good to go."

What she said made a whole lot of sense, and Colton knew in the back of his mind she was right on some level. The thought of dropping her off at the RV to fend for herself after witnessing the way she'd gobbled down food last night and cleaned her plate this morning wasn't something he could stomach doing.

He wanted to help her, but he didn't want to hurt her pride. He needed to be tactful. "Since you're going to be resting for a few days anyway, why not do it here?"

The question surprised even him. But it was the logical thing to do. He had plenty of room here. He could sleep on the sofa. He'd done that countless times before, unable and unwilling to face an empty bedroom.

"That's a really kind offer. Maybe under different circumstances I could take you up on it..."

"I didn't want to have to pull this card out, but since you mentioned it, you're leaving me no choice." He caught hold of her gaze and tried his level best not to give himself away by laughing. "If you don't stay here and let me help you heal, I might be forced to handcuff you."

He mustered up his most serious expression.

Makena's jaw nearly dropped to the floor, and a twinge of guilt struck him at tricking her.

"That's blackmail. You wouldn't do that to me.

Would you?" Her question was uncertain and he suspected she'd figured out his prank.

"I don't know." He shrugged. "Is it working?"

She walked straight toward him with her slight limp on the left side and gave him a playful jab on the shoulder. "That wasn't funny."

"Actually, I thought it was ingenious of me." Seeing the lighter side of Makena and her quick wit reminded him of why he'd been willing to walk away from the relationship he'd known his entire life, for someone he'd met in biology lab.

Deep down, behind those sad and suspicious eyes, she was still in there. Still the playful, intelligent, perceptive woman he'd fallen for.

"I'm probably going to regret this, but I'll think about staying here until I get better. Maybe just a day or two. But…"

"Why is there always a *but*?" He rubbed the day-old scruff on his chin.

"But I sleep on the couch. You only have two bedrooms here. One is yours and the other has two cribs in it. The door was open on the way to the bathroom. I couldn't help but notice," she said in her defense.

"Yes, you can stay here. Thank you for asking. And who sleeps on the couch is up for debate. We'll figure out a fair way to decide." There was no way he was going to let her curl up on the sofa when he had a king-size bed in the other room. Most of the time, he nodded off with a laptop open next to him and a phone in his hand anyway. It was easier than facing an empty bed on his own.

"And hey, thanks for considering my proposal," he added.

Colton appreciated how difficult her situation must be for her to feel the need to hide in a random stranger's RV, and he appreciated the confidence she put in him by staying with him last night.

In the ultimate display of trust, she'd fallen deeply asleep.

She didn't speak, but he could see the impact of his words. Sometimes, silence said more than a thousand words ever could.

Colton put his hand on the small of Makena's back as he escorted her to the elevator. Emotions seemed to be getting the best of her, because she'd gotten all serious and quiet on him again. The lighter mood was gone and he wondered if it had something to do with what he'd said or the simple fact they were going back to the RV where she'd been staying.

There were so many unanswered questions bubbling up in his mind about Makena and her need to hide. Abusive exes he understood. But she'd been in hiding for months, and he wondered how much of it had to do with losing her mother. He knew firsthand what it was like to have a close bond with a parent who died. Colton and his siblings were still reeling from the loss of their father. Worsened by the fact none of them could solve the decades-old mystery about their only sister's abduction from her bedroom window.

Frustration was building with each passing day, along with the realization their father had gone to his deathbed never knowing what had happened to Caroline. Plus, there was the whole mess of Caroline's kidnapping being dredged up in the news ever since there'd been a kidnapping attempt in town a couple of months ago.

Renee Smith, now Renee O'Connor after marrying his brother Cash, had moved to Katy Gulch with her six-month-old daughter, Abby, in order to start a new life. Her past had come with her and it was a haunting reminder of what could happen when a relationship went sour.

Renee's ex had followed her to Katy Gulch unbeknownst to her and tried to take away the one thing she loved most, in order to frighten her into coming home.

Was Makena in the same boat?

At least in Makena's case, she knew what she was dealing with. Renee had been caught off guard because her ex had cheated on her and was having a child with a coworker before deciding no one else could have Renee. That was pretty much where the comparisons between the two ended.

He'd brought up a good point, though. Colton wanted to know more about Makena's ex so he could determine just how much danger she might be in.

The fact she'd left the man a year ago stuck in Colton's craw. The way he'd found her and discovered how she'd been living made him think that she'd either run out of money or couldn't get to hers.

But then, he didn't know many people who could go a year without working and survive. Colton may have come from one of the wealthiest cattle ranching families in Texas, but all the O'Connors had grown up with their feet on the ground and their heads out of the clouds. Each one was determined to make a mark on this life and not rely on the good graces of their family to earn a living despite loving the land and the family business.

Colton helped Makena into the passenger seat,

where she buckled herself in. The drive to Mrs. Dillon's place was short. Colton checked in with Gert on the way and the rest of the car ride he spent mulling over what he already knew.

He hoped Makena was seriously considering his offer to let her stay at his apartment. He couldn't think of a safer place for her to heal. It dawned on him that he hadn't even asked her if she liked children. He just assumed she did.

That was one of the funny things about becoming a parent: he was guilty of thinking that everyone loved kids. Growing up in Katy Gulch didn't help, because most people were kind to children in his hometown.

Colton had to stop a couple of times to clear the road of debris. So far, it was looking like Katy Gulch had been spared the storm's fury.

Gert had reported in several times last night and first thing this morning to let him know that very few people had lost power. Neighbors were pitching in to make sure food didn't spoil and people had what they needed. It was one of the many reasons Colton couldn't imagine bringing up his boys in any other place.

The twins were fifth-generation O'Connors, but whether or not they took up ranching would be up to them. Both seemed happiest when they were outdoors. Colton prayed he could give them half the childhood he'd been fortunate to have. He and his brothers had had the best. Of course, they'd also had their fair share of squabbles over the years.

Garrett and Cash seemed to rub each other the wrong way from just about the day Garrett was born. Make no mistake about it, though. Either one would be there for the other in a snap. Help needed? No questions asked.

Was it strange that Colton wished the same for Makena? He wished she could experience being part of a big family. It sounded like since losing her mother, she'd lost all the family she had. He couldn't even imagine what that would be like.

She'd remained quiet on the way over. They were getting close to Mrs. Dillon's and the river.

"Everything all right over there?" he asked her.

"Yeah, I'm good." The words were spoken with no conviction.

From the way she drawled out those three words, he could tell she was deep in thought. Her voice always had that sound when she was deep in concentration. He'd once accidentally interrupted her studying and heard that same sound.

He'd given her a lot to think about. To him, it was a no-brainer decision. Knowing Makena, she wouldn't want to live off him for free even for a few days.

It occurred to him that he was momentarily without a sitter. He wasn't even sure if she was up for the job, considering her left hip. She was walking better today, but she would know better than anyone else if she'd be able to keep up with the boys.

For the time being, it was a lot of bending over and letting them hold your fingers while they practiced walking. They also had swings and walkers and every other kid device his mother could think to buy for them.

He could put gates up to make it easier for her. More and more, he liked the idea. It would give her some pocket money and a legitimate place to stay. She wouldn't have to feel like she was imposing, if she took a short-term job with him just until he found someone permanent.

"How are you with children?"

"They seem to like me. I have been a music teacher in an elementary school. I don't know about little-littles. I don't have much experience with anyone younger than the age of five. But I do seem to be popular with eight-year-olds." Hearing her voice light up when she talked about her career warmed his heart. "Why?"

"It's just an idea. I already told you my babysitter had an emergency in Austin and had to quit. I also mentioned having my boys with my mom at the ranch isn't ideal for anything less than short-term. We have a lot going on in our family right now with our father passing recently. I was just wondering if you'd be interested in helping me out of a pinch. Would you consider taking care of the boys until I could find someone else full-time?"

He gripped the steering wheel until his knuckles went white, as he waited for an answer.

"When would you need me to start?"

Was she seriously considering this? Before she could change her mind, he added, "Now would be good. My mom can hang on for a couple more days if needed."

"Can you give me a few hours to think about it?"

"Take all the time you need, Makena. I don't have any interviews set up just yet. Mom is on board with helping for a few days. I'm just trying to lighten her load."

"Okay." She nodded, giving him the impression that she liked the idea. "It's definitely something to think about. Maybe I could just meet the boys and see if they even like me."

"That's a good first step. I'm sure they will, though. They're easygoing babies. It might be good for you to see if that age scares you, without the pressure of signing on for a commitment." He liked the idea of taking some of the burden off his mother, considering everything she was going through. And the thought of Makena sticking around for a while.

"I've been so focused on my situation that I haven't considered what your family must be going through," she said. The conversation ended when Colton parked at Mrs. Dillon's house.

Makena had opened the passenger door and was out of the vehicle before Colton could get around to help her. "I just want to pick up the few things I always have with me."

As she walked toward the RV, a bad feeling gripped him.

He glanced around, unable to find the source that was causing the hairs on the back of his neck to tingle.

Why did it feel like they were walking into a trap?

Chapter Eight

The silver bullet–style RV sat on a parking pad behind the farmhouse and near the river. Makena had placed a foot on the step leading into the RV when she heard Colton's voice in the background, warning her. She craned her neck to get a good look at him.

"Stop." That one word was spoken with the kind of authority she'd never heard from him before. It was the same commanding cop voice she'd heard from River.

Colton locked gazes with her. "Take your hand off the handle slowly. Don't put any pressure on the latch. And then freeze."

Makena stood fixed to the spot as a chill raced up her spine at the forceful tone. The "cop voice" brought back a flood of bad memories.

Would it always remind her of River when she heard Colton talk like that? Even a simple friendship, let alone anything more, was out of the question if her body started trembling when she heard him give an order.

She also knew better than to argue with him. He'd obviously seen something and was warning her.

"Stay right where you are. Don't move." He was by her side in a matter of seconds.

Makena's heart hammered against her rib cage, beating out a staccato rhythm. Panic squeezed her chest, making inhaling air hurt.

"Stay steady. Don't shift your weight." Colton dropped down to all fours. In that moment, she knew exactly what he was looking for.

A bomb.

Sweat beaded on her forehead and rolled down her cheek. She focused on her breathing and willed herself not to flinch. She reminded herself to slowly breathe in and out. Her hands felt cold and clammy.

Although she couldn't exactly say she'd been living the past six months, she didn't want to die, either. And especially not here.

Her mouth tried to open but her throat was dry, and she couldn't seem to form words. Fear was replaced with anger. Anger at the fact that by hiding, she'd allowed River to run her life all these months. She'd been miserable and lonely, and had nearly starved because of him. But she'd survived. Now there'd be no going back.

Makena decided by sheer force of will that she would live. No matter what else happened, she would make it through this. It was the only choice she would allow herself to consider.

"There's a device strapped to the bottom of this step. Stay as still as you possibly can. We're going to get through this." Colton pushed up to standing and quickly scanned the area. Based on the expression on his face, which was calmer than she felt, she knew the situation was bad. He was too calm.

From the few action movies she'd seen, it seemed like if she moved, she'd be blown sky-high. She was afraid even to ask, because a slight shift in her weight, no matter how subconsciously she did it, would scatter her into a thousand tiny bits. More of that ice in her veins was replaced by fire.

River didn't get to do this. If anything happened to her, she needed Colton to know who was responsible. "My ex." She slowly exhaled, careful not to move so much as an inch.

"His name is River Myers. He works at the Dallas Police Department as an officer. He's the reason I've been on the run for the past six months. He has threatened me on numerous occasions. I walked away from a man who is armed and dangerous. He's calculating. He'll destroy me if he finds me before I locate evidence against him," she said in a voice as steady as the current in the river next to them.

"Don't you give up on me now. You're going to be fine. But the clock is ticking. I have no idea how much explosive is here and we're running out of options."

With that, he literally dove on top of her, knocking her off the step and covering her with his own body. When a blast didn't immediately occur, he said, "Let's get out of here."

With one arm hooked under her armpit, he scrambled toward a tree near the riverbank. He rounded the tree, placing it in between them and the RV. He hauled her back against his chest. He leaned back against the tree and dropped down, wrapping his arms around her.

Not two seconds later, an explosion sounded.

Her first thought was that she was thankful for Colton. If he hadn't been there, she'd be dead. Her brain couldn't process that information. It was going to take a while for that to sink in. Her second thought, as Colton's arms hugged her in a protective embrace, was that everything she'd owned in the past few months was gone.

The guitar her mother had given her had been blown to smithereens. The few clothes she had were gone along with it. It wasn't much but it was all she owned in the world.

A few tears of loss leaked out of her eyes. She sniffed them back, reminding herself this could've been a whole lot worse. It was hard to imagine, though. She had so little left from her mother.

She brought her right hand up, tracing the rose necklace with her fingers. Thankfully, she had at least one thing left from her mother.

A little voice in the back of her head pointed out that she had someone in her corner for the first time in a very long time. It wasn't the security of her mother's guitar or the few articles of clothing that meant something to her. But she had the necklace and she had Colton.

She would have to rebuild from there.

And then another thought struck. She was in danger. Real danger. Colton had a young family, and because of her, his twins had been almost orphaned. She'd never been more certain of the fact that she couldn't accept his help any longer.

Moving forward, she planned to ask him for a loan, some kind of cover identity and a ticket out of town. She'd been crazy to stay in Texas. It was only a matter of time before River and his buddies would find her there. She'd adopted the hiding-in-plain-sight strategy and it had backfired big time.

Staying in the country was no longer an option. Since Mexico bordered Texas, she could slip across the border and make a new life. Maybe she could get down to one of the resorts and work in a kitchen or someplace where she'd be hidden from view.

A ringing noise in her ear covered the sound of Colton's voice. The only reason she realized he was talking at all was because she felt his chest vibrate against her back. The blast had been deafening. And at least temporarily, she'd lost hearing. Bits of metal had blown past her and the last thing she'd heard was the bomb detonate.

Everything felt like it was moving in slow motion. It was like time had stopped and everything around her moved in those old-fashioned movie frames and some mastermind stood behind a curtain clicking slides.

When the last of the debris seemed to have flown past and everything was still, Colton scooted out from underneath her and whirled around to check the damage.

Her heart went out to the owner, the sweet woman who'd just lost a remnant from her past.

Makena balled her fists and slammed them into the unforgiving earth in frustration.

Colton had disappeared from view. She rolled around onto all fours to see for herself. The door had been blown completely off its hinges. Many of the contents had gone flying. The RV was on fire. Colton had raced to his sport utility and returned with a fire extinguisher before she was able to get to her feet.

River hadn't just sent a potent message. His intention had been to kill her. All those times he'd threatened her came racing back. And so did the memory of the pair of men she'd seen the other day.

WITHIN THE HOUR, Colton had cordoned off the crime scene. A few of his deputies arrived on-site to aid in the investigation. There was no need to call in a bomb expert. The one that had caused the kind of damage the RV had sustained was a simple job. One that anyone could've logged onto the internet and bought materials to make.

Hell, any person old enough to know how to use a phone and have access to a credit card could grab the materials used here. The bomb was crude but would've done the job of killing Makena if he hadn't been there.

A ringing noise still sounded in Colton's ears, but his hearing was coming back at least. People didn't have to shout at him anymore for him to hear what they were saying.

Deputy Fletcher walked over. He had on gloves. His palm was out, and a key chain was on top. It was a classic hotel style, with the words *Home sweet home* inscribed on the black plastic.

"What's this?" Colton asked his deputy.

Fletcher shrugged. "Found it about fifteen feet from the RV."

"Let's check with Makena to see if she recognizes it." He led Fletcher over to the spot where she was being examined by EMT Samantha Rodriguez. There were no visible signs of bleeding, so she'd been spared being impaled by debris. Colton, on the other hand, hadn't been so lucky. He'd taken a nick to his shoulder, and he was holding a T-shirt pressed to the wound to stem the bleeding.

Samantha's partner, Oliver Matthew, had tried to get Colton to stop long enough for treatment, but he had a

crime scene to manage and wouldn't take any chance
that evidence could end up trampled on.

"Does this look familiar to you?" he asked Makena,
pointing toward the key chain on Fletcher's palm.

She gasped.

"I bought one just like that for River after moving in together. He kept losing his key, so I ordered
a key chain for him. That looks exactly like the one I
bought," she stated.

"Bag it and see if you can lift a print," he said to
Fletcher.

"Yes, sir." Fletcher turned and walked toward his
service vehicle after thanking Makena for her confirmation.

Although any Joe Schmo could make this bomb,
Colton had zeroed in on one name: River Myers. And
now he might have proof. Colton was a little too familiar with the law enforcement statistics. Police officers
battered their spouses in shockingly high numbers.
The stress of the job was partly to blame and the reason why Colton, as a law enforcement leader, went to
great lengths to offer programs and resources to help
combat a pervasive issue with his deputies and employees. He saw it as his responsibility to ensure the
mental and physical fitness of the men and women who
served under him.

However, he could only keep an eye on his employees and do his level best to ensure they had plenty of
tools to manage the stress that came with a career like
theirs. He couldn't force them to take advantage of a
program. An old saying came to mind: "You can lead
a horse to water but you can't make it drink."

One of the advantages of running a smaller department like his office came in the form of being able to be up-front and personal with each one of his employees. A large department like Dallas wouldn't have that same benefit. Running an organization that large presented challenges.

In no way, shape or form was Colton condoning or justifying what a cop under duress might do. He held his people to the highest standards. Part of the reason why he was so selective in the hiring process. In a bigger setup, it would be easier to slip through the cracks.

When the site had been secured and medical attention given, he made his way back to Makena. Samantha turned to him.

"Her hearing should return to normal in a few days. Other than that, she was very lucky."

The last word Colton would use to describe Makena was *lucky*. Bad things happened to good people sometimes. But he understood what Samantha meant. The situation could've been a whole lot worse, with neither one of them walking away from it.

They'd also been fortunate that the pressure on the step had set off a timer and not a detonator. Those critical fifteen seconds had saved both of their lives.

"I'm so sorry, Colton. I should've known something like this would happen." Makena's pale blue eyes were wide. Fear flashed across them for a moment, followed by anger and determination. Two emotions that could get her in trouble.

"You know this isn't your fault." He needed to reassure her of the fact. He thanked Samantha.

The EMT folded her arms, put her feet in an athletic stance and shot him a death glare. "You are going to let me check out that shoulder now. Right?"

Samantha knew him well enough to realize he would put up a fight. Colton always made sure everyone around him was okay first.

"I'm standing here right now, aren't I?"

"Good." She didn't bother to hide the shock in her voice. She bent down to her medical bag and ordered him to take off his shirt, which he did.

"This is the only injury I sustained other than the ears, just like Makena."

Samantha stood up and made quick work tending to the cut in his shoulder. Within minutes, she'd cleaned the wound, applied antibiotic ointment and patched it up with a butterfly bandage.

"This should help it heal up nicely. I'd try to talk you into stopping by the ER for a few stitches, but I didn't want to push my luck."

"I appreciate the recommendation. This should be good." He'd grown up working a cattle ranch, so it wasn't the first time he'd ended up with a scar on his body. Nor would it be the last. He thanked Samantha for doing a fine job, which she had.

She told him it was no trouble at all before closing up her bag and heading toward the driver's seat of her ambulance. He would've just patched himself up but didn't want to appear a hypocrite in front of Makena after urging her to seek care.

Before he could open his mouth to speak, Makena threw herself into his chest and buried her face. He stroked her long, silky hair, figuring this was a rare show of emotion for her.

He couldn't be certain how long they stood there. Being with her, it was like time had stopped, and nothing else mattered except making sure she was okay.

When she pulled back, his heart clenched as he looked at her. She wore the same expression as she had that last day of biology lab. He'd been so tempted to ask her out despite the fact that it had been made clear she was with someone else. It would've gone against everything he believed in. Honor. Decency. He'd never break the code of asking someone out who was married, in a relationship, or dating someone else.

He'd cleaned up his own relationship at home, realizing that he and Rebecca would never have the kind of spark that he'd felt with Makena. He'd decided right then and there, with his nineteen-year-old self, that he'd hold out for that feeling to come around again. Little did he know just how rare it could be.

All these years later, he'd never felt it again until recently. It was then he realized what he and Makena had had was special.

"It's not safe for me to be here anymore, Colton. I know you need a statement from me, but I'd like to keep my name as quiet as possible. He obviously found me here and he'll find me again. I'll be ready next time. I took his threats too lightly. Not anymore."

"I do need a statement from you. And I have no authority to force you to stay in Katy Gulch. Whether or not you do, a crime happened here in my jurisdiction. Someone's property was damaged and there was an attempted murder and that makes it my responsibility. So, whether you're here or not, I plan to investigate." Why did the news of her wanting to run away impale him?

She had every right to do what she felt was necessary to protect herself. Now that he knew her ex was in law enforcement, so many of her reactions made sense to him. That fact alone made a relationship between them practically impossible.

Given Colton's line of work, she would always be reminded of her ex.

Makena shook her head furiously. "I understand you have to file a report. Believe me when I say you don't want to chase this guy down. Look what he's capable of, Colton. You have a family. You have young boys who depend on you. I won't have your life taken away from them because of something I did."

"Is that what you believe? That any of this is somehow your fault?"

"I didn't mean it like that. I know what River did in the past and now is completely on him. I didn't deserve it then and I don't deserve it now. I won't take responsibility for any of his actions. That's all on him. But *I* brought that man to your doorstep. That's the responsibility I feel."

"You're right about one thing. You did nothing wrong."

Her chin quivered at hearing those words, so he repeated them. "You did nothing wrong."

She was nodding her head and looked to be fighting back tears. "I know."

"Sometimes we just need to hear it from someone else."

"Thank you, Colton. You have no idea what you've done for me in the past twenty-four hours and how much that has truly meant to me, which is why I can't burden you any more than I have."

Colton had his hands up, stopping her from going down that road again. "In case you hadn't noticed, Makena, this is my job. This is what I do. And yes, there are personal risks. Believe me when I say that I don't take them lightly. Also, know that I take safety very personally. I have every intention of walking through the door every night to my boys as I watch them grow up. There is no other option in my mind. And if this had been anyone else but you in this situation, I would still be following the same protocol. Most law enforcement officials are there for all the right reasons. It's rare for them to go completely rogue or off the chain. But when they do, they aren't just a danger to one person. They will be a threat to women, to children and to men. That's not something I can live with on my conscience. Not to mention the fact that I'm a law enforcement officer. Being on this job is in my blood."

He stopped there. He'd said enough. He gave her a few moments to let that sink in while he walked her over to his SUV.

Makena took in a deep breath. "Okay."

She blew the breath out.

Colton hoped that meant she'd heard what he said and was ready for him to continue his investigation.

"Let's do this. Let's make sure that River Myers never hurts another soul again. I'll tell you everything I know about him."

Colton helped her into the passenger seat before closing the door and claiming his spot. Pride filled his chest. It wasn't easy for anyone to go against someone they'd cared about or, worse yet, someone they were afraid of. It took incredible courage to do what she was doing, and he couldn't be prouder of her than he was right then.

After giving Colton a description of her ex, his

badge number, his social security and his license plate, she dropped another bomb on him.

"Abuse is not the only thing he's guilty of. I don't know the names of the people he was talking to one night in my garage but I'd heard a noise and when I went to investigate, River flipped out. He rushed me back inside the house and threatened me. He told me that I had no idea what I'd just done. All I can figure is that I walked in on some kind of meeting between the three of them."

"Did you hear what they were talking about, by chance?"

"I wish I had. He rushed me out of there too early and I was too chicken to go back." Her hands were balled fists on her legs. "I guess they were planning something or talking about something they didn't want anyone else to know about. They sounded threatening and there was a handprint around River's throat. I thought I overheard something about getting someone to pay but I have no idea what that means."

"Were the other men in uniform?"

"No. They weren't. They were in regular street clothes but they acted like cops." That didn't mean they weren't officers.

"Did you get a good look at them?"

"Yes. As a matter of fact, I did. And I saw them here three days ago. It's the reason I ducked into the RV and didn't leave for three days straight."

That explained why she'd practically starved to death by the time she'd walked out to find food. So many things clicked in the back of his mind. Like the fact that she'd gone out in a driving rain when there were no cars out. It must have been to forage for food.

The way she'd gobbled down that sandwich and apple made more sense to him now.

He'd wondered how long it had been since she'd had a meal.

"I knew I'd stuck around too long and I was preparing to move on. Seeing them scared me to the core. River had always been clear. If I left him, he would hunt me down and kill me. He would see the divorce as the ultimate betrayal."

Another thought dawned on Colton. River may not have been trying to kill her. His cohorts, on the other hand, seemed ready to do the job.

They could be in league with River. They may or may not be cops themselves, but they definitely could be doing his dirty work.

"Describe them to me in as much detail as you can remember."

Chapter Nine

"The first one I saw was around six feet tall. He had a football-player build, with a clean-shaven face. His hair was light red…kind of strawberry blond. He had a thick neck and big hands. Other than that, I remember that he had light skin and freckles." Makena remembered the men vividly because they were so different.

Colton nodded.

"The second guy had one of those 1970s mustaches on an otherwise clean face. Black hair with big bushy eyebrows. He had these puffed-out cheeks like he had a big wad of gum or tobacco in his jaws. His hair was short and thick and a little wavy. I remember that he was several inches shorter than Red. They were so distinct-looking and oddly matched. Opposites. That's what I remember about them from that night."

"Did you have a chance to hear their voices? Would you recognize them if you heard them?"

She shook her head.

"Cops?" he asked.

"I don't know for certain. I can't be one hundred percent sure. They looked like they were law enforcement. They had that cop carriage, if you know what I mean."

Colton nodded. He seemed to know exactly what she

was talking about. There was just a cop swagger. Being on the job, wearing a holster for long shifts day in and day out caused them to hold their arms out a little more than usual. They also walked with the kind of confidence that said they could handle themselves in almost any situation. They had the training to back it up.

"What shift did your ex work?" Colton asked.

"Deep nights. He requested them. Said he liked to be out and about when everyone else was asleep." She couldn't imagine anything had changed in the past few months since she'd been gone, considering the fact that River had been on deep nights for almost fifteen years.

"A couple of my brothers work in law enforcement," he said.

"Oh yeah?"

"U.S. Marshals. They would help if we brought them up to speed." Colton had scribbled down descriptions of Red and Mustache Man. He also made notes about River's shift preference. Considering it was only ten thirty in the morning, River would be home and still asleep.

"I'm not sure it's such a good idea." A lot was coming at her, fast. She needed a minute to process. "Can I think about it first?"

He nodded and then moved on. "Could he afford the residence you shared on his own?"

"I moved into his bachelor pad and fixed it up. It's likely that he's still there. He doesn't really like change."

Colton checked the clock on his dashboard. It was almost like he read her thoughts. He started the engine of his sport utility. "I have a few calls to make that might go a little easier in my office. You okay with that?"

What he was really asking was would she stay with him? She could read between the lines. Since she had nowhere to go, literally, and no friends in town, she nodded. The honest truth was that she didn't feel safe with anyone but Colton. Being with him was warmth and campfires despite the dangers all around.

She leaned her head back and brought her hands up to rub her temples. Her head hurt. A dull ache was forming between her eyes. The headache distracted her from her hip pain. Now, there was something. She was getting punchy.

Makena appreciated the fact that the ride to Colton's office was short. She climbed out of the sport utility, her hip reminding her that it wasn't quite finished with her yet.

The driver's-side door of a blue sports sedan popped open two spots down, the driver having cut off the engine almost the minute she stepped out of the SUV. Makena flinched.

The person held something toward Colton. As the youngish man, early thirties if she had to guess, bumrushed them, Colton tensed. His gaze bounced from being locked onto the guy he seemed to recognize and then across the rest of the cars in the lot. The way he watched anything that moved reminded her just how out in the open they were in the parking lot.

The jerk with what she recognized as his phone in his hand caught up to them. "Sheriff O'Connor."

"Mike."

"Sir, do you care to comment on your sister's kidnapping and the recent crime wave in Katy Gulch?"

Colton stopped dead in his tracks. He turned to face the guy named Mike, who Makena assumed was a reporter. "That story has been dead for decades, Mike. What's wrong? Slow news week?"

"Sir, I—I—I…"

"I accept your apology, Mike. Now, if you don't mind, I have business to attend to in my office." Colton turned his back on the reporter and started walking toward the building. He said out the side of his mouth, "But if there are any new leads, you'll be the first to know."

Considering Colton's stiff demeanor, it was clear to Makena the story about his sister's kidnapping was off-limits.

Mike stood there, looking dumbfounded.

Makena heard what was said, and she couldn't help but think about the fact that Colton's father had just died. She wondered if the two incidents were connected in some way. That had to be unlikely, given that Colton himself had said his sister's kidnapping was decades old. Colton had also mentioned a kidnapping attempt on his newly minted sister-in-law's adopted daughter and then there was his father's death. A family like the O'Connors could be a target for any twisted individual who wanted to make a buck. A shudder raced through her. She could only imagine based on her experience of living in fear for the months on end what it must be like living on guard at all times.

Colton had mentioned that a couple of his brothers had gone on to become US marshals. He was sheriff. She had to wonder if their choices to go into law enforcement had anything to do with a need to protect each other and keep their family safe.

The minute Colton walked through the front door and into the lobby, a woman who seemed to be in her

late sixties popped up from her desk, set the phone
call she'd been on down, and ran over to give Colton
a warm hug. The moment was sweet and the action
seemed to come from a genuine place.

"Thank heavens you're okay." The woman had to be
Gert, Makena guessed from the sound of her voice. It
also made sense that she would be at Colton's office.

When Gert finally released him from the hug, he
introduced her to Makena.

"I'm pleased as punch to meet you. I'm sorry for
the day you've had. Can I get you anything? Coffee?
Water?"

"Coffee sounds great. Just point me in a direction
and I can get my own cup." Makena echoed Gert's sen-
timents. Now that she'd had a minute to process the
fact that her ex had tried to blow her to smithereens,
she needed a strong cup of coffee.

"Don't be silly. I'd be happy to get you a cup. I just
put on a fresh pot."

"If you're offering, I'll take a cup of that coffee, too."
He placed his hand on the small of Makena's back and
led her through a glass door that he had to scan his
badge to enter. He hooked a right in what looked to be
a U-shaped building and then led her halfway down
the hall. His office was on the right.

"Make yourself comfortable," Colton said. "Is there
anything else you'd like besides coffee?"

"No, thank you." The shock of the day's events was
starting to wear off. The annoying ringing noise was
a constant companion as she moved to the leather sofa
and then took a seat.

Colton moved behind his desk. "Professional courtesy dictates that I make a call to Mr. Myers's chief before questioning him."

"Won't that give River a heads-up that you want to speak to him?" The thought of being in the same room again with her ex fired more of that anger through her veins. It needed to be a courtroom, the next time. And he needed to be going to jail for a very long time. One way or another, she would find a way for justice to be served and keep him from harming other innocent people. But the River she knew wouldn't exactly lie down and take what was coming his way. Without a doubt, he'd deny any involvement.

The explosion and fire would have made certain there were no fingerprints. When she really thought about the crime, it was an easy way on his part to get away with murder. No one would know her in Katy Gulch. That meant she would most likely have ended up a Jane Doe. She'd quit her job and disappeared. No one would miss her.

She could vanish and there was no one to notice. How sad had her life become since marrying him, since her mother's drawn-out illness, that Makena could die at the hands of her ex and no one would know?

The only person she knew in Katy Gulch was Colton. He would have had no reason to suspect a blast from the past. He wouldn't have been looking for her. And if she'd been badly burned, which seemed like the plan, her face would have been unrecognizable anyway. It had been a near-perfect setup.

She flexed and released her fingers a couple of times to work out some of the tension. She rolled her shoulders back and took in a couple of deep breaths. She

couldn't imagine trying to hurt someone she supposedly cared about.

Colton's voice broke through her heavy thoughts.
She realized he was on a call.

"Yes, sir. My name is Sheriff Colton O'Connor and
I need to speak with Chief Shelton. This is a professional courtesy call and I need to speak to him about
one of his officers." Colton was silent for a few beats.
And then came, "Thank you, sir."

A few more beats of silence, and then someone
must've picked up on the other line. Gert walked in
about that same moment with two mugs of coffee in
her hands. She set the first one down on Colton's desk,
which was the closest to her. The other one she brought
over to Makena, who accepted the offering and thanked
Colton's secretary for her kindness.

Gert produced a couple packets of sugar and a pack
of creamer from her pocket and set them down on the
coffee table along with a stir stick. Gert made eye contact and nodded. The sincerity, warmth and compassion
in her gaze settled over Makena. It was easy to see the
woman had a heart of gold. She disappeared out of the
room after Makena mouthed a thank-you.

"As I said before, this is a professional courtesy call
to let you know that the name of one of your police officers came up in the course of an investigation today."
Colton was silent for a moment. "Yes, sir. The officer's
name is River Myers. A few more seconds of silence
followed. "Is that right?" A longer pause. This time the
silence dragged on. Colton glanced at her, caught her
eye and then nodded. She could tell there was a storm
brewing behind his cobalt eyes.

After Colton explained to the Dallas police chief

that he wanted to speak to River in connection with an attempted murder case, there was even more silence.

Colton ended the call by thanking the chief for his time and by promising that he would keep him abreast of his investigation.

"What did he say?" She waited for Colton to hang up before asking the question.

"He wished me luck with my investigation. He said his office was fully prepared to cooperate. And then he informed me that River Myers is on administrative leave pending an investigation."

Makena gasped as all kinds of horrible thoughts crossed her mind. "Did he say what River was being investigated for?"

Colton's earlier words that she needed to speak up so she could prevent anyone else from getting hurt slammed into her. Had River done something to another woman he was in a relationship with?

"The chief said he really can't share a lot of details for an ongoing investigation, but in the spirit of reciprocity, he said an internal affairs division investigation was underway on two counts of police brutality and one count of extortion."

Relief washed over Makena that River wasn't already being looked at for murder. He was, now. "What does being placed on administrative leave mean?"

"It's basically where he would be required to hand in his department-issued weapons along with his badge until the investigation is over and it's decided whether or not any criminal charges would be filed." Colton took a sip of coffee.

Makena brought her hand up to her mouth. If River had still been on the job, they would know exactly where to find him. "Does this mean what I think? That he's out there somewhere? Going rogue?"

"That is a distinct possibility." Colton's grip on his coffee mug caused his knuckles to go white. With his free hand, he drummed his fingers on his desk. "I need to issue a BOLO with his name and description. I don't want my deputies being caught unawares if they happen to run into him personally or on a traffic stop."

Colton mentioned a couple of other things before jumping into action. Not five minutes later, he'd had Gert issue the BOLO, he'd started the report on the explosion, and he'd nearly polished off his second cup of coffee. Once he'd taken care of those preliminary details, he looked at her. "My next call needs to be to my mother. But first, I want to know where you stand. Will you stay with me until the investigation runs its course?"

The look on his face suggested he expected an argument. She had none.

"I appreciate the offer. You already know my concerns about bringing danger to your doorstep. And then there's your boys to consider."

"Don't worry about my sons. For the time being, they'll be safe at the ranch. I know my mom will pull through and yet she's the one I worry about the most. I have two new sisters-in-law I forgot about before, who I can ask to pitch in. The ranch has a lot of security in place already, and I don't mind adding to it. In fact, it might not be a bad idea for me to take you to my home there. Times will come up when I have to leave for the investigation or for work, and I want to know that you're safe."

Makena could stay on the ranch safely with all the

extra security. She could not live with bringing danger around Colton and his children. "I'll stay with you at your apartment or I'll wait here at your office if you need to investigate someone without me there. But I won't go to the ranch. It's too dangerous for the people."

Colton rubbed the scruff on his chin. He took a sip of coffee. "That's fair."

She hoped so, because it was the only offer on the table. If she had to sit in the office for an entire day, she would. There was no way in hell she was going to risk his family. Granted, River wanted her. But she couldn't be certain that he wouldn't use one of them to draw her out. It was a gamble she had no intention of taking.

Makena rolled up her sleeves and drained her cup. She set the mug down on the coffee table. She placed her flat palms on her thighs and looked at Colton.

"What's next?"

"You tell me everything you can think of about your ex. His favorite restaurant. Whether or not he's a fisherman and has a fishing lease. Is he a hunter? Does he have a hunting license? Who are his friends? And then, I go track him down."

"Hold on there. I'm the best person to help find him. I want to go to Dallas with you."

"Not a chance. The agreement we just made was that you would stay here while I investigate. It's either here or my apartment. I need to know that I can trust you to do what you say you're going to do."

"I wouldn't lie to you. I just thought it would be easier to track him down with me involved."

"If you're his target and he sees you, it could be game over."

"I'm not arguing. However, trying to blow me to pieces on a timer once I thought I was safely inside an RV doesn't exactly make me feel like he wants to be connected to my murder in any way. In fact, he seems to be taking great pains to kill me without leaving any trail back to him."

"True enough. The explosion was most likely meant to cover his tracks. We also have to broaden the scope. You saw his friends…or…acquaintances might be a better word. You said yourself they were speaking in hushed tones. We can go after them, too. They might be acting on his behalf or they might be on their own."

"Oh, I doubt anyone would do that. Not with River's temper. He never struck me as the type to step aside."

"We have to keep unbiased eyes on the case and we have to follow the evidence. Right now, you saw two people from your past in town three days ago and that spawned you to disappear into the RV."

"Allegedly saw. I mean, they were far away and I can't be one hundred percent certain it was them."

"Okay. What are the chances the two guys you saw, even at a distance, weren't the men you saw in your garage?" He was playing devil's advocate. She could see that. Looking at the case from every angle probably made him a good investigator.

It was impossible for Makena not to lead with emotions in this case. For one, the explosion was targeted at her. And for another, River's threats echoed in her mind. To her thinking, he was delivering on threats he'd made six months ago.

Chapter Ten

Colton spent the next hour getting to know River
Myers. He then made a quick call to his mother, and
she agreed the twins staying on with her would be for
the best, at least for a couple of days.

He knew better than anyone that investigations often
took far longer than that, but he hoped for a break in
this one. If Makena's ex was determined to erase her
and she was constantly at Colton's side, he would have
to get through Colton first. Makena had made a list of
River's known hangouts. Colton had handed the list
over to Gert, who'd meticulously called each one to
ask when the last time River had been in.

So far, no one had seen or heard from River for the
past month. Of course, the couple of places that were
known cop hangouts most likely wouldn't admit to
seeing him if he was standing in front of their faces.

Other than that, he frequented a popular Tex-Mex
restaurant and a couple of taco chains. None of the
managers or employees admitted to seeing the man in
the past few weeks if not a month.

The timing of River sticking to himself coincided
with when he was put on leave according to the chief.
It was odd, since the guy would've had more free time

on his hands. Usually, that meant being seen in his favorite haunts more often. In River's case, he seemed to be hunkering down.

A call to one of his neighbors revealed that it didn't seem like he'd been home, either. There were no lights left on in the evenings, and the neighbor hadn't seen his truck in a couple of weeks.

"What are the chances he has a new girlfriend?" Colton asked Makena.

She looked up from her notebook, where she'd been trying to recall and write down all the places he could've possibly gone to.

"Anything is possible. Right?" She tapped her pencil on the pad. "I mean, he's not really the type to be alone and he was served with divorce papers not long after I disappeared. I worked through my lawyer to finish up the paperwork."

"If River is spending all his time at a new girlfriend's house, it might be harder to track him down." His personal phone number had changed. Colton had his guess as to why that might have happened.

As word spread about the morning's incident, Colton's phone started ringing off the hook. Everyone in the community wanted to pitch in and help find the person responsible for blowing up Mrs. Dillon's RV. Colton couldn't give any more details than that and it was impossible to keep this story completely quiet considering how much neighbors watched out for each other in Katy Gulch.

After hours of receiving and making phone calls, Colton realized it was past dinnertime. Not a minute later, Gert knocked on the office door. It was a courtesy knock because Colton had a long-standing open-door policy.

"It might be time to take a break," Gert said. They both knew she would go home and continue working on the case, but it was her signal she was heading out.

"Let me know if you get any leads or figure out anything that I've missed," Colton said. He stretched out his arms and yawned, realizing he'd been sitting in the same position for hours. It was no wonder his back was stiff. His ears were still ringing from the explosion this morning but there was improvement there, too.

"You know I will, sir." Gert waved to Makena before exiting the room. Before she got more than a few steps down the hall she shouted back at them. "I'll lock the front door."

Colton turned to Makena. "What do you think about taking this back to my apartment? We should probably get up and get our blood moving. And then there's dinner. You must be starved by now."

"That's probably a good idea. I'm not starving, but I could eat. The bags of nuts and trail mix that Gert has been bringing me have tided me over."

"I'll just close up a couple of files and log out and then we can go." Colton tried not to notice when Makena stood up and stretched just how long her legs were. She had just the right amount of soft curves, and all he could think about was running his hand along those gorgeous lines…

He forced his gaze away from her hips—a place he had no business thinking about. He straightened up his desk and then closed out of the files on his desktop. His laptop had access to the same system, and he could get just as much done at home. He figured Makena would be more comfortable there anyway.

It also occurred to him that she'd lost everything she owned except the clothes on her back. He stood up and pushed his chair in. He gripped the back of his chair with both hands. "We can stop off anywhere you need on the way to my house. I'm sure you want a change of clothes and something to sleep in."

"I appreciate the offer, but pretty much everything I own was blown up. I don't have any ID or credit cards with me." He realized that she wouldn't want to carry ID in case she got picked up. Now that he knew her ex was a cop, he understood why she'd gone to the lengths she had to keep her identity a secret.

"How about I take care of it for you? It really wouldn't be any trouble—"

"You're already doing so much for me, Colton. It's too much to ask. I'll be fine with what I have."

"I promise it isn't. We don't have to do anything fancy. We can stop off at one of those big-box stores. There's one on the way home. We can let you pick up a few supplies. It would be a loan. Just until you get back on your feet. I have a feeling once we lock this jerk away for good, you'll get back on your feet in no time. For old times' sake, I'd like to be the one to give you a temporary hand up."

Colton hoped he'd put that in a way that didn't offend her. He wasn't trying to give her a handout. All he wanted was to give her a few comfort supplies while they located the bastard who'd tried to kill her.

She raked her top teeth over her bottom lip, a sure sign she was considering his offer. Then again, with her back against the wall, she might not feel like she had any options.

"I promise it's no trouble, and if you don't want to take the stuff with you, you could always leave it at my place. One of my new sisters-in-law will probably fit the same clothes. Renee looks to be about your size, if leaving them would make you feel better. It would certainly make me feel better to be able to help you out. Besides, you're probably the only reason I passed biology lab."

That really made her laugh. "I was terrible at biology lab. If you hadn't helped me, I would've failed and I'm pretty certain I dragged your grade down."

"I might have been better at the actual work than you were, but you were the only reason I kept going to class."

Her smile practically lit up the room. It was nice to make her smile for a change after all she'd been through. She deserved so much better.

"I tell you what. I'll let you buy me some new clothes. But once this is over, maybe I can stick around a few days and watch the boys for you as a way to pay you back. I'm not sure I'm any good with kids that age and they might not even like me, but I'm willing to try. And who knows, we might actually have some fun. It would make me feel so much better if I can do something nice for you."

"Deal." He wouldn't look a gift horse in the mouth. This was something nice, and she made a good point. He was halting his nanny search so he could throw himself completely into this investigation. As much as the process would take time, he was also keenly aware that the colder the trail, the colder the leads. His best bet at nailing the bastard would come in a window of opportunity he had in the next seventy-two hours. If the investigation dragged on longer than that, the apprehension rate would drop drastically.

Unless there was another attempt. Colton didn't even want to consider that option.

"Do you want to take a minute to order a few things on the laptop? We can put a rush on the order, and they'll have it ready by the time we swing through. I just need to turn off a few lights and double-check the break room." He handed his laptop over.

"Sure." She sat down in one of the leather club chairs across from his desk and studied the screen as he headed down the hallway.

Turning off the lights had been an excuse to give her a few minutes alone to order. In reality, he didn't like the idea of her going out in public where she'd be exposed. A skilled rifleman could take her out from the top of a building or beside a vehicle.

And then there was the gossip mill to consider. Most of the time, he didn't mind it. For the most part, people were trying to be helpful by sharing information. Being seen with him would be news. Like it or not, the O'Connors were in the public eye and people seemed to enjoy discussing the details of his family's private lives.

He took his time checking rooms before returning. The laptop was closed. She stood up the minute she heard him come in the room. "Ready?"

"All set," she said, handing over the device. He tucked it under one arm before placing his hand on the small of her back and leading her out the rear of the building. He guided her down the hall and outside, deciding it would be safer to take his personal vehicle home.

His pickup truck was parked out back.

"I don't want to run into Mike or anyone else sniffing around for a story." It was true. But he also didn't want to risk going out the same way he'd come in, just in case River or one of his cohorts was watching. That part Colton decided to keep to himself.

Colton finally exhaled the breath he'd been holding when they were safely inside his truck and on the road. It was past seven o'clock, and it wouldn't be dark for another hour and a half this time of year.

Being out in the daylight made him feel exposed. He kept his guard up, searching the face of every driver as he passed them. He stopped off at the box store and pulled into the pickup lane. A quick text later, an employee came running out to the designated curbside area.

Colton thanked the guy and handed him a five-dollar bill. The rest of the ride to his apartment took all of ten minutes. He pulled up to the garage and punched in the security code before zipping through the opened gate.

From a security standpoint, the place wouldn't be that difficult to breech on foot. But the gate kept other drivers from coming in and closed quickly enough after he pulled through that it would be impossible to backdraft him.

Colton had spent part of the drive thinking through something that had been bugging him since he'd gotten off the phone with the DPD chief. If River was being investigated for serious charges like police brutality and extortion, there had to be a reasonable complainant involved. Considering there were several charges against him, he wondered what kind of huddle Makena could've walked into that night, when she'd interrupted River and the other two men.

It was obviously a meeting of some kind. The fact that River had ushered her away so fast meant that he was trying to protect his group, or her. Possibly both. In his twisted mind, he probably believed that he loved his wife.

Abusers usually thought they cared for their partners. Forget that their version of caring was tied up with control and abuse, sometimes physical. When they realized that, they seemed to have some sense of remorse. For others, it was just a way of life.

Thinking back, Colton wondered if Makena's life would've turned out differently if he'd somehow plucked up the courage to ask her out.

But then, his own life might've turned out differently, too. Having the twins was one of the best things that had ever happened to him. He wouldn't trade his boys for the world. And even though his wife had died, he wouldn't trade the years of friendship they'd had, either.

Since regret was about as productive as stalking an ant to find cheese, he didn't go there often. Life happened. He'd lost Rebecca. He'd gained two boys out of their relationship.

Makena's life might not have turned out differently even if they had dated. There was no way to go back and find out. And even if they could…change one thing and the ripple effect could be far-reaching.

Returning his focus to the case, he thought about Red and Mustache Man. The what-if questions started popping into his mind.

What if Red and Mustache had been working to shake someone down? Considering one of the charges against River was extortion, it was a definite possibility.

If Mustache and Red had come to Katy Gulch, were they sticking around? Were they acting alone? Were they after her because they thought she'd heard something in her garage that night?

Alarm bells sounded at the thought. He felt like he was onto something there.

This could've been an attempt to…what?

Hold on. Colton had it. If River had gone into hiding and the guys blew up Makena, would that be enough to bring him out?

COLTON THREW A PIZZA in the oven while Makena mixed together a salad from contents she'd found in the fridge. Working in the kitchen with her was a nice change to a frozen dinner in front of his laptop after the boys were in bed.

They'd just sat down at the island to eat when his cell phone buzzed. He glanced at the screen and saw Gert's name. Makena was sitting next to him, so he tilted the screen in her direction before taking the call. He held the phone to his ear.

"This is Colton. I'm going to put you on speaker. Is that okay?" There was some information that was sensitive enough that Makena shouldn't hear.

"Fine by me, sir."

Colton put the call on speaker and set it in between him and Makena on the island. "Okay. Makena and I are listening."

"Sir, Deputy Fletcher was canvassing in Birchwood

and stopped off at a motel along the highway. He got a hit." Her voice practically vibrated with excitement. Gert loved the investigation process. "The clerk told Deputy Fletcher a man matching River Myers's description had been staying at her motel for the past four days. The clerk's name is Gloria Beecham and this place is a rent-by-the-hour type, if you know what I mean. She said he was a cash customer. Given the amount of time he'd been there and the fact that he kept the Do Not Disturb sign on the door the whole time, housekeeping was freaked out by the guy."

Colton wasn't surprised. Hotels and motels had tightened up their processes to ensure every room was checked.

"Housekeeping alerted the clerk to the fact. She made a call to let him know that housekeeping had to check his room every twenty-four hours by law. She said that when they came to clean, he would stand in the corner of the room with the door open and his arms crossed over his chest."

"Odd behavior," Colton noted.

"It sure is." She made a tsk noise. "They never did find anything suspicious, and honestly, admitted to getting in and out of there just as fast as they could."

"And this mystery man matched River's description?" he asked.

"Yes, sir."

"He was staying in the room alone?" This could be a solid lead. Colton looked at Makena, who was on the edge of her seat.

"Yes, sir."

"Did they say whether anyone else ever came in or out of the room?"

"No. No one to her knowledge. She started keeping an eye on the room by the camera mounted outside. This place has no interior spaces. It's the kind of place where you park right in front of your door and use a key to go straight inside. So there are cameras along the exterior overhangs. She said it was something the owner had insisted on installing over a year ago. The funny thing is, he struck her as odd because his face was always pointed the opposite direction of the nearest camera."

"He was smart enough to realize that cameras might be in use."

"So much so, in fact, he wore a ball cap most of the time. He kept his chin tucked to his chest as he walked in and out of the building."

"Did they, by chance, get a make and model on his vehicle?" Colton asked.

"No, sir. They did not. He never parked close enough to the door for the cameras to pick up his vehicle."

Colton wished there were parking lot cameras. Even a grainy picture would give him some idea of the kind of vehicle River was driving, if that was in fact him. The coincidence was almost too uncanny.

The possibility the clerk could've picked up on any details of the bombing case from the media was nil. He'd kept a very tight rein on the details of the morning's event on purpose. He'd released a statement that said there had been an incident involving an RV and a homemade explosive device, and there'd been no casualties or injuries. Technically, that part was true. The scratch on his arm would be fine and his hearing would return to normal in a few days. The ringing was already easing.

Evidence was mounting against River.

"And this witness was certain, without a shadow of a doubt, that the man at the motel matched the BOLO?"

"Not one hundred percent," Gert admitted. "She said she wouldn't exactly bet her life on it, but it was probably him."

Colton cursed under his breath. He needed a witness who would testify they were certain it was River, not someone who *thought* it might be him.

"This is something. At least we have someone who can most likely place him in town or at least near town. Birchwood is a half-hour drive from here."

"That's right, sir."

"Is he still there, by chance?" He probably should've asked this already, except that Gert would've known to lead with it.

"That's a negative sir." Gert's frustration came through the line in her sigh. "You're going to love this one. He checked out first thing this morning, at around six thirty."

Colton had figured as much, even though he'd hoped for a miracle. River, or anyone in law enforcement, would be smart enough to stay on the move. "You mentioned the place was basically a cash-and-carry operation. Is that right?"

"Yes, sir. And I confirmed that the person who'd stayed in room 11 paid with cash."

"Good work, Gert." Colton pressed his lips together to keep from swearing.

Makena issued a sharp sigh. "So close."

"Thanks for the information, Gert. It gives us confirmation that we're on the right track."

"My pleasure, sir. And you know me. Once I'm on a trail, I stick with it."

"I've never been sure who was the better investigator between the two of us. I appreciate all your efforts." He knew it made Gert's chest swell with pride to hear those words. He meant them, too. She was a formidable investigator and she'd proven to be invaluable in many cases.

Colton thanked her again before ending the call.

"I knew it was only a matter of time before he caught up to me." Makena's voice was a study in calm as she stabbed her fork into her salad. Almost too calm. And yet, Colton figured she was much like the surface of the river. Calm on top with a storm raging below the surface.

If River checked out at six o'clock this morning, he could've set the bomb at the RV. He'd had a specific detonation in mind. It made sense to Colton that he'd wanted Makena to be stepping on the platform as she headed inside the RV to blow her up. Otherwise, if she stepped on the platform to go outside, then the bomb could've been a warning. It was possible, maybe unlikely, the ordeal was meant to be a scare tactic.

Without knowing much about River, it was difficult to ascertain which. But what would he have to gain by scaring her months later?

River had had some time on his hands recently to stew on his situation. It was clear the guy had a temper. He'd used that on Makena during their marriage. And yet a hothead didn't tend to be as calculating. That type was usually more spontaneous.

In Colton's years of investigating domestic violence cases, of which there'd been sadly too many, it was generally a crime of passion that led to murder. A spouse walked in on another spouse having an affair. The unsuspecting spouse got caught up in the moment, grabbed a weapon and committed murder.

Makena had not had an affair in this case. She'd left. That was a betrayal someone like River wouldn't take lightly.

Chapter Eleven

Makena pushed around a piece of lettuce on her plate. The fact that River had been in town at the very least on the morning someone had attempted to take her life sat heavy on her chest. It wouldn't do any good to look back and question how on earth she'd ever trusted him in the first place.

It was time to move forward. And then something dawned on her. "Did I hear right? Did Gert say River checked into that hotel four nights ago?"

"That's the same thing I heard. Gert will write it all up in a report, but yeah, that's what I heard." Colton rocked his head. He pushed the phone away from their plates.

"So River shows up four days ago. It's now been four days since I saw Red and Mustache Man." A picture was taking shape, but it was still too fuzzy to make out all the details.

"So these three have met in your garage and now they are in town at the same time without staying in the same room. We don't know if they rented a room next door." Colton got up, found a notepad and pen and then reclaimed his seat. He scratched out a note for them to check with the early-morning-shift clerk to see if anyone matching the description of Red or Mustache had checked in or been seen coming into or out of River's room.

"Gert said River had no visitors," she corrected, distinctly remembering Gert's words.

"True." He scratched out the last part. "Which didn't mean they didn't meet up somewhere."

She was already thinking the same thing.

"Maybe they thought I overhead them and that's why I left my husband. Maybe in their twisted-up minds they think I know something, which meant the meeting in the garage could've been some kind of planning meeting."

Colton was already nodding his head. "It makes sense. When we look at murder or an attempted murder case, we're always looking for the motive. In your case, one could make the argument that River was still jealous months after you left and that it took him that long to hunt you down. That would make sense. It's a story that, unfortunately, has been told before. The twist in this case is Mustache and Red. If River was here because of a jealousy that he couldn't let go of or because he didn't want you to ever be with anyone else, which is another motive in domestic cases, there wouldn't have been anyone else with him."

"That's exactly my thinking. So if I did walk in on a meeting that day and they think I know something, which I assure you I don't no matter how much I wish I did, they're willing to kill me to make sure I'm silenced. River has already gotten in trouble with his department for extortion. At least, he's under investigation for it." They were finally on a path that made some sense to her. Granted, it was still twisted and unfair, and she didn't like anything about it, period, but it made sense. "Okay, what do we do next?"

"Tonight? We eat. We try to set the case aside at least for a little while. Overly focusing on something and overthinking it only creates more questions. Tomorrow, six a.m., we pay a visit to Gloria Beecham and see if she remembers seeing Red or Mustache anywhere in the area. If we can link those three up, it's a story that makes sense."

Colton was holding something back.

"What is it?"

"There's another story that says all three of them are in town and in a race to see who gets to you first."

Makena shuddered at the thought. It was a theory that couldn't be ignored. It would still take a while to wrap her thoughts around the fact that anyone would want her dead, let alone three people. But it was possible each person was acting on his own, trying to be the one to get to her first to see what she knew and if she had evidence against any one of them.

"Think you can eat something?" Colton motioned toward her plate. "It's important to keep up your strength."

"I can try." She surprised herself by finishing the plate a few minutes later. Colton was right about one thing—overthinking the case would most likely drive her insane.

When the plates were empty, she picked up hers and headed toward the sink. She stopped midway. "I can clean yours while I'm up." At least the ringing noise in her ears was substantially better if not her left hip. The bruise was screaming at her, making its presence known. Colton was right. All she wanted was to stand under a warm shower and to curl up on the couch and watch TV to take her mind off the situation.

Colton was on his feet in the next second, plate in hand. He was such a contrast to River, who, in all the years she spent with him, basically set a plate down wherever he was and got up and walked away without a thought about how it got cleaned and ended up back in the cabinet the next day. He'd blamed his disinclination to do the house chores on being tired after working the deep night shift. The truth was that he thrived on that schedule. And the other truth was that he was lazy.

"It's not that hard for me to rinse off a second dish and put it in the dishwasher."

Colton set his dish down next to the sink. "For the last year, I've done everything for myself. Well, for myself and two little ones. I'm not trying to be annoying by doing everything myself, but I can see how that might get on someone's nerves. Especially someone who is strong and independent, and also used to doing things for herself. The truth is, being in the kitchen together making dinner tonight, even though it was literally nothing but pizza and salad, was probably my favorite time in this kitchen since I moved in."

Well, damn. Colton sure had a way with words. His had just touched her heart in the best possible way and sent warmth rocketing through her. She stopped what she was doing, turned off the spigot and leaned into him.

"It's been a pretty crazy twenty-four hours since we literally ran into each other, but it's really good to see you again, Colton."

It was so easy in that moment to turn slightly until her body was flush with his and tilt her face toward him. She pushed up on her tiptoes and pressed a kiss to his soft, thick lips. Being around Colton again was the easiest thing despite the electricity constantly pinging between them. Instead of fighting it…she was so very tired of fighting…she leaned into it.

Colton took a deep breath. And then he brought his hands up to cup her face. He ran his thumb along her jawline and then her chin as he trailed his lips in a line down her neck. He feathered a trail of hot kisses down her neck and across her shoulder. She placed the flat of her palms against his solid-walled chest, letting her fingers roam.

She smoothed her hands toward his shoulders and then up his neck, letting her fingers get lost in that thick mane of his as he deepened the kiss.

There was so much fire and energy and passion in the kiss. Her breath quickened and her pulse raced. Kissing Colton was better than she'd imagined it could be. No man had ever kissed her so thoroughly or made her need from a place so deep inside her.

He splayed one of his hands across the small of her back and pressed her body against his. Then his hands dropped, and she lifted her legs up and with help wrapped them around his midsection. He dropped his head to the crook of her neck.

Colton held onto her for a long minute in that position before he released a slow, guttural groan and found her lips again.

He fit perfectly and all she wanted to do was get lost with him.

THE ATTRACTION THAT had been simmering between Colton and Makena ignited into a full-blown blaze.

He wanted nothing more than to strip down and bury himself deep inside her.

Her fingernails dug into the flesh of his shoulders. Considering her injury, this was about as far as he could let things go between them. There was another reason. A more obvious one. He knew without a doubt that taking their relationship to the next level would be a game changer for him, and he hoped it would be for her, too.

But she had trust issues and he still hadn't gotten over the loss of his best friend. Besides, as much as Makena fit him in every possible way, he had zero time to commit to a new relationship. He had the boys to think about and the fact that they might not be comfortable with him moving a stranger into the house. Somewhere in the back of his mind, his brain tried to convince him these were excuses. Maybe they were.

But if he was ready, he doubted his mind would try to come up with reasons they shouldn't be together. The biggest of which was the fact that she hadn't gotten over the experience with her ex.

Colton had seen that fear in her eyes one too many times. Granted, her anxiety had never been aimed at him and he would never do anything knowingly to hurt her. He wouldn't have to. His badge and gun might prove to be a problem for her.

Plus, she'd changed her life in every sense of the word. She needed to reemerge and find a footing in her new life.

Makena moaned against his lips, and it was about the sexiest damn thing he'd ever heard. Let this go on too much longer and no cold shower in the world would be able to tame the blaze. Because he was just getting started.

He dropped his hands from her face, running his finger down to the base of her neck. He lowered his hand to her full breast and then ran his thumb along her nipple. It beaded under his touch and sent rockets of awareness through his body. Every single one of his muscles cried out for the sweet release only she could give. His need for Makena caused a physical ache.

Sleeping together at this point would only complicate the relationship. She was beginning to open up to him more and more. He sensed she was beginning to lean on him, and he liked the fact her trust in him was growing.

She needed to be sure how he felt about her before taking this to the next level. And since he was just now trying to figure that out himself, he pulled back and touched his forehead to hers. Their breathing was raspy. A smile formed on his lips.

Having twin sons had sure made one helluva grown-up out of him. Not that he'd taken sex lightly in the past. He preferred serial dating before he married Rebecca, and always made certain that his partners knew one hundred percent that the relationship would be based on mutual physical attraction. The likelihood anything emotional or permanent would come out of it was off the table.

"What is it, Colton? What's wrong? Did I do something?"

"You? Not a chance. It's me. And before you think I'm giving you the whole 'it's not you, it's me' speech, it really is me. I think whatever we have brewing between us could turn out to be something special. But the timing is off. I think we both realize that." He almost couldn't believe those words had just come out of his mouth. They were true. They needed to be said. But, damn.

He felt the need to explain further, because he didn't want her to be embarrassed or have any regrets. "For the record, I think that was probably up there with the best kisses of my life."

He could feel her smiling.

"Okay, I lied. That was the best kiss of my life. And it gets me in trouble because I don't want to stop there. I want more. And when I say more, I don't just mean physical." He could almost hear the wheels spinning in her brain and could sense she was about to do some major backpedaling.

"I hear what you're saying, Colton. I feel whatever this is happening between us, too. I don't exactly have anything to give right now." Ouch. Those words hurt more than he was expecting them to.

"You don't have to explain any of that to me. I feel the same."

"I'm sorry. This is the second time I've put you in this position. I promise not to do it again." She pulled back and put her hands up in the surrender position, palms out.

"Well, that's disappointing to hear." Colton laughed, a rumble from deep in his chest rolling up and out.

She looked at him with those clear blue eyes, so honest and still glittering with desire. The way his heart reacted, he thought he might've made a huge mistake in pulling back. Logic said that he had done the right thing in preparing her. His life didn't have room for anyone else, and she was just about to figure out what her new life was going to be. She didn't need him inserting himself right in the middle and possibly confusing her.

A sneaky little voice in the back of his mind said his defense mechanisms were kicking into high gear. He hushed that because it was time to think about something else.

"We could watch a movie to take our minds off things. We could talk." Normally, that last option would've felt like pulling teeth with no Novocain. But he actually liked talking to Makena. Go figure.

"I think what I would like more than anything is to curl up on the sofa with you and turn the fireplace on low. And maybe have something warm to drink. Maybe something without caffeine."

"Sounds like a plan. As far as the hot beverage without caffeine, I'm kind of at a loss on that one."

It was her turn to laugh. She reached up and grabbed a fistful of his shirt and tugged him toward her. She stopped him just before their lips met. "Thank you, Colton. You've brought alive parts of me that I honestly didn't know existed anymore. You've shown me what a strong, independent man can be."

This time she didn't push forward and press a kiss to his lips, and disappointment nearly swallowed him.

He smiled at her compliment and squeezed her hand, needing to refocus before he headed down that emotional path again.

"Good luck if you want something warm in this house that doesn't have caffeine."

"If you have water, a stove and maybe a lemon or honey, I can get by just fine."

"I definitely have honey. It's in the cupboard. Gert

makes a point of bringing some back for everyone in the office when she visits honeybee farms. She's made a goal to visit every one in the state before the end of the year. I should have a few bottles in there to choose from. As far as lemons go, I actually might have a few of those in the bin inside the fridge. I'll just make a call and check on my boys. I really want to hear their voices before they go to sleep. So if you'll excuse me, I'll take the call in the other room while you make up your warm batch of honey-lemon water."

His smile was genuine, and when she beamed back at him his heart squeezed. His traitorous heart would have to get on board with the whole "he needed to slow the train down" plan. It was on a track of its own, running full steam ahead.

Makena pushed him back a little bit in a playful motion. He hesitated for just a second, holding her gaze just a little too long, and his heart detonated when he turned to walk away. He exhaled a sigh and grabbed his phone off the granite island before heading into the bedroom.

He gave himself a few moments to shake off the haze in his mind from kissing Makena. He was still in a little bit of shock that one kiss could ignite that level of passion in him. He chalked it up to going too long without sex. That had to be the reason. He hadn't felt a flame burning like that in far too long.

After a few more deep breaths, he was at a ready point to hear his sons' little babbling voices. He pulled up his mother's contact and let his thumb hover over her number.

He dropped his thumb onto the screen and put the phone to his ear. It took a couple of rings for his mother to pick up. When she did, he could hear the sounds of his little angels in the background, laughing. He'd recognize those voices anywhere.

"Hi, son. I was just drying off the boys after their baths. How are you doing?" she asked. He listened for any signs of distress in her voice that meant taking care of the boys was too much for her right now.

"All is well here. We're moving forward with the investigation and I'll be up and out early tomorrow morning to go interview a potential witness. Making progress." Hearing his sons' laughter in the background warmed his heart.

"Colton, what's really wrong?" His mom could read him and his brothers better than a psychic.

"The case. I know the intended target from college. We go way back and she's a good person. She definitely doesn't deserve what's being handed to her." It would do no good to lie to his mother. She'd be able to hear it in his tone and he wouldn't feel good about it anyway. He'd been honest with her since seventh grade, after he'd hidden his phone in his room so he could call Rebecca when they were supposed to be asleep.

A young Colton hadn't slept a wink that night. He'd come clean about the deception in the morning and his mother said he'd punished himself enough. She expected him to leave his phone downstairs before he went up to bed just like the others did. Garrett had always sneaked back down to get his, but that was Garrett and beside the point.

Lying had taught Colton that he was an honest person.

Plus, his mother had been around him and his brothers who worked in law enforcement long enough to realize they wouldn't be allowed to divulge details about an ongoing investigation. She wouldn't dig around.

And she wouldn't ask. There were lines families in law enforcement never crossed.

"I'm sorry to hear such a nice-sounding person is having a rough go of it." He could hear more of that innocent laughter come across the line and he figured his mother knew exactly the distraction he needed. "The boys have had a wonderful day. They've been angels with just enough spunk in them for me to know they're O'Connor boys through and through."

"That's good to hear."

"Do you want me to put them on the line? I can put the phone in between them. They're here on the bed. Well, mostly here on the bed. Renee is here helping me and they keep trying to move to get away from the lotion." His mom laughed. It sounded genuine, and there'd been too much of that missing in her life over the past few months. It made him feel a lot less guilty about having the boys stay over with her for a few days. They might be just the distraction she needed.

"I would love it. Put them on." He could hear shuffling noises, which he assumed was her putting the phone down.

Her mouth was away from the receiver when she said, "Hey, boys. Guess who is calling you? It's your Dada."

It warmed his heart the way his family had accepted Silas and Sebastian despite the circumstances of their birth.

"Hey, buddies. I hope you are behaving for your Mimi and Aunt Renee." In truth, there wasn't a whole lot to say to one-year-olds. All he really wanted to hear was the sound of their giggles. Knowing how well they were being cared for and how much his mother loved them. It was kind of Renee to help.

One of the twins shrieked, "Dada!"

The other one got excited and started chanting the same word. Colton didn't care how or why his boys had come into his life. He was a better man for having them. He kept the phone to his ear and just listened.

A few minutes later, his mother came back on the line.

"Well, these two are ready for a little snack before bedtime," she said.

"Sounds good, Mom." He wanted to ask how she was really doing but figured this wasn't the time. Instead, he settled on, "They really love you."

"Well, that's a good thing because I love them more. And I love you." There was a genuine happiness to her tone that made Colton feel good.

They said their goodbyes and ended the call. Colton glanced at the clock. It was after eight. He needed to grab a shower and get some shut eye soon. Four o'clock in the morning would come early and he wanted to be at the motel the minute the clerk started work.

Colton took a quick shower, toweled off and then threw on some sweatpants and a T-shirt. By the time he joined Makena in the other room, she was curled up on the couch. She'd figured out how to flip the switch to turn on the fireplace. He didn't want to dwell on how right it felt to see her sitting there in his home, on his sofa, looking comfortable and relaxed.

If it was just the two of them and she was in a different mental space, letting this relationship play out would be a no-brainer. But he had his children to think about and how the loss of their mother at such a young age would affect their lives. He also had to consider how bringing someone into their lives who could leave again might impact them. He couldn't see himself getting into a temporary relationship or introducing them to someone who might not stick around for the long haul.

"Shower's free. I left a fresh towel out for you and a washcloth. It's folded on the sink," he said, trying to ignore his body's reaction to her. His heart—traitor that it was—started beating faster against his rib cage.

Sitting there, smiling up at him, Makena was pure temptation. A temptation he had to ignore—for his own sanity.

Chapter Twelve

The shower was amazing and quick. Makena couldn't help but think about the case, despite trying to force it from her thoughts. It was impossible for questions not to pop into her mind after the update they'd received from Gert.

It was probably odd to appreciate the fact that she knew River. He had a physical description and a job. She couldn't imagine being targeted by someone without any idea who it could be or why.

Granted, in her case, the why was still a question mark. It could be his jealous nature. Or it could be that he believed she'd overheard something.

At least she wouldn't walk down the street next to the person targeting her without realizing it. Even Red and Mustache were on her radar.

And then there was Colton. She couldn't imagine having a better investigator or a better human being on her side. He'd grown into quite an incredible person, not that she was surprised. His cobalt blue eyes had always been just a little too serious and a little too intense even in college. He saw things most people would never notice. After hearing more about his family, she was starting to get a better understanding of him and what made him tick.

To say her feelings for him were complicated barely scratched the surface. She got dressed and brushed her teeth before venturing into the living room.

Colton sat in front of the fire, studying his laptop. Her heart free-fell at the sight of him looking relaxed and at ease. Butterflies flew in her stomach and she was suddenly transported back to biology lab at the time they had first met. Those feelings were very much alive today and sent rockets of need firing through her.

"Hey, I thought we agreed. No more working on the case tonight." She moved to the kitchen and heated more water. The lemon and honey water had done the trick earlier.

"I was just mapping out our route to the motel tomorrow morning. I wanted to be ready to go so that we're there the moment Gloria Beecham checks in for work."

"That sounds like a plan." The buzzer on the microwave dinged and she poured the warm water into the mug she'd used earlier.

"It's about a half hour's drive, so we should probably get on the road at five thirty at the latest."

"In the morning?" She gripped the mug and added a slice of lemon along with another teaspoon of honey. After stirring the mixture, she made her way back to the sofa, noticing how badly her attempt at humor had missed the mark.

Colton continued to study the screen without looking up. She hoped she hadn't offended him earlier before the showers but the air in the room had definitely shifted. A wall had come up.

Makena pulled her legs up and tucked her feet underneath her bottom. She sat a couple of feet from Colton and angled herself toward him. From this distance, she'd be less likely to reach out and touch him. The feel of his silk-over-steel muscles was too much temptation. It would be so easy to get lost with him.

But then what?

There was no way she wanted to do anything that might drive a wedge between her and Colton. He was her best and only friend right then. She had no plans to cut off her lifeline. An annoying voice in the back of her head called her out on the excuses.

"So, the way I understand it, there's a story behind why everyone in law enforcement got there. What's yours?" She wanted to know why he'd chosen this profession versus taking up ranching.

He chuckled, a low rumble in his chest. "Do you mean more than the fact that I grew up with five brothers, all of whom were close in age?"

"That would challenge anyone's sense of justice," she laughed.

"I think it was always just inside me." He closed the laptop and shifted it off his lap and onto the sofa. Then he turned to face her. "We all used to play Cops and Robbers. Growing up on a ranch, we had plenty of room to roam and enough time to use our imagination. I was always drawn to the cop. For a while, I tried to tell myself that I was a rancher. Don't get me wrong, ranching is in my blood and it's something I think I've always known I'd do at some point. We all pitch in, especially me before the boys came. I think I always knew it was just a matter of time. I want to take my place at the ranch. Later. I'm just not ready.

So in college, when my parents tried to get me to go to the best agricultural school in the state, I rebelled. Our university had a pretty decent business school, and that's how I convinced my parents it was right for me. They weren't really trying to force me into anything so much as trying to guide me based on what they thought I wanted."

"They sound like amazing parents."

"They were…my mom still is," he said.

"I'm guessing by that answer there's no news about who is responsible for your father's death. I'm really sorry about that, Colton. About *all* of it."

"Before I checked the map, I was digging around in the case file. I couldn't find anything else to go on."

"Maybe no one was supposed to find him," she offered.

"It's possible. There are just so many unanswered questions. When I really focus on it, it just about drives me insane."

She could only imagine someone in his shoes, someone who was used to giving answers to others in their darkest moments, would be extremely frustrated not to be able to give those answers to his own family. She figured that between him and his brothers who worked for the US Marshal Service, they wouldn't stop until they found out why their father was killed. Their sister's kidnapping must have influenced their decisions to go into law enforcement in the first place. "How long has it been?"

"A couple of months now. He was digging around in my sister's case."

"You mentioned that she was kidnapped as a baby.

Thirty-plus years is a long time. Wouldn't any leads be cold?"

"Yes. The trail was almost instantly cold and has remained so to this day. We're missing something. That's what keeps me up at night. It's the thing that I don't know yet but know is out there, which gives me nightmares. It's the one piece that, when you find it, will make the whole puzzle click together. That's been missing in my sister's case for decades."

This was the first time she'd ever heard a hint of hopelessness in Colton's voice. Despite knowing just how dangerous this path could be, she reached over and took his hand in hers. He'd done so much for her and she wanted to offer whatever reassurance she could. The electricity vibrating up her arm from their touch was something she could ignore. She needed to ignore it. Because it wasn't going to lead her down a productive path.

She couldn't agree more with Colton about timing.

"I wish there was something I could say or do to help."

"Believe it or not, just being able to talk about it for a change is nice. We never talk about Caroline's case at home. Our mother has a little gathering every year on Caroline's birthday and we have cake. She talks about what little she remembers about her daughter. It isn't much and it feels like Caroline is frozen in time. Always six months old. I've already had more time with my sons than my mother did with my sister. And I can't imagine anything happening to either one of my boys."

"It hardly seems fair," she agreed.

Colton rocked his head and twined their fingers together.

"We better get some sleep if we intend to be out the door by five thirty." He squeezed her fingers in a move that she figured was meant to be reassuring. He got up and turned off the fireplace. From the other room, he grabbed a pillow and some blankets. "For tonight, I'll take the couch."

"I thought we already talked about this." The last thing she wanted to do was steal the man's bed. It was actually a bad idea for her to think about Colton and a bed because a sensual shiver skittered across her skin.

"We did. I said I'd take the couch tonight and you'll take the bed. If I have to, I'll walk over there, pick you up and carry you to bed." At least there was a hint of lightness and playfulness in his tone now that had been missing earlier. There was also something else…something raspy in his voice when he'd mentioned his bed. And since she knew better than to tempt fate twice in one night, she pushed up to standing, walked over and gave him a peck on the cheek…and then went to bed.

COLTON SLEPT IN fifteen-minute intervals. By the time the alarm on his watch went off he'd maybe patched together an hour of sleep in seven. It was fine. He rolled off the couch and fired off a dozen pushups to get the blood pumping. He hopped to his feet and did a quick set of fifty jumping jacks. He'd been sitting way more than usual in the past thirty-six hours and his body was reminding him that it liked to be on the move.

He followed jumping jacks with sit-ups and rounded out his morning wake-up routine with squats. As quietly as he could manage, he slipped down the hall past his master bedroom, past the boys' room, where he lingered for just a second in the doorway of the open door.

And then he made his way to the master bath where he washed his face, shaved and brushed his teeth.

Makena didn't need to be up for another hour. There was something right about her being curled up in his bed. He didn't need the visual, not this early in the morning. So he didn't stop off at the master bedroom on his way to the coffee machine.

The supplies were all near the machine, so he had a cup in hand and a piece of dry toast in less than three minutes. It didn't take long for the caffeine to kick in or for questions to swirl in the back of his mind.

At first, he thought about his father's case. Colton had a dedicated deputy to untangle Mrs. Hubert's financials and the contact information that had been found in her computer. Her files were all coded and his deputy was presently on full-time duty trying to crack the code. The older woman who was murdered a few months ago had ties to a kidnapping ring. Had she been involved in Caroline's case?

As a professional courtesy, and also considering the fact they were brothers, he was sharing information with Cash and Dawson. Those two were working the case in their spare time, as well. Even with a crack team of investigators, it would take time to unravel Mrs. Hubert's dealings. Time to get justice for Finn O'Connor was running out. A cold trail often led to a cold case. It occurred to Colton that his mother could be in danger, too.

There could be something hidden around the house, a file or piece of evidence their father had been hiding that could lead a perp to her door.

Colton tapped his fingers on his mug. He thought about time. And how short it could be. How unfair it could be and how quickly it could be robbed from loved ones.

It was too early in the morning to go down a path of frustration that his boys would never know their mother. Besides, as long as he had air in his lungs, he would do his best to ensure they knew what a wonderful a person she was.

Colton booted up his laptop and checked his email. Several needed attention, so he went ahead and answered those. Others could wait. A couple he forwarded on to Gert. She'd been awfully quiet since the phone call last night, which didn't mean she wasn't working. It just meant she hadn't found anything worth sharing.

He pinched the bridge of his nose to stem the headache threatening. Then he picked up the pencil from on top of his notepad. He squeezed the pencil so tight while thinking about the past that it cracked in half. Frustration that he wasn't getting anywhere in the two most important cases of his life got the best of him and he chucked the pencil pieces against the wall.

Colton cursed. He looked up in time to see a feminine figure emerge from his bedroom. Makena had on pajama bottoms and a T-shirt. The bottoms were pink plaid. Pink was his new favorite color.

"Morning." She walked into the room and right past the broken pieces of pencil.

"Back atcha." He liked that she knew where everything was and went straight to the cabinet for the coffee. She had a fresh cup in her hands and a package of vanilla yogurt by the time he moved to the spot to clean up the broken pencil.

"How'd you sleep?" he asked her as he tossed the bits into the trash.

"Like a baby." She stretched her arms out and yawned before digging into the yogurt. The movement pressed her ample breasts against the cotton of her T-shirt.

Colton forced his gaze away from her soft curves. "How's your hip today?" He'd noticed that she was walking better and barely limped.

"So far, so good," she said. "I don't think I'm ready to run a marathon anytime soon, but I can make it across the room without too much pain. The bruise is already starting to heal." She motioned toward her hip, a place his eyes didn't need to follow.

Colton made a second cup of coffee, which he polished off by the time she finished her first.

"I can be dressed and ready in five minutes. Is that okay?" she asked.

"Works for me." He gathered up a few supplies like his notebook and laptop and tucked them into a bag.

Makena emerged from the bedroom as quickly as she'd promised, looking a little too good. He liked the fact that she could sleep when she was around him, because she'd confessed that she hadn't done a whole lot of that in recent months.

He smiled as he passed by her, taking his turn in the bedroom. He dressed in his usual jeans, dark button-down shirt and windbreaker. He retrieved his belt from the safe and then clipped it on his hip.

He returned to the kitchen where Makena stood, ready to go.

The drive to the motel took exactly twenty-nine minutes with no traffic. The place was just as Gert had described. A nondescript motel off the highway that fit the information Gert had passed along—that it rented rooms by the hour. There was an orange neon sign that had M-O-T-E-L written out along with a massive arrow pointing toward the building. Colton had always driven by those places and wondered why people needed the arrow to find it. He could chew on that another day.

"It's best if you stick to my side in case anything unexpected goes down. I'm not expecting anything, but should River still be in the area or pop in to rent another room, I want you to get behind me as a first option or anything that could put the most mass between you and him. Okay?"

She nodded and he could see that she was clear on his request. She'd been silent on the ride over, staring out the window, alone in her thoughts. Colton hadn't felt the need to fill the space between them with words. It had been a comfortable silence. One that erased the years they'd been apart.

The office of the motel was a small brick building that had a screen door in front of a white wooden one. The second door was cracked open enough to see dim lighting. He opened the screen door as he tucked Makena behind him.

With his hand on her arm, he could feel her trembling. River's connection to this place seemed to be taking a toll on her. A renewed anger filled Colton as he bit back the frustration. Of course, she'd be nervous and scared. She'd been running from this guy for literally months and here she was walking inside a building where he'd recently stayed.

Inside, they were greeted by a clerk whose head could barely be seen above the four-and-a-half-foot counter. The walls were made of dark wood paneling. The worn carpet was hunter green, and the yellow laminate countertop gave the place a leftover-from-another-era look.

"How can I help you, Sheriff?" The woman didn't seem at all surprised to see him, and he figured his deputy might've let her know someone would most likely swing by to speak to her.

"Are you Gloria?" he asked. Aside from the long bar-height counter that the little old lady could barely see over, there were a pair of chairs with a small table nestled in the right-hand side of the room. To his left, in the other corner, a flat-screen TV had been mounted.

"In the flesh." She smiled.

"I understand you spoke to one of my deputies yesterday. My name is Sheriff Colton O'Connor." He walked to the counter and extended his right hand. "Pleased to meet you."

The little old lady took his hand. Her fingers might be bony and frail but she had a solid handshake and a formidable attitude.

"Pleased to make your acquaintance, Sheriff. You're in here to talk to me about one of my clients." She had the greenest eyes he'd ever seen. He didn't get the impression she'd had an easy life. The sparkle in her eyes said she'd given it hell, though.

"Yes, ma'am. This is a friend of mine and she's familiar with the case." He purposely left out Makena's name.

Gloria nodded and smiled toward Makena. "My name might be Gloria but everyone around here calls me Peach on account of the fact I was born in Georgia.

I've lived in Texas for nearly sixty years but picked up the name in second grade and it stuck."

Peach's gaze shifted back to Colton. She nodded and smiled after shaking hands with Makena.

"Can you tell me everything you remember about the visitor in room 11?" Colton asked, directing the conversation.

"The name he used to check in was Ryan Reynolds. I can get the ledger for you if you'd like to see it."

"I would." Ryan Reynolds was a famous actor, so it was obviously a fake name. Colton figured that Makena could confirm whether or not the handwriting belonged to River.

Peach opened a drawer and then produced a black book before finding a page with the date from five days ago.

"I get folks' information on the computer usually, but my cash customers like to sign in by hand the old-fashioned way." He bet they did.

She hoisted the book onto the counter and, using two fingers on each hand, nudged it toward Colton. He looked at the name she pointed at. Ryan Reynolds. The movie star. Somehow, Colton seriously doubted the real Ryan Reynolds would have come all the way to this small town to rent a motel room. Last he'd checked, there were no movies being made in the area. But this wasn't the kind of place where a person would use his or her real name, and Peach clearly hadn't asked for ID.

Colton leaned into Makena and said in a low voice, "Does that handwriting look like his?"

"Yes. He always makes that weird loop on his Rs. I mean, wrong name, obviously. But that's his handwriting."

"Do you mind if I take a picture of this?" Colton glanced up at Peach, who nodded.

Colton pulled out his phone and snapped a shot.

"I'd also like to keep this book as evidence. Did Mr. Reynolds touch the book or use a pen that you gave him?"

"Now that I really think about it, I don't think he did touch the book. I can't be sure. But the pen he used would be right there." She reached for a decorated soup can that had a bunch of pens in it.

"If you don't mind, I'd like to admit that as evidence." Colton's words stopped her mid-reach.

"Yes, sir. I'm happy to cooperate in any way that I can."

"Thank you, ma'am." Colton tipped his chin. "Has anyone else who looked suspicious been here over the last week or two?"

"You'll have to clarify what suspicious means, sheriff. I get all kinds coming through here," she quipped with a twinkle in her eye.

Chapter Thirteen

Okay, bad question on Colton's part. "Let me ask another way. Did you have anyone new show up?"

"I have a couple of regulars who come in once a month or every other week. This is a good stop for my truckers who are on the road."

"Anyone here you haven't seen before other than Mr. Reynolds?" he clarified.

"I've had a couple of people come through. I'd say in the last week or so there've been four or five, but we've been slower than usual."

"Has anyone say around six feet tall with light red hair, maybe could be described as strawberry blond, been in?"

She was already shaking her head before he could finish his sentence. "No. I would remember someone like that."

"How about anyone with black hair and a mustache?" he asked.

"No, sir." Her gaze shifted up and to the left, signaling she was trying to recall information. So far, she'd passed his honesty meters.

"I can't really recall anyone who looked like that coming through recently."

"Is it possible for me to view the footage from the occupant of room 11 as he came and went?" Colton asked.

"I can pull it up on the screen behind you now that I have here one of those digital files." She smiled and her eyes lit up as she waited for his response.

"That would be a big help." Colton turned his head and shifted slightly to the left. He put his right elbow on the counter, careful not to disturb the cash ledger.

The next few sounds were the click-click-clicks of fingers on a keyboard.

"Here we go," she said with an even bigger smile. "It should come up in just a second."

Colton's left hand was at his side. He felt Makena reach for him and figured she must need reassurance considering she was about to see a video of the man she'd been in a traumatic relationship with. He twined their fingers together and squeezed her hand in a show of support.

She closed what little distance was between them, her warm body against his. He ignored the frissons of heat from the contact. He'd never get used to them, but he had come to expect the reaction that always came and the warmth that flooded him while she was this close.

The TV set came to life and the sound of static filled the room. The next thing he knew, the volume was being turned down on the set. There was a large picture window just to the left of the TV screen and Colton surveyed the parking lot of the small diner across the street. There were five vehicles: two pickup trucks, a small SUV and a sedan. He figured at least one of those had to belong to an employee, possibly two.

"Here it is. Here's the day he checked in." Peach practically beamed with her accomplishment of finding his file.

Just as Gert had explained, the video was grainy as all get-out. The man in the video wore a Rangers baseball cap and kept his chin tucked to his chest. Out of the side of his mouth, Colton asked, "Is that about his height and weight?"

"Yes." There was a lot of emotion packed in that one word and a helluva lot of fight on the ready. He couldn't help being anything but proud of her. When some would cower, she dug deep and found strength.

"I don't have a whole lot of video of him, just his coming and going." Peach fast-forwarded, pausing each time his image came into view. The time stamps revealed dates from five days ago, four days ago and three days ago. Then it was down to two days and the same thing happened every time. He'd walk in or out of the room with his chin-to-chest posture. He didn't receive any visitors during that time except for daily visits from housekeeping. He didn't come and go often, mostly staying inside. He didn't have food delivered, which meant he either packed some or went out for food once a day. His eating habits would definitely classify as strange.

And then on the last day, the morning he checked out, he did something out of character and strange. He took off his hat as he left the room and glanced up at the camera, giving the recording device a full view of his face.

Makena's body tensed and she gripped Colton's hand even tighter.

River, she'd said, was a solid six-foot-tall man with a

build that made it seem like he spent serious time at the gym. He had black hair and brown eyes. And was every bit the person who'd looked straight at the camera.

From the corner of Colton's eye, he now saw a man matching the description of River exit the diner and come running at full speed toward the motel office. He put his hands in the air, palms up, in the surrender position to show that he had no gun in his hands and he was surveying the area like he expected someone to jump out at him.

MAKENA HAD NOTICED the moment she and Colton had exited the vehicle earlier that he'd rested his right hand on the butt of his gun. Having been married to someone in law enforcement, she knew exactly the reason why. It was to have instant access to his weapon. The seconds it took for his hand to reach for his gun, pull it out of the holster and shoot could mean life or death for an officer. It also reminded her of the risks they were taking by visiting the place River had been in twenty-four hours ago.

As she followed Colton's gaze, she saw her ex-husband, to the shock of her life. Her body tensed. River was running straight toward them, hands high in the air, no doubt to show that he wasn't carrying a weapon.

Colton drew his, like anyone in law enforcement would.

"Get down and stay below the counter, Ms. Peach," he directed the clerk.

He tucked Makena behind him and repositioned himself so they were behind the counter. She wanted to face River and ask him why in hell he'd tried to blow her up yesterday morning, but she wasn't stupid. She wanted to make sure she did it safely. Colton had told her to either hide behind him or put some serious mass between her and River.

She dropped Colton's hand as it went up to cup the butt of the weapon she recognized as a Glock. She glanced around, looking for some kind of weapon. There was a letter opener. She grabbed it and tightened her fist around it.

If River somehow made it past Colton to get to her, she'd be ready.

Her left hand was fisted so tightly that her knuckles went white. Anger and resentment for the way she'd had to live in the past six months bubbled up again, burning her throat.

Colton crouched so only a small portion of his head and his weapon were visible as River opened the door.

Her ex was out of breath, and the expression on his face would probably haunt her for months to come. She expected to find hurt and anger and jealousy, emotions that had been all too common during their marriage. Instead, she found panic. His eyes were wide, and he kept blinking. He was nervous.

"I swear I'm not here to hurt anyone. You have to believe me," he said. He still had that authoritative cop voice but there was a hint of fear present that was completely foreign coming from him.

"Give me one good reason we should listen to you." Colton didn't budge. "And keep your hands up where I can see them.

Colton had that same authoritative law enforcement voice that demanded attention. Hearing it from River had always caused icy fingers to grip her spine, but her body's reaction was so different when she heard it come from Colton.

All the angry words that Makena wanted to spew at River died on her tongue. It was easy to see the man was in a panic. Whatever he'd done was catching up to him. That was her first thought.

"I swear on my mother's life that I'm not here to hurt anyone." His face was still frozen on the TV that was positioned behind him. He'd taken a couple of steps inside the room and then stopped in his tracks.

"How'd you know I was here?" Makena asked.

"I saw you come in, and they will, too," came the chilling response.

"Who are *they*?" Colton asked.

"I can't tell you and you don't want to know. Believe me. The only thing you need to be aware of is that your life is in danger." River's voice shook with dread and probably a shot of adrenaline.

A half-mirthful, half-frustrated sigh shot from Makena's throat. He wasn't telling her anything she didn't already know.

Makena locked eyes with the terrified older woman at the other end of the counter. Peach kept eye contact with Makena when she pointed at something inside a shelf. It was hidden from view and Makena had a feeling it was some kind of weapon, like a bat or a shotgun.

Makena shook her head. Peach nodded and tilted her head toward it.

"Talk to me, River. Tell me why they would be after me. Is it because of you?" As much as Makena didn't believe that anymore, she had to ask. She needed to hear from him that wasn't the case, and she needed to get him talking so she could understand why it seemed like the world was crumbling around her.

"It's not important *what* you know. It's what they *think* you know. Even more important right now is that you get the hell out of here. Stay low. Stick with this guy." He motioned toward Colton. "He can probably protect you if you stay out of sight. Just give me time. I need time to straighten everything out."

"Time? To what? Plant another bomb?" she said.

She'd never seen River look this rattled before. And also…something else…helpless? His eyes darted around the room and he looked like he'd jump out of his skin if a cat hopped up on the counter.

This close, she could see his bloodshot eyes and the dark circles underneath. They always got that way when he went days without sleep. He was almost in a manic state and part of her wondered if deep down he actually did care about her well-being or if this was all some type of self-preservation act. To make it seem like he was a victim. But to what end?

"I knew they were planning something, but I had no idea…" River brought his hands on top of his head. His face distorted. "Everything's a mess now. I made everything a mess. I never meant for you to get caught up in this. Bad timing. But just do what I say and lie low. Trust me, you don't want to get anywhere near these guys."

His words sent another cold chill racing down her spine.

"You're not getting off that easy, River," Colton said. "Start talking now. I can work with the DA. I can talk with your chief if you give me something to take to him."

River's emotions were escalating, based on the increasing intensity of his expression.

This was not good. This was so not good.

"Are you kidding me right now? It's too late for me. It's too late to go back and fix what's wrong. I messed up big-time. There's not going to be any coming back from this for me but there's still time for me to fix it for you."

"Hold on. Just do me a favor and slow down." Colton's deep voice was a study in calm. "This doesn't have to end badly. Whatever you've done… I can't promise any miracles, but I can say that I'll do everything in my power if you talk. You need to tell us what's going on. You need to tell us who those men are and exactly why they're after Makena. It's the only way that I can help you."

River seemed more agitated. "You just don't understand. You don't get this and you don't realize what I'm going through or what I've done. It's too late. It's too late for me. I can accept that. But not her. She didn't do anything wrong."

The fact that River was concerned about her when it appeared his own life was on the line told her that she hadn't married a 100 percent jerk all those years ago. There had been something good inside him then and maybe she could work with that now.

Makena stood up taller so that she could look River in the eye, hoping that would make a difference. "I don't know what happened, River. But I do know there was a decent person in there at one time. The person I first met—"

"Is gone. That guy is long gone. Forget about the

past and forget that you ever knew me. Just lie low and give me some time to get this straightened out."

"I've been in hiding for half a year, River. How much more of my life do I need to give up for whatever you did?" she asked.

Instead of calming him, that seemed to rile him up even more. She'd been truthful and her words seemed to have the effect of punching him.

"I know, Makena. I realize that none of this makes sense to you, and it's best for everyone else if it doesn't. If I could go back and change things, I would. Time doesn't work like that and our past mistakes do come back to haunt us."

Makena remembered that he was on leave for some pretty hefty charges. Maybe if she pretended like she already knew, he would come clean. "The men who are after me, who tried to blow me up…are they related to your administrative leave?"

River issued a sharp sigh and then started lowering his hands.

"Keep 'em up, high and where I can see them." Colton's voice left no room for doubt that he was not playing around. He could place River under arrest, she knew, but he seemed to be holding off long enough to get answers. She took it as a sign he believed River might give them useful information.

River's hands shot up in the air. Being in law enforcement, he would be very aware just how serious Colton was about those words. Colton's department-issued Glock was still aimed directly at River. All it would take was one squeeze of the trigger to end River's life.

Considering the man was standing not ten feet away, Colton wouldn't need a crackerjack shot to take him out.

"What did you do, River?" Makena asked again, hoping to wear him down and get answers. "You can help me the most if you tell Colton what you're involved in."

Hands in the air, River started pacing. He appeared more agitated with every forward step. His mood was dangerous and volatile. Deadly?

She scanned his body for signs of a weapon, knowing full well there had to be one there somewhere. On duty, he'd worn an ankle holster. It wasn't uncommon for him to hide his Glock in another holster tucked in the waistband of his jeans.

He mumbled and she couldn't make out what he was saying. And then he spun around to face them. "Did you say his name is Colton?"

"Yes, but I don't see how that has any bearing on anything."

"Really? Isn't that your ex-boyfriend from college? I used to read your journals, Makena."

Her face burned with a mix of embarrassment and outrage. She hadn't kept a journal since their early years of marriage. And yes, she had probably written something in it about Colton. But it had been so long ago she couldn't remember what she'd written.

"Colton was never my boyfriend. He wasn't then and he isn't now. But even if he was, that's none of your business anymore. In case you forgot, we're divorced. And this is my life, a life that I want back." She'd allowed him to take so much time of hers. No more.

Makena took in a deep breath because the current assertiveness, although she deserved to stand up for herself, wasn't exactly having a calming effect on River.

In fact, she feared she might be making it worse. She willed her nerves to calm down and her stress levels to relax.

"I won't pretend to know what you're going through right now." Colton's voice was a welcome calm in the eye of the storm. "I know you're facing some charges at work but if you help in this case it'll be noted in your jacket. It won't hurt and might convince a jury to go easier on you."

River looked at Colton. His gaze bounced back to Makena.

"Man, it's too late for me now."

And then the sound of a bullet split the air, followed by glass breaking on the front door.

The next few minutes happened in slow motion. Out of the corner of her eye, Makena saw Peach reach into the shelf. The older woman came up with a shotgun in a movement that was swift and efficient. It became pretty obvious this wasn't the woman's first rodeo.

She aimed the barrel of the gun right at River. But it was River who caught and held Makena's attention. As she ducked for cover, the look on his face would be etched in her brain forever.

At first his eyes bulged, and he took a step forward. She could've sworn she heard something whiz past her ear and was certain it was a second bullet. Before she realized, Colton positioned his body in between her and River.

River's arms dropped straight out. His chest flew toward her as he puffed it out. It was then she saw the red dot flowering in the center of his white cotton T-shirt. His mouth flew open, forming a word that never came out.

Shock stamped his features. He looked down at the center of his chest and said, "I've been shot."

He looked up at Makena and then Colton before repeating the words.

Colton was already on the radio clipped to his shoulder, saying words that would stick in her mind for a long time. She heard phrases like "officer down" and "ambulance required." This was all a little too real as she saw a pair of men, side by side and weapons at the ready, making their way across the street and toward the motel.

"I have to get you out of here," Colton said to Makena. The truck was parked behind the motel and she saw the brilliance of his plan now.

"Okay." It was pretty much the only word she could form or manage to get out under the circumstances. And then more came. "What about River?"

"There's nothing we can do to help him right now. The best thing we can do is lead those men away from the motel." Colton turned to Peach. "Is the back door locked?"

"Yes, sir." She ran a hand along the shelf and produced a set of keys. She tossed them to Colton, who snatched them with one hand. "You need to come with us. It's not safe here."

Peach lowered her face to the eyepiece of the shotgun. "I'll hold 'em off. You two get out of here while you can. I'll hold down the fort."

"I'm not kidding, Peach. You need to come with us now."

The woman shook her head and that was as much as she said.

"Help is on the way," Colton shouted to River, who'd taken a few steps back and dropped against the door, closing it. He sat with a dumbfounded look on his face.

"Reach up and lock that," Peach shouted to him.

Surprisingly, he obliged.

"We have to go." Colton, with keys in one hand and a Glock in the other, offered an arm, which Makena took as they ran toward the back.

He unlocked a key-only dead bolt and then tossed the keys into the hallway before fishing his own keys out of his pocket. The two of them ran toward the truck, which was thankfully only a few spaces from the door.

Once inside, he cranked on the ignition and backed out of the parking spot. "Stay low. Keep your head down. It's best if you get down on the floorboard."

Makena did as he requested. She noticed he'd scooted down, making himself as small as possible and less visible, therefore less of a target. He put the vehicle into Drive and floored the gas pedal.

In a ball on the floorboard as directed, Makena took in a sharp breath as Colton jerked the truck forward. It was a big vehicle and not exactly nimble. Size was its best asset.

"They have no idea who they're dealing with," Colton commented, and she realized it was because they were in his personal vehicle and not one marked as law enforcement.

A crack of a bullet split the air. It was then that Makena heard the third shot being fired.

Chapter Fourteen

Colton tilted his chin toward his left shoulder where his radio was clipped on his jacket. His weapon was in the hand that he also used to steer the wheel after they'd bolted from around the back of the motel.

Peach would be safe as he drew the perps away from the building and onto the highway. River had been shot and it looked bad for him, but he was still talking and alert, and that was a good sign.

Getting Makena out of the building and Birchwood had been his first priority. River was right about one thing. She'd be safer if she kept a low profile.

Colton also realized the reason the perps were shooting was probably because they didn't realize they were shooting at a sheriff. Even so, it had been one of his better ideas to slip out the back of his office yesterday and take his personal vehicle, because it seemed as though the perps had zeroed in on Makena's location at the RV.

They also seemed ready and able to shoot River though he was an officer of the law. With River's professional reputation tarnished, plus the charges being lobbed against him, they must think they could get away with shooting him.

"Gert, can you read me?" He hoped like hell she could, because she was his best link to getting help for River and for him and Makena.

Birchwood was in Colton's jurisdiction. One of his deputies passed by this motel on his daily drive to work, and Colton hoped that he was nearby, possibly on his way into work.

Gert's voice came through the radio. "I read you loud and clear."

"I have two perps who have opened fire on my personal vehicle. And an officer is down at the motel. Makena is in my custody and we're heading toward the station, coming in hot."

"Do you have a vehicle or a license plate or can you give me anything on who might be behind you?"

"The shooter was on foot." Colton took a moment to glance into his rearview mirror in time to see the pair of perps running toward a Jeep.

With the weight of his truck, he didn't have a great chance of outrunning them. "It's looking like a Jeep Wrangler. White. Rubicon written in black letters on the hood. I don't have a license plate but I imagine it won't take them long to catch up to me. If they have one on the front of their vehicle, I can relay it."

He heard Makena suck in a breath. She scrambled into the seat and practically glued her face to the back window. "What can I do?"

"Stay low. Stay hidden. I don't have a way to identify myself in the truck. My vehicle is slow. But I'm going to do my level best to outrun them."

Makena didn't respond, so he wasn't certain she bought into his request. He was kicking up gravel on the service road to the four-lane highway. He took the first entrance ramp, and despite it being past seven o'clock in the morning on a Friday, there were more cars than he liked.

"Where are they now?" Makena asked.

"They're making their way toward us on the service road." Colton swerved in and out of the light traffic, pressing his dual cab truck to its limits. What it lacked in get-up-and-go, it made up for in size. If nothing else, he'd use its heft to block the Jeep from pulling alongside them.

Of course, the passenger could easily get off a shot from behind.

Colton leaned his mouth to his shoulder. "Where's the nearest marked vehicle?"

"Not close enough. I'm checking on DPS now to see if I can get a trooper in your direction. How are you doing? Can you hold them off until I can get backup to you?"

"I don't have a choice." Colton meant those words.

The Jeep had taken the on-ramp onto the highway and it wouldn't be long before it was on his bumper. He glanced around at the traffic and figured he'd better take this fight off the highway rather than endanger innocent citizens.

River was in trouble at work. Colton knew that for certain. What he wasn't sure of was his partners.

Colton relayed the description of the perps to Gert. "Call Chief Shelton at Dallas PD and see if any of his officers matching those descriptions have been connected in any way to River Myers. I want to know who River's friends were. Who he hung out with in the department and if any of them had visited the shooting range lately."

Most beat cops couldn't pull off the shot Red had at that distance and through a glass door. Whoever made the shot would get high scores in marksmanship at the range. Other officers would take note. Someone would know.

Between that and the physical descriptions, maybe River's supervising officer could narrow the search.

"Hold on, I'm going to swerve off the highway," he said, noting his chance.

At the last minute, he cranked the steering wheel right and made the exit ramp. It was probably too much to hope the perps lost him in traffic. There were plenty of black trucks on these roads.

He cursed when the Jeep took the exit.

"Gert, talk to me. Do you have someone at the motel?" Colton's only sense of relief so far was that he'd drawn the perps away from Peach and River. He also had a sneaky suspicion that Peach could take care of herself and could keep River there at gunpoint. Colton had no doubt the woman could hold her own until River received medical attention.

He could only hope that River would come clean with names.

Again, all they needed was a puzzle piece. At least now they knew that River had some connection to Red and Mustache. There was something the three of them had concocted or were doing they believed would land them in jail if someone found out. That someone, unfortunately, ended up being Makena. And again, he was reminded of how timing was everything.

If Makena had gone out to that garage five minutes before, maybe the men wouldn't have been there yet. Maybe River could've convinced her to go back to bed and she could be living out a peaceful life by now after the divorce.

His mind stretched way back to college. He'd wanted to ask her out but hadn't. Again, the ripple effect of that decision caused him to wonder about his timing. Now was not the time to dredge up the past. Besides, the Jeep was gaining on him. At this pace, it would catch him.

There were fields everywhere. One was a pasture for grazing. The other was corn stalks. The truck could handle either one and so could the Jeep. Colton couldn't get any advantage by veering off road. Except that in the corn, considering it was already tall, maybe he could lose them.

The meadow on the other side of the street was useless. The last thing he needed was more flat land. And while he didn't like the idea of damaging someone's crop and potential livelihood, he knew that he could circle back and make restitution. What was the point of having a trust fund he'd never touched if not for a circumstance like this one?

"Hang on tight, okay?" he said to Makena.

When she confirmed, he nailed a hard right. The truck bounded so hard he thought he might've cracked the chassis but stabilized once he got onto the field. The last thing he saw was the Jeep following.

Colton's best chance to confuse them was to maybe do a couple of figure eights and then zigzag through the cornfield. It would at the very least keep the perps from getting off a good shot. He was running out of options.

So far, the Jeep hadn't gotten close enough to them for him to be able to read a license plate if there was one on the front. Law required it to be there. However, many folks ignored it.

Considering these guys had good reason to hide any identifying marks, they most certainly wouldn't have a plate up front.

Gert's voice cut through his thoughts. "I got you pulled up on GPS using your cell phone. I have a location on you, sir. Can you hold tight in the area until I can get someone to you?"

"That's affirmative. I can stick around as long as I keep moving." He tried to come off as flippant so Gert wouldn't worry about him any more than she already was.

Makena was getting bounced around in the floorboard. At this point, it would be safer for her to climb into the seat and strap in. So that was exactly what he told her to do.

She managed, without being thrown around too much.

The crops had the truck bouncing and slowed his speed considerably. He cut a few sharp turns, left and then right…right and then left. A couple of figure eights.

There was a time in his life when a ride like this might've felt exciting. His adrenaline was pumping and he'd be all in for the thrill. Even having a couple of idiots with guns behind him would've seemed like a good challenge. A lot had changed in him after he'd become a dad last year.

He took life more seriously and especially his own. Because he knew without a shadow of a doubt those boys needed their father to come home every night. And he would, today, too.

He checked his mirrors and was feeling pretty good about where he stood with regard to the perps. Until he almost slammed into the Jeep that had cut an angle right in front of him.

Slamming the brake and narrowly avoiding a collision, Colton bit out a few choice words.

Gert's voice came across the radio again. "Sir, I have names. Officer Randol Bic and Officer Jimmy Stitch were known associates of River Myers and fit the descriptions you gave. Bic is a sharpshooter. They're partners in East Dallas and both of their records are clean."

A picture was emerging. Was River taking the fall for Bic and Stitch?

Had they threatened him? Were they holding something over his head?

"I've heard those names before," Makena said.

Gert's voice came across the radio. "Sir, I think the GPS is messing up. It looks like you're driving back and forth on the highway."

Colton couldn't help himself; he laughed. "Well, that's because I'm presently driving in a cornfield near the highway. GPS probably can't register that location."

"I feel like I should have known it would be something like that." Now Gert laughed. It was good to break up some of the tension. A sense of humor helped with keeping a calm head, which could be the difference between making a mistake or a good decision.

The Jeep circled back, and Colton could hear its engine gunning toward him. He cut left, trying to outrun the perps.

"Gert, how are you doing over there?" Colton needed an update. Actually, what he needed was a miracle. But he'd stopped believing in those after losing Rebecca, and he figured it was best to keep his feet firmly planted on the ground and his head out of the clouds.

"Sir, I have good news for you. Do you hear anything?"

Colton strained to listen. He didn't hear anything other than the sound of his front bumper hacking through the cornfield. He hated to think what he was doing to this farmer's crops. But again, he would pay restitution.

"I don't hear much more than the noise I'm making and the sound of an engine barreling toward me." He was barely cutting around.

The Jeep was close, he could hear and feel it, if not see it.

"Well, sir, the cavalry is arriving. If you roll your window down, I think you'll be happy with what you hear. DPS got back to me and a trooper should be on top of you right now."

Well, maybe Colton had been too quick to write off the likelihood of miracles happening.

"That's the best news I've heard all day." When he really listened and got past the sounds of corn husks slapping against his front bumper, he heard the familiar wails of sirens in the distance.

Makena was practically glued to her seat, with her hands gripping the strap of her seat belt.

"If you like that news, I've got more. An ambulance is en route to the motel. Help is on the way, sir."

"Gert, remind me the next time I see you that you deserve a raise."

"Sir, I'm going to hold you to that when it's time for my review." Again, lightening the tension with teasing kept his mind at ease and his brain able to focus. The minute he thought a situation was the end of the world was the minute it would be true.

Colton circled around a few more times, ensuring that he was on the move and as far away from the Jeep as possible. He figured the perps had probably given up once they'd heard sirens.

Since they were cops with clean records, they would want to keep them that way. When he really thought about it, they'd concocted the perfect scenario. The puzzle pieces clicked together in one moment.

They had some type of hold over River. That was obvious and a given. They believed that Makena could possibly link them to River and so they would get rid of her. All the while implicating River, who was already known to have a temper and a bad relationship with his wife.

When the different parts of their plan made sense like that, he realized the genius of their plot. However, he had seen them. He knew who they were. That was where they'd messed up. Now they'd gone and left a trail.

"Are they gone?" Makena looked around as Colton slowed down.

"I believe so."

Makena sank back in the chair. "I hear the sirens."

Colton nodded as he tried to navigate back toward the highway.

"I can patch you through to Officer Staten," Gert said.

"Ten-four. Great work, Gert." But before Colton could speak to the highway patrolman through the radio, he saw the cruiser. Colton flashed his headlights and cut off his engine.

Hands up, he exited his truck and told Makena to do the same.

After greeting Officer Staten, Colton said, "It's a shame I didn't get a plate. A white Jeep Rubicon in Texas doesn't exactly stand out."

"The two of you are safe. That's the most important thing to me right now," Officer Staten said.

There was no arguing with that point.

"Do you need assistance getting back to your office?" Staten was tall and darker-skinned, with black hair, brown eyes and a deceptively lean frame. Every state trooper could pull his own weight and more in a fight. These officers traveled long distances with no backup in sight. To say they were tough was a lot like saying Dwayne Johnson had a few muscles.

Colton looked to Makena. "Any chance I can convince you to take a ride back to my office with the officer?"

Makena was already vigorously shaking her head before he could finish his sentence. He figured as much. It was worth a try. He wanted her to be safely tucked away while he circled back and checked on River and Peach.

She seemed to read his mind when she said, "I'm going with you."

There was so much determination in her voice he knew better than to argue. No use wasting precious time.

Colton turned to Officer Staten and said, "Can I get an assist to the motel where an officer was fired on? I'd like to go back and investigate the scene. And considering I have a witness with me, I think it might be best if I have backup."

Staten seemed to catch on, because he was already nodding. "I'm happy to help in any way I can."

Professional courtesy went a long way and Colton had gone to great lengths to build a cooperative relationship with other law enforcement agencies.

Once their destination was agreed upon, Colton retreated to his truck with Makena by his side.

The drive back to the motel surprisingly took half an hour. Colton didn't realize they'd gotten so far from the motel, but then he was driving back at normal speed limits, whereas he'd flown to get away from there.

There was a BOLO out on the Jeep. If they were as smart as they appeared to be, they would ditch the vehicle. The new problem was that they'd been made and now they had nothing to lose. Dangerous.

They couldn't possibly realize that Colton had figured out who they were. So Colton had that on his side.

By the time they reached the motel, it looked like a proper crime scene. An ambulance was there. The back had been closed up and it looked as though they were about to pull away.

"Hold on a sec," Colton said to Makena.

He hopped out of his pickup, knowing that Makena would want to know River's status.

He jogged up to the driver's side of the ambulance and the driver rolled down the window. Fortunately for him, he still had on his windbreaker that had the word SHERIFF in big bold letters running down his left sleeve, so it was easy to identify that he was in law enforcement.

"How is your patient in the back?" Colton asked.

"I was here at the time of the shooting. I had to get a witness out of the building. What is the status of your patient?"

"GSW to the back, exit wounds in his chest. We need to rock and roll, sir. No guarantees on this one. Still breathing, but a lot of blood loss by the time we got here."

Colton took a step back and waved them on. "Go."

It wasn't good news, but River was still alive and Colton had learned that even a tiny bit of hope was better than none. As done as Makena was with the relationship, and he had no doubt in his mind the marriage had been over for a very long time, she was the type of person to be concerned for someone she'd once cared about.

He wished he could give her better news.

Glancing toward the truck, he expected to see her waiting there. A moment of shock jolted him when he saw that she was gone. Then, he knew immediately where she would go. He raced inside to see her standing next to Peach, who was sitting in one of the chairs on the right-hand side.

Makena was offering reassurances to the older woman while rubbing her shoulders. Peach had blood all over her flowery dress.

"I did everything I could to help him, but there was so much blood. He was already pale by the time we got help. His lips were turning blue." The anguish in the older woman's voice was palpable.

"Peach, what you did was admirable. If he has any chance at all, it's because of you," Colton said.

Peach glanced up at him, those emerald green eyes sparkling with gratitude for his comments.

"I mean it. You very well could've saved his life here and I know you saved ours. I would work beside you in law enforcement any day." He meant every word.

Her chin lifted with his praise.

"I appreciate your saying so, Sheriff. It means a lot."

Colton crouched down to eye level with her before taking her statement. And then Makena took Peach into a back room where she washed up.

Makena stayed by the elderly woman's side long after the blood had been rinsed off and Peach had changed clothes.

The highway patrolman stayed outside, guarding the front door in case the perps returned. The front door was cordoned off with crime scene tape.

"My deputy here is going to process the scene. Can one of us give you a ride home?" Colton asked Peach.

"I'll be all right in a few minutes," Peach said. Her hands had steadied. "I have my car out back and I don't want to leave it here overnight."

"What's the owner's name? I'll give 'em a call and ask for someone to cover your shift."

Whatever he said seemed to tickle Peach.

"You're looking at the owner. I owned this place with my husband, God rest his soul."

"Can I call someone? It's not a good idea for you to be alone right now." The shock of what had happened would wear off and her emotions could sneak up on her. Colton didn't want her to suffer. She'd shown incredible bravery today.

"I have a daughter in town," she said. "I'll see if she'll make up the guest bedroom for me tonight."

"Any chance you could get her on the phone now?" Colton asked.

"My purse is underneath the counter where Rapture was hiding." She motioned toward her shotgun that was sitting on top of the counter. It had been opened and the shells looked to have been removed.

As he waited for Peach to call her daughter, Colton took stock of the situation. He now had names. He had motive. All he needed was opportunity to seal Bic and Stitch's fate.

Chapter Fifteen

Makena heard Colton's voice as she sat with Peach. He was talking about shock and the need to keep an eye on her. The concern in his voice brought out all kinds of emotions in Makena. She could tell that he genuinely cared about Peach and it was just about the kindest thing Makena thought she'd ever witnessed. But that was just Colton. He was genuine, kind and considerate wrapped in a devastatingly handsome and masculine package. There was nothing self-centered about him. In fact, there was a sad quality in his eyes that made him so real.

"Bernard and I spent our whole lives here at this motel. He never would take a vacation. I used to tease him about what he'd turn into with all work and no play." A wistful and loving look overtook Peach's face when she spoke about her husband.

"He sounds like an honest, hard-working man," Makena said.

"That he was. He was good to me and I was good to him. We had two daughters. One who succumbed to illness as a child, and the other who your boyfriend is on the phone with now. She looks after me. She's been on me to sell the business for years." Peach exhaled.

"It's difficult to let go. Here is where I feel Bernard's presence the most. I always thought I'd start a little restaurant. Even had a name picked out, but I never did find the time. I always would rather be feeding people. The motel was Bernard's baby."

The fact that Peach had referred to Colton as Makena's boyfriend didn't get past her. She didn't see this as the time to correct the elderly woman.

She glanced up, and it was then that the flat-screen TV caught her attention. She remembered the date stamp and the time stamp on the screen when River had looked up. He'd looked up at exactly 6:12 a.m., which meant he was at the motel and not anywhere near Katy Gulch and he must have known something was going to happen even if he didn't know what because he'd given himself an alibi. Birchwood was a solid half hour from town. He'd been inside his room the entire night, based on the camera footage. The only window was in front, next to the door. If he'd tried to climb out, the camera would've picked it up.

As far as she knew there were no other exits in the room, which pretty much ensured that he was innocent.

A flood of relief washed over her that he hadn't been involved in the bombing attempt. Bic and Stitch's whereabouts had yet to be known, and she had plenty of questions for the pair.

Makena sat with her hands folded in her lap. She refocused on the story Peach was telling her about how her beloved Bernard had singlehandedly patched up a roof after a tornado. Peach was rambling and Makena didn't mind. The woman's smooth, steady voice had a calming effect, and she figured Peach needed to keep her mind busy by talking.

Colton stepped back into the room and then handed the phone to Peach, who took it and spoke to her daughter.

While Peach was occupied, Makena motioned for Colton to come closer. He bent down and took a knee beside her. She liked that he immediately reached for her hand. She leaned toward his ear and relayed her discovery.

He rocked his head. "That's a really good point. If he was here all night, he couldn't have been the one to set the bomb. We have two names, and their department will want to be involved. I promise you here and now justice will be served."

Makena hoped he could deliver on that promise before they could get to her. Bic and Stitch had proven they'd go to any length to quiet her.

"I already figured out they were setting River up. It's a pretty perfect setup and that's the reason we found the black key chain at the scene." After everything she'd been through with River, she probably shouldn't care one way or the other about it. She just wasn't built that way. She did care. Not just about him but about anyone who'd taken a wrong turn.

"Any chance we can stop by the hospital when we leave here?" Makena asked.

"I think that can be arranged."

She really hoped so, because she wanted to see with her own eyes that River was okay.

"Since we know he's a target, will there be security? How will that work?" she asked.

"I just called in a report that he's a material witness in an attempted murder case. One of my deputies is with him and we'll make sure he's not left unattended in the hospital while he fights for his life." Colton's words were reassuring.

"Excuse me, sir." Trooper Staten stepped inside the room.

"How can I help you?"

"Since you have a deputy here, I'd like to offer backup to one of my buddies who has a trucker pulled over not far from here. If you think you'll be good without me, I'd like to assist."

"We're good. Thank you for everything. Your help is much appreciated." Colton stood up, crossed the room and shook the state trooper's hand.

Deputy Fletcher worked to process the scene while Colton and Makena waited for Peach's daughter to show. She did, about twenty minutes later. The young woman, who looked to be in her late twenties, had a baby on her hip and a distressed look on her face as she approached the motel.

Rather than let her step into the bloody scene before it could be cleaned up, Colton met her at the door. He turned back in time to say, "Makena, do you want to bring Peach outside?"

"Sure. No problem." She helped Peach to her feet.

The older woman gripped Makena's arm tightly and it gave her the impression Peach was holding on for dear life. It was good that her daughter was picking her up. She needed someone to take care of her.

Seeing the look on her daughter's face as soon as they stepped outside sent warmth spreading through Makena. The mother-daughter bond hit her square in the chest, and for the first time, Makena thought she was missing out on something by not having a child of her own.

When Peach was settled in her daughter's small SUV and the baby had been strapped in the back seat, the older woman looked up with weary eyes.

"Maybe it is a good idea for me to sell. My handyman, Ralph, can keep things running until the sale. He can see to it if anyone needs a rental. You were right to have me call my daughter," she said to Colton. "Good luck with everything. Take care of yourselves." Peach glanced from Makena to Colton and back. "And take care of each other. If you don't mind my saying, the two of you have something special. That's probably the most important thing you can have in life."

"Thank you, ma'am," Colton said.

Again, Makena didn't see the need to correct Peach despite the thrill of hope she felt at hearing those words. Peach had been through a traumatic experience and Makena wasn't going to ruin her romantic notions by clarifying her relationship with Colton. He had become her lifeline and that was most likely the reason the thought of being separated from him at some point gave her heart palpitations, not that she'd reactivated real feelings for him. The kind of feelings that could go the distance.

COLTON CHECKED HIS WATCH..He surveyed the area, well aware that it had only been a short while ago that two perps had been walking across that same street.

A second deputy pulled up. Colton motioned for him to go on inside. He didn't want anyone working alone on this scene or this case.

He turned to Makena. "River is probably still in surgery. Do you think you could eat something?"

Peach wasn't the only one in shock. Makena was

handling hers well, but she'd had months of being on the run and hiding to practice dealing with extreme emotions.

Makena closed the distance between them and leaned against him.

Colton looped his arms around her waist and pulled her body flush with his. This time, he was the one who dipped his head and pressed a kiss to her lips. He told himself he did it to root them both in reality again, but there was so much more to it, to being with her.

The thought of how close he'd come to losing her sent a shiver rocketing down his back. He'd lost enough with Rebecca and he didn't want to lose another friend.

Makena took in a deep breath. "How do you think he knew?"

Colton knew exactly what she was talking about. She was picking up their conversational thread from a few minutes ago.

"It's possible he didn't. It's likely he assumed that something could happen. He might have followed them here. Maybe they disappeared for a couple of days, and he realized they were searching for you and had found you. So he must've decided following them was his best chance at finding you. You were the wild card. They had no idea when you were going to show up and what evidence you might bring with you. They've probably been looking for you this entire time, and the fact that you disappeared when you did made it look that much more like you had something to hide or fear."

"Timing," she said on another sigh. It was a loaded word.

She blinked up at him and those crystal clear blue eyes brought out feelings he hadn't felt since college.

He had no idea what to do with them. Complicated didn't begin to describe their lives. But he liked her standing right where she was, her warm body pressed against his and his arms circling her waist.

Colton glanced around, surveying the area. Even with two deputies on-site he couldn't let his guard down.

"What do you say we eat at the cafeteria in the hospital?" Makena asked.

"I need to let these guys know where we're headed and communicate with Gert so she can keep someone close to us." Traveling this way was cumbersome and frustrating. An idea sparked. He twined his and Makena's fingers before walking back inside the building. "How about one of you gentlemen lend me your service vehicle? I can leave my truck here. I don't want either one of you driving it. I'll have it towed back to my office. And then the two of you can buddy up on the way back to the office, where you can pick up another vehicle."

Both of his deputies were already nodding their agreement.

Deputy Fletcher pitched a set of keys to Colton, which he caught with one hand. He figured that he and Makena would be a helluva lot safer in a marked vehicle than his truck. Not to mention Bic and Stitch knew exactly what he drove. They may have even pulled some strings and run the plates by now, which would work in Colton's favor. He highly doubted they would've shot at a sheriff if they'd known.

Colton led Makena out to the county-issued SUV.

The drive to the hospital was forty minutes long. Colton located a parking spot as close to the ER doors as he could find. He linked his and Makena's fingers before walking into the ER bay. He was ever aware that a sharpshooter could be anywhere, waiting to strike. But what he hoped was that Bic and Stitch had gone back to Dallas to regroup.

Now that their chief was aware, they would be brought in for questioning. It would have to be handled delicately. Their plan to set up River had blown up in their faces, as had their plans to erase Makena.

The strangest part about the whole thing was that they were targeting her based on what they thought she knew, while she really knew nothing. But now Dallas P.D and the sheriff's office knew what the men were capable of.

On the annual summer barbecue night, Colton and his staff would sit around a campfire way too late and swap stories. Conversation always seemed to drift toward what everyone would do if it went down, meaning they had to disappear.

The first thing people said was obvious. Get rid of their cell phone. The next was that they'd stay the heck away from their personal vehicle. Another thing was not to go home again. That seemed obvious. Most of the deputies said they'd go to the ATM and withdraw as much money as they could before heading to Mexico. At least one said she would head toward Canada because she thought it was the opposite way anyone would look for her.

Bic and Stitch had to have a backup plan. It was just a cop's instinct to talk through worst-case scenarios. And if they thought like typical cops, like he was certain they did considering they had twenty-six years of police experience between them, he figured they had an escape plan, too.

So the thought of them going back to their homes or to Dallas was scratched. Their cover was blown.

But did they realize it?

One thing was certain: they didn't have anything to gain sticking around town. In fact, it would do them both good to hide out until this blew over. And then take off for the border.

What would their escape plan be? He wondered where they'd been hiding while River booked the motel room.

It was a lot to think about. Colton needed a jolt of caffeine and he probably needed something in his stomach besides acid from coffee. The piece of toast he'd had for breakfast wasn't holding up anymore.

He stopped off at the nurses' station in the ER.

"Can you point me to the cafeteria?" It wouldn't do any good to ask about River yet and these women most likely wouldn't know. He would go to the information desk, which would be in the front lobby.

"Straight down this hallway, make a right and then a left. You'll find a lobby, which you'll need to cross. You'll get to a hallway on the exact opposite side and you'll want to take that. You can't miss it from there."

Colton thanked the intake nurse and then followed her directions to a T. A minute later, they were standing in front of a row of vending machines that had everything from hot chocolate to hot dogs.

"Does any of this look appetizing?" he asked Makena.

She walked slowly, skimming the contents of each vending machine. She stopped at the third one and then pointed. "I think this ham sandwich could work."

Colton bought two of them, then grabbed a couple bags of chips. She wanted a soft drink while he stuck with black coffee.

There was a small room with a few bright orange plastic tables and chairs scattered around the room. Each table had from three to six chairs surrounding it. There were two individuals sitting at different tables, each staring at their phone.

Makena took the lead and chose a table farthest away from the others. The sun was shining, and hours had passed since breakfast.

"So I noticed you didn't ask about River." Makena took a bite and chewed on her ham sandwich.

"No, the intake nurses either wouldn't have information or wouldn't share it. There's an information desk we can stop at after we eat. I know most of the people who work there and figured that would be the best place to check his status" He checked his smartwatch. "Gert would let me know if the worst had happened, if River had died."

"Have you given much thought to what your life might look like once this is all behind you?" Colton asked Makena after they'd finished eating.

"Every day for the past six months I've thought about what I would do once this was all over. To be honest, I never really had an answer that stuck. I went through phases. One of those phases was to just buy a little farmhouse somewhere away from people and live on my own and maybe get a golden retriever for company."

"There are worse ways to spend your life."

She smiled and continued. "Then, I had a phase where I wanted to move far away from Texas and live in a major metropolitan area where there would be people everywhere, but no one would bother me unless I wanted them to. If I wanted to be left alone, people would respect that. But I would be around life again. I'd be around people doing things and being busy. I wouldn't have to hide my face." She looked out the window thoughtfully. "None of those things stuck for more than a month."

"And how about now?"

"I have a few ideas." She turned to face him and looked him in the eyes. "Now I feel like I know what I want, but that maybe it's out of reach."

Before he could respond, a text came in from Gert that River was out of surgery. Gert had connections in most places and the hospital was no different. Glancing at his watch, he realized an hour had passed since they'd arrived at the hospital.

Colton made a mental note to finish this conversation later, because a very large part of him wanted to know if she saw any chance of the two of them spending time together. It was pretty much impossible for him to think about starting a new relationship while he had one-year-old twins at home, especially with what was going on with his family.

His mind came up with a dozen reasons straight out of the chute as to why it was impossible and wouldn't happen and could never go anywhere. Why he couldn't risk it.

But the heart didn't listen to logic. It wanted to get to know Makena again. To see if the fire in the kisses they'd shared—kisses he was having one helluva time trying to erase from his memory—could ignite something that might last longer than a few months.

Logic flew out the window when it came to the heart.

"River is out of surgery and I can probably get us up to his floor if not his room."

Makena looked like she wanted to say something and then thought better of it.

"Let's do it." She took in a sharp breath, like she was steadying herself for what she knew would come.

Colton cursed the timing of the text, but it was good news. He led them to the information desk where he could get details about which floor River was housed in. Trudy, a middle-aged single mother who lived on the outskirts of Katy Gulch, sat at the counter.

As sheriff, Colton liked to get to know his residents and look out for those who seemed to need it. Trudy had been widowed while her husband had been serving in the military overseas. She'd been left with four kids and not a lot of money. Colton's office led a back-to-school backpack drive every year in part to make sure her children never went without. Gert always beamed with pride when delivering those items.

Gert organized a toy drive every year for Christmas, a book drive twice a year and coats for kids before the first cold snap.

"Hey, Trudy. You have a patient who just got out of surgery, and we'd like to go up to his floor and talk to his nurse and possibly his doctor," Colton said after introducing Trudy to Makena.

"Just a second, Sheriff. I'll look that up right now," Trudy said with a smile. Her fingers danced across the keyboard.

Makena's gaze locked onto someone. Colton followed her gaze to the man in scrubs. The doctor came from the same hallway they'd entered the lobby from, and then headed straight toward a bank of elevators.

The hair on Colton's neck prickled. Trudy's fingers worked double time. Click-click-click.

As the elevators closed on the opposite side of the lobby, something in the back of Colton's mind snapped.

"The patient you're looking for is on the seventh floor. He's in critical condition. No visitors are allowed." She flashed eyes at Colton. "No normal visitors. That doesn't mean you. He's in room 717."

Colton thanked her for the courtesy and realized what had been sticking in the back of his mind. The doctor who'd crossed the lobby wore a surgical mask and regular boots. Every doctor Colton had seen had foot coverings on their shoes. They usually wore tennis shoes with coverings over them for sanitation purposes.

This guy had on a surgical mask and no boot covers?

One look at Makena said she realized something was up. Colton looked at Trudy before jumping into action the minute he made eye contact with Makena and realized she was thinking along the same lines.

"Trudy, call security. Send backup to the seventh floor and help to room 717." Colton linked his fingers with Makena and started toward the elevator. Of course, he had a deputy on-site and the hospital had its own security. So imagine his shock when the elevator doors opened and his deputy walked out.

"Lawson, what are you doing?"

His deputy seemed dumbfounded as Colton rushed into the elevator.

"What do you mean? I'm going to get a cup of coffee. Hospital security relieved me and said you authorized a break."

"And you didn't think to check with me first?" Colton asked.

Lawson's mistake seemed to dawn on him. He muttered a few choice words as he pushed the button for the seventh floor, apologizing the whole time.

It seemed to take forever for the elevator to ding and the doors to open. At least, they knew where one of the men was; the other had to be close by. The two seemed to travel as a pair.

As soon as the doors opened, Colton shot out. He shouted back to Lawson, "Make sure no one comes down this hallway."

There were two hallways and several sets of stairs, but Lawson could make sure no one followed Colton.

Unwilling to let Makena out of his sight, Colton held on to her hand as he banked right toward room 717. As suspected, there was no security guard at the door.

Colton cursed as he bolted toward the open door.

Inside, he interrupted a man in a security outfit standing near River's bedside. The man in uniform had a black mustache, neatly trimmed.

"Sheriff, I saw him. Someone was in here. He ran out the door."

"Put your hands where I can see them," Colton demanded.

Chapter Sixteen

From behind the curtain dividing the room, a window leading to the outside opened.

"Hands where I can see them," Colton repeated, weapon drawn, leading the way. River lay unconscious with a breathing tube in his mouth as multiple machines beeped.

The security guard dropped down on the opposite side of the bed. And then, suddenly, an alarm began to sound on one of the machines. Was it unplugged?

Another wailing noise pierced the air.

Colton kept Makena tucked behind him as he took a couple of steps inside the room. He planted his side against the wall, inching forward.

A nurse came bolting in and froze when she saw Colton with his gun drawn. The divider curtain blew toward him with a gust of wind. Colton saw a glint of Mustache as he climbed out the window.

Red must've been on the other side of the divider all along. He must've made it inside the room. Colton assumed he'd be the one wearing the surgical gear.

"Freeze." Colton took a few more tentative steps before squatting down so he could see underneath the curtain. He saw no sign of shoes and assumed both men had climbed out the window and onto the fire escape they'd seen earlier. And since assumptions in his life of work could kill, he proceeded with extra caution. Someone could be standing on the bed or nightstand. Hell, he'd caught a perp climbing into the ceiling tiles at the bank before.

There was no more sound coming from that side of the room. He took a few more steps until he was able to reach the curtain and pull it open. He scanned the room before checking on the other side of the bed.

"Clear. Nurse, you're okay." It was all Colton could get out as he heard the sounds of feet shuffling and her scurrying to plug in the machines that were most likely the reason River was still breathing.

Colton rushed to the window and looked out in time to see someone wearing scrubs along with Security Dude climbing down the fire escape and around the side of the building.

He glanced back at Makena.

"Stay here. Someone will come back for you. Stay in this room. Nurse, lock this room and stay with her. As soon as I'm out of this window, I want you to lock it."

A moment of hesitation crossed Makena's features. She opened her mouth like she was about to protest and then clamped it shut.

Colton climbed out the window and followed the path of the perps. He climbed down to the corner, stopping before risking a glance.

The second he so much as peeked his head a shot rang out, taking a small chunk of white brick before whizzing past his face.

Colton quickly jerked back around the side of the

building and pulled himself back up. His body was flat against the building, his weapon holstered.

There was no way these guys were escaping him twice.

He scaled the wall a couple more floors, refusing to look down. He wouldn't exactly say he was afraid of heights, but he wouldn't call them his friend, either.

When Colton made it to the third story, gripping the windows for dear life, he risked another glance around the side of the building, hoping they would still be looking for him on the seventh floor. This time, thankfully, Red and Mustache were too busy climbing down to realize he'd looked. They probably still thought he was up on the seventh.

Colton continued his climb down with his stomach twisted in knots, but he made it to the ground. Without a doubt, they'd made it to the ground first. There were also two of them and only one of him. Not the best odds. One was a sharpshooter. That would be the person who would most likely wield the weapon.

And then there was the fact that they were both cops. Maybe he could find a way to use that to his advantage.

With his back against the wall and his weapon extended, Colton leaned around the building. The pair of men were making a beeline for the parking lot. He scanned the area for the Jeep but didn't see it.

They could have another vehicle stashed by now. Since it was early evening, there was a little activity. He wouldn't risk a shot. He, like every law enforcement officer on the job, was responsible for every bullet he fired. Meaning that if he accidentally struck a citizen, he was answerable, not to mention it would be horrific.

When Red and Mustache made it to the lot, one turned around.

They took cover behind a massive black SUV. One turned back, Red, and Colton figured that of the two, he was the marksman. He had his weapon aimed at the seventh floor, where he must expect Colton to be.

He figured Mustache was looking for a vehicle to hotwire, since they didn't immediately go to a car.

Colton figured his best line of defense was to get to his county-issued vehicle and try to circle around the back and come at them from a different direction. He got on his radio to Lawson and Gert as he bolted toward his SUV.

He slid into the driver's seat and blazed around the opposite side of the lot as he informed Gert of the situation. Lawson chimed in, stating that he was on his way down and heading to the spot Colton had just left.

Colton slowed his SUV down to a crawl as he made his way around the back of the parking lot. He located a spot in the back of the lot and parked. He slipped out of his windbreaker, needing to shed anything that drew attention to him. He toed off his boots as he exited the vehicle.

As the shooter's attention was directed at the building, Colton swung wide to sneak up on him. He was ever aware that Mustache was creeping around the lot, likely looking for a vehicle.

Lawson peeked his head around the building and Red fired a shot. While Red's attention was on Lawson, Colton eased through cars and trucks.

With Red distracted by Lawson, Colton came in stealth. He rounded the back of the SUV and dove at Red, tackling him at the knees. His gun went flying as Colton wrestled him around until his knee jabbed in the center of Red's back. As tall and strong as Red was, he was no match for a man of Colton's size.

Face down, Red spit out gravel as he opened his mouth to shout for help. Colton delivered a knockout punch. The man's jaw snapped.

From there, Colton was able to easily haul Red's hands behind his back and throw on zip cuffs.

It was then that Colton heard the click of a gun's hammer being cocked.

"Make one move without me telling you to, and you're dead."

Out of the corner of his eyes, Colton could see Mustache. He cursed under his breath.

"Hands in the air where I can them." Mustache was in authoritative cop mode.

Colton slowly started lifting his hands, his weapon already holstered. And at this rate, he was as good as dead. His thoughts jumped to Lawson. Where was he?

"Uncuff my friend. You're going to help me get him into my vehicle."

The retort on Colton's lips was, *like hell.* However, he knew better than to agitate a cop on the edge.

"You won't get away with this. Your superiors know what you've done and they know you're connected to Myers. But you can get a lighter sentence. You haven't dug a hole that you can't climb out of yet. No one's dead. A murder rap is not something you can ever come back from."

"Shut up. I don't need to hear any more of your crap. The system pays criminals better than it pays us. When Bic's kid needed medical care and his insurance ran out, who do you think covered his mortgage?" Stitch grunted. "It sure as hell wasn't the department."

Psychological profiles were performed on every officer candidate to ensure a cop could handle the pressures that came with the job. The tests could give a snapshot of where a candidate's head was at the time of his or her hiring. What it couldn't do 100 percent accurately was predict how someone would handle the constraints of the job over time.

The stress could compound and end up looking something like this.

"I never said it was easy being on the job. But you and I both know you didn't get into it for the money."

Mustache laughed. "Yeah, I was a kid. What did I know about having real bills and a father-in-law with dementia who lost his business and I had to support?"

"This isn't the answer. You can still make this right. You can still go back and untangle this. Make restitution."

A half laugh escaped Mustache.

"You know what? I think I'm just going to kill you instead. Not because I have to but because I can."

Colton had no doubt Mustache was trigger-happy. A man with nothing to lose was not the kind of person Colton needed to have pointing a gun at him.

"You're going to help me put my friend in my vehicle and then I'm going to give you ten seconds to run."

Colton knew without a doubt that the minute he put Red into a vehicle, his life was going to be over. He needed to think fast. Stall for time. He glanced over to see if Lawson was on his way.

Mustache laughed again.

"Your friend isn't coming. I don't know if you noticed but he's bleeding out over there. Guess it's too late for me after all."

Colton slowly stood with his hands in the air.

"Keep high and where I can see them. I'm going to relieve you of your weapon."

The crack of a bullet split the air.

Colton flinched and dropped to his knees. When he spun around, it was Mustache taking a couple of steps back. With his finger on the trigger, all it would take was one twitch for Colton to be shot at in point-blank range.

He dove behind the sport utility and came up with his weapon. It would take Mustache's brain a few minutes to catch up with the fact that he'd been shot. Right now, he was just as dangerous as he had been, if not more so.

Using the massive sport utility for cover, Colton drew down on Mustache.

"Hands up, Stitch." All Colton could think of was securing the area and getting to Lawson.

Another shot sounded.

Colton glanced around and saw Lawson's body. As he rounded the back of the vehicle, he heard a familiar voice.

"Drop your weapon *now.*" From behind a vehicle, Makena had her arms extended out with a Glock in her hands. Red's weapon? The barrel was aimed at Mustache.

Colton was proud of the fact she'd listened to his earlier advice and used the vehicle to protect her body.

Mustache seemed dumbfounded as he took a couple of steps and locked onto her position. "You."

He brought up his weapon to shoot her and she fired

again. This time, the bullet pinged his arm and his shoulder drew back. His weapon discharged, firing a wild shot, and his shoulder flew back. His Glock went skittering across the black tar.

Colton dove toward it and came up with it after making eye contact with Makena. He tucked and rolled on his shoulder and then popped up in front of the vehicle Makena used as cover.

There was no way to know if Mustache had a backup weapon, which many officers carried in an ankle holster.

"You just saved my life," Colton said to Makena. He moved beside her and realized that her body was trembling.

Her eyes were wide.

"You're okay," he said to soothe her before turning to Mustache, who was slumped against the back tire of a vehicle. "Get those hands up."

Much to his surprise, Mustache did.

It was probably the shock of realizing he'd been shot multiple times. Colton immediately fished out his cell and called Gert, telling her the perps had been subdued and that Lawson was down. She reassured Colton a team of doctors was waiting at the ER bay for word.

Before Colton could end the call, he saw the doctors racing to save Lawson's life.

Mustache's once light blue shirt was now soaked in red. Colton ran over and cuffed Mustache's hands. After a pat-down, he located a backup weapon.

"If either one of these men moves, don't hesitate to shoot," he said to Makena.

Lawson was flat on his back as he was being placed on a gurney.

"I'm sorry. I let you down," Lawson said.

"No, you didn't. I'm alive. You're alive. Those bastards are going to spend the rest of their lives behind bars. You did good."

In less than a minute, Lawson was on his way to surgery. The bullet had nicked his neck.

Colton bolted back to Makena.

"It's over," Makena said. She repeated herself a couple more times as Colton took her weapon before he pulled her into an embrace, keeping a watchful eye on the perps.

"You did good," he whispered into her ear as she melted against him.

"I found the gun on the ground," she said quietly.

Red popped his head up and shook it, like he was shaking off a fog.

"What the hell happened?" His gaze locked onto his partner, who had lost a lot of blood.

"You and your partner are going away for a very long time," Colton said. He held Makena, trying to calm her tremors.

An emergency team raced toward Mustache. In another few minutes, he was strapped and cuffed to a gurney with security in tow and another deputy on the way.

Colton pulled Red to standing after patting him down. He walked the man over to his service vehicle. "You're taking a trip in the back seat for once."

Makena climbed into the passenger side and kept silent for the drive back to Katy Gulch.

Deputy Schooner met them in the parking lot and took custody of the perp.

"You would do what you had to if your kid was

sick," Bic practically spat the words. "Look as sancti-
monious as you want, but I had bills stacking up and
a mortgage to cover. I did what was necessary to take
care of my family."

"There are other ways to accomplish the same thing
and stay within the law," Colton said.

"That's what you say. Don't you get tired of watching them get away with crimes every day? Don't you
get sick of seeing criminals drive better cars and wear
better clothes than us?"

"Fancy clothes were never my style," Colton said.
"But why River?"

"He was on to us, so we turned the tables on him.
His nose wasn't clean, either. He liked to play it rough,"
Bic said. "She was the problem. She threatened everything we were doing. It took months to track her down
but she made mistakes and River led us right to her."

Colton was done talking. He turned to Makena. "Are
you ready to go home?"

She stood there, looking a little bit lost.

"I don't have a home to go to, Colton."

"Then come home with me while you figure out
your next move." He brushed the backs of his fingers
against the soft skin of her face. He'd missed his opportunity with her once and did not intend to do so
again. "Come home with me and stay."

"And then what?" She blinked up at him, confused.

"Stay. Meet my boys. See what you think about
making a life together. I know what I want and it's you.
I love you, Makena. And I think I have since college. I
was too young and too dumb to realize what was happening to us in college. I had no idea how rare or spe-

cial it was. But I do now. I'm a grown man and I won't make that same mistake twice."

He looked into her eyes but was having trouble reading her. Maybe it was too much. Maybe he shouldn't have thrown this all at her at once.

"But if you don't think this is right, if you don't feel what I'm feeling, then just stay with me until you get your bearings. I don't care how long. You'll always have a place to stay with me."

"Did you say that you love me?"

Colton nodded. "Yes, Makena. I love you."

"I love you, too, Colton. I think I always have. Seeing you again brought me back to life. But then what? You have boys. You have a life."

"I'd like to build a life with *you*."

"Are you sure about that, Colton? Because I have no doubts."

"I've never been more certain of anything in my life other than adopting my boys," he admitted.

She blinked up at him, confused.

It dawned on him why. He'd never told her about his twins.

"Rebecca and I had been high school sweethearts. We didn't know anything but each other. We decided to take a break in college and see if this was the real deal. I loved her and she was my best friend. But then I met you and it was different. I felt things that I had never felt with Rebecca. There was a spark inside me that said you were special and then I wanted more than a best friend as a partner. I went home and told Rebecca that I didn't think I was coming back to her."

"But you ended up together?"

"Yes, but not for years. We went our separate ways

as a couple but stayed close as friends. Years later, long
after she and I broke up, she ended up in a bad relationship with a man who didn't treat her right. When he
found out she was pregnant he accused her of cheating
on him. He questioned whether or not the boys were
his and that crushed her. She said she couldn't come
home pregnant to her father's house without a husband or a father for her kids. We'd always promised
to have each other's back, so that's what I did. Her father, who's the mayor of Katy Gulch, got over the fact
she was pregnant and still not married as soon as he
found out she was marrying an O'Connor. I felt like I
could've done a lot worse than marry my best friend.
I figured that what you and I had was a one-and-done
situation. So I asked Rebecca to marry me. I loved her,
but there was no spark in our marriage, not like what
I'd experienced with you. But then, no one else made
me feel that way. And make no mistake about it, those
boys are my sons. They are O'Connors through and
through, and always will be. Can you live with that?"

"Colton, you are the most selfless man I've ever met.
I think I just fell in love with you even more."

"Just so you're clear, we can take a little time for
you to get to know the boys, and we can make certain
this is the life you want. But I'm in this for the long
haul, and I have every intention of asking you to be
my bride," he said.

"If your sons are half the person you are, I already
know that I'll love them. And just so you know, when
you ask me to marry you, I'll be ready to say yes. I
never felt like I was home around anyone until I met
you and then I lost it. I've definitely been in the wrong

relationship and that taught me exactly what I wanted in a person. And it's you. It's always been you."

Colton pulled Makena into his arms and kissed his future bride, his place to call home.

"I have one condition," she warned.

"Anything." He didn't hesitate. He wanted to give her the world.

"You asked me before if I had any idea what I wanted to do once I had my freedom back."

He nodded.

"I want to volunteer at the motel to help out Peach. She told me about her and her husband building that place together and that the motel made her feel closer to him. She's considering selling, but I could tell nothing in her heart wanted that to happen. It would cut her off from the man she built a life with and she deserves so much more than that. She deserves to have her memories of him surrounding her until she takes her final breath."

"It sounds like the perfect plan to me." Colton kissed his future, his soon-to-be bride, his home.

Epilogue

"I have news."

Makena sat on the kitchen floor, playing with her favorite boys in the world. She'd taken them into her heart the minute she'd looked at those round, angelic faces. Someday, she wanted to expand their family, but after living with twins 24/7 for the past month, she realized her hands were full.

"What is it?" she asked Colton as he walked into the kitchen wearing only jeans hung low on his hips. He was fresh from the shower, hair still wet. Droplets rolled down his neck and onto his muscled chest.

She practically had to fan herself.

"Myers has agreed to testify against Bic, who will be put away a very long time for attempted murder and police corruption, among other charges."

Stitch hadn't made it, but Bic was the brains of the operation.

"Good for him," she said. "I'm so ready to close that chapter of my life. I'm done with running scared and I'm done hiding. He put me through hell and I'm just ready to move on and never look back."

Colton walked over to her and sat down behind her, wrapping his arms around her. He feathered kisses along the nape of her neck, causing her arms to break out in goose bumps and a thrill of awareness to skitter across her skin.

"I can't wait to be alone after we put the boys to bed tonight," he whispered in her ear.

She smiled as she turned her head enough for him to find her lips. The kiss sent more of that awareness swirling through her. Tonight felt like a lifetime away.

One of the boys giggled, which always made the other one follow suit. Their laughs broke into the moment happening between Makena and Colton.

"What's this?" she asked as she witnessed one pick up a block and bite it before setting it down only for the other to copy him.

Laughter filled the room and her heart.

This was her family. These were her boys. This was her home.

* * * * *

He was challenging her already and they hadn't even really started working together, but if they were going to survive several weeks of training, honesty was going to be the best policy.

"My husband was a marine," Piper said, but didn't make eye contact with him. Instead, she whirled and started walking back in the direction of the outdoor training ring.

He turned and kept pace beside her, his gaze trained on her face. "Was?"

Challenging again. Pushing, but regardless of that, she said, "He was killed in action in Iraq. Four years ago and yet..."

Her throat choked up and tears welled in her eyes as she rushed forward, almost as if she could outrun the discussion and the pain it brought.

The gentle touch of his big, calloused hand on her forearm stopped her escape.

She glanced down at that hand and then followed his arm up to meet his gaze, so full of concern and something else. Pain?

"I'm sorry. It can't be easy," he said, the simple words filled with so much more. Pain for sure. Understanding. Compassion. Not pity, thankfully. The last nearly undid her, but she sucked in a breath, held it for the briefest second before blurting out, "We should get going. If you're going to do search and rescue with Decoy, we'll have to improve his obedience skills."

Rushing away from him, she slipped through the gaps in the split-rail fence and walked to the center of the training ring.

Shane hesitated, obviously uneasy, but then he bent to go across the fence railing and met her in the middle of the ring, Decoy at his side.

"I'm ready if you are," he said, his big body several feet away, only he still felt too close. Too big. Too masculine with that kind of posture and strength that screamed military.

She took a step back and said, "I'm ready."

She wasn't and didn't know if she ever could be with this man. He was testing her on too many levels.

Only she'd never failed a training assignment and she didn't intend to start with Shane and Decoy.

"Let's get going," she said.

Don't miss
Decoy Training *by Caridad Piñeiro,*
available April 2022 wherever
Harlequin Intrigue books and ebooks are sold.

Harlequin.com

Love Harlequin romance?

DISCOVER.

Be the first to find out about promotions, news and exclusive content!

Facebook.com/HarlequinBooks

Twitter.com/HarlequinBooks

Instagram.com/HarlequinBooks

Pinterest.com/HarlequinBooks

YouTube.com/HarlequinBooks

ReaderService.com

EXPLORE.

Sign up for the Harlequin e-newsletter and download a free book from any series at
TryHarlequin.com

CONNECT.

Join our Harlequin community to share your thoughts and connect with other romance readers!
Facebook.com/groups/HarlequinConnection

HARLEQUIN

HSOCIAL2021

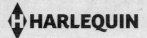

HARLEQUIN

Heartfelt or thrilling, passionate or uplifting—Harlequin is more than just happily-ever-after.

With twelve different series to choose from and new books available every month, you are sure to find stories that will move you, uplift you, inspire and delight you.

SIGN UP FOR THE HARLEQUIN NEWSLETTER

Be the first to hear about great new reads and exciting offers!

Harlequin.com/newsletters